Richard Laymon wrote over thirty novels and seventy short stories. In May 2001, *The Travelling Vampire Show* won the Bram Stoker Award for Best Horror Novel, a prize for which Laymon had previously been shortlisted with *Flesh*, *Funland*, *A Good, Secret Place* (Best Anthology) and *A Writer's Tale* (Best Non-fiction). Laymon's works include the books of the Beast House Chronicles: *The Cellar*, *The Beast House* and *The Midnight Tour*. Some of his recent novels have been *Night in the Lonesome October*, *No Sanctuary* and *Amara*.

A native of Chicago, Laymon attended Willamette University in Salem, Oregon, and took an MA in English Literature from Loyola University, Los Angeles. In 2000, he was elected President of the Horror Writers Association. He died in February 2001.

Laymon's fiction is published in the United Kingdom by Headline, and in the United States by Leisure Books and Cemetery Dance Publications. To learn more, visit the Laymon website at: http://rlk.cjb.net

'If you're not already well acquainted with Richard Laymon, get to know him now' *Manchester Evening News*

'A gut-crunching writer' *Time Out*

'In Laymon's books, blood doesn't so much as drip as explode, splatter and coagulate' *Independent*

'This author knows how to sock it to the reader' *The Times*

'No one writes like Laymon and you're going to have a good time with anything he writes' Dean Koontz

'A brilliant writer' *Sunday Express*

'Stephen King without a conscience' Dan Marlowe

'This is an author that does not pull his punches . . . A gripping, and at times genuinely shocking, read' *SFX Magazine*

'Incapable of writing a disappointing book' *New York Review of Science Fiction*

'One of the best, and most underrated, writers working in the genre today' *Cemetery Dance*

Also in the Richard Laymon Collection published by Headline

The Beast House Trilogy:
The Cellar
The Beast House
The Midnight Tour

Beware!
Dark Mountain*
The Woods are Dark
Out are the Lights
Night Show
Allhallow's Eve
Flesh
Resurrection Dreams
Darkness, Tell Us
One Rainy Night
Alarums
Blood Games
Endless Night
Midnight's Lair*
Savage
In the Dark
Island
Quake
Body Rides
Bite
Fiends
After Midnight
Among the Missing
Come Out Tonight
The Travelling Vampire Show
Dreadful Tales
Night in the Lonesome October
No Sanctuary
Funland
The Stake
Amara
The Lake

* previously published under the pseudonym of Richard Kelly
Dark Mountain was first published as *Tread Softly*

The Glory Bus
and
Friday Night in Beast House

Richard Laymon

<u>headline</u>

THE GLORY BUS first published in Great Britain in 2005 by
HEADLINE PUBLISHING GROUP

FRIDAY NIGHT IN BEAST HOUSE first published in Great Britain in 2007 by
HEADLINE PUBLISHING GROUP

First published in this omnibus edition in 2008 by
HEADLINE PUBLISHING GROUP

5

ISBN 978 0 7553 3186 4

Typeset in Janson by Palimpsest Book Production Limited,
Grangemouth, Stirlingshire

Printed and bound in Great Britain by
CPI Antony Rowe, Chippenham and Eastbourne

Headline's policy is to use papers that are natural, renewable and recyclable
products and made from wood grown in sustainable forests. The logging and
manufacturing processes are expected to conform to the environmental regulations
of the country of origin.

HEADLINE PUBLISHING GROUP
An Hachette Livre UK Company
338 Euston Road
London NW1 3BH

www.headline.co.uk
www.hachettelivre.co.uk

The Glory Bus

The Glory Bus

Chapter One

'You were it. Do you know what I mean? There was never anyone else, not for me. Do you know when it was, the first time I ever saw you? Sally Harken's thirteenth-birthday party. I hardly even knew Sally, since we didn't go to the same school. The only reason I got invited to her party, my mom and dad were friends with Sally's parents. I didn't want to go, can you believe that? They had to make me go.

'And then you walked in. I'll never forget it. You had bangs that hung down almost to your eyes, and those blue eyes shining out, and those white teeth. You wore a white blouse. It had short sleeves but you had them rolled way up high on your arms. And you had the cuffs of your shorts rolled up, too. The shorts were blue denim, and looked brand new. The legs must've been too long to suit you, so you turned them up. It was like you were all cuffs. Cuffs and smooth, tan skin.

'Speaking of cuffs, how are you doing?'

Pamela, sitting in the passenger seat with her cuffed hands resting on her lap, stared out the window and didn't answer.

'Are they too tight?'

They *were* too tight. The sharp edges of the bracelets dug into her wrists, and her fingers tingled. But Pam didn't want Rodney to fool with them. 'They're fine,' she said. She wanted him to leave her alone.

'You sure?'

'Yes.'

'Anyway, that's when I fell in love with you. We were thirteen, and you walked into Sally's party and . . . It hurt me to look at you, you were so cute and beautiful and . . . you had a freshness, an innocence, something like that. And you also had that twinkle in your eyes. A kind

1

of glint. You've still got that. Not at the moment, of course. But it'll come back. Once you get used to things, it'll come back.

'Of course, you lost most of that freshness I was talking about. It's a shame. Everyone loses it, though. Maybe it goes when you start in with sex. Or maybe it's when some special sort of dream dies in you. Who knows? You kept it longer than most girls. You still had it in your junior year. Your first year as a varsity cheerleader. Oh God, the way you used to look . . . that pleated skirt, that sweater. When you jumped, the sweater would come up just an inch or two above the top of your skirt, so there'd be a little strip of bare skin showing. I used to watch you at the games, and want to kiss you there. I knew just how it would feel, and how it would smell.

'Anyway, that freshness thing was gone when we started our senior year. Even without it, you were . . . wonderful. But a different kind of wonderful. Not so much like an innocent, eager kid, more like a woman. And you sure hadn't lost that sparkle in your eyes. It's sort of as if, everywhere you look, you're seeing things that amaze you. And like maybe you're hoping to throw in a quip.

'Of course, too, you just got more and more beautiful. I couldn't believe it when I saw your picture in the newspaper. The picture sure didn't do you justice, but it about tore me apart. To look at your face again, after so many years. I thought to myself what a fool I'd been, depriving myself of you, making do with a string of gals that were nothing but lousy imitations of the one and only *you* I longed for in my heart. They were available, that's all they had going for them. They hadn't gone off to some damn college halfway across the country, like some people I could name. So I just had to make do with them. I tried to make them look like you. Silly, huh? I made them wear a wig that looked like how you wore your hair. I dressed them up like you, too. And I called them Pamela. Sometimes, when I tried really hard, I could sort of trick myself into thinking they *were* you. It wasn't an easy trick, though. Mostly, I was just disgusted by myself. You know? That I'd let myself get so obsessed with you and couldn't let it go and had to trick myself with a bunch of crummy substitutes.

'So when I saw your picture in the paper, it was like a sign that I oughta quit all that and go after the real thing. So that's just what I did.

'Bet you must be wondering what took me so long. They ran that picture six months ago, didn't they? And it gave your husband's name, and even the address of the newlyweds' home. So why did it take me six months to show up and claim you? Is that what you're wondering?'

'I'm wondering what you did to those girls.'

'Oh, mostly the same as what I plan to do to you. Except for one difference, which is that I'm going to *keep* you. I've bought us a house. It's a fine little place where nobody'll ever bother us. It'll be our home. We'll have a wonderful time.'

'Did you kill them?' Pamela asked.

He smiled. 'I put them out of their misery.'

'Oh, God.'

'I guess one might say it's your fault. All those girls *and* that husband of yours, all of them died because you went on your merry way just as if old lardass Rodney Pinkham was a nobody. Should've paid me more attention, maybe. Should've maybe *dated* me.'

'*Dated* you? You never even asked!'

'You would've laughed in my face.'

'I've never laughed in *anyone*'s face!'

'Bet you called me Piggy behind my back.'

'I didn't.'

'*They* all did.'

'I never heard *anybody* call you Piggy behind your back.'

'Liar.'

'If you wanted to go out with me so badly, why didn't you just *ask*!'

'Told you why.'

'I might've gone out with you. You didn't have to *kill* people. My God . . . how many were there?'

'Including your husband? Oh, sixteen.'

It numbed Pamela's mind. Fifteen girls had died because of this man's obsession with her?

Not just Jim.

She'd thought it couldn't get any worse than last night. *It can always get worse*, she realized.

'It's not all that many, fifteen,' Rodney explained. 'I mean, it *sounds* like a lot when you just blurt it out like that. But what you've gotta remember, it went on for five years. That only averages out to three a year. That's not so many. Would've been plenty more, except you went and got yourself married and they ran your picture in the paper.

Now that I've got you, the rest of it's gonna stop. I mean, why would I want them when I've got you? You're all I ever wanted.'

He turned his head and smiled at Pamela. It was the way he had smiled ever since she'd known him: an odd, quick lift of the upper lip that showed not only his front teeth but the gums above them. The crevices between his teeth always used to be packed with crud from old meals, and all the snacking in between.

Which was one of the reasons why everyone had called him Piggy. They'd called him Piggy not only because of his obesity, but also because of his tiny eyes and his filth and body odor and the remains of food decorating his clothes and teeth.

Pamela had always figured that the nickname was an insult to swine everywhere. She preferred to call the creep Rotney because everything about him seemed rotten, repulsive. Hoglike. Among her friends she'd said terrible things about him. She had always been kind to him, though.

Maybe that had been a mistake. Not hurrying away whenever he approached, the way most kids used to do. Smiling at him. Talking to him. Treating him like a human being, even though his disgusting appearance and sour smell had sometimes made her eyes water. A couple of times, she had actually gagged in the middle of chats with him. Wanting to spare his feelings, she'd claimed it must've been something she ate.

Maybe she *should* have avoided him, laughed at him, called him Piggy or Rotney to his face. If she'd been really bad to him, maybe none of this would've happened.

All those girls . . . Jim.

Went away Jim, came back Rodney.

That's how it had seemed, anyway.

The room had been dark last night except for the light from the television. Pamela was in bed, propped up with pillows, watching the tail end of the eleven o'clock news and waiting for Dave to start. Jim had gone off to the bathroom. He seemed to be taking longer than usual. Pamela hoped he was shaving. He usually shaved before bed if he planned to fool around. The VCR was already set, so they would be able to watch the tape if they missed some of Dave's show.

When she heard Jim's footsteps outside the room, she drew the top sheet up to cover her bare shoulders. She wanted it to be a surprise that she had dispensed with her nightshirt. Jim walked into the bedroom. He was wearing his paisley bathrobe, the same robe that he'd been wearing ten minutes ago, but he had *grown*. He looked as if he'd somehow swollen up – grown taller, spread out until he was so fat that his robe wouldn't shut all the way. The front of his belly bulged through the gap and looked like uncooked bread dough. Only for an instant did Pamela's mind stumble with confusion about the sudden change in her husband.

Then she realized that the man in Jim's robe wasn't Jim. He reached toward a light switch.

The bedside lamps came on and made the room bright. Pamela recognized the man in Jim's robe. She hadn't seen him in five years, not since her high-school graduation, but he hadn't changed very much. His smile was *exactly* the same – a lift of the upper lip. Same piggy eyes. He raised his arms and spread them wide. 'My dear! Have you missed me?'

Pamela could hardly breathe. She felt as if a mallet was pounding her heart. She wanted to call out for Jim.

But Jim had to be dead, didn't he? Dead.

Rodney took a step toward her.

She whipped the sheet away, flung herself over, squirmed across Jim's side of the bed and reached down for the nightstand drawer. She grabbed its handle. Jerked it open. Drove her hand down inside the drawer toward the Sig-Sauer .380 that Jim kept there for emergencies.

Before she could touch the pistol, Rodney kicked the drawer shut. It slammed on her forearm. As Pamela cried out, her arm was grabbed and jerked away from the drawer. Rodney shoved it up high on her back, driving her face into Jim's pillow. Then he climbed onto her.

The weight of his body mashed her against the mattress. The robe must've come wide open. She could feel his bare, greasy skin all down her back and rump and legs. With her face in the pillow and his massive weight on her back, she couldn't breathe. She couldn't scream. She could hardly move. She fought to suck air into her lungs, but failed. *This is it*, she thought. *Oh Jesus, I'm gonna die.*

When Pamela woke up, she was surprised to find herself alive. And spent the next several hours wishing that she were dead. Rodney finally dragged her out of the bedroom. In the bathroom he showed her Jim's body. Then she watched him set the house on fire. She remembered being carried outside in Rodney's arms, but nothing after that.

She came awake in the passenger seat of his car. The sun was low and shining in her eyes. Her hands rested on her lap, shackled together with handcuffs as if she'd been arrested by the police. She ached almost everywhere. In some places, she felt raw pain. Rodney must've dressed her. She couldn't remember it, though. It seemed as if she'd still been naked on her way out of the house.

She was wearing a green pleated skirt. It was very short. It reached only halfway down her thighs, and she could feel the upholstery of the car seat against her bare rump. She was also wearing a gold pullover sweater. It had a crew neck and long sleeves. The wool felt heavy and hot. It was scratchy against her skin. All the outfit really needed was a big green-felt 'J' sewn to the chest of the sweater, and it would be a pretty fair replica of the varsity cheerleader costume that she'd worn at Jackson High. Rodney seemed unaware that she'd awakened, so she closed her eyes again and pretended to sleep. She thought about what had happened last night.

Jim was dead.

At twenty-three, Pamela was a widow. She'd been beaten savagely and half suffocated. In his grunting, hog-man voice Rodney promised to do so many things to her. He mentioned some of them. With gloating relish. *Dirty* fucking pervert!

What if I just throw myself out of the car? Probably bust my head open, but that might be better than going on. At least it'll be over and done with. In some ways, the idea appealed to her. But she knew that she wouldn't hurl herself out of the car – not while it was speeding along at sixty. *Not gonna kill myself. No way, no how. I'm gonna live through this.*

Right. That's what they all think.

Pamela had no confidence that she could live through this. But she knew that she would try. She would be patient and wait for just the right time to save herself. And so she sat motionless, head down, eyes shut, cuffed hands resting on her lap. For a long time, Rodney drove along in silence. Maybe he thought she was sleeping. Maybe he was preoccupied with plans or fantasies.

When he finally started to talk, the words came out in a heavy rush that seemed to have no end.

'You were it. Do you know what I mean? There was never anyone else, not for me.'

Then he fell silent, and she wondered: *When he stops the car – what's he going to do to me?*

Chapter Two

'Now that I've got you, the rest is gonna stop. I mean, why would I want them when I've got you? You're all I ever wanted.' Rodney turned his head and smiled at Pamela.

She turned her face away from him. She stared out the window. All she could see beyond the edge of the road was desert. Not a desert of sand, but of hard gray ground that looked like a mixture of dry mud and gravel. She knew the brush was mesquite. The stubby trees were yuccas. Some of the cacti were prickly pear, cholla and saguaro. The saguaros looked like giant men with their arms raised in surrender. But she didn't see any men out there. The only animals in sight were a few hawks or buzzards floating across the sky on outstretched wings. Except for the road, the area seemed to be a wasteland. There was bound to be civilization ahead, though. At the very least, a service station. Rodney hadn't stopped for gas yet, so he would have to get a fill-up soon.

I'll make my break when he stops for gas, Pamela thought. She wondered if he had a gun. He might've taken Jim's pistol out of the drawer. He might've had a gun of his own, last night, when he broke into the house.

For all she knew, he might be armed to the teeth.

She hadn't seen any guns on him, but that didn't mean much. The little .380 could fit in a pocket of his pants.

I don't want anybody getting killed. But I can't let him take me to his hideout, she told herself. *Have to make my getaway before that. What if his next stop is the hideout? Maybe he found a place that he could reach on a single tank of gas. Or maybe he has a couple of jerry cans stowed in his trunk.*

Pamela suddenly found herself peering past Rodney at the gas gauge.

The Glory Bus

The red needle pointed to E. She felt a lurch of fear. *Take it easy*, she told herself. *My angle makes it look worse than it is. It's not really on empty yet. We've probably got twenty or thirty miles to go. We could be in a city by then. And if we do run out of gas here in the middle of nowhere it might give me a chance to get away.*

'Am I going too fast for you?' Rodney asked.

Apparently, he thought that she was staring at the speedometer. 'I'm worried about the gas,' she said.

'We're fine.'

'Will there be a gas station pretty soon?'

'Nope. Nothing between us and home.'

Home. Coming from him, the word made her feel sick. 'Will we have enough gas to reach it?' she asked. 'Our home?'

'Sure. We oughta be coming up on the turn-off in another fifteen miles, and then it's only twelve to go.'

'That's almost thirty miles.'

'Twenty-seven.' Rodney looked at her and raised his upper lip. 'We might have to go the last bit on fumes. Maybe even on foot. It won't matter, though, long as we make it to the turn-off. We can always walk from there, if we have to. Nobody'll come along and bother us. It's just an old dirt road that doesn't go anywhere. It goes to our house, and noplace else.'

'What about a gas station?' Pamela asked.

'We don't need one, like I told you.'

'I do. I have to use a restroom.'

Rodney looked very interested. 'Number one or number two?'

'Number one.'

'Ahhh. You don't need a restroom for that.'

'Where am I supposed to go?'

'Anywhere you like. Except the car.'

'Then you'd better pull over.'

'Wait till we get to the dirt road.'

'I can't.'

'Sure you can.'

'I'm telling you. I have to go *now*.' She saw him glance at the rearview mirror. Apparently, the road behind them was as empty as the road ahead. Rodney stepped on the brakes. As his car slowed down, he steered to the right. The tires bumped down off the pavement. The ride became bumpy, and the tires made crunching sounds on the rough surface of the shoulder.

After a few seconds, the car stopped.

'Don't move,' Rodney said. He shut off the engine, pulled out the ignition key, and swung his door open. Hot, dry air swept into the car. He climbed out. His door thunked shut. Pamela watched him walk toward the front of the car.

In spite of the heat, she felt loose and shivery inside.

I'd better just pee and let it go at that, she told herself. *I don't have to do anything crazy.*

If I don't do something crazy, he'll have me. He'll get me to his place and that'll be it.

As Rodney walked past the front of the car, he watched Pamela through the windshield. He had an eagerness in his tiny pig eyes. Sweat glistened on his nose.

He's planning to watch.

He turned and came toward her door. Reaching into the left front pocket of his pants, he pulled out a small black pistol. The Sig-Sauer. He'd taken it, after all. He opened the passenger door.

'What're you gonna do, shoot me?'

'That'll be up to you.'

'I won't try anything.'

'Hope not.'

'Will you take the cuffs off?'

'What do you think?'

'Please?'

'You must think I'm pretty stupid.'

'What are you scared of? What could I possibly do to you? My God, you're twice my size. *And* you've got the gun. So just take the cuffs off me, okay?'

'No-kay. Come on, out.'

Pamela scooted to the edge of her seat. Rodney was staring at her legs. Keeping them together, she turned sideways and swung them out the doorway. She used her cuffed hands to stop her skirt from climbing too high when she squirmed forward.

Rodney laughed. 'Who you trying to hide it from?'

Ignoring him, she stretched her legs down. She couldn't quite touch the ground, so she scooted off and dropped the rest of the way.

The ground felt rough and hot under her bare feet. She stood up straight in the V of the open door.

The heat of the desert sun was so great that Pamela felt as if she were standing in the midst of a fire – a blaze that seemed only moments away from igniting the hair on her head, the shoulders of her sweater. Her body suddenly ran with dribbles and trickles of sweat as if her skin were melting.

'My God,' she muttered.

'Soon as you're done with business,' Rodney said, 'we'll climb back into the car and be on our merry way. In air-conditioned comfort, such as it is.'

'Better than this.'

'You're the one who wants to pee.'

She hobbled clear of the open door. Rodney threw it shut. Squinting against the afternoon brightness, she looked for a place beyond the roadside where she might have some privacy.

None of the nearby cactus plants were high enough. There was a good-sized organ-pipe cactus, but it was at least a hundred feet away. She'd destroy her feet, going that far.

This isn't about peeing, she reminded herself. *It's about escaping. If I can get to that organ pipe, I'll have that much of a head start.*

Unless he comes with me.

She squinted at Rodney. He was grinning at her, enjoying her discomfort. 'Could I borrow your shoes?' she asked.

'What do you want shoes for?'

'So I don't kill my feet. I want to go over there.' Pamela pointed at the cactus. It was tall and green. It looked like a saguaro, but it had no arms.

'What do you wanta go over there for?'

'To relieve myself.'

'Forget it. Do it here.'

She shook her head.

'Do it.'

'No. Somebody might come along.'

'Think so?'

She swiveled her head from side to side. Nothing was approaching from either direction. But the highway had dips and bends. 'What if I start to go, and a car comes?'

11

'Isn't gonna happen. And so what if it does? They get a free peek, so what? If they stop and try to mess with us, I'll blow their heads off.'

Facing him, Pamela stiffened her back. 'I'm not going to do it here. Just let me go over to that cactus. I can get behind it and nobody'll be able to see what I'm doing.'

'What a kick. You care? After last night?'

'Yeah, I care.'

'Okay, okay. What the hell, why not? Anything for my honey.'

'How about shoes?'

He coughed out a laugh. 'Anything but that.'

'Just let me borrow your shoes for two minutes, okay?'

'What am I supposed to wear?'

'You can sit in the car.'

'What's this, Fantasy Land? I'm going with you.'

Of course he is, she thought. *What did you think, he'd give up his chance to watch?*

'Go on,' Rodney said. 'I'm right behind you.'

Pamela started walking toward the cactus. She moved slowly, picking her way with care to avoid stepping on any of the shiny bits of broken glass that littered the roadside, then keeping her distance from the prickly pears and cholla. In spite of her care, bits of rock jabbed the bottoms of her feet. She winced when they stabbed her. She kept her teeth gritted. Sometimes, the scorching heat of the ground made her hiss. But she kept on walking all the way to the organ-pipe cactus.

She stepped behind it.

Rodney halted beside her. 'Did you notice?' he asked. 'Nothing came by.'

'Really,' she muttered. She didn't care.

'Could've saved yourself all that hurt.'

Pamela looked back at the road. It still appeared to be empty in both directions. The only car was Rodney's. It sat there, hunched in the sunlight, like some species of metal beast. A beast with a foul, rancid soul. Just biding its time, waiting for them to come back so that it could bear them away to Rodney's den.

I'm not getting back in.

'Come on and do it,' Rodney said.

'Not with you watching.'

His lip slid up. 'Get outta here. You forgetting about last night? I saw all your iddy-biddy bits and pieces.'

'That was last night, this is today.'

'Lift your skirt and squat, honey.'

Squinting into his eyes, she slowly shook her head from side to side.

Rodney laughed softly. Then he pressed the muzzle of the pistol against the bridge of her nose. The feel of it made her eyes ache as if she had crossed them.

'Do you want to die?' he whispered.

'No.'

'Do you want me to hurt you so bad that you'll wish you *were* dead?'

'No.'

'Good.' Rodney took two steps backward. Keeping the pistol aimed at her face, he sank to a crouch. 'How about doing me a cheer?' he said.

'*A what?*'

'I was gonna wait till we got home, but I wanta see you do one now.'

'A cheer?'

'A good one. Pretend it's a night game at good old Jackson High, it's fourth down and goal to go, and our guys just *gotta* make it.'

'My feet.'

'You're the one who had to make us stop. You're the one who had to walk all the way out here barefoot so you could have the privacy of a cactus. You wreck up your feet, whose fault is it?'

'I can't do a cheer with my hands cuffed.'

'Sure you can.'

'Not a good one. You want me to jump, don't you? You want me to make my skirt and sweater fly up. That's the idea, isn't it? Well, I can't really make them fly unless my arms are free.'

Rodney's tiny eyes stared at her. 'The only problem,' he said, 'is you'll try to run away if I take off the cuffs.'

'No, I won't.'

'Yes, you will. I'm not an idiot. Do I look like an idiot?'

'Where would I run to? We're out in the middle of nowhere.'

'You might run to the car.'

'You've got the gun.'

'That's very true.' His eyes narrowed to pink slits. 'Have you ever been shot?'

'No.'

'It hurts. If you make me shoot you, it'll hurt *a lot*. Because I won't kill you. I'm not going to ruin it all and kill you, no matter what you do. But I'll shoot you just enough to stop you so you can't get away. And it'll hurt. And that'll only be the *start* of the pain for you, because I don't like traitors.'

'I won't try to get away,' Pamela said. 'Okay?'

'Better not.'

She raised her outstretched arms.

Rodney stood up. He switched the pistol to his left hand. With his right, he dug into the front pocket of his pants. He came up with the leather key-case that had been swaying under the ignition during the trip. One-handed, he flipped it open, shook the keys free and took hold of the one he wanted.

Pamela stood motionless while he unlocked the cuffs and removed them. He slipped the cuffs and key-case into his pocket as he stepped backward again. Then he crouched and nodded up at her.

'Ready,' he said.

She nodded. She took a deep breath. She stood at attention. Then she clapped her hands four times. Smack, smack, smack, smack. With each clap, she took a big step backward. After the fourth, she halted. Legs together, shoulders back, chin up. She tried to make herself smile. And her eyes filled with tears as she suddenly thought about Maui. She had run through most of her best cheerleader routines for Jim during their honeymoon there. They'd had a picnic lunch – and a couple of beers – on a hidden beach they'd discovered along the road to Hana. Afterward, they'd taken a stroll along the beach. She'd done a few cartwheels on the sand and Jim's enthusiasm had prompted her to give him a major show. Her only audience had been Jim. Halfway through, she'd taken off her bikini. Jim had looked stunned, ecstatic, watching her prance about naked – leaping, kicking high, twirling, doing handsprings and flips. At the end of her performance she'd thrown her arms around him, exhausted and gasping. While she hung on him, he'd pulled down his trunks. Then he'd clutched the backs of her thighs, lifted her, and lowered her slowly, going up into her high and deep.

Pamela sniffed. With the sleeves of her sweater, she wiped the tears from her eyes.

'What'cha waiting for, crybaby?' Rodney said. 'Let's go.' He clapped four times.

Smack, smack, smack, smack.

'We got *pep*!' Pamela shouted. She kicked her right leg high and clapped. 'We got *steam*!' She kicked up her other leg and clapped. 'We are the boys on the *Jackson team!*'

She leaped, throwing her hands overhead and flinging her legs out high to the sides. The jump tossed her skirt up and slid the sweater up her midriff.

That's the way. Give him what he wants.

She landed with a harder jolt than she expected.

Rodney, squatting close to the ground, looked sweaty and a little stunned – as if he had trouble believing his luck. He was silent for a few seconds. Then he applauded.

'Go, Pam, go!' he called. 'Let's have another one!'

Pamela shot her fists into the air and shouted, 'Our team is red hot!'

'Yeah!'

She twirled, making her skirt rise high as she shouted again, 'Our team is red hot!' She halted, facing Rodney. Clapping hard and stomping her feet, she yelled, ''Cause we got killer instinct – and they do not!' She ran at Rodney, yelling one long 'Yaaaaaay!' as she dived into a handspring, did another one and another, her skirt and sweater flying up and down to let Rodney see more than he had ever seen at any football game, letting him see it all as she kept on yelling 'Yaaaaaay!' and flipped her way closer to him. Landing just in front of him, feet together, she cried out, *'Team!'* She clapped once more, then shot both fists into the air and kicked with her right leg.

The kick was meant for Rodney's face. He gasped. Flinched backward.

Chapter Three

Pamela watched her bare foot flash up past Rodney's face, and knew she'd missed.

Oh, God! I blew it!

Her leg kept rising.

I'll be high-kicking when he shoots me.

But Rodney wasn't shooting, not yet. He was tumbling backward, arms flung out, the gun pointing off to the side. As his back hit the ground, Pamela reached the top of her kick.

She brought her leg down, lunging forward at the last moment to stomp Rodney's knee.

He cried out.

She dropped with both knees onto his belly. It was big and soft. A hog belly full of meat and cheese fried in grease. Her knees sank in halfway to the ground. Rodney's eyes bulged. Air exploded from his mouth and nose, blasting out spittle and snot.

His left hand came up, clutched the sleeve of her sweater.

His right hand started to raise the pistol.

Pamela dropped straight forward. The sweater in Rodney's grip stretched and pulled away from her shoulder but couldn't stop her falling. She fell onto him, her belly on his face. He pressed the pistol against her ear.

She grabbed his wrist and forced his hand away. He didn't seem to have much energy. The smell of fried food belched from his mouth.

He writhed beneath her. His face felt like a soccer ball under her belly. A soccer ball with a hard, jutting chin – with breath that seeped through her sweater and felt like hot water against her skin. That smell

16

of grease would contaminate the material. Stay there. Maybe even saturate her skin.

She wondered if she could smother him this way. *Just stay on his face till he dies.*

It would be a good way to get him – suffocate him with the very body that had been his obsession, the body that he'd killed Jim for, the body that he intended to use and hurt and soil so badly.

Kill him with it!

His face pushed up at her belly and he began to snap, chin jerking up and down, teeth clamping shut on her sweater, biting and biting, going for her. Pamela sucked in her belly. He kept after it, snapping. His spit soaked through the fabric to her flesh.

As she started to push herself up, Rodney nipped her skin through the sweater.

'Ahhh!' she cried out.

She got away from his teeth but he sat up, snapping. Her left hand was busy trying to keep the pistol away. With her right, she grabbed his face and tried to push it down. His face kept coming at her, forcing her hand back, lifting her until she was perched on her knees and starting to slip down the hill of his stomach. She was only moments from falling.

'NO!' she yelled – and dug her thumb into his eye. His body jerked rigid and he shrieked.

Teetering on her knees, Pamela lunged for the pistol. Before she could reach it with her right hand his fat paw jumped out of her grip. He smashed the pistol against her cheekbone.

She toppled sideways.

As she fell, she thought, *Blew it again. I'm dead meat.* Her shoulder struck the ground. The blow seemed to shake her whole body. She felt sharp bits of gravel digging into her arm and hip and the side of her leg. But only for an instant, because she was rolling. Her back slammed the ground and she skidded.

The moment her skid stopped, she lifted her head and looked at Rodney. He was curled on his side, left hand cupping his face as if he hoped to catch whatever might spill from his eye socket. His right hand swayed, trying to aim the pistol at her. He made a high-pitched humming noise.

'Would you like another cheer?' Pamela gasped as she sat up. 'I'll do you another cheer.' She leaned forward, drew in her legs, and got her feet underneath her. 'Which cheer would you like?' She stood up. The pistol kept pointing at her, but Rodney didn't seem able to hold it steady. 'Do you want my favorite?'

Without waiting for an answer or a shot, she clapped her hands and started marching backward as she chanted, 'U! G! L! Y! You ain't got no al-i-bi! You *ugly*! You *ugly*!'

The gunshot kicked up dirt beside her right foot. Grit whipped the side of her leg.

She turned her back on Rodney and broke into a sprint. With the next shot, dirt exploded from the ground a few yards ahead of her and off to the left.

Two down, five to go. *Just keep missing! Please keep missing!*

Pamela dodged a cluster of prickly pear, then poured on the speed again: chin tucked down, back hunched, arms pumping, legs kicking out, reaching . . .

But never far enough. Never fast enough.

She huffed for air. Sweat poured down her body. She knew that she had to be running faster than she'd ever run before, but it seemed so terribly *slow*. A plodding pace. No more than a trudge!

Not fast enough to outrun a bullet. Not by a loo-oong shot.

But Rodney was blind in one eye, had to be in awful pain, and maybe he wasn't such a great marksman in the first place. He had already missed her twice at fairly close range. And she was a lot farther away from him now.

Why isn't he firing? She looked back.

He was on his feet, chasing her, pistol in his right hand, his left hand clenched in a fist and jabbing forward as he ran. One side of his face was an eyeless slick of blood. Pamela heard herself let out a whimper.

I'm not gonna get away, she thought. *He's gonna keep coming and keep coming till he gets close enough and then he's gonna use the gun on me.*

That's what he thinks. He's fat and out of shape and hurt bad. I can outrun him till hell freezes over.

If I don't keel over from heat prostration, she thought. *If my feet don't bleed me dry.*

She glanced at the ground behind her. She was leaving spots of blood on the desert floor. *He can follow those till hell freezes . . .*

Maybe she could make it to the car.

What good would that do? she wondered. *He's got the keys.* Pamela didn't even know anymore where the car *was*. The highway was off to her right – the car didn't seem to be there. Looking back over her right shoulder, she spotted it far off in the distance.

Good thing I don't have the keys, since I'm running away from the damn thing!

She considered changing direction and making a run for the road: a car was sure to come along, sooner or later. Anybody seeing her would know that she needed help and would probably give it to her. But if she went for the road, Rodney might run for his car. It wasn't *that* far behind. He could just hop in and chase her down with it.

Better not go any closer, she thought. She twisted around to make sure that he wasn't gaining on her. He was sprawled on the ground, far back. Pamela stopped running. Standing still, she gasped for breath and wiped the sweat out of her eyes.

Rodney looked as if he'd flopped facedown. He didn't seem to be moving at all.

All right! Pamela turned away from him and ran as hard as she could, dodging cacti and mesquite, sometimes leaping over rocks that got in her way. Rodney, she supposed, had been brought down by the heat, too much exertion and the pain or shock of losing his eye – but he would probably recover soon and come after her again.

At the edge of an arroyo she stopped to catch her breath. The slope was fairly steep. She wondered if she should try to climb down, or slide to the bottom on her rump.

Slide, she decided. *You don't wanna lose your footing and take a header.*

Pamela bent over and clutched the sides of her skirt. Then she looked back to see if Rodney was after her yet. And couldn't see him at all. Suddenly scared, she turned around and stood on tiptoes. No sign of him.

Maybe he's still down, she told herself. *I just can't see him because of all the rocks and bushes and stuff.*

Off to her right a cluster of rocks jutted up from the floor of the desert to a height of about twenty feet. She hurried toward it. It seemed to be farther away than she'd first supposed. Farther away, and higher.

As she ran, she began to think that she was making a mistake. She should've kept on running *away*. This detour was stealing her advantage. Rodney might be up and gaining on her – closing in with every step she took toward this damn pile of rocks. But she'd already come this far. So far, no sign of Rodney.

At last, Pamela reached the foot of the rocks. She was breathless, worn out, sodden with sweat. But she didn't pause to rest; she began to scurry upward. When she was halfway to the top, she decided that she was probably high enough for a good view. She crawled onto a stone slab that looked fairly smooth and didn't have much of a slant. She sat on it, knees up, feet against the surface to keep her from sliding down.

Hands cupped around her eyes, she squinted off across the desert. After a while, she spotted Rodney. Still sprawled on the ground.

Sighing, she wiped the sweat off her face.

For a while, she simply watched him and savored the knowledge that she was safe. Rodney was down. He was far away. As long as they both stayed put, he couldn't hurt her. She looked at the road.

Nothing was coming.

Why did they even put it here if nobody uses it? she wondered. *Put it here just for Rodney.* Then she thought, *Maybe so.* The idea spooked her a little. 'Just kidding,' she muttered. A road bound for nowhere. *That's ridiculous*, Pamela told herself. *It's not some sort of a phantom highway, it's just out in the middle of nowhere and probably goes between a couple of Podunk towns that nobody ever goes to, so it doesn't get used much.* Somebody would be along, sooner or later. Pamela tried to remember if she'd seen any other vehicles since they'd made the turn-off onto this stretch. None that she could recall.

What if nobody does come along? she wondered. Then she told herself, *I'm safe here. That's what counts. He can't get me. Just oughta make myself comfortable and wait things out.*

Her sweater felt like a heavy, damp coat. She pulled it off and sighed. The breeze was hot and dry against her skin, but it felt wonderful.

She folded the sweater and sat on it. The thick wool pad made a good cushion.

Rodney still appeared to be lying motionless out there. She checked the road. Still deserted.

If somebody does come along, Pamela thought, *it won't do me any good. Not while I'm up here. He probably won't see me, and I sure can't get down to the road in time.*

That's okay. I'm fine right here. For now.

But the sun felt awfully hot, so she tugged the sweater out from under her rump and draped it over her head. Some of it hung down her back; some of it shrouded her face. She lifted the part that hid her face and held it up with both hands to make a sunshade.

She gazed out from under it. Rodney was still sprawled on the ground.

Had he moved at all since going down? She didn't think so.

Maybe he's dead?

Maybe he's not.

With her sweater off and her arms raised, there was nothing to stop the dribbles of sweat that ran down Pamela's body. They slid all the way down to the waist of her skirt, tickling as they went. Every so often, when the itching became intolerable, she let the sweater flop down over her face and used both hands to rub herself.

Relieving the itches felt wonderful. But she hated to do it because she couldn't see Rodney while the sweater covered over her face.

Each time she lifted it, she was afraid that he might be gone.

He isn't going anywhere, she finally told herself. *He's all done chasing me.*

But is he dead? Pamela was pretty sure that a poke in the eye could be fatal – if you got in deep enough to hit the brain. Had she jabbed her thumb sufficiently far in for that? She doubted it. But if the gouge hadn't killed him, maybe he'd been dropped by a heart attack. A big fat guy like him running around the desert, fighting with her, getting plenty of shocks to his system from all the damage she'd inflicted . . . not to mention the fact that he'd probably been exhausted to start with. Driving for hours. Awake all night, first killing Jim, then wearing himself out with taking Pamela captive, then burning the house. She'd spent much of the night hoping that he would be knocked dead by a heart attack. *If he is dead now*, she thought, *I can get hold of his car keys and drive away. But if he's not dead and I go for the keys . . .*

She let the sweater flop in front of her face. Using both hands, she rubbed her itchy sides and belly and breasts. Her skin felt hot and slippery. With the fabric down, her face seemed to bake. She lifted the garment and sighed at the good feel of the breeze. *The car has air-conditioning. But what if Rodney's faking?*

He can't be faking the eye. If he isn't dead, he's messed up very badly. Still, I'd have to be nuts to go for his keys.

Pamela waited. She watched Rodney. She watched the road. More and more often, she found herself staring at Rodney's car. Imagining herself sliding into the driver's seat, slipping the key into the ignition and taking off. Leaving Rodney behind. Heading for a town just up the road (there must be one) while cool air poured onto her from the vents.

Only one way to make it happen, she told herself. *Go for the keys.*

He'll kill me!

Only if he can.

Chapter Four

Pamela went for his keys.

First, she pulled the sweater on. The heat of it made her grimace. But she kept it on and made her way down from her perch on the rocks.

She hobbled over the burning ground.

I'll take his shoes, too, she thought. *His shoes, his keys, his shirt.*

A nice lightweight shirt with short sleeves. But she remembered that it had gotten all bloody because of his eye, so she decided against taking it.

Just his shoes and keys, she told herself. Eventually, his body came into view. Pamela made her way toward it, limping, wincing each time she set down a foot. When she was only a few yards away she stopped. She stood motionless and gazed at Rodney.

Is he breathing? Not that she could see.

Maybe this is exactly what he's been waiting for, she thought. *He knew I'd come back for the keys if he stayed still long enough. And now I've done it. Walked straight into his trap.*

He lay facedown, his head turned to the right, both arms up and bent at the elbows. His right hand, on the ground a few inches from his forehead, still held the pistol. His grip on the pistol didn't look firm. As if he'd fallen asleep with the gun in his hand. *Maybe that's what he wants me to think?*

To shoot her, Rodney would only need to raise the pistol off the ground, move its barrel a couple of inches, and pull the trigger.

Slowly and silently, Pamela circled around him. Finally, she was standing a distance beyond his feet. She stood motionless and watched him while she tried to catch her breath.

If he was going to shoot me, she thought, *he would've done it when I was in front of him. Wouldn't have let me get behind him like this.*

But I didn't go very close to him. Maybe he didn't know I'd shown up. Maybe he still doesn't know I'm here. But he'll know when I try for his stuff. Unless he's out cold or dead.

To get the car keys, she would need to reach into the right front pocket of his trousers.

Squeeze her hand in between his thigh and the ground. He would feel it. And he would feel it when she tugged off his shoes.

Maybe he isn't feeling anything?

Pamela took a small step and crouched. Reaching down between her knees, she wrapped her fingers around a lump of rock. She tried to pick it up, but the rock was embedded in the dirt. So she shook it and jerked it, and soon worked it loose.

She lifted it.

The rock was about the size of a steam iron, and heavier. Raising it to shoulder height, she walked slowly toward Rodney. She stopped near his feet.

What do I do now? she wondered. *Drop it onto his back and see if he says 'ouch'? Brilliant idea*, she thought. *He says 'ouch,' then turns over and shoots me.*

Pamela could think of only one smart thing to do: *Bash his head in.*

Don't try to do it by throwing *the rock, either. Keep hold of it, dive onto his back, and bust his head open before he knows what's happening.*

I can't do that, she thought. *Oh, yeah? Why not! The dirty bastard murdered Jim. Not just Jim, but all those girls. And don't forget what he did to ME. He kidnapped me and shot at me. It's self-defense if ever there was a case of self-defense. On top of which, the dirtbag* deserves *to die!* She hurled herself at Rodney.

When her rump dropped onto his back, he let out a grunt. *Not dead! NOT YET!*

Pamela hoisted the rock high, ready to slam it down against the back of Rodney's head. He made a quiet whimper. She hesitated. *Do it!*

But he wasn't trying to fight, wasn't even trying to grip on the pistol. He was just lying there, making little whimpery sounds.

Then he murmured something.

She hissed, 'What?'

'I give.'

He gives? That's what a kid says when he's wrestling with his brother!

'You *give?*' Pamela blurted. 'You GIVE? When you killed my husband!' *He wants to quit. Like this is a game that just got too rough.*

'Please,' Rodney murmured. 'Don't . . . don't hurt me. My eye!' He started to sob.

Do it, she told herself. *Just do it. Get it over with.* But she couldn't force herself to strike.

Wait till he tries something. That way it won't be so much like a cold-blooded killing.

'If you move a muscle,' she said, 'I'll kill you, so help me God.'

'Don't . . . Please. I'll do . . . anything.'

'Let go of the gun. Take your hand away from it.'

Rodney's fingers trembled and opened. His hand slid off the pistol.

Pamela wanted to pick it up, but her right hand was holding the rock. She switched the rock to her other hand, then leaned forward and reached out past Rodney's shoulder.

Her fingertips were about to settle on the pistol when he grabbed her wrist. She swung the rock at his head, but he was already bucking beneath her, already jerking her arm.

She felt the rock connect with him. The blow made him cry out. It didn't stop him.

Pamela hurtled headlong past his shoulder. She landed on her side, skidding. He let go of her wrist. She rolled onto her back, hoping to start a quick series of rolls that would put her out of reach.

But she was still on her back when his fist came down, hammering her belly. Her breath exploded out. She *had* to keep rolling and get away from him, but all she could do was hug her belly and bring her knees up and try to suck air into her lungs. Then her arms were pinned to her sides by Rodney's knees. He was sitting on her chest.

'Get off! I can't breathe!'

He hunched down so that his face loomed over Pamela's face.

'Look!' he gasped. 'What you . . . did to me.' Rodney hunched lower.

His empty socket looked like a bloody gash. It dripped foul fluid onto Pamela's cheek and nose. His upper lip twitched. He altered his position slightly, and the socket dripped toward her right eye. She shut her eyes fast. She felt warm patters on her right lid. Rodney uttered laughs that sounded like choking noises.

Then something went into her mouth. It knocked against her upper teeth, thrust against her tongue. She opened her left eye. Rodney had thrust the pistol into her mouth.

'Blow your . . . fuckin' brains out,' he muttered.

He shoved the barrel deeper. It pushed against her uvula, and she started gagging.

Pamela didn't hear the gunshot. Not at first. What she heard first was a sound like a whip cracking. Then came a noise like a mallet smacking meat. Rodney's head jerked up and she caught a glimpse deep into his forehead through a hole the size of a shirt button. *Then* she heard the gunshot. It sounded like distant thunder echoing through a canyon of clouds. An instant later, a jet of gore spouted out of the hole in Rodney's forehead. It arced past Pamela's face, then curved lower and splashed her straight between the eyes as he crumpled forward.

Chapter Five

Pamela didn't know why the ground was vibrating underneath her, or what the loud windy roaring sound might be.

She wondered where she was. She wondered what day it was.

Then she suddenly remembered that Jim was dead, and her whole life seemed to collapse into bleak rubble. She remembered about Rodney. She supposed that she was in his car, maybe stretched out on the back seat, and he was probably driving her the rest of the way to—

No! She'd seen a deep hole in the middle of Rodney's forehead. *He's dead*, she realized.

She opened her eyes. She was stretched out on a seat, all right. But not the seat of Rodney's car.

Pamela was in a bus – on one of those long cushioned benches where people sit just behind the driver, facing the aisle. The windows above the back of the seat were covered with yellow fabric that muffled the sunlight and gave the air a murky golden hue. The air felt warm, but not terribly hot. She guessed that the bus's air conditioner must be going.

She turned her head. The long seat across the aisle was empty.

Lowering her gaze, she looked down at herself. She was still wearing the cheerleader sweater and skirt. Most of the sweater was caked so thickly with blood that very little of its original gold color was visible. It was neatly arranged, however, and so was the skirt. Somebody must've taken care to straighten her clothes after placing her on the seat.

Someone had also cleaned her face, apparently. It had a freshly washed feel. Exploring it with her hand, she found no trace of stickiness.

27

Not on her face, and not in her hair, which felt slightly damp. She checked her hand. There was no blood on it.

Someone had done a good job of washing her, at least from the neck up.

Looking past her feet, Pamela saw a couple of passengers in the first row of forward-facing seats. A man and a woman. They sat rigid and stiff, secured by safety belts that crossed their chests and laps. They both seemed to be gazing straight forward. They were dressed very well to be on a bus in the middle of the desert: the man in a jacket and tie, the woman in a flower-patterned dress.

This must be a charter bus, she thought. *Maybe taking a church group on some sort of excursion.*

Got lost on their way to the Grand Canyon? Besides, religious groups don't usually go around putting bullets into people's heads.

Then who just shot Rodney?

Pamela doubted if she'd been saved by either of these two people. They sat there like a couple of statues.

She nodded a greeting at them, but they didn't respond. She turned her head. Across the aisle from the couple sat a kid. Maybe their son. About eight or nine years old, he wore a baseball cap, blue jeans and a T-shirt. Pamela tried to read the slogan on his T-shirt. Parts of a few words were hidden under the chest strap of his safety belt, but she pieced together a message that seemed rather odd: 'I've been to Pits. It IS the Pits. Pits, CA, pop. 6.'

Though the boy seemed to be dressed like a normal kid, he sat rigid by the covered window, arms at his sides, face forward, and didn't move.

'Hi,' Pamela said, hoping that her voice was loud enough to be heard over the noise of the bus.

The kid didn't even look at her.

Real friendly people, she thought. *Probably a religious group, she mused again, a bunch of holier-than-thou fanatics. Maybe they're practicing a vow of silence.*

Yeah, but somebody *shot Rodney. Somebody saved my life.* She sat up. Turning toward the aisle, she lowered her legs. The bottoms of her feet felt stiff and sore, so she eased them down gently against the floor. The rubber mat on the floor felt cool and smooth, a little gritty. She waved at the kid.

He ignored her.

So Pamela turned her head to the left. Just past the arm-rail of the seat where she'd been lying a metal partition rose from the floor to about the height of her shoulders. She supposed that it was there to shield the back of the driver's seat, though the top of the seat showed – and so did the driver's head.

He wasn't wearing a hat. His black hair was cut so short on the back and sides that his scalp showed through. The close trim made his ears seem way too large. On top, his hair stuck straight up like the bristles of a brush. 'Hello,' Pamela said.

He didn't answer.

'Driver?' she asked, raising her voice.

'No talking, ma'am,' he called without looking back. He didn't sound angry, just like a man stating a plain fact.

'What?' she asked. 'What do you mean, no talking?'

'No talking to the driver while the bus is in motion. Company policy.'

'Oh. Okay.' She supposed it must be a safety rule. 'Sorry,' she added.

'No problem.'

Pamela wondered if the bus company also had a rule against standing up while the bus was in motion.

Soon find out.

Leaning forward, she reached out for a shiny support pole. She clutched it and pulled herself off the seat. Pain surged up from the bottoms of her feet. She stood hunched over, clutching the pole, her mouth torn open in a silent outcry. The worst of the pain didn't last long. She straightened her body. As she took deep breaths, she noticed that the window shades across the aisle appeared to be strips of yellow blankets. They were secured to the windows with broad silvery strips of duct tape. *Real classy*, she thought. *What sort of bus is this? Probably one of those rat-trap death machines without any brakes – the sort you hear about when they crash in the mountains on the way to a revival weekend or Bible camp or something.*

And the pilgrims get to heaven a little sooner than they expected. Amen. Maybe we are on our way to a Bible camp. If we don't crash and die first.

Moving only her head, Pamela looked toward the front of the bus. The brightness from the windshield made her squint. Ahead of the bus was a two-lane road through the desert.

The same road she'd been traveling with Rodney? She couldn't tell. But it sure looked like the same desert.

She could see the driver's face in the rearview mirror, but sunglasses hid his eyes. She nodded a greeting, in case he was looking at her. He didn't react.

At least he's not ordering me to sit down.

With his sunglasses and flattop and the lean, rough features of his face, he looked like he ought to be a motorcycle cop.

A cop moonlighting as a church-bus driver. That'd be a good one. Might explain what happened out there with Rodney.

'Hello?' Pamela said.

The face in the mirror turned slightly. As patiently as before, the driver explained, 'I can't talk just now, ma'am. Not while the vehicle is in motion. It's for the safety of everyone aboard.'

'Okay. Sorry.'

The hell with it, she thought. Then she stepped to the center of the aisle, turned away from the brightness of the windshield, and peered toward the back of the bus. In the hazy yellow glow, she saw that many of the seats seemed to be occupied. She guessed that there must be fifteen or twenty passengers.

None of them talked. None of them moved, except for rocking and shaking a little with the motions of the bus.

What a lively crew, Pamela thought.

With so many passengers, however, there must be at least one who would open up and tell her what was going on.

Grimacing and flinching with every step, she hobbled down the aisle. The pair in the first seat didn't even turn their heads as she approached them.

What's the matter with these people! A few paces away from them, she saw what the matter was. She halted.

She moaned.

She grabbed the nearest support pole to hold herself steady, and heard herself mutter, 'Isn't *this* wonderful? Isn't *this* just what the doctor ordered? What the hell *is* this?'

The couple hadn't been ignoring her, hadn't been snubbing her, hadn't even known that she existed.

'Dummies,' she muttered.

The kid across the aisle was also a dummy. So were the two women sitting side by side in the next row of seats. They looked like a pair of mannequins heisted from a department store. Maybe they'd been modeling casual wear at J.C. Penney's. Both wore colorful outfits that looked cool and comfortable: knit pullover shirts, Bermuda shorts, knee-high socks and white tennis shoes.

Nobody sat across the aisle from them, but behind them was a male mannequin dressed in a pinstriped suit and tie.

From where she stood, Pamela could now see at least a dozen more passengers scattered here and there among the seats. Some sat alone, others in pairs. None of them moved.

They're all dummies. Every last one of them. She felt goose bumps scurry up her body. They started at her knees and crawled up her legs and buttocks. They raced up her spine to the nape of her neck. Her arms and breasts went prickly. Her nipples squirmed and grew stiff. Her scalp crawled. Her legs began to shake.

Stop it! she told herself. *It's not that big a deal! Last night was a big deal. Rodney was a big deal. This is nothing. It's just creepy.*

That's the thing, she thought. *It's no big deal, but it's too damn weird. Creepy, eerie, spooky. Like something out of an old* Twilight Zone – *but no big deal.*

No big deal, my ass. I'm the only real person on a busload of dummies!

Maybe I'm dead, she speculated. *Nice thought.*

Maybe Rodney killed me, after all, and this is some sort of soul-bus taking me wherever it is that souls get taken to. Like the train in that song – the one that's 'bound for glory.' Only this isn't a train, it's a bus. The Glory Bus.

'Bull,' she muttered.

I've gotta stop scaring myself, she thought, *and find out what's really going on.*

Pamela looked over her shoulder at the bus driver. *Won't say much, but at least he's real. My old buddy Charon. Ferryman of the dead.*

'Cut it out,' she muttered, and faced the rows of mannequins. 'There's got to be a logical explanation,' she whispered, and felt a smirk come to her face. 'Right,' she said. 'Sure. That's what they always say: "Gotta be a logical explanation." Yeah, a logical explanation, all right – el shitto has hit el fanno, that's the logical explanation.'

She decided to take a closer look at her fellow passengers, so she continued toward the back of the bus. As she hobbled along, she spoke softly to them. 'Anybody here *not* a dummy? Speak up. Anybody wanna offer me a logical explanation as to what you're doing here? Nothing about me being dead and on my way to hell, please. And I don't want to hear that the driver's a lunatic, either. Understood? Perhaps he's a traveling dummy salesman? How about it? Anyone? How about you?' she asked the final passenger.

This one wasn't sitting up like the others. He was stretched out on the long seat at the very back of the bus. Approaching him, Pamela could see only his legs. He wore dark trousers and his feet were crossed at the ankles. The back of the seat in front of him blocked the rest of her view.

'Hello?' she asked. 'Cat got your tongue?' *What if this was a real person?*

Fat chance, she told herself. Then she stepped past the last seat-back, looked down through the murky yellow light and saw that she'd made a good guess: the figure lying on his back, feet crossed, was a real person. She figured out who he was when she saw his bloody shirt. Then she recognized the neat round hole in his forehead, and the pit where his eye should've been.

He looked as if he'd been laid out to dry a while ago, after being dipped headfirst into a vat of blood. Pamela gagged. She turned away from the body. She began staggering down the aisle, hurrying past row after row of mannequins.

He brought Rodney! Why did he bring Rodney? What's going—?

A sudden braking of the bus shoved Pamela forward. About to fall, she stretched out her arms and grabbed seat-back handles on both sides of the aisle. From behind her came a thudding sound. She looked back. Rodney had been thrown to the floor.

The bus continued to lose speed for a while, then made a right turn that thrust Pamela sideways. She kept her grip on the seat handles and stayed on her feet through the turn.

Now the bus was on an unpaved road. Pamela saw the strip of rough dirt through the windshield. And she felt it. The floor shuddered under her sore feet. The whole bus bounced and lurched and vibrated. It shook so hard that she thought it must be falling apart. She pictured it leaving a trail of pieces to mark its passage: a tailpipe, a hubcap, a muffler, a drive shaft.

From what she could see through the windshield, the terrible road seemed to be leading toward nothing except more mesquite and cacti and brush, ravines and jagged dry piles of rock and a mountainous area that looked just as desolate as the desert. *Not taking me to a town*, she thought.

Maybe he's got a house out here, same as Rodney. A fun house where he's gonna have the same kind of fun with me that Rodney planned. She twisted her head around. Rodney was still on the floor. His body seemed to be trapped, facedown, between his seat and the legs of the seat in front of him.

Going nowhere.

The feel of the floor pounding against her feet made Pamela want to cry.

Gotta sit down.

She belonged on the long seat near the front of the bus. That was where someone – most likely the driver – had put her, so that was where she ought to be. Besides, it was a good distance from Rodney's body. When she let go of the seat handles, however, the lurching bus tossed her forward. She landed on her hands and knees in the middle of the aisle.

She supposed she could *crawl* to the front. *The hell with that*, she thought.

Pamela climbed onto the nearest empty seat. This entire row was clear of mannequins. Across the aisle a couple of bundles were piled on the seat. One of them appeared to be a sleeping bag, while the other was a large fabric satchel with handles. *The driver's stuff*, she supposed. *He must sleep on the bus. Maybe it's his home, and he lives on it with his dummy collection.*

Now he's collected me.

He saved my life, she reminded herself. *Someone did, anyway. And the driver seems to be the only person around who might've done it.*

She guessed it was possible that her rescuer had shot Rodney and vanished, that the bus had come along later and that there was no direct connection between the two events.

That didn't seem terribly likely, though.

The driver almost *had* to be the one who'd saved her. Leaning on the arm-rail, she peered up the aisle. All she could see of the driver was the back of his head.

What if he's not a good guy? she wondered. *He's prowling around the desert with a bus full of dummies and probably some sort of high-powered rifle.* Pamela hadn't seen the gun but he must've fired it from awfully far away; the bullet had struck Rodney a long time before she'd heard the shot. *The guy has to be weird,* she thought. *But he saved me. Then again, maybe he wants to have me. Let's face it, what's he doing on a dirt road like this? He should be driving me to the nearest town, not deeper into the desert.*

'This doesn't look real good,' she muttered.

Chapter Six

They were in a canyon when the bus finally stopped. The driver reached out to his right and shoved a handle, opening the front door. Then he shut off the engine.

To Pamela, the sudden quiet seemed enormous.

The driver stood up and turned around. Pamela stared at him.

She felt scared, but weary. They'd spent at least half an hour on the rough dirt road. She'd worn herself out with wondering about the driver, imagining all the things that he might want to do with her, and trying to figure out the best course of action for herself.

Her most recent conclusions: he might or might not intend to rape or murder her; she shouldn't try to attack him or escape until she knew more; by then, it might be too late; sit tight and see what happens; he might be a friend; if he turns out to be a bad guy, fight him to the end.

He started walking up the aisle. *Oh God, here he comes.*

He wasn't a large man like Rodney. Medium height, and slim. He wore a gray short-sleeved shirt. It was tucked into blue pants that were cinched around his waist with a black leather belt.

A bus-driver uniform?

Why isn't it all rumpled and sweaty and bloody? Pamela wondered. *It would have to be, if this is the guy who hauled Rodney into the bus. Not to mention hauling me in too. But his uniform looked neat and clean, as if he'd done nothing more than sit behind the steering—*

Almost here. Get ready.

The driver walked past Pamela as if he hadn't noticed her. She couldn't believe it. She twisted in her seat to watch him. At the back of the bus he crouched and took hold of Rodney's ankles.

35

Go!

She lurched out of her seat and raced down the aisle. The nearest exit was the side door, just ahead and down a short stairwell to the right. But it was shut and might give her trouble, so she ran past it. Dashed for the open front door. Each footfall made her wince with pain. She gritted her teeth and tried to run faster.

'Don't fall and hurt yourself,' called the driver.

When she reached the front she glanced back. He wasn't even watching her. He was still at the rear of the bus, bent over, dragging Rodney's body into the aisle.

Doesn't he care that I'm getting away? Maybe not. Maybe he doesn't care because he knows I can't really escape. Nowhere to go.

We'll see about that, Pamela told herself. She charged down the steps and leaped off the bus. The desert heat slammed down on her.

Here we go again, she thought. She started running toward the nearest high ground, a rocky butte not too far away. If she could get up there, she might be able to pull a disappearing act among the boulders and crevices. At its foot she looked back.

No sign of the driver.

Pamela couldn't see inside the bus because of the makeshift yellow curtains on the windows. But the side door was still shut and the driver wasn't at the front door yet. She didn't know whether the bus had an emergency exit at the very back. She hadn't noticed one there, but she'd been awfully distracted at the time because of Rodney's body.

School buses usually had an emergency exit at the rear and this looked like an old, medium-sized school bus. It wasn't painted like one, though. Only the curtains were yellow. The rest of the bus – what Pamela could see of it – was painted a dull gray color that reminded her of how a lake looks on a gloomy overcast day.

It had a word painted in black above the windows where the name of the school district had probably once been.

PEQUOD

Terrific, Pamela thought. *I've been captured by Captain Ahab.*

She turned away from the bus and hurled herself at the rocky slope. She scrambled upward, climbing higher and higher, huffing and sweating, her throat clenched because of the pain shooting up from her feet.

'Be careful you don't hurt yourself,' the driver called. 'I didn't shoot this feller just to have you fall and crack your head open.'

Stopping at the top of a boulder, Pamela put a hand against a steep wall of rock and turned sideways. She was surprised to find herself so high above the floor of the canyon.

The driver was just outside the front door of the bus, bent over and walking backward, dragging Rodney's body by the wrists. The head, face up, wobbled from side to side between the driver's straight arms. The body skidded along on its back. The feet shook and bounced.

'What're you doing?' Pamela called.

Not bothering to look up, the driver answered, 'Gotta dump him.' Beyond the front of the bus he started dragging the body uphill. 'It'd be a sight easier if you gave me a hand,' he announced. 'Not that I'm complaining. I killed him, after all – my duty to deal with his mortal remains. But a helping hand'd be appreciated.'

'Where are you taking him?'

'Up yonder.' He dropped Rodney's arms, then tilted back his head. Pamela supposed he was looking at her, but she couldn't see his eyes because of the sunglasses. Raising an arm, he pointed in the direction he'd been dragging the body. 'Yonder there,' he said. 'I'll just give him the old heave-ho down the glory hole.'

'What were you going to do with me?' Pamela asked.

'Take care of you, I reckon. Take you on down the road, soon as I'm done with my business here.'

'How do I know you won't . . . do something to me?'

'What do you mean, *hurt* you?'

'Yeah.'

'Why would I wanna go and do that?'

'Some men do.'

'You mean like him?'

'Yeah.'

'Look what I done to him.'

'Why'd you do it?'

'You wanna gab, come on down so I ain't gotta yell.' With that, he picked up Rodney's arms and resumed dragging the body. Pamela watched him labor with it. She shook her head. Rodney was a lot bigger than the driver. It had to be a tough job, struggling uphill with a heavy body on a hot day like this.

He shot him for me. I'd be dead right now.

'Hold on,' she called. 'I'll come down and help.'

'Much obliged.' He dropped Rodney's arms and sat down on a nearby rock.

I must be out of my mind, Pamela thought as she began to make her way down from the rocks. *He's out of his, for sure. But he* did *save my life. And he seems pretty much okay except for the fact that he drives around the desert with a bus full of dummies. Maybe there's a good reason for that,* she told herself. *Right. A logical explanation. Even if he is nuts,* she thought, *maybe I can stay on his good side and he'll treat me okay.*

Near the bottom, she leaped the rest of the way to the ground. The hard earth smacked her wounded feet. She cried, 'Ahhh!' and hobbled over to the bus. She leaned against its side, propped a foot across her knee and inspected the damage. The sole was filthy, scratched and bloody. She supposed her other foot was just as bad, or worse.

'Go on in the bus,' the driver called, 'and grab yourself some shoes.' He was still sitting on the rock.

'Really?' Pamela called.

'Just take 'em off a passenger. I'll wait.'

'Thank you!' Pamela hobbled to the open front door, climbed aboard and stopped. The key was in the ignition. She stared at it.

I'll never get another chance like this. She glanced through the windshield. The driver, sitting on the rock near Rodney's body, wasn't even watching. His head was turned away and tipped back as if he might be admiring the scenery.

Did he leave the key here on purpose? she wondered. *Maybe it's a trick or a test or something. To see if I try to make a getaway. Maybe he's just careless, forgot to take the key with him. Or maybe it's his way of telling me that I'm not his prisoner.*

Who knows?

The hell with it, she thought. *I told him I'd help with the body, so that's what I'll do.*

She limped down the aisle to the seat behind the boy dummy. Both the young female mannequins wore knee socks and white sneakers.

The driver hadn't said anything about taking socks. Would he mind?

Pamela pulled the shoes and socks off the nearest figure. Sitting on the aisle floor, she put them on. The socks felt almost as good a band-ages. When she stood up, her feet still hurt but they felt protected. The socks' arid soles made a springy cushion for them.

Would the driver get angry if she borrowed more? The rest of the mannequin's outfit, for instance?

The plaid shorts and lime-green polo shirt looked cool and fresh. And clean.

Pamela felt miserable in the clothes she had on. They made her sweat. They made her itch. The sweater and skirt were not only heavy and hot but filthy. And covered with Rodney's blood.

Besides, they'd been a gift from him.

An imitation of her high-school cheerleader costume, put together by Rodney so that he could get himself all turned on.

He had dressed her in it. Maybe he had dressed his other victims in it, too. Some might've been wearing it while he did horrible things to them. Perhaps some had even worn it after they'd been killed – the inside of the sweater and skirt touching their dead skin.

Pamela wished she hadn't thought of that. *Now I have to get out of this stuff.*

She spotted the driver outside, still sitting. He seemed to be paying no attention to her or the bus. She crouched slightly, and couldn't see him anymore. Staying low, she unfastened the Bermuda shorts and drew them down the mannequin's legs. Then she unbuckled the safety belts, pulled the figure into the aisle and stripped off its knit shirt. Standing, she glanced at the driver. He was still sitting on the rock. So she tugged her skirt down. Squatting, she pulled the sweater off.

Pamela looked at herself. A lot of bruises and scratches and weals, but they didn't concern her. What did concern her was the blood. She supposed that nearly all of it was Rodney's blood. It must've soaked through the sweater. She didn't want it getting on her clean clothes. Quickly, she turned the cheerleader skirt inside-out. She used both hands to towel off her skin with the skirt. The blood was damp, maybe kept moist by her sweat, so she was able to wipe off most of it. Then she tossed the skirt aside and slipped into the bright green polo shirt. Holding the mannequin's shorts, she stood.

The driver was sitting on the rock, head down.

Pamela stepped into the shorts, pulled them up and fastened them. A bit loose, but not enough to matter. She tossed the old sweater and skirt onto an empty seat, then walked toward the front of the bus. Though her feet still hurt, this was the best they'd felt in a long time. The best *she*'d felt. The clothes were light. They seemed to float against her, not wrap her in heat and load her down. She wished there'd been undergarments to wear. This was like being half-undressed. The shorts were certainly better than the skirt had been, but the clinging knit shirt made it very obvious that she wasn't wearing a bra.

She supposed she could find something to wear over the shirt. *Too hot around here already. The hell with it.* She climbed down the stairs and stepped to the ground.

The driver raised his head. 'Look at you,' he said.

Pamela grimaced at him. 'I grabbed a bit more than just shoes,' she said. 'I hope that's okay. I mean, my stuff was horrible, and . . .'

'You take whatever you want, girl. You're welcome to it.'

'That's really nice of you. Thanks.'

This guy isn't going to attack me, she thought. *He's nice. Except maybe he's just in a calm period right now between his fits of homicidal frenzy.*

No, no, no, she told herself. *He's okay, he's fine.*

As she approached him, she held out her hand. 'I'm Pamela,' she said.

The driver stood up. He took her hand and gave it a small squeeze. His grip felt solid but restrained. 'Pleased to meet you,' he said. 'My name's Sharpe. Walter Sharpe.' He released her hand. 'You call me Sharpe.'

'I go by Pamela, mostly.'

'Howdy, Pamela.'

'Howdy, Sharpe.'

'That outfit there, it sure looks better on you than it did on Fran.'

'Fran?'

'The gal you took it offa. Fran Lowry.'

Oh wonderful, he's got names for them.

'Well, time's a-wasting,' he said. 'What's say we dump this ol' boy? Pick an arm.'

Pamela chose Rodney's left arm. She lifted it by the wrist. Sharpe, at her side, picked up the right arm. They began walking backward, dragging him.

'I want to thank you for, you know, saving me. He was about to kill me.'

'Figured he weren't up to much good.'

'He murdered my husband last night.'

For a few moments, Sharpe didn't say anything. Then he shook his head. 'That's a real shame. I'm sorry to hear it. My God, he made a widow outta you. Makes me double-glad I put that bullet through his skull.'

'We'd only been married for six months.'

'A real shame,' Sharpe said.

'He showed me Jim's body.' Pamela was a little surprised to hear herself telling Sharpe about such things. Dragging Rodney and telling her secrets. 'It was . . . in the bathroom. He showed it to me on the way out . . . when we were leaving. Jim was on the floor, but . . .'

The memory suddenly made her retch and double over. As she heaved, she saw through teary eyes her vomit cascading down onto Rodney's face.

'That's all right,' Sharpe murmured, gently patting her back. 'Get it all out. You'll feel a whole lot better, you just dump it all out on him.'

When Pamela was done vomiting, she remained bent over with her hands on her knees. Her vision was blurry with tears. Her chest hurt. Her throat and nasal passages felt scorched.

'Here,' Sharpe said, 'I got a hanky for you.'

'I'll . . . mess it up.'

'You need it more than me.'

He held a red bandanna under her face, so she took it. She wiped her face and blew her nose, then straightened up and stepped a couple of paces backward. Rodney's face was carpeted with colorful, chunky glop.

Last night's pizza.

Jim had phoned Pizza Guy to order it for home delivery. Pepperoni and sausage, thin crust, with extra cheese. They'd eaten it in the living room on TV trays, drinking beer and watching a tape of the previous night's Letterman show. Jim's last meal. His last Letterman show. His last everything.

Pamela started to weep, but then she saw how Rodney's open mouth was full to the brim.

She suddenly lost interest in crying.

She turned away and gagged again. It hurt her in the chest and

41

across her back. She wondered if she'd somehow damaged herself with all the vomiting. She concentrated, trying not to gag anymore.

Just don't think about the puke in his mouth. She retched all over again.

'You okay?' Sharpe asked.

'No,' Pamela gasped.

'Don't look at him. Tell you what. You just stay here and take it easy. I'll see to this feller.'

Without looking around, she nodded.

'Good thing he's already dead,' Sharpe announced. 'If he weren't, he'd likely be wishin' he was.'

Pamela laughed. She couldn't help it. Just a small laugh. It hurt, but not as much as the gagging.

She heard Rodney being dragged away. Then she felt guilty about making Sharpe do all the work, so she hurried after him.

Keeping her gaze on him, she said, 'I'll take a hand.'

'You don't have to.'

'I just won't look at him.'

So Sharpe turned an arm over to her. She clutched its wrist with both hands. Side by side, she and Sharpe trudged backward, dragging the body. She stared off to the left to avoid looking at Rodney.

'Where did you say we're taking him?' she asked.

'Up to the glory hole.'

'The glory hole?'

'Used to be a lot of mines round these parts. Some of the pits, they just got left behind, open and all, when the ore played out. I found this here glory hole a few years back. I doubt much of anyone knows it's here, 'cept me and maybe a couple of old prospectors.'

'Do you live somewhere nearby?'

'Yup. In yonder bus.'

Don't ask! But she couldn't seem to help herself. 'With the others?'

'That's about the size of it.'

Don't, don't, don't! 'With ... Fran and ... uh ...' she said. She turned her head the other way, forcing herself not to focus on Rodney, and looked at Sharpe's face. 'Who are they?'

'Well, they ain't so much *whos* as they're *whats*.'

'Oh. Okay. *What* are they?'

He turned his head and smiled at her. 'You telling me you don't know?'

'Well . . .'

'They're *store* dummies,' Sharpe said, and looked over his shoulder.

'Well, I know *that*. But . . .'

'Better hold up, we're here.' Sharpe let go of Rodney's arm.

Keeping her gaze away from the body, Pamela crouched and set the other arm on the ground. Then she stood and turned around.

'That's it there,' Sharpe said, nodding.

The hole just a little farther up the slope from them looked like the mouth of a cave.

A vertical cave. Pamela walked slowly toward it. Sharpe stayed by her side.

'You don't wanna get too close,' he warned.

A few strides more, and Pamela suddenly found that she *couldn't* walk any closer to the hole. Her legs, going shaky and weak, seemed to know they were near enough. They stopped her. She had an urge to back away, but she fought it. Bending her knees slightly, she stood her ground.

Sharpe stopped beside her.

'It's a hole, all right,' she said.

'Goes straight down,' Sharpe told her.

'Very far?'

'Far enough.'

'It seems like . . . a horrible place to leave someone.'

'No more than what I reckon he deserves. 'Sides, he's dead. He won't know no better. You just stand pat, and I'll take care of him.'

Sharpe went to get Rodney.

From where Pamela stood, she could see only partway down the mouth of the hole. The far wall of it was bright with sunlight. She supposed that the sunlight must peter out, farther down. Get dimmer and dimmer until there was none at all – blackness. Sharpe stepped past her. He was bent over and trudging backward, dragging Rodney by the wrists.

'Be careful,' Pamela said.

'Yup.'

He kept walking backward, closer and closer to the edge of the glory hole.

'Sharpe!'

His head lifted, but he didn't stop.

'Watch where you're going!'

'Oh, don't worry about this ol' boy.'

He was only about two paces from the pit, and still backing up.

'Damn it, Sharpe! You're gonna fall in!'

At the very rim of the pit, he halted and let go of Rodney's wrists. He stood up straight. He grinned at Pamela. 'No need to fret. I ain't exactly a novice at this.'

'Would you *please* get away from the edge!'

'Sure.' He stepped over Rodney's body.

Pamela took a deep, trembling breath.

Standing over Rodney's feet, Sharpe turned his head toward her. 'I already emptied his pockets for him, back on the bus. Anything you want before I give him the ol' heave-ho?'

'I don't think so.'

'Well, then.' He lowered himself to his knees, clutched Rodney around the ankles, and pushed. The body started scooting headfirst toward the pit.

Pamela looked at Rodney's face. Much of the mess must've slid off, but he still had gobs of vomit clinging to his face. It still filled his open mouth. It covered his one remaining eye and was packed in the socket where his other eye used to be. She imagined cold pizza hurl trickling down his throat. Thick cheesy lumps of it.

Pamela swallowed hard and looked away.

He deserves it, she told herself. *He deserves everything.* When she looked again, his head was over the hole, tipped way back. His shoulders were at the edge.

Sharpe kept shoving.

Rodney's arms flopped into the hole. Soon, his back was bent so much that he looked as if his spine might snap. Sharpe let go of the body's ankles.

Rodney's feet kicked toward the sky. Heels up, he plunged straight down and vanished.

'Jesus,' Pamela muttered. A moment later there came a thudding sound.

Sharpe stood up. 'What was the feller's name?' he asked. 'I like to know their names.'

'Rodney Pinkham.'

'Mind if I say a few words over him?'

'Whatever you want.'

'Much obliged.' Cupping both hands to the sides of his mouth, Sharpe lowered his head and called, 'Good riddance, Rodney Pinkham. Rot in peace.'

Chapter Seven

Norman nearly always locked his car before leaving it. This time he decided not to bother.

Norman climbed out, shut the door without locking it, and stepped to the gasoline pump marked REGULAR UNLEADED. After filling his tank, he walked no more than fifty feet to the gas-station office. No waiting. Stepped right up to the counter, gave his pump number, handed over a twenty-dollar bill, accepted his change and headed for the door.

In and out, just like that.

Away from the car for two minutes, maybe less.

But on his way out of the office, Norman thought about the container of teriyaki beef jerky that he'd noticed on the counter while paying for the gas.

The label on the tall plastic jar had caught his eye: 'Wolfbane – you'll *howl* for more.'

He loved teriyaki jerky.

He'd never heard of Wolfbane.

All the best jerky was the kind you'd never heard of, the kind you found in out-of-the-way places like gas stations in small towns you were passing through on your way home from college.

Only a stride from the door, Norman halted. *Screw my diet*, he thought. *One or two jerkies aren't going to make any big difference in the great scheme of things.* So he returned to the counter.

Ahead of him was a woman buying a pack of cigarettes. It didn't take her very long. When she left, Norman stepped up to the counter. 'Guess I'll have some of this jerky,' he said.

'Help yourself,' the clerk told him.

Norman opened the clear plastic jar and took six strips of Wolfbane teriyaki beef jerky. The clerk held out a paper sack and Norman slid them in. Then he screwed the lid back on to the container.

He paid.

More than twelve dollars, but when did good jerky ever come cheap? Finally, he walked out the door.

When he looked at his car, he thought he'd made a mistake. This couldn't be *his* red Jeep Cherokee. It was a popular model and color. Another one must've pulled in.

One with a man in the passenger seat. Norman looked for his.

There wasn't another Cherokee on the gas station's lot. There wasn't *any* other car. Besides, this one was stopped at the pump where he'd filled up. And it had his license-plate number.

He suddenly felt cold and crawly in his bowels. *It's mine, all right.*

He should've locked up. He *always* locked up. But this was a nice little town on the Oregon coast, where you'd have to be paranoid to lock your car when you were just leaving it for two minutes to pay for your gas.

Would've only been two minutes, he reminded himself, *except you had to have the jerky. Just had to have it.*

One or two jerkies won't make any big difference in the great scheme of things.

Right.

Just if some jerk climbs in your car while you're buying the damn things. Now what? he wondered.

He took a deep breath, let it out slowly, and walked toward his car. The guy in the passenger seat smiled and waved at him. Norman decided not to approach the passenger door. He went to the driver's door instead. Breathing hard, shaking, angry and scared, he swung the door open. He ducked slightly and peered in at the stranger.

At least he hasn't got a gun, Norman thought. *Thank God for that, anyway.*

The man didn't have any visible weapon at all.

He turned toward Norman, gave him a smirk and a nod, then lifted an elbow and rested it on the back of the seat.

Though he couldn't have been much older than twenty-one, he looked as if he'd stepped out of the 1950s. Like he thought he was *The Wild One* or James Dean or Charlie Starkweather or Elvis or something. His blond, greasy hair was swept high. His blue eyes had a movie-tough-guy nonchalance. His sideburns stretched down to his earlobes. He wore a white T-shirt that hugged his muscles, and faded blue jeans. Below the cuffs of the jeans, Norman could see a pair of black motorcycle boots, complete with side buckles.

'Hello,' Norman said, trying to sound calm.

The guy winked at him. 'Hello, good buddy.'

'Uh . . . you're in my car.'

'And a very fine vehicle it is. My name's Duke.' With that, he swung his right shoulder forward and extended his hand past the steering wheel.

Norman kept his own hands at his sides. 'I think . . . maybe you'd better get out.'

'Figured you'd give me a lift.'

'Well . . . I don't think so.'

'Why not?'

'Because.'

'Because why?'

'Please,' Norman said, 'just get out. I'm not going anywhere till you get out, okay? I'm sure you can find somebody else to ride with.'

Duke seemed somewhat amused. 'But I want to ride with you, big fella.'

'Come on. Get out. Please.'

'What am I hurting? Just let me ride . . .'

'Look, you don't want to make me do something, do you? Do you want to make me go back in the office and have them call someone?'

'Like the cops?'

'I guess so. I don't want to get you in any trouble, but you're in my car. What am I *supposed* to do? I can't go driving off down the road with a complete *stranger* in my car.'

'Told you, I'm Duke.'

'But I don't *know* you. For all I know, you might be some sort of a . . . a criminal, or something.'

Duke smirked. 'Do I look like a criminal to you?'

Damn right you do, Norman thought. But he didn't dare say it. 'I don't know. Are you on your way to audition for *Grease* or something?'

Duke let out a quick laugh. 'Hey! That's a good one! *Grease*. I seen that movie. The Olivia! The Newton! The John! What a babe! Is she a babe, or what?'

'Yeah,' Norman muttered. 'She's a babe.'

'But you're not saying I look like *her*. You're saying I look like the guy. Travolta.'

'I'm not saying that. I'm just saying I wish you'd ... It's not even my car. It's my father's car, and he's really strict about not giving rides to strangers.'

'You do everything your daddy tells you?'

'Look . . .'

'How old are you, anyhow? Wait, let me guess. Sixteen?'

'Very funny. Get out, okay?'

'You're a college boy, right? Going home for spring break.'

'So what?'

'Ah, I'm right. I'm always right. How come you aren't on your way to Palm Springs for the big spring bash?'

'I don't go in for that kind of stuff.'

'Surprise, surprise. Bet you live off your old man. He pays for everything, right? You drive his car. You do whatever he says. Him or mama. You never worked a day in your life, and you've never gotten in a single little bit of trouble.'

Screw you, Norman thought.

'Haven't gotten into much fun, either, I bet.'

Norman glanced toward the office, but a gas pump blocked his view. *Great. They can't even see what's going on. Won't even see if I get a switchblade in my guts . . . if he's got a switchblade, that is. But with his looks he's bound to have one. Maybe slipped down the side of one of those motorcycle boots.* He thought for a moment, then an idea cheered him. *Another car's bound to come along pretty soon*, he told himself. *Then Duke might just sidle away.*

'Got a girlfriend?' Duke asked.

'None of your business.'

'Didn't think so.'

'Get out of my car, okay? Please?'

'You could learn a lot from a guy like me. Course, you already know that, don't you? That's how come you're so scared.'

'I'm not scared.'

'You're scared of everything.'

'I am not.'

'That's your main problem.'

49

'You don't even know me.'

'Don't kid yourself. What's your name?'

'That's my business.'

'See that? You're scared to even tell me your name. What do you think, I'll look you up sometime? Drop in on you?'

'I don't have to tell you anything.'

'It's probably some sort of sissy name. What is it? Melvin?'

'No!'

'Elroy?'

'None of your business.'

'Susie?'

'It's *Max*!'

Duke smiled. 'Max. As in Maxwell. Knew it.'

'As in *Mad Max*,' Norman said. He wished he hadn't just blurted out the first name he thought of that didn't sound geeky.

'Okay, Max. Here's the deal. I've got your registration in my pocket.'

Norman opened his mouth. He didn't know what to say.

After a moment, he said, 'No, you haven't.'

'Oh yes, I have.' Duke patted a front pocket of his jeans. 'Is your old man called Kenneth?'

Norman moaned. He heard himself murmur, 'God.'

'No, your dad ain't God. Sorry to disappoint you on that score, Maxwell.'

'Give it back,' Norman said.

'If I give it back, how will I be able to look you up and drop in on you?'

'Hey. Please.' Tears suddenly came. They made Norman's eyes feel hot and blurred his vision.

'Aw, don' cwy.'

'You'd better give it to me!'

'What'oh baby dooo?'

'I'm gonna get the cops on you! I swear! If you don't hand it over by the time I count to three, I'm gonna call the cops.'

Duke smiled, nodded.

Norman wiped his eyes, but more tears came. He could feel his chin jumping up and down.

Don't start bawling!

'One,' he said.

'Two,' said Duke.

'Two and a half,' Norman said.

'Two and three-quarters.'

'You'd better give it back! I'm warning you!'

'We're just a wee bit nervous about saying "three," aren't we?'

'Am not!'

'Cool your jets, pal. You can have it back. All I want's a ride, know what I mean? I don't want you throwing fits.'

'I'm not throwing fits!' Norman sniffled, then wiped his eyes again.

Duke jammed his right hand down inside the pocket of his jeans. He plucked out the registration slip. 'This what you want?'

Norman nodded. Duke reached past the steering wheel, the paper pinched between his thumb and forefinger.

He won't really let me have it, Norman thought. *When I go for it, he'll jerk it away.*

Norman went for it fast. Grabbed it and tugged. It came free.

Yes!

Quickly, he tucked it into a rear pocket of his shorts.

'What do you say?' Duke asked.

'Thanks,' Norman muttered. He took a deep breath. His lungs seemed to tremble as he inhaled.

'I'm not such a bad guy,' Duke told him. 'How about that ride?'

Norman shook his head. 'Just get out now, okay? I'm not asking again. If you don't get out right now, I'm gonna—'

'Wait.'

'No more waiting. Out!'

'3219 Avenida del Sol, Tiburon.'

Norman shriveled inside.

'I got it right?' Duke asked.

Norman stared at him.

'What about the cops, Maxwell? You suppose they've got some sorta technique that'll wipe that address out of my mind? 'Cause if they don't, I might just end up dropping in. Know what I mean?'

Norman just kept staring at him. He didn't know what to do.

'Get in the car, Maxwell. Let's blow this one-horse town.' Duke grinned. 'It'll be fine. I'm not gonna hurt you. Give me a ride where I wanna go, I'll climb out, and that'll be the end of it. No midnight visits to 3219 Avenida del Sol, Tiburon.'

'Promise?' Norman asked. He had a feeling that someone else was asking the question but he knew it came from him.

'In.' Duke patted the driver's seat. Norman obeyed. He pulled the door shut, set the paper sack of jerky on his lap, fastened his seat belt and slid the key into the ignition. He twisted it and the engine kicked into life.

'Where do you want to go?' he asked, his voice distant and hardly familiar.

'The coast highway's fine by me. You were heading south, weren't you?'

'Yeah.'

'South's fine by me.'

Norman drove away from the gas station. Soon he'd left the town behind. Duke found a country music station on the radio and turned the volume high. That was good, because Norman didn't want to talk to him. He wanted to get rid of him, but he felt trapped. He wished that he had never stopped at that gas station. *That wasn't the mistake*, he realized. *You can't exactly avoid stopping for gasoline. The mistake was leaving the car unlocked so the bastard could climb in and make himself at home and get his paws on the registration. That was mistake number one. Mistake number two was buying the jerky.* Norman thought about how nice it would be to go back in time and try again.

Do it the right way. But he had done it the wrong way and ruined everything. *At least I've got the jerky*, he thought. Steering with his left hand, he reached down with his right and opened the paper sack. He pulled out a long, dark strip. Duke looked at him.

'Want one?' Norman asked.

Duke reached out and took it from his hand. 'You're a bud.'

Norman drew another strip out of the sack. He clamped it between his teeth and ripped the end off it. The slab in his mouth felt very firm. But not hard and dry, like some jerky. As he chewed, the meat softened. His teeth squeezed out rich, sweet juices. He moaned with pleasure.

'*This* ain't bad,' Duke said.

Norman moaned again. *This* was, by far, the best teryaki jerky that he'd ever tasted.

'What's this stuff called?' Duke asked.

'Wolfbane teriyaki beef jerky.'

'Wolfbane?'

'You'll howl for more.'

Duke tossed back his head and howled.

Norman smiled.

Maybe this guy isn't so bad, he thought. *Hell, can't be all bad if he goes and howls like that over my jerky. He probably is a cool guy if you get to know him.*

Are you nuts! Norman asked himself. *This guy as good as kidnapped you!*

Yeah, but he hasn't done anything. So far, so good. And the jerky is incredible.

'You can have some more when you're done,' Norman told him.

'Don't mind if I do. You're okay, Max. You know that? You're an okay guy.'

'Thanks.'

'I think we're gonna get along real good.' Duke reached out and gave Norman's thigh a couple of solid, friendly slaps.

'It's Norman, actually.'

'What's Norman?'

'My name. It isn't Maxwell, it's Norman. I sort of lied about it before.'

'Why'd you wanna do that, Norman?'

'I guess I was afraid you'd make fun of it.'

'Norman ain't a bad name.'

'Thanks.'

Chapter Eight

Norman drove past the girl who was walking backward along the side of the road, her thumb out.

'You gotta be kidding me,' Duke said.

'What?'

'Passing up a babe like that? You some kind of a fag?'

'No!'

'Pull over!'

'I don't pick up hitchhikers.'

'This one you do. What are you, nuts? Didn't you look at her?'

'Yeah, but—'

'Don't be a loser all your life.'

'It's stupid and dangerous to pick up hitchhikers,' Norman blurted.

'Don't worry, I won't let her hurt you.'

'Very funny.'

'Pull over.'

The southbound side of the road had no breakdown lane and its hard shoulder was narrow. It was bordered by a low steel guardrail to keep cars from flying off the coastline cliffs.

'There *isn't* anyplace to pull over,' Norman said. He glanced at the rearview mirror. 'And I can't just stop. There's a truck behind us.'

'U it.'

'I can't just U it.'

'Why not? Nothing coming. Do it.'

'Are you nuts?'

'Show some *hair*, Norman!'

Norman wasn't sure what that meant, but he liked the sound of it.

He checked the traffic. Then he hit the brakes. As his speed fell, the truck bore down on his rear. Its horn blasted. He whipped the steering wheel over and cut hard to the left. The Jeep swung toward the middle line. Crossed it. Skidded. Found traction again in the northbound lanes and kept turning. Though the right-side tires went off on the gravel, he knew he had control. He'd made it!

'Way to go,' Duke said.

'Thanks.' Norman started to steer back onto the pavement.

'This is good enough. Just stop here and we'll wait for her.'

That sounded fine to Norman. He pulled the rest of the way off the road and shut off the engine. He felt happy with himself for doing the U-turn so well.

'There she is,' Duke said.

Norman spotted her. She was quite a distance away.

'Nobody better pick her up before she gets here,' Duke said.

The girl swaggered along the road as if she owned it. A big denim bag, suspended from her shoulder by a strap, swung beside her hip.

Cars, trucks and a couple of big recreational vehicles drove past her, and all of them had to swing wide. Norman wondered if he, like the other drivers, had veered to go around her. He couldn't remember doing it. His mind must've been on something else.

'That babe's got balls,' Duke said.

'I doubt it,' Norman said.

Duke laughed. 'Hope you're right, Normy! What a waste that'd be, huh? 'Cause it sure looks like the rest of her's top-drawer.'

'Yeah,' Norman said.

'You don't think so?' Duke asked.

'She looks fine.'

'What a babe. Give the horn a toot.'

Norman beeped the horn. The girl didn't break stride, but her head turned. Duke waved. She gave a quick nod, then stopped and faced the highway and watched for a break in the traffic.

Norman didn't like the looks of her. Even from this distance, he could see her eye makeup and flashy lipstick. Though she appeared to be no older than eighteen, her hair was white. *A bleach job*, Norman figured. And he didn't like the way it was cut so short. That pixie style was meant for slim, delicate girls. Not someone like this.

She had a wide face with blunt features. Her shoulders and hips were very broad. Her arms and legs were thick – not quite fat, but so heavy and solid that it seemed crude of her to show them off by wearing such skimpy clothes.

Her tank top exposed her arms entirely and left her shoulders bare except for narrow straps. It was so tight that it hugged every curve and bulge. It didn't reach down far enough to meet the waistband of her jeans, so Norman could see her skin there – and her belly button.

She wore the blue jeans low on her hips. They were faded almost white. The legs were cut off at the crotch, and the side that wasn't blocked from sight by the denim bag had a slit going halfway up. Norman supposed she must have a matching slit on the other side though he couldn't see.

He wondered if the slits were meant to be sexy. Maybe they were just there to make room for her thighs.

Her stocky legs were bare to mid-calf. That was where the boots began. Dirty white cowgirl boots with high heels and pointy toes.

Hasn't she ever looked in a mirror?

If she's 'top-drawer,' Norman thought, *I'd hate to see what's in the bottom.*

An RV the size of a railroad boxcar came roaring down from the north. It angled across the centerline to give the girl some space. She vanished. The wind of the passing RV shook Norman's Jeep. When he could see again, the girl was running across the highway.

A very controlled, measured run. As if she felt that running was required, but wanted to show that she was in no great hurry.

One hand, bunched in a loose fist, swung forward and back. The other clutched the shoulder strap of the denim bag that lurched and swayed at her hip. Her breasts seemed small for someone with such wide shoulders and full hips. She looked as if she had a couple of oranges trapped inside her tank top. They leaped around quite a lot.

'Look at 'em go,' Duke said.

'What?'

'What do *you* think? Man, I wouldn't mind sucking on one of those.'

Before quite reaching their side of the road, the girl stopped running. A couple of casual strides and she stepped off the pavement. She turned and walked straight toward them. Smirking, swaggering, swinging her hips.

'What a piece of work,' Duke muttered.

'A piece of work, all right.'

'You're a fag, all right.'

'Am not. And look, don't do anything . . . weird. Just leave her alone, okay?'

'Oh, yeah. Right. Want her for yourself, huh?'

'I'm a fag, remember?'

'Yeah, we both know better than that. Tell you what.' Instead of telling Norman anything, Duke swung open his door and climbed out.

'Howdy!' he called to the girl.

'Howdy right back at you, guy.'

'Your chariot awaits.' He patted the top of the Jeep. 'We'll let you sit up front. Give me your bag, there.'

'Thanks.' She lifted the strap off her shoulder and swung the bag toward Duke.

He caught it. Climbing into the front seat, the girl smiled at Norman.

Her stare was fixed on him, so he couldn't check her out the way he wanted to.

'Hey,' she said.

'Hi.'

She smelled fresh and clean in a way that made Norman think of a breeze coming in off the ocean. Duke shut her door. He opened the back door, then flung himself in and set her bag on the floor.

'Thanks for stopping,' she said to Norman.

'Glad to help.'

Duke's face appeared between the seat-backs. 'They call me Duke,' he said.

The girl turned her head, and her nose almost touched his. 'That's a dog's name, ain't it?' she asked.

Duke let out a howl.

She laughed and mussed his hair. Then she pushed his head out of the way. 'Now, who are you?' she asked, turning to Norman.

'Norman.'

She repeated his name and slipped her hand up the short sleeve of his shirt. Her fingers curled under, nails lightly scraping his upper arm. Goose bumps scurried over him. He squirmed.

He gave her a nervous smile. 'What's *your* name?' he asked.

'Boots.'

'Boots?' Duke said. 'What kind of a name is that?'

'You're someone to talk, aren't you? *Duke*.'

'I guess we oughta get going,' Norman said, and started to check the traffic. When an opening came, he swung out, made a tight U-turn, and stepped on the gas.

Duke leaned forward. 'Where you going, Boots?' he asked.

'No place much.'

'You must be going *somewhere*,' Norman said.

'Nope. I just follow my boots. Get it?'

'I guess.'

She raised her right leg and crossed it over her left knee.

She was looking at her foot, not at Norman. So he stared at the raised side of her thigh. It looked pale and very smooth. He wondered what she would do if he reached out and put his hand on it.

Not about to find out. No way!

She wiggled her boot. 'See how it's pointing? Down the road. That's where I'm going now. With you guys.'

Norman glanced again at her thigh, then forced himself to look through the windshield. 'Don't you have some kind of a destination in mind?' he asked.

'What for?'

'I mean, aren't you trying to *get* someplace?'

'Anywhere I am, that's fine with me.'

Norman smiled at her. She smiled back.

Her eyes give me the creeps. And it's not just the makeup, he told himself. *Something was wrong with the eyes themselves*. In a way, they looked like perfectly normal brown eyes. They had no physical defect that he could see. But they seemed to have an emptiness.

Cow eyes, Norman thought. *Cow eyes and a pig face*.

Cut it out. She's not so bad. Maybe she's just dim-witted or something.

He returned his gaze to the road, but his mind stayed on Boots.

Why on earth, he wondered, *does she want to use all that makeup?*

Maybe to hide the emptiness. Instead of hiding it, though, the gaudy makeup seemed to highlight it. Like an elaborate frame around a blank canvas.

Bull. She's some sort of low-life white trash. Probably thinks gobbing her eyes with that stuff makes her look glamorous. Bet I could screw her.

Who'd want to! She's creepy, repulsive, and probably diseased.

The Glory Bus

I oughta try and get rid of her, Norman told himself. *Her and Duke. What am I doing with these creeps in my car? Get rid of them both. And soon, before they pull something.*

'I've got an idea,' he said. 'Since we aren't in a big hurry to get anywhere, why don't we stop for a while next time we come to a decent stretch of beach?'

Duke clapped him on the shoulder. 'Good thinking. Let's do it.'

'Can we have a picnic?' Boots asked. She sounded as if she'd always wanted a picnic. But had never had one.

'Sure,' Norman said. 'We'll have a picnic on the beach.'

'Let's stop and pick up some stuff,' Duke said. 'We'll have us a real party – beer, the whole nine yards.'

Boots clapped her hands. 'This'll be *wild*. Oh, you guys are the greatest!'

Her enthusiasm made Norman feel a little sad. The whole point of the picnic was to get her and Duke out on the beach so that he could lose them. But here she was, acting like a waif who'd been cheated out of every picnic ever promised.

Probably never had a Christmas, either.

She'll get her picnic on the beach, Norman told himself. *I won't ruin that for her. Snacks, a few beers. Then Duke'll probably start putting some moves on her . . . and then it'll be so long, been good to know ya.*

The gas station where they stopped for their picnic supplies had a full-size convenience store. Instead of pulling up to a pump, Norman swung into a parking place near the front door.

With any luck, he might miss out on the picnic after all. He shut off the engine, then reached into his back pocket and took out his wallet. He removed a twenty-dollar bill. He held it toward Boots.

She plucked it free. 'Twenty buckaroos!'

'Why don't you go in and pick out whatever you want?' Norman looked over his shoulder. 'What sort of beer should she get?'

Frowning, Duke scratched at one of his sideburns. 'Can't go wrong with Bud.'

'Maybe you should go in with her.' To Boots, he said, 'You aren't twenty-one, are you?'

'I've got a license says I am.'

'You can help her pick something, Duke.'

Duke reached between the seats and squeezed Boots's shoulder. 'You got something you want me to *pick*, darling?'

Grinning, she tilted back her head. 'Wanna pick my nose?'

God, Norman thought. *She's a regular Dorothy Parker.*

Boots and Duke both seemed to find the exchange hilarious. Norman shook his head. He had to smile, but only because they were being so moronic.

After they'd settled down, Norman said to Duke, 'While you're in there, why don't you see if they have any of that Wolfbane jerky?'

'You'll *howl* for more!' Duke blurted, and then howled hysterically. Boots joined in with a shrill howl of her own.

These two are meant for each other, Norman thought.

But then Duke said, 'Let's *all* go in.'

'Yeah!' Boots cried out. 'That way, we can *all* pick what we want.' She waved Norman's twenty-dollar bill. 'I'm buying!'

As Norman entered the store with his laughing companions, he supposed that it was just as well he hadn't been left in the Jeep. He *would've* sped off – and he'd have missed out on the picnic.

In a way, he was looking forward it.

He looked forward to it even more when Boots stopped in front of a sunblock display.

'Let's get some of this,' she said.

'Okay.'

'I like the oily kind,' she explained.

Norman and Duke looked at each other.

With their help, she picked out a coconut oil that promised 'a full, rich tropical tan' but not much protection against the sun.

Roaming the aisles, they came upon a section with beach gear: plastic buckets and shovels, beach balls, goggles and snorkels, and a small assortment of towels and swimsuits.

'Do you have . . . something to wear?' Norman asked. Boots nudged him with her elbow.

'I got me a *fab*ulous little bikini. Just you wait!' She winked at Duke, and he winked back at her.

Oh, man, Norman thought.

Turning to Duke, he asked, 'Need anything?'

'You mean like trunks? You kidding me?'

'Maybe we should get some beach towels,' Norman said. 'Even if nobody goes in the water, we can use them to sit on.'

'And lie on,' Duke added, glancing at Boots. They each chose a towel.

After wandering through the rest of the store and picking out what they wanted, they went to the counter.

That was where the jerky was. While they waited in line, Norman studied the labels on the containers. He couldn't find any Wolfbane so he decided against buying jerky here.

They bought the towels and suntan oil, two cold six-packs of Budweiser, packets of pre-sliced hard Italian salami and sharp cheddar cheese, a box of Ritz crackers, sacks of Cheetos and onion-flavored potato chips, and a package of chocolate-covered Oreo cookies.

When Boots saw the total price, she made a face and waved the twenty-dollar bill at Norman. 'I don't think this'll do it,' she said.

'Not even close,' Norman admitted. As he slipped his MasterCard out of his wallet, Boots shrugged and stuffed the twenty down a front pocket of her cutoffs. He raised his eyebrows.

'I'll keep it warm for you,' she said.

Chapter Nine

Norman drove slowly past a sign that read BEACH PARKING. He steered onto the unpaved lot. Except for a couple of cars, a van and a small RV, the lot was deserted. He could see several people scattered about on the long stretch of beach. The sky was almost cloudless. The Pacific looked deep blue, the curling ridges of the incoming combers as white as snow.

'Ooo,' Boots said. 'This is so *fab*ulous. I just can't hardly wait to sprawl out in the sun. Now you guys run along and set up the picnic, and I'll just change in the back seat and catch up to you in a little bit.'

'We better stay and guard you,' Duke said, smirking.

'Yeah,' Norman said. 'It might not be safe.'

'You guys.' She shook her head. 'Shame on the both of you. You're just angling for a peek.'

'Us?' Norman asked. He smiled and hoped that his disappointment didn't show. Despite his negative feelings for Boots he wanted very badly to stay – to stand 'guard' outside the Jeep and sneak glances at Boots while she stripped butt-naked in the back seat.

She knows that's what we want, he realized. *Maybe she isn't as stupid as she looks. Or sounds.*

'You guys just go on and take all the goodies with you, and I'll be along in a minute.'

'Let's go, Norm.'

Norman frowned over his shoulder at Duke. 'Are you sure it'll be safe to leave her alone?'

'Aah, nobody's around. Come on.'

'Don't go and worry about me,' Boots told them. 'Any fool tries to jump on me, he's gonna die screaming.'

The words shocked Norman. 'Jeez,' he said. 'You're a mighty tough little thing, Bootsy-girl.'

'I ain't so little, but I'm plenty tough.'

'We better haul ass, Norm, 'fore we make her mad.' Then Duke reached over the seat-back and mussed her hair.

She laughed. 'Quit it!'

After raising the windows, Norman shut off the engine. He pulled out the ignition key and stuffed the key case into the front pocket of his shorts.

Then they all got out of the car. After the paper sacks were unloaded, Boots climbed into the back seat. Duke started to shut the door for her, but she stopped it with her foot.

'You want me to smother to death in here?' she asked. 'Norman rolled up the windows, you know. It's not that I'm *fond* of having a door open while I strip down bare-ass, but I sure don't aim to *bake* to death.'

'Roll your window down,' Duke told her.

She thumbed the switch. Nothing happened. 'See? I can't.'

'It doesn't work when the key isn't in,' Norman explained.

'See?' she said again to Duke.

'So put the key back in,' Duke told Norman.

'I can't. Not if I'm leaving. You know? Somebody might steal the car.'

'Not with me in it,' Boots said. 'I'll just lock up and bring you the key when I'm done.'

'I don't . . . uh, think that'd be a very good idea.'

'He's scared you'll take it,' Duke said.

'Me?'

'No,' Norman said. 'It's not that.'

'Like hell it's not.'

'I'd just be awfully nervous. I mean, somebody might come along and . . .' He shrugged. 'Anyway, it's my dad's car. If it was my car, you know . . . but it isn't.'

'Norman's a very nervous guy,' Duke pointed out.

'I could *stay* until you're ready,' Norman offered. 'I could just sit in the front seat, you know, and run the windows for you. And I wouldn't have to *look* at what you're doing back there. I could even do something like cover the rearview mirror, if you want, or . . .'

'Cover the mirror with what? Your underpants? Never you mind about that,' Boots told him. She didn't seem angry. Smiling, she flapped a hand at him. 'You just take your keys with you and go on. I'll be just fine here with the door open.'

'I'd *like* to help.'

'I know. That's all right. Everything's dandy. You guys, get!'

'Come on,' Duke said.

Arms loaded with the paper sacks from the store, Norman and Duke turned their backs to the Jeep and headed for the beach. Norman had an urge to look over his shoulder, but he fought it. What was the point, anyway? He wouldn't be able to see anything, not with Boots in the back seat.

As they walked onto the sand, he said, 'Don't you think we should've stayed?'

'Nah. She knew we wanted to get our jollies watching her strip. She just don't trust us enough yet. For all she knows, we might be the sort who'd jump her.'

Norman forced himself to smile. 'If we did that, she'd make us die screaming.'

'Tough little bitch. Love it. You get a look at her eyes?'

'You mean the makeup?'

'I mean the whole nine yards, buddy. She's not a gal you'd wanna piss off, if you know what I mean. What we gotta do is play along with her. She'll loosen up, once she gets to know us. Before we know what's hit us, we'll be fucking her lights out.'

'You think so?'

'I know so.'

'Jeez.'

'You bet.'

Not me, Norman thought. *I'll be jumping in the Jeep and taking off, first chance I get.*

They walked a distance farther before Duke said, 'Here looks good to me.'

'Me, too,' Norman agreed.

They were about fifty feet from the water; the sand was dry and soft. They put down the sacks, spread out the towels, and sat down. Right away, Duke peeled off his T-shirt. He had a very good tan, for April in Oregon. *He's probably been traveling around*, Norman thought. *Out in the sun a lot. Lifting weights, too.*

On Duke's left upper arm was the tattooed slogan BORN TO RAISE HELL.

Figures.

The only real surprise was that a guy like Duke didn't have more tattoos. He must've decided that BORN TO RAISE HELL said it all.

Unless he's got others somewhere I can't see them. Norman decided to keep his own shirt on, at least for now. A cool breeze was blowing, so he didn't feel hot in spite of the bright sun. And he knew he wouldn't look good, shirtless next to Duke. He had no tattoo, no tan, and no prominent muscles. He did remove his shoes and socks, though. He looked at Duke's heavy black motorcycle boots. The side buckles gleamed like silver.

'Are you a biker?' he asked.

'Not anymore. Not since I totaled my Harley.'

'You had a Harley?'

'You gotta be kidding. What else is there?'

'Hondas . . . ?'

Duke sneered at him. 'I look like the kinda guy'd get himself caught dead on a rice rocket?' He tossed a can of Budweiser to Norman and took one for himself. They popped open the beers. As they started to drink, Boots came striding toward them.

'Whoa, mama,' Duke muttered. Norman stared at her.

She smiled and waved. He returned the wave. *Doesn't she know how awful she looks?* Her shoulders and hips seemed even broader than he remembered them – her arms and legs thicker. She also had a bit of a paunch. She had no business wearing such a skimpy bikini. It was black, which made her skin look very pale and pasty. As she swaggered closer, Norman saw that the bikini was knitted. Its top looked tired and loose. Limp strings held triangular patches of black yarn across her breasts. The patches bobbed and jiggled and swayed as she walked.

Black cords strained down over her hips to pull at a V of yarn that came up from between her legs.

'Bitchin' bikini, babe,' Duke said.

'Yeah,' Norman added. *Hideous!* he thought.

'You like?' Boots asked. Stopping in front of them, she flung up her arms and cocked a hip. 'Da-dahhh!'

Her bikini top was too small and too loose. Half an inch of skin showed under each breast. Before Norman could get a good look, however, she turned around.

Black cords were tied in bows behind her neck and back.

'Da-dahhh!' she proclaimed again, and swished her butt to one side.

Her ass cheeks were wide, white and smooth – and mostly bare. A couple of cords slanted down from her hips. They met a narrow patch of yarn that stretched tautly down the center. Through the tiny holes in the knitting Norman glimpsed the crack between her buttocks. His heart thudded.

If the front's like that . . . Boots continued her slow turn. Seconds later she was facing him again.

Oh my God, Norman thought. The view ripped his breath out and pumped heat into his groin. He didn't want to be caught staring, so he forced himself to look at her face.

'Very nice,' he said. 'Is it . . . is it homemade?'

Boots beamed. 'How'd you *guess*?' Not waiting for an answer, she pranced over to the third towel. She sat down on it, cross-legged, one knee pointing at Norman and the other at Duke. Duke tossed her a beer.

As she snatched it from the air, Norman watched her breasts. There was no doubt about it: her nipples were actually jutting out through artfully contrived small holes in the knitting. Their tips were sunlit and pink as tongues.

I've gotta stop looking, he told himself. *Gotta. Gotta!* He raised his beer. The top of the can flashed in his eyes. It blocked his view of Boots while he drank. When he lowered the can, he tried to keep his gaze on her face.

She was smiling, her attention on the beer that she was about to pop open.

She really is ugly, Norman thought. *Very piglike.*

Boots tilted back her head and drank, so he dropped his gaze to sneak a look between her legs.

Doesn't she know? he wondered. *My God, it's sticking out like she's got it mashed up against a tiny little chain-link fence.*

She knows, all right. She has to know. She's just some sort of weird pervert, or nympho, or something. Or maybe she doesn't know, or doesn't think it matters. Any way you slice it, Norman thought, *she's definitely not operating with a full deck. She wears a thing like that in front of us. Why the hell didn't she let us watch her change? She's showing off every-thing she's got anyhow.*

She's nuts, that's why.

'You lookin' at me?' Boots asked.

Norman couldn't believe it. She'd caught him! Heat surging to his face, he met her stare and shook his head.

'No,' he said. 'I wasn't looking at anything.'

'You were, too.'

'No. Honest.'

Duke smirked. 'Busted.'

Suddenly grinning, Boots said, 'Well, don't.' She reached out and gave Norman a playful slap on the knee. 'Ain't polite to stare at a lady's cooz.'

She burst out laughing, and so did Duke. After a moment or two, Norman joined in. He wasn't amused, but he laughed with a mixture of relief and nerves. And gratitude.

She isn't so bad, he thought. *Most gals would've torn me apart for doing something like that.*

Most gals don't wear a bikini like that.

She doesn't mind me looking, he told himself. *That's the thing. She likes it. She wants me to do it.*

All the more reason to get the hell out of here.

Norman took a few more swallows of beer, then set his can on the towel by his hip.

He shoved it to make it stand upright.

'I'm getting pretty hot,' he said.

Duke and Boots laughed about that.

'Yeah yeah yeah,' Norman said, grinning. 'Anyway, just watch my beer for me, okay? I'm gonna get into my trunks after all. You guys can go ahead and break out the food if you want. I'll be right back.' He got to his feet and stepped off the towel. 'Either of you need anything from the car?'

Boots shook her head. Duke waved him off.

'Right back,' Norman said, and started toward the parking area. Halfway there he had a strong urge to glance over his shoulder. *Don't! You'll blow it. Duke'll come running. Just play it cool. Walk slow. Don't look back.*

He listened but he didn't look. He heard the squeal of seagulls, the rush of the surf, but he didn't hear anyone coming.

What's to hear? Footsteps in the sand? The click of a switchblade spring?

They aren't coming, he told himself. *They bought my story. Hook, line and sinker.*

Maybe.

Then he was so close to the Cherokee that he knew he'd made it.

Unless they're right behind me ... He'd heard that gals like Boots made trophies out of fellas' gonads. His shriveled up tight.

As Norman reached into his pocket for the keys, he leaned toward the driver's door and turned his head.

They were both still sitting on the towels! Not even looking at him!

Head down, Duke was reaching into a grocery sack on his lap. Boots appeared to be watching him.

I made it!

Norman unlocked the door, swung it open, and climbed in behind the wheel. Hand trembling, he slid the key into the ignition. A buzzer sounded. The noise made him cringe, but he told himself that Duke and Boots couldn't possibly hear it. They might hear the door thud shut, though, so he left it open.

Don't close it till the engine's going, he told himself. *You'll be outta here before they can even get off their butts.* On the beach, Duke took something out of the sack.

A brown bottle. The coconut oil. *For a full, rich tropical tan.*

Norman felt a tightness in his throat. He'd wanted to be there when she slicked herself up with that oil. Wanted to watch, and smell it, and maybe give her a hand.

Boots took the bottle of oil but didn't open it. Instead, she set it on the towel by her side.

Of course, Norman thought. *She's gonna wait till I get back. She doesn't want me to miss the show.*

Little does she know ... He started the engine. Their heads turned.

'Sorry,' he muttered. He shifted to reverse. Duke and Boots stayed sitting on their towels, staring at him.

They aren't even gonna try to stop me, he realized. *It's like they don't even care.*

Why should they care? Three's a crowd, right?

That isn't it, he told himself. *The thing is, they know there's no point.*

They can't possibly stop me. They wouldn't stand a chance. That's why they aren't trying.

As Norman started to back up, Boots raised a hand. The same hand that had patted his knee after she'd caught him looking. It flapped up and down, waving good-bye.

Chapter Ten

Pamela sat up. She'd spent long enough stretched out on the seat, sometimes gazing up at the ceiling of the bus, sometimes sleeping. She didn't mind the sleeping. But she was wide-awake now.

If she stayed on her back, she would start dwelling on Jim and Rodney – *Rotney!* – and all the terrible things that had happened. Or she might start wondering about Sharpe again. What was his problem? Where was he taking her?

She sat up, swung her legs off the seat, and gently placed her feet on the floor. Leaning forward, she peered through the windshield.

Still in the middle of nowhere.

It looked nice out there now. The bright, hot glare of the sun had mellowed. The pavement, the whole desert landscape, was awash with a rosy glow.

Must be almost sundown, Pamela thought. Her mouth was dry.

Sharpe had given her a plastic bottle full of water after they'd finished dumping Rodney's body. She'd been sipping at it, off and on. Between drinks, she'd kept it trapped between her hip and the seat back. It must've rolled against her rump when she sat up. She could feel it there now.

Reaching behind herself, she picked it up. She twisted off the cap and took a drink. Her stomach growled. She looked at Sharpe. From where she sat, she could see only the top of his head. So she stood up. Wincing with each step, she limped across the aisle. She swung around and dropped into a seat. Now she had a side view of Sharpe. She took another sip of water.

'Where are you taking me?' she asked.

He didn't so much as glance her way. 'No talking to the driver while the bus is in motion, Pamela.'

'Oh, give me a break.'

'Company policy.'

'*What* company? This is *your* bus, isn't it?'

'Sorry.'

'Okay, okay.' Pamela sighed. Turning her head, she gazed down the aisle. Back there, the bus was dim with murky golden light. She could make out the blurred shapes of the mannequins. They seemed to be bouncing and swaying a little with the motions of the bus.

She faced Sharpe. 'Is it against the rules if I chat with the other passengers?'

This time, his head tilted back. Checking her out in the rearview mirror. Pamela saw the reflection of his face. He still wore the sunglasses.

His thin lips didn't smile. 'They don't say much,' he said.

'What are you doing with them?'

'Driving 'em.'

'Why?'

He shook his head.

'None of my business?'

Sharpe didn't answer.

'You've got to admit,' she said, 'it's pretty strange.'

'Quiet, now,' he said. 'That's too much talk already.'

'I'm a little hungry, you know.'

'Can't be helped.'

'You don't have any food in here?'

He shook his head again. 'We'll be stopping by and by. Now, cut out the talk.'

'Okay.' Pamela settled back in the seat, sipped water, and wondered what he meant by 'by and by.' To her, it meant 'soon.' But maybe it didn't mean that to Sharpe.

Maybe it's like 'In the sweet by and by.' She tried to sing the old hymn in her mind.

In the sweet by and by, we will come to that beautiful . . . something. Shore? Cross? Sky?

That sort of 'by and by' – the hymn sort – didn't seem to mean 'soon' at all. It had to do with when you're dead; she was pretty sure.

Terrific, Pamela thought. *We'll all just gather at the river.*

Richard Laymon

'I know,' she said. 'Those things aren't mannequins back there. They're just former passengers you starved to death. Petrified passengers.'

Sharpe didn't look at her, but his back seemed to stiffen slightly. A jaw muscle bulged.

Uh-oh, Pamela thought.

'Just kidding,' she said.

He acted as if he hadn't heard her. His back remained rigid, and the muscle in his jaw stayed knotted.

'I'm just hungry,' she explained. 'I didn't mean to say anything wrong.'

Sharpe's head lifted slightly. 'Never mind,' he said. Moments later he raised an arm to point out a roadside billboard. 'We'll stop there,' he said.

The big white sign had red lettering.

MAKE A PIT STOP AT PITS
IT'S REALLY THE PITS
PITS, CA, pop. 6

Pamela had heard of Pits, but she couldn't remember. *No. Wait. The T-shirt on the kid.*

She peered down the aisle at the boy dummy. His T-shirt looked dark and rusty in the gloom, and she couldn't make out the words. She was sure, though, that they were about the same place as the billboard. Pits, California, population six.

Leave it to California, she thought, *to have a town with only six inhabitants AND still make a big deal out of it.*

At least one of them apparently had a sense of humor. The kid bought his T-shirt there, so . . .

The kid did not *buy his T-shirt there. The kid is a dummy: he's never bought anything anywhere, period.*

Sharpe must've bought the T-shirt, Pamela told herself. *Or he got hold of it one way or another. The same with the clothes on all the other dummies . . . And me.*

She felt a corner of her mouth stretch. *I'm just one of the gang. Sharpe's gang.* With one minor or significant difference, depending on how you look at it.

She shook her head and wondered how she'd digressed to such a level.

72

The T-shirt on the kid. Sharpe must've gotten it at Pits, which meant that there had to be a store – some sort of gift or souvenir shop. And a place like that was almost certain to carry food.

A whole assortment of snack food would probably be sold at a place with souvenir T-shirts for sale. Pamela longed for an actual meal, but anything would do: potato chips, popcorn, pretzels, peanuts, candy bars, jerky. And a good cold beer to wash it down. Though a soda would be fine. Probably can't get beer at a gift shop.

A few minutes later, they drove past another billboard.

IT'S THE PITS GAS! FOOD! FUN!
ONLY TEN PITIFUL MILES TO GO
PITS, CA, pop. 6

Things are looking better and better, Pamela told herself. The place wouldn't advertise food if you couldn't get an actual meal there. A cheeseburger, for instance. Or a hot dog. Maybe pizza. And only ten miles away.

About fifteen more minutes, at the speed Sharpe seemed to be driving.

Pamela spotted another billboard in the distance and watched it grow until she could read it.

IT'S NOT PITTSBURGH
IT'S JUST THE PITS
COME SEE OUR
PALACE
!!!THE EIGHTH WONDER OF THE WORLD!!!
PITS, CA, pop. 6

Soon another billboard appeared.

ASK TO SEE OUR PITS
FREE LOOKS
JUST ASK!!
FIVE MILES TO GO
PITS, CA pop. 6

Smiling, Pamela shook her head. *Ask to see our pits? What does that mean?* Next came the best of the billboards.

EAT! EAT! EAT! THE PITS CAFE
BREAKFAST, LUNCH, DINNER
DOWN-HOME COOKING
!!!PLUS OUR FAMOUS BOTTOMLESS PIT OF COFFEE!!!
PITS, CA, pop. 6

A real cafe! Thank God, Pamela thought. But she suddenly realized that she wouldn't be able to pay for a meal. She had no money.

Or anything else.

She had nothing at all of her own. She'd been naked when Rodney had attacked her. Later, he had dressed her in the costume that he'd brought with him. He'd dragged her out of the house without her purse. And now she was wearing clothes from one of Sharpe's mannequins.

She didn't even have her engagement and wedding rings. At the bathroom door last night, Rodney had pulled them off her finger. 'We don't want *these*! They're *his*. He can *have* them.' One at a time, Rodney had hurled the rings at Jim's body. The engagement ring had hit Jim in the forehead and bounced into the bathtub behind him. In the tub, it had made a sound like a coin clinking and rolling around. The diamond wedding ring had landed with a quiet little *plip* sound on the intestines bulging out of the slit in Jim's belly.

Pamela pressed a hand against her mouth. Her eyes watered. *Why did I have to think about that? Get used to it.*

I am *getting used to it*, she thought. *Must be. I didn't throw up this time.*

Didn't even gag.

But she did feel ashamed of herself. For the past half-hour or so she'd been thinking about almost nothing except where and when she would get her next meal.

Jim's dead. He's never going to eat again. And I'm worried about being a little hungry. What the hell is the matter with me?

I'm alive, she reminded herself. *What am I supposed to do, give up eating?*

'I don't have any money,' Pamela said. Before Sharpe could respond, she hurried on. 'I know I'm not supposed to talk to the driver while the bus is in motion, but I'm starving and we're almost to this cafe and I haven't got a dime on me. But I want to eat. Okay? I mean, I *will* be able to pay you back. It just might take a while. I've got a bank account and credit cards, but I don't have anything *with* me. Rodney didn't exactly let me pick up my purse while he was dragging me out of the house last night. And also, he burnt the house *down* so there went everything. Like my checkbook and credit cards? But I'm not poor. I have a job. I can pay you back if you'll buy me something to eat. Okay?'

Sharpe's head lifted slightly. 'It'll be on me.'

'That isn't necessary, but . . .'

'I saved your life, so I reckon you're family now. I take care of my own.'

'Well, thanks,' Pamela said. She wasn't sure about having Sharpe think of her as 'family.' Before she could give it much thought, however, Pits came into sight beyond the windshield. *It really is the pits*, she thought.

What she saw was a roadside conglomeration consisting of a run-down gas station and a small cafe surrounded by a vast parking area that seemed to double as a junkyard. There were a few old mobile homes scattered around the rear. Between the gas station and the cafe but back a short distance was a fenced area that appeared to be a grave-yard. On a rise beyond the graveyard was a Victorian house that looked as if it had been uprooted from a movie-studio back lot where it might've been used decades ago as a setting for haunted-house flicks.

That must be the Palace, Pamela thought. 'What a dump,' she said.

'Home, sweet home,' Sharpe said.

'I thought you lived in your bus.'

'That's right.' He slowed down, then steered off the pavement. As he rolled toward the gas station an old geezer near the pumps saw him coming and waved. Sharpe tooted the horn. A moment later a woman in a white dress came running out of the station's office.

Sharpe drove past the pumps, then swung to the right and eased into an empty space that seemed to be precisely the size of the bus.

Looking over his shoulder, he said, 'Welcome to Pits, pop. six.' Then he reached out and worked the chrome door handle. The bus's main door wheezed open.

75

Pamela leaned forward, ready to stand.

But she stayed in her seat when the woman leaped into the doorway and bounded up the steps. Sharpe climbed out of the driver's seat. The woman took a quick look at Pamela, then threw herself into Sharpe's arms. They stood at the front of the bus, embracing each other. Sharpe seemed to be returning the hugs in a fairly perfunctory way – gently, but without much passion, as far as Pamela could tell.

He ought to be a little more enthusiastic, she thought, *having a gal cling to him as if he were a long-lost lover who'd just returned from the wars.*

While he did little more than stand there with his arms around her back, the woman moaned, kissed him over and over again on his mouth and cheeks and neck, ran her hands up and down his back, caressed his face and stroked his hair, all the while squirming and rubbing herself against him.

Finally, she separated herself from Sharpe. Flushed and a little breathless, she straightened her dress and turned toward Pamela.

'Hi,' she said.

'Hi.'

'Sorry about that. I don't usually . . . I haven't seen him in a while.'

'No problem.'

Sharpe still had an arm across the woman's back. He squeezed her shoulder and said, 'This here's Lauren. Lauren, meet Pamela.'

'Nice to meet you,' Lauren said.

'Same here.'

Very nice to meet you, she thought.

Even though Sharpe had saved Pamela's life and hadn't abused her in any way, he was definitely strange. Being alone with him had kept her uneasy. So the very presence of Lauren was a relief.

And it was very good to find that Sharpe had a woman in his life. *Wasn't after my bod after all. All that worry for nothing.*

'Welcome to Pits,' Lauren said.

Pamela stood up as she approached. They shook hands. Lauren had a strong grip. She looked sturdy, but also delicate: tall and wide-shoul-dered, though extremely thin; thick hair the color of straw; amazing eyes of forest green. Her face, bony and hollow-cheeked, was saved from looking cadaverous by the tawny glow of her skin. Her complexion made her seem more like an athlete than a corpse.

Pamela guessed that Lauren was no older than thirty. And probably descended from hippies, by the looks of her granny dress. The white garment, short-sleeved, shapeless and loose, was buttoned up the front almost to her throat, and was so long that it reached down almost to her ankles. *All she needs is a flower in her hair.*

Stop that, Pamela told herself. *She probably wears a dress like that because it's nice and cool. Just the thing for dwelling in the middle of a desert. Same goes for her sandals. At least she's not barefoot.*

Fixing her deep green-eyed stare on Pamela's face, Lauren said, 'You've been through some tough times.'

'That's for sure.'

'Well, you'll be fine, now.' Lauren smiled. 'You've been saved.'

Chapter Eleven

'I'll show you around,' Lauren said, 'and then—'

'We better get some grub in her, first,' Sharpe broke in. 'Take her on over to the cafe, and I'll be along by and by.'

Smiling, Lauren said, 'Come along.'

Pamela followed her down the stairs at the front of the bus. When she stepped to the ground, pain shot up from her feet. She sucked in air, hissing.

'Your feet?' Lauren asked, frowning.

'They're a little beat up. But I'm fine.'

'I know just the thing. Wait here.' Lauren started to hurry away.

'It's fine,' Pamela protested. 'I don't need anything.'

'Yes, you do. This'll be just the ticket.' A moment later, Lauren disappeared around the corner of the gas-station office. Pamela, embarrassed, wanting to tell her not to bother with whatever she had in mind, limped after her.

And almost collided with the old geezer she'd seen earlier by the pumps.

As she stepped out of the bus's shadow, he came around the corner.

She gasped and jerked to a halt.

'Howdy do.' He gave her a big grin. His gums were interrupted by a few brown, twisted teeth.

'Hello,' Pamela said.

My God, she thought. *What is this guy?* A few terms came quickly to mind. *Old-timer. Prospector. Mule skinner. Desert rat. Snake rustler. Sand bandit.* The only thing that looked worse than his dental situation was his cowboy hat.

The Glory Bus

The ancient, filthy hat sat crooked atop his head, its brim turned up in front. It might've been a good hat at about the time of the Alamo's fall. In the years since, it had apparently been slashed, shot, stomped, kicked, burnt . . . and drenched thousands of times with the old coot's sweat – or worse. It was decorated with so many stains that Pamela couldn't even guess at its original color. She imagined that the sorry old hat, if caught in a rainstorm, would likely have yellow runoff.

Not much of the old man's face showed. Most of it was hidden behind his wild gray hair, his heavy eyebrows, his thick mustache and beard. But his eyes showed. They were squinty, with blue irises and bloodshot whites. His nose showed. It looked like a strawberry that had been kicked around on a dusty road. His lower lip was cracked and peeling.

The guy's a walking ruin, Pamela thought. But she had to change her mind about his age. He wasn't quite the old coot that she had supposed. Probably in his middle fifties. With the exception of his hat, his clothes looked reasonably clean. But heavy and hot. His plaid flannel shirt had long sleeves, and Pamela could see the neck of a faded red T-shirt that he was wearing underneath it. The shirts were tucked into his blue jeans. His belt had a big silver buckle. On his feet were a pair of scuffed and dusty black cowboy boots.

Giving Pamela an odd lopsided smile, he lifted the hat off his head. 'Name's Hank,' he said. 'Honorary mayor of Pits, chief guide, Man Friday, you name it and I'm it. Hank.'

'I'm Pamela.'

'Yer a dish.' He winked.

'Thanks.'

'A real hot tuh-matuh.'

'Well . . .'

Hank narrowed an eye. 'Show you my pits?'

Trying to smile, she shook her head. 'Not right now.'

'It's my job. Chief guide. How about the Dillinger Death Car? Wanna see her?' He pointed at the rusted ruin of an ancient automobile near a far corner of the lot.

'Is that it?' Pamela asked.

'Yessiree. Wanna see her?'

'Maybe later.'

'Don't miss her.'

She couldn't help but smile. 'Is that really the Dillinger Death Car?' It certainly looked like a vehicle that might've been around back in the 1930s.

'You can see the bullet holes,' Hank said, and winked. 'The baby's *peppered* with 'em.'

'Are you trying to trick me?'

'How d'ya mean, there?'

'You're talking about *John* Dillinger?'

'None but.'

'I don't think he was in a car when he was killed.'

'Ya don't, huh?'

'I think he was standing outside the Biograph Theater in Chicago.'

'*Haw!*' Hank reached out and clutched her shoulder. 'Can't fool *you*! Nosirree! You're a smart cookie, yes, you are! I like you.'

'Thanks.'

He leaned in close to her. As if sharing a dark secret, he said, 'You got no idea how many plug-fuck ignoramuses come along here and *believe* every dang thing I tell 'em. *No idea!*' He cackled. Then he stepped back, scowled, and nodded. 'That ain't no *Dillinger Death Car*. It's the *Jesse James Death Car!*'

Surprised, Pamela found laughter bursting out of her. She was even more surprised to find herself reaching out and slapping Hank on his shoulder. A puff of dust rose off his shirt.

'What's your name?' he demanded. Hadn't she already told him?

'Pamela.'

'Pamela! Good for you!

'Well, thanks.'

'Ya gonna stay?'

She shrugged. 'For a while, maybe.'

'Good deal! I stayed. Aim to keep stayin', too, till the day I go toes-up and then I'm gonna have 'em plant me over yonder on Boot Hill with the dogs and monkeys. Been here since seventy-two.'

'That's a long time.'

'You betcha!'

Lauren came riding around a far corner of the gas station office. She was on the front seat of a bicycle built for two.

'Hank!' she called out. 'Have you been bothering the lady?'

He cackled. 'Making a plug-fuck nuisance outta myself, and you know it.'

Lauren pedaled toward them, a big smile on her face. 'Hank is an inveterate bushwhacker. We keep him around to scare the children off.'

'Haw!'

'Are you one of the "pop. six"?' Pamela asked him.

'You better betcha, baby!'

'Which are you?'

He winked. 'Some folks take me for number two.'

'You're terrible!'

'Ain't I?'

Lauren stopped her bike just beyond Hank. She put her feet on the ground and held the bike steady by its front set of handlebars. 'Climb on aboard, Pamela, and I'll pedal you over to the cafe.'

'Well . . . okay.' She limped toward the bike's second seat. 'Nice to meet you, Hank.'

'You know it!'

Laughing, she shook her head.

Hank stepped backward, out of the way. He leaned against the rear of the bus and watched her mount the bike.

'Don't be no stranger,' he said.

'See you around, Hank. *Mayor* Hank.'

He guffawed so loud she thought he'd up-'n-out of one of his lungs.

'Ready?' Lauren asked. 'Here we go.'

They both pushed at the ground to get the bike rolling. Then they put their feet on the pedals and started to pump.

'Beats walking,' Pamela admitted. 'I was afraid you might show up with a wheelchair or something.'

'Nope.'

From behind them came a raspy, almost tuneless voice singing, 'Mademoiselles got derrieres, whoop-de-doo. Mademoiselles got—'

Cheerfully, Lauren called over her shoulder, 'Put a lid on it, you raunchy old sidewinder!'

'*Pardonnez-moi!*' Hank yelled.

Lauren glanced back at Pamela, smiled, then faced forward. 'He's about as addled as they come,' she said.

'I sort of like him.'

'Well, I'm glad to hear it.'

'Is he really the mayor of Pits?'

'He's pretty much whoever he says he is, I guess.'

A dusty old pickup truck swung off the highway and rolled slowly across the dirt. It seemed to be heading for the cafe. Lauren raised an arm and waved. The driver tooted his horn. He stopped in the midst of fifteen or twenty other vehicles that were scattered about near the cafe: an odd assortment of cars, trucks, vans, and even a couple of motorcycles. Some looked fairly new and roadworthy, but quite a few didn't seem to be in much better shape than the Dillinger/James Death Car.

Lauren dodged several as she and Pamela pedaled toward the cafe.

They glided very close to the remains of an old Pontiac. It had no windows. Pamela felt heat coming out of it. A smelly heat that made her think of melting rubber. On the dashboard was a plastic Jesus.

The plastic Jesus looked almost new.

Parked near the front entrance of the cafe was a Toyota Land Cruiser, its cargo space loaded with luggage.

They steered past it. Then Lauren swerved away from the cafe door, braked, and lowered her feet to the ground. She held the bike steady while Pamela dismounted. After that, she leaned it against a stucco wall.

The man from the pickup swung the door open for them. He looked like a younger version of Hank, but with better teeth, whiskers instead of a full beard, and a fairly presentable outfit – cowboy hat, plaid shirt, blue jeans and boots. Smiling, he lifted his hat.

'Thank you,' Pamela said as she entered.

'Mah pleasure, ma'am. Howdy, Lauren.'

'Howdy, Wes. This is Pamela. Sharpe just now brought her in.'

Wes followed them into the cafe. 'Reckon yer a lucky gal,' he told her. To Lauren he said, 'She's, what, the seventh?'

'Yep.'

'Sharpe's got himself a long ways to go.'

'Afraid so.'

'Pleasure to meet ya, Pamela.'

'Nice to meet you, Wes.'

He sauntered toward the counter.

Pamela saw four other customers at the counter. A family with two kids sat at one of the booths, an elderly couple at another, and a group of four teenagers at a corner booth. There were several wooden tables scattered about the area between the booths and the L-shaped counter but they weren't being used. 'Would you like a booth?' Lauren asked.

'That'd be fine.'

Lauren led her to one at the front of the cafe. They slid in across from each other. The table between them had a green Formica top and looked clean. A couple of menus were propped up behind the napkin holder. Lauren took them and handed one to Pamela.

'We've got good food here. Terry's a whiz in the kitchen. Sharpe brought him in, and he stayed. Our vittles were mighty poor till he showed up.'

'Has Sharpe brought in *everybody*?'

Smiling slightly, Lauren shook her head. 'Terry's the only one who's stayed. He didn't have anywhere better to go and found out he liked it here.'

'Wes said something about me being the seventh.'

'There were six before you.'

'Six what?'

'People Sharpe has saved since he started the mission.'

'*Saved?*'

'Like you.' Lauren turned her head and smiled at the approaching waitress. 'Nicki, I want you to meet Pamela. Sharpe saved her today.'

'Hey, great!' Nicki beamed. 'He's moving right along.'

'I'll be an old lady in a wheelchair,' Lauren said.

'No, you won't!' Nicki set down the water glasses and reached a hand toward Pamela. 'Pleased to make your acquaintance,' she said as they shook.

Nicki looked as if she belonged in a ski lodge, not in a cafe in the middle of the Mojave Desert. Her blond hair was arranged in a braided ponytail behind and a thick curtain of bangs in front. The bangs hung almost to her pale blue eyes. Her face had a Nordic look, in spite of its dark tan.

She wore a knit pullover shirt similar to the one that Pamela had taken from the dummy in the bus. Nicki's was white, not lime green, and had her name in red stitches above her left breast. It appeared to be a few sizes larger than Pamela's, too. Filled with mounds and curves and slopes.

Around Nicki's waist was a blue apron with pockets for her order pad and tips. It hung down like a very short skirt, ending just above the cuffs of her shorts. The shorts were bright red. They looked snug around her thighs.

'Ready to order?' she asked.

'Give us a few more minutes,' Lauren said.

'Can I bring you something to drink while you're deciding?'

'Do you have beer?' Pamela asked.

'You bet.' Nicki flashed her white teeth. 'All we got's Bud, but that suits most folks.'

'That's fine.'

'One for me, too,' Lauren said.

'You got it.' Nicki headed for the counter.

'She seems nice,' Pamela said.

'A good kid. But she drives Terry crazy. He's got it really bad for her but she won't have a thing to do with him.'

Pamela felt a quick shiver. *Rodney and me.*

'A thing like that can be dangerous,' she said.

'Keeps the place lively.' A corner of Lauren's mouth tilted upward. 'We'll have to make up some sort of billboard about this place being a "passion pit." You just wouldn't believe all the lust and unrequited love we've got around here.'

Shaking her head, Pamela made a wry half-smile of her own. 'That's how I got here, I guess. A guy had the hots for me and wouldn't let it go. Killed my husband,' she added quickly.

The last three words were enough to shut her throat and fill her eyes with tears. Across the table, Lauren blinked. She pressed her lips together. They formed a tight, straight line. Leaning forward, she reached out and squeezed Pamela's hand.

'Nothing bad'll happen to you here. We take care of each other, and you're welcome to stay just as long as you want.'

Chapter Twelve

Pamela cried softly, head down, trying to stop. Hoping that everyone in the cafe wasn't staring at her. Lauren kept hold of her hand, and said nothing.

Nicki showed up with the beer. She set two frosty glass mugs on the table. Then she put a hand on Pamela's shoulder. Pamela looked up at her.

'Whatever it is,' Nicki said, 'I'm sure sorry. You gonna be all right?'

'She's been through some rough times,' Lauren said. 'That beer's bound to help.'

Nodding, Pamela murmured, 'Thanks.' She sniffed. With the back of her hand, she wiped her eyes. 'I haven't . . . had a chance to look at the menu.'

'No problem.'

'Do you like burgers?' Lauren asked.

Pamela nodded.

'Get her a Pitsburger Deluxe and chili cheese fries. Same for me.'

Nicki let go of Pamela's shoulder and started to turn away. Before she could leave, Pamela said, 'I don't . . . have any money.' She sniffed again. 'Where's Sharpe?'

'He'll be along.'

'He said he'd pay.'

'Don't worry about anybody paying,' Lauren told her. 'I own the joint.'

'The cafe?'

'Everything.'

'Oh. Neat.' Pamela lifted the heavy mug and drank some beer. The beer was very cold.

'We like it here,' Lauren said.

'Pop. six?'

'That's me, Hank, Nicki, Terry and Sharpe when he isn't on the road.'

'That only makes five.'

'Six is just sort of a general estimate.'

Pamela laughed. It felt strange to laugh when she was hardly done crying. She wiped her eyes again and drank some more beer. It quenched the fire in her throat.

'We can't go changing everything each time we have a minor fluctuation in our population.'

'I guess not.'

'It stays roughly in the area of five or six, and none of us are sticklers for detail. Besides, as long as you and Sharpe hang around, we've got our full complement.' Lauren lifted her mug. It left a wet ring on the tabletop. Most of the frost on its sides had melted, leaving the mug clear and dripping. But a few small white patches slipped down its exterior like the last remnants of snow sliding down a car's windshield. When she lifted the mug toward her mouth, the bottom of it dripped cold drops of water onto the front of her white dress. She didn't seem to notice.

With the rim at her lips, she sucked at the frothy head. Then she tipped the mug back and drank.

In a way, Lauren seemed too willowy and ethereal to be drinking a mug of beer. A delicate glass of white wine might've been more appropriate. On the other hand, a hefty mug of beer seemed just about right for the Lauren who was weathered, gaunt and earthy. Somehow she seemed like two different people rolled into one. The first delicate, fey, spirit-like, the second – the outer shell – made tough by life: strong enough to fight back if fighting was required.

Lauren set the mug back down on the table, smiled at it, and rubbed the back of a brown hand across her lips. 'You're welcome to stay,' she said. 'You can sleep in Mosby's trailer. He hasn't got any use for it.'

'Well . . . thank you. I don't know.'

'Sharpe won't be going anywhere tonight, if that's what you're wondering about. He'll probably stick around for a day or two – longer, if I have any say in things.' Lauren raised her eyebrows. 'Are you in a rush to get home?'

'He burnt it. Rodney. The man who killed my husband. The house is gone. My home. Everything.' Pamela stared at her beer and struggled not to start crying again.

'Pamela? Do you have family?'

'In Chicago.' She took a drink. The mug dripped onto the front of her pullover. The drops felt ice-cold. 'I don't want to go there. My job . . . I work in LA.'

'What do you do?'

'Just . . . I'm a teacher. A substitute.'

'Oh, dear God. A sub in Los Angeles? That must be about the nearest thing to hell on earth.'

'It's not much fun. It's a way to work into a . . . a real teaching position. You know, you get your foot in the door. Jim had a good job, though, so . . . I don't know what I'll do, but I've gotta go back. I mean, that's where I live, and guess I'll have to find an apartment, or something.'

'It doesn't sound as if you've got much to go back to.'

'Well, not much.'

'Sharpe'll drive you back to LA when he's ready to go, if that's what you want. But there's no law that says you've gotta go with him. You can stay here just as long as you want. I'd recommend it for a while, anyway, after what you've gone through. It's peaceful here. It's a good place for getting over troubles.'

'Thanks. I don't know . . .'

'Play it by ear. But figure on staying tonight, at least. I always keep Mosby's trailer up in case of company.'

'Okay. Thanks.' Pamela looked out the window. Long shadows stretched across the dirt lot in front of the cafe. 'Where do you suppose Sharpe is?'

'Oh, he'll be in my trailer taking a shower, I guess. That's usually the first thing he does when he comes back.'

'He told me he lives in the bus.'

'His bus doesn't have a shower.'

Pamela glanced at Lauren's hands to double-check. No rings. But she supposed that didn't prove anything; Lauren didn't seem to be wearing any jewelry at all.

'Are you and Sharpe married?'

'Afraid not.'

'But you're . . . something?'

'I guess we're something, all right.'

Pamela waited. When Lauren didn't go on, she decided not to push. She drank some more beer instead. The mug dripped chilly water onto her.

She put the mug down.

Across the table Lauren sat motionless, one hand on her own beer mug, her eyes lowered and staring blankly, her straw-colored eyebrows drawn together just enough to carve a pair of small grooves into the skin between them. *It's my fault*, Pamela thought. *I shouldn't have asked about Sharpe. I must've hit a sore spot.*

Bumbled right into it.

Should've known better.

One of thsoe 'unrequited love' things she was talking about, probably.

'Are you okay?' Pamela asked.

'Huh? Sorry. What did you say?'

'Is something wrong?'

'No. No. I wonder what's keeping the burgers.' Lauren flashed a smile at Pamela. 'Maybe I'll have to give someone the boot.'

'It hasn't been so long.'

'But you must be starving.' Lauren peered off across the cafe, her eyes narrow. 'Ah, here they come now.'

Turning, Pamela saw Nicki hurry around the end of the counter with a big loaded tray.

'I'm going to marry Sharpe,' Lauren said.

Pamela looked at her, surprised.

The other woman nodded, smiling. 'Soon as he's done with his mission. By then, of course, I'll probably be an ugly old hairless hag . . . and too old to have babies.' As she spoke the last part, her smile trembled and her eyes suddenly brimmed with tears.

Nicki arrived at their booth and began to unload the food. 'That's two Pitsburger Deluxes, chili cheese fries . . . Lauren?' Nicki crouched slightly and peered into her boss's eyes. 'What's the matter, honey?'

'Just the usual.'

'Damn that man.'

'Don't say that. He can't help it.'

'He sure can help it, too. Jesus H. Christ, there's no excuse. The dead don't mean squat. Somebody oughta tell him that.'

'He has to do it.'

'Bullshit, if you'll pardon my French.'

Lauren fixed her wet-eyed gaze on Pamela. 'He saved your life, didn't he?'

'Sharpe? Yes.'

'What sort of danger were you in?'

'Rodney . . .' Pamela looked at Nicki, then back at Lauren. 'He was going to kill me. He killed my husband last night.'

'Oh, God,' Nicki muttered.

'And he . . . threatened he'd do a lot of things to me. Anyway, then he kidnapped me. He wanted to take me to a place in the desert, but I sort of escaped. Almost. The thing is, he finally got me down on the ground and stuck a pistol in my mouth. I'd hurt him bad. He was going to kill me. I mean, he would've pulled the trigger in about one more second. And suddenly he got shot in the head. Sharpe shot him right in the middle of the forehead.'

'Wow,' Nicki said.

Lauren simply nodded. Then she turned to Nicki. 'See? It's not exactly bullshit. If it hadn't been for Sharpe and his mission, Pamela'd be food for buzzards about now. Instead, she's about to partake of a Pitsburger Deluxe.'

'Well,' Nicki said. 'I know. It's just maddening, though, that's all.'

'I've noticed,' Lauren said.

Nicki shook her head at Pamela. 'It's not that I'm not really glad he saved your life. I mean, that's great. But he's just so obsessed, and here's poor Lauren who loves him like crazy, but off he goes anyhow just as if he didn't give a rat's hairy behind, if you know what I mean, and one of these days he'll probably wind up getting himself killed . . .'

'Stop it,' Lauren told her.

'Well, it's just so *maddening*.'

'Don't you have some other customers you might want to go and bother, Nicole?'

Nicki rolled her eyes upward. 'Well, I *suppose* so.'

Lauren reached out and squeezed her forearm. 'Get out of here, okay?'

'Somebody oughta pound some *sense* into that lunkhead, that's all.'

'Go.'

'I'm going, I'm going.' Nicki stepped backward with the empty tray. 'I'm just saying he oughta think about *you*, for a change, and quit—'

'Hey!'

'Okay, okay.' Nicki shrugged at Pamela, smiled at both the women, then turned around and hurried off.

Lauren was the next to shrug at Pamela. 'Better dig in,' she said. 'All this talk, our food's gonna get cold.'

'Yeah.'

'Eat it.'

Pamela looked down at her meal. A Pitsburger Deluxe and chili cheese fries.

The fries were hidden completely beneath thick blankets of chili and melted yellow cheese. So much steam curled off the concoction that Pamela knew she'd be risking a mouth burn if she didn't wait a few minutes before taking a taste. She turned her attention to the Pitsburger.

The bun was nearly as large as the plate. Its top was brown, shiny, and striped with dark grill marks. Lettuce leaves and curls of onion stuck out beneath the bun's top, but only here and there, not enough to hide the crispy edges of the hamburger patty.

Edges that dripped with cheese.

'It sure looks good,' Pamela said, and had to shut her mouth quickly to prevent drool from spilling out.

'Just wait'll you sink your teeth in,' Lauren said. 'The patty's partly sausage, by the way. It's my recipe. A mixture of ground beef and sausage.'

'Ah. Sounds great.'

Pamela needed both hands to pick up her Pitsburger Deluxe. The bun felt both slippery and crisp under her fingertips. Afraid of losing it, she tightened her hold before biting in. Warm juices and cheese spilled down her palms and wrists.

She opened her mouth wide and took her first bite. Her teeth crunched through the bun, lettuce and onions, then sank into the meat. A wonderful assortment of sweet, tangy flavors filled her mouth.

Moaning with pleasure, Pamela began to chew.

Chapter Thirteen

When Boots bit into her hamburger, red juice dribbled down her chin.

'Are you sure that thing's done enough?' Norman asked.

Chewing, she turned her burger around and showed it to him. The inside of the patty looked like a raw, bloody wound. The sight of it disgusted Norman.

'You oughta have them cook it some more,' he said. 'You could catch a disease, or something.'

'This is just how I like it,' Boots said, her words muffled. She opened her mouth wide. It was full of mushy, partly chewed burger.

Norman looked away.

Boots laughed. 'You're funny,' she said. She ran the back of her hand across her chin to stop the dribble. When she lowered her hand, her chin was shiny.

She's so repulsive. Norman thought.

Right. But here I am.

Back at the beach parking lot, hours ago and fifty miles north of where they now sat eating supper, he'd had a perfect chance to get away from her and Duke. He could've driven off and never seen either of them again. But what had he done? He'd shut off the engine and gone to the back of the Cherokee and searched through his luggage until he found his swimming trunks.

In the back seat, where Boots had changed into her tiny little knitted bikini, he'd taken off his shorts and underwear and put on his trunks. Then he'd hurried back to where Boots and Duke were sitting on their beach towels.

'Thought you were gonna split on us,' Duke had said, smiling.

'It crossed my mind. But I just couldn't drive off and leave you two stranded. Thought it would've been a dirty trick.'

'Like we don't *know* how come you came back,' Boots had said. Tongue protruding between her lips, she'd somehow made her breasts hop and shake inside the flimsy bikini – without apparently moving the rest of her body.

'That isn't why.'

'Like fun.'

'Glad to have you back, bud,' Duke had said. 'It don't matter how come you stuck, just matters you done the right thing.'

The right thing, my ass.

The one thing certain to Norman, as he'd sat down on his towel and picked up his beer, was that sticking with these two had *not* been the right thing. It was probably the least right thing he'd ever done. He *should*'ve driven away.

He'd come back to them only because of Boots, because of her knitted bikini, because of what he'd been able to see through its artful holes.

And because he'd wanted to be there when it came time to work the suntan oil into her sun-heated skin.

Sitting across from her now in the diner, Norman shifted uncomfortably as he remembered.

Soon after his return to the beach, Boots had squirted the coconut oil onto her palm and spread it on the front of her body. It had a strong, sweet scent. Her hand had slipped underneath the bikini – both the top and the bottom – and Norman had been able to watch it through the meshwork of black yarn. Watch it slick her skin with shiny oil. Watch it linger inside the bikini, fingertips roaming and stroking as she glanced from Norman to Duke with her lazy, blank eyes.

Done, she'd sprawled on her back. Legs apart. Hands folded beneath her head.

Gleaming in the sunlight from face to feet. He was sure he could see her—

'*What?*' Boots asked, lowering her hamburger.

'Nothing.'

'Tell.' She smiled, but she didn't look amused. 'You're thinking about me, aren't you?'

'Yeah, I guess so. About the beach.'

'I knew it.' She took another bite of her hamburger. After a few chews, she said, 'Probably spoiled yer eyes, you was staring at me so hard.'

'Well . . .'

'I was gonna let you do my back, but then you went and walked off. How come you walked off?'

I was about to explode, that's why. 'I just felt like taking a walk,' he said.

'Duke was kinda rough. He kinda hurt me. Hope he didn't leave no bruises.'

'Well . . .'

'I kinda like it when it hurts. Don't like bruises, though. I got me real delicate skin, in case you didn't notice. I bruise easy. Burn, too. Sunburn? Wonder if I got me a burn out there today.'

With the hand that wasn't holding her hamburger, Boots plucked out the front of her tank top and peered down inside. She shook her head and pursed her lips. 'Reckon *they* got some sun. Wanna see?' She met Norman's stare.

Blushing, he glanced around the diner. It was fairly crowded. He smiled at Boots. 'I don't think so. Not right now, anyway.'

'Later, then.'

'Well . . .'

'We'll get a room, the three of us.'

The suggestion stunned him, excited him, frightened him. *The three of us in a motel room. My God!*

Privacy. Beds.

'What?' he asked her. Maybe he'd misunderstood what she was getting at.

'We'll get us a room.'

'What kind of a room?'

'A lecture room in a flicking museum. *Duh!* A motel room, dummy.' Smiling, she shook her head. 'What'd you think we was gonna do, spend the whole night in your car?'

'I don't know. I guess I hadn't really thought about it.'

'Thought about what?' Duke asked, coming back from the diner's restroom and pulling out his chair.

'Everything come out all right?' Boots asked him.

Duke smirked. 'Can't complain.' He sat down. He studied his cheese dog and French fries, then picked up the squeeze-bottle of catsup and covered the fries with a mat of thick red sauce. 'So,' he said, 'what'd I miss? What's going on?'

'I was just saying to Norm how we oughta get us a room at that motel right across the street there.'

'Hey. Yeah.'

'I don't know,' Norman said. 'I don't have a whole lot of money.'

'You got plastic,' Duke reminded him.

'I know, but . . . I can't use a credit card for something like that. My father'll get the bill.'

'You gotta sleep.'

'But I've only made about a hundred and fifty miles today. I should've gone twice that far. When he sees . . .'

'Hey, use your head. All you gotta do is say you got a flat.'

'No,' Boots said. 'We don't wanna go and use no credit cards. It's like telling who we are. Anyhow, we don't need one. I can get us a room, and it won't cost us nothing.'

They both stared at her.

'I just bet you can,' Duke said.

'You better believe it.'

'You mean like . . . use your charm on the desk clerk?' Norman asked.

'Whatever,' Boots said.

'That'll only work if it's a guy,' he pointed out.

She grinned. 'Oh, don't be too sure.'

'Anyway, it wouldn't be legal. Not if he doesn't *charge* us anything.'

'So?' Boots said.

'I don't want us getting into trouble,' Norman muttered.

'Don't be such a wuss all your life,' Duke told him. 'Boots here, she's offering to get us a free room. You *really* got a problem with that? Just take a second and think about what's gonna *happen* in that room, know what I mean?'

'I just don't think we should do something that might be against the law. I don't want to end up in jail.'

Duke suddenly looked dead serious. 'Nobody's gonna end up in jail. I don't do jail. That's for losers. So, long as you stick with me, you got nothing to worry about.'

'You guys wait here,' Boots said. 'I'll come back and get you when it's all set.'

'No big rush,' Duke told her. 'Finish your burger.'

'I'll take it with me.' Holding the hamburger in one hand, she stood up. She shoved her chair away with the backs of her legs. 'You guys can fight over the end of my Pepsi. It'll be watered down anyhow by the time I get back.'

'I don't know about this,' Norman said.

'Face it,' Duke said, 'you don't know about much.'

'I know, but . . .'

'Don't you worry about anything,' Boots told him. She squeezed his shoulder. 'I'm gonna show you boys the best time you ever had.'

She released his shoulder.

On her way toward the door, she sashayed past several crowded tables. Conversations stopped. Customers turned their heads. Stares latched onto her from every direction.

'Look at 'em,' Duke said. 'The gals, they all hate her, figure her for a tramp. The guys, they're thinking how they'd give their left nut to shack up with her for a night. They hate us just as much as the gals hate Boots. We're the guys that *have* her, know what I mean?'

'I guess so.'

'We're gonna have her all to ourselves, and those poor bastards know it. They can't stand it. They're ready to blow their pants right now.'

'I really don't know if we should do this.'

'The room?'

'Everything.'

'Man, you're a case.' Shaking his head, Duke fixed Norman with a look of exaggerated disgust and pity. 'You don't watch out, you're gonna go *through* your whole life and get to the end of it and find out you never done nothing. You gotta go for it, man. That's what life's all about.'

'If you're living a beer commercial.'

'Ha! Good one.'

'Maybe I should just go ahead and *pay* for a room,' Norman suggested. 'I mean, I don't like this idea of trying to get a freebie.'

'Take what you can get,' Duke said. 'Somebody wants to hand us a room for the night . . .'

'But—'

'Look, you're just scared of getting caught. But the thing is, so what if we do get caught? Say Boots finds herself a horny clerk at the front desk – she gives him some head or whatever – he lets her have a room for the night and the boss shows up and finds out all about it. The *clerk's* the guy that gets his ass reamed. We walk. The worst that happens, maybe we have to fork over whatever it would've cost us to get the room legitimate. See?'

'I guess so. But it still seems like a bad idea.'

'That's 'cause you're also scared to fuck her.'

Norman's face flooded with heat. 'I am not.'

'Sure you are. Shit, she's a scary bitch any way you slice it, but it's gotta be *real* scary for a guy like you.'

'What do you mean, like me?'

'A guy that's never done it before.'

'Who says I've never done it?'

'You told me.'

'No, I didn't.' Norman frowned. Had he admitted such a thing to Duke? *No! No way!* He'd never told that to anyone, much less to Duke.

'You want a piece of advice?' Duke asked.

'I don't need any advice.'

'Sure you do.'

'Yeah, sure.' Norman rolled his eyes upward. 'Okay. Let's hear it.'

'First thing you gotta know, dames aren't the same down there as guys.'

'Very funny.'

Duke tried to look offended. 'No! I mean it! Seriously. They haven't got tools.'

'Ha ha.'

'You think I'm joking? I mean it!'

Norman started to laugh for real.

Leaning forward, Duke whispered, 'It's like their tools got cut off, and all they've got left is just this gash. Now, what you've gotta do is put your tool in *her* gash. Get it?'

'I get it. Jeez!'

'And you gotta make sure you stick it in the front. You don't wanna stick it in the back by mistake, you know what I mean? That's a good place to stay away from.'

Norman, shaking his head, tried to stop laughing.

'Stick it in the right spot, and you got nothing to worry about.'

'Except maybe for the clap and a few other things.'

'No *problemo*, good buddy. They got a vending machine in the john.'

'You mean, like for condoms?'

'Right on. They got three varieties. We'll go in and stock up, soon as we get done eating.'

Norman nodded, but wrinkled his nose. 'Those things aren't all that safe, you know.'

'Sure they are. Ain't you never heard of "safe sex"?'

'I heard the things don't work too well. Like they break when you're inside her, or sometimes come off . . . that sort of stuff. A *lot* of the time. Like once out of six. I mean, that's not very good odds. That's the same sort of odds as playing Russian roulette with a six-shooter.'

Duke frowned. 'So what? Just fuck her five times, you're okay.'

Duke looked quite pleased with himself.

Norman laughed a bit, then said, 'Good one.'

'Yeah, I know. I'm a card. Fact is, though, you gotta lighten up. Who's to say she's even infected? It might be as sweet as a rose garden down there.'

'Can we ask her?'

'Like anyone's gonna admit it.'

'Do *you* have it?'

'You mean AIDS?'

'Yeah.'

'Like I'd admit it?'

'Do you?'

'Don't know, don't care.'

'How can you not care?'

'I don't worry about shit like that. I live how I wanna live. And I know one thing for sure – I ain't ever gonna let no disease nail my ass. When I go out, I go out quick in a blaze of glory.'

'Not with a whimper, but a bang.'

'Right on.'

'I think I'd rather live to a ripe old age and die in bed,' Norman said.

'Yeah? Gee whiz! How come that doesn't just surprise the everlasting shit outta me?'

'Make fun all you want. I don't intend to go around risking my life for a few minutes of . . . screwing Boots, or whatever.'

'So you're telling me you ain't gonna fuck her?'

'It just isn't worth it.'

'What're you aiming to do, stand around and watch us?'

Another blush scorched Norman's face. 'I don't know,' he muttered. 'I figured I'd . . . just sort of go along to the room and see what happens.'

'I *know* what'll happen. We better load up on rubbers.'

By the time they were done eating, Boots still hadn't returned. They asked for coffee. Then Norman gave Duke a five-dollar bill.

'What's this for?'

'Why don't you go up to the cashier and get some change? Whatever you need for the vending machine.'

'Quarters.'

'Yeah. Then, you know – go in the john and buy whatever we need.'

'We? Changed your mind already?'

'Okay, whatever *you* need.'

'Sure you don't wanna come along?'

'No, that's all right.'

'Aren't gonna run out on us, are you?'

He hadn't thought of that.

I could!

Yeah, right, he thought. *I couldn't even make myself drive away from the beach, so I'm sure I'm gonna take off when I've got a chance to end up in a motel room with her.*

Duke stood up from the table, his chair scooting back, its legs squawking against the floor. Breadcrumbs speckled his pants. Norman watched him walk toward the cashier's counter. The five was in Duke's left hand. His right hand was shoved partway down the seat pocket of his jeans. He walked with a swagger. Norman couldn't see his face, but he knew there had to be a smirk on it. *Guy acts like he owns the world.*

Norman tried to picture himself walking like Duke, dressing like him, smirking like him.

I'd look like a total dork, he decided. *I just haven't got what it takes.*

What does *it take?* he wondered. *Does it have to be in the genes to be able to wear jeans like that? Like you're James Dean. Better yet, would I really* want *to be like him? Let's face it, the guy's a macho jerk and not all that bright.*

But he sure is cool. What does it take to be that cool? Plenty of time attending the school of hard knocks, Norman supposed. *More balls than brains. I wouldn't want to be that way,* he told himself. And a voice in a shadowy corner of his mind whispered, *What good are brains if you're a gutless wonder who hasn't got any balls at all? You've gotta take chances sometimes or what's the point?* Carpe diem! *Seize the day! Seize the babe! If you chicken out with Boots tonight, you'll regret it the rest of your life.*

Chapter Fourteen

Flushed and a little breathless, Boots dropped into her chair. She smiled at Duke and Norman in turn.

'We was starting to take you for missing in action,' Duke said.

'Not me.'

'How'd it go?'

She shifted onto her left buttock, reached behind the right, and pulled something out of the rear pocket of her jeans. A big green plastic tab with a key dangling from its end.

A smile spread across Duke's face. 'All *right*!'

'Jeez,' Norman gasped. 'You did it?'

'Told you I was gonna, didn't I?' Boots glanced around the diner as if worried about spies, then quickly returned the motel key to her seat pocket. 'It was a cinch.'

'Really?' Norman asked. He found himself leaning toward her and whispering. 'You really got it for free?'

She beamed at him.

Duke grinned. 'I think Normy here wants all the juicy details.'

'That so, Normy?'

'Well . . .'

'You wanna sit here and listen to how I got the room for us, or you wanna go over and get into it?'

'You betcha,' Duke said

Norman felt as if his face might burst into flame. 'Well . . .'

'I think Normy's got the jitters.' Duke winked.

'Would you quit calling me "Normy"? Please?'

The Glory Bus

His eyes on Boots, Duke said, 'Normy's got such a bad case of the jitters, he's about ready to shit.'

Boots reached out and took hold of Norman's hand. 'What're you scared of?'

Norman shrugged.

'He's scared of getting in trouble with the law,' Duke explained. 'And he's scared of you. *He's a virgin.*'

'Good deal!' She squeezed Norman's hand. 'I'll break you in.'

'That's what scares him.'

'Well, it ain't like I'm gonna *hurt* him.' To Norman, she said, 'You got nothing to be scared of, honey. This is gonna be the night of your life. Now, come on. Let's get the show on the road.' She took her hand away and stood up.

'Are you sure you don't want anything else before we go?' Norman asked her. 'Did you get enough to eat? Do you need a Pepsi, or something?' To Duke he said, 'How about you? Don't you want another hot dog, or something?'

'Only one thing I'm hankering to eat, good buddy, and it ain't a doggie.'

Boots laughed. She leaned over the table and slapped Duke's shoulder.

Giving her a smirky grin, Duke got to his feet.

'Just a minute,' Norman said. He took out his wallet and removed a few dollars for the tip. His hands trembled as he folded the bills. He tucked them under a corner of his coffee mug. When he stood up, his legs were shaking. *My God, I can't believe I'm really gonna go through with this.*

I'm not going through with anything, he told himself. *Not yet, anyhow. Just gonna pay the tab and go outside. Which I'd be doing anyway. Then maybe I'll go over to the motel with them, or maybe not. I can do whatever I want. Nobody's holding a gun to my dick . . . Dick? I mean head. I wonder if she gives head . . . Oh Christ, I'm rambling . . .*

Duke and Boots waited by the cashier's counter while Norman paid. Then they walked ahead of him to the door.

As he followed them he gazed at Boots. She wore her tank top, cutoff jeans and white boots. In the beach parking lot, by the side of the Cherokee, Norman and Duke had watched her put them on. Still

101

in her black-knit bikini, she'd stepped into the shorts and pulled them up. Then she'd slipped the tank top down over her head. After putting her boots back on she had untied the yarn at the nape of her neck, then reached up under the back of the tank top, fiddled around in there, and finally plucked out the upper part of her bikini.

It had gone into her big denim bag. But her bikini pants had stayed on.

Norman wondered if she was still wearing them, just as he was still wearing his swimming trunks underneath his shorts. He stared at the seat of her cutoffs. The blue denim, faded almost white, was packed tight with her buttocks. No telltale lines to indicate that she was wearing the bikini pants underneath.

Maybe they're in her bag by now.

Maybe she took them off for the benefit of the motel's desk clerk.

She's such a slut, he thought. *Not to mention ugly. I'd have to be nuts to mess around with her. She doesn't even seem like a real human being. Maybe she's the result of a laboratory experiment. A fusion of human and pig DNA. Now she's broken free. She's making men pay for the result of the obscene experiment. The Revenge of the Pig Woman . . . Oh Christ, I really am rambling . . .*

But it excited him, knowing that her breasts were loose inside her tank top and that she was probably naked underneath the ragged cutoff jeans. *Wow, gonna make bacon tonight . . . with the Pig Woman. Gonna make a hog of myself, too . . .* The excitement made Norman dizzy.

Duke stepped outside the diner and held the door open. Boots walked out. Norman followed her.

The sun must've just gone down. When they'd entered the diner, the town had been aglare with sunlight flashing off glass and chrome. Now all the harsh brightness was gone. The white rocks of the parking lot had a mild blue tint. Boots rubbed her arms.

She started to turn around, so Norman glanced at the slit side of her cut-offs. Bare skin was all he saw.

Nothing under there but Boots, he thought. *I'd bet on it. Pure pork belly . . . Stop it,* he told himself. *You're making crap jokes because you're nervous. Stick around and find out what's under those tight clothes of hers.*

'Wait'll you get a look at the room,' she said. 'It's a real peach.'

'You're the peach,' Duke told her.

Lame, Norman thought.

102

Duke stood there in a slouch, a smirk on his face, both arms up as he ran a comb through his greased waves of hair.

If he doesn't watch out, Norman thought, *he'll get mobbed by autograph hounds.*

Except there seemed to be no one nearby.

And the stars Duke seemed to be copying were long dead: Elvis, Dean, Brando.

'You gonna stick around?' Duke asked.

Norman looked across the road at the Golden Anchor Inn and felt himself go squirmy inside.

A nice place. A long, two-story complex, with stairways going up to the second level. Freshly painted. Lights aglow in some of the big picture windows of the guest rooms. The parking lot was about half-full, and the red neon VACANCY sign seemed shockingly bright in the mellow dusk. 'Well . . .'

'Come on,' Boots said. Turning away, she sashayed toward the Cherokee. The blue-white stones of the parking lot made crunching sounds under her boots.

'How about it, Norm?' Duke asked. 'Ready to turn the boy into a man?'

'We'll see. I don't know yet.'

Boots smiled over her shoulder. 'If you don't, you're gonna be sorry.'

Either way, he thought, *I'm gonna be sorry*. They climbed into his car.

Boots, in the back seat, leaned forward as Norman started the engine. He saw her face beside his shoulder. 'We even got cable TV and a thingy . . . a channel-changer.'

Norman started to back up. 'What should we do about parking?' he asked.

'Just do it.'

'Maybe we shouldn't use the motel parking lot. Since we aren't registered?'

Duke snorted. 'You worry too much. Or have I already mentioned that?'

Norman shifted, and steered toward an opening near the far end of the lot. 'Maybe *you*'d worry,' he said, 'if it was your car.'

'Your old man's car, you mean?'

'Which is even worse,' Norman pointed out. 'I'm just saying maybe we should leave it on the next block, or something. Just in case something *does* go wrong.'

Boot's fingers slid gently up the back of Norman's head. 'Nothing's gonna go wrong, honey.' The fingers felt awfully good. They made him squirm. But then she took them away.

'Let's put it smack in front of the room so we don't have to walk so far.'

'I don't know.'

Maybe that isn't such a bad idea, he thought. *If we're right at the door, we can hurry into the room really fast. Less chance of being spotted. Not to mention how convenient it'll be if we need to make a quick getaway. What if somebody takes down the license plate?*

Big deal, Norman told himself. *I do worry too much. My God, it's not like we're committing a federal offense or something. We're getting a free room for the night, that's all. It's no big deal, so lighten up.*

No traffic was coming, so he steered onto the road and drove slowly back toward the Golden Anchor.

'Don't take the first entrance,' Boots told him.

Norman saw that it led directly to the portico in front of the motel office.

'There's another way in,' she added. 'Down at the other end of the lot.'

'Scared your clerk might wanna join the party?' Duke asked.

'He ain't on duty now. His boss was coming on.'

Norman groaned.

'Don't worry, hon. What he don't know ain't gonna hurt him.'

'What if he checks somebody into our room?'

Duke laughed.

'I don't see what's so funny. It could happen.'

'It ain't gonna happen,' Boots said. 'My guy took care of it.'

'Oh. You mean we *are* checked in?'

'Not as us. But the room's signed up for.'

That was certainly good news.

Maybe I'll stay, after all, Norman thought. *I've gotta spend the night somewhere. Now, at least, there won't be much danger of getting into trouble about the room.*

Just have to stay away from Boots. And keep her away from me.

He drove slowly alongside the motel's parking lot, keeping watch for the second entrance. When he spotted it he flipped his turn signal on. He swung in.

'It's one-forty,' Boots said. 'That's the last room on this end. See it?' Her arm stretched past the side of his face, her finger pointing. 'That one right there. Where that car is.'

Norman drove straight toward it. But he asked, 'Are you sure? I mean, somebody's parked there.'

'Those guys, they went upstairs.'

'Oh. Okay. Are you sure?'

'Yeah, I'm sure. Good golly, Norman.'

'Just pull in next to it,' Duke said.

'Okay.' Slowing, he eased his Cherokee into the space to the right of the other car.

'Brand new Caddy,' Duke muttered. 'Wonder how much these rooms go for?'

'Plenty, I'll bet,' Boots said. 'It's a real dandy place – just wait, you'll see.'

Norman shut off the engine. 'Let's get in fast before someone spots us,' he hissed.

Boots put her hand against the back of his head and gave it a gentle shove. Then she climbed out.

Norman cringed when she slammed her door. It sounded like an explosion. He expected faces to suddenly appear at room windows. He grimaced at Duke. 'Shouldn't we try and be *quiet*?'

'Got a lesson for you, bud. When you're up to sneaky shit, the last thing you wanna do is *act* sneaky. If you're going in a place, you go in acting like you own it.'

Boots strode past the front of the Cadillac and stopped at the door of room 140. She slid her key into the lock.

'Let's go,' Duke said.

They climbed out of the Cherokee and Duke flung his door shut. Norman shut his door gently. In spite of Duke's lesson on sneakiness, he just couldn't bring himself to slam it.

Boots was stepping into the room by the time they reached her. They hurried inside and Duke shut the door. The room was dark except for a slice of gray dusk-light coming in through a gap between the edges of the curtains.

Duke flicked a switch. A lamp came on. It stood atop a round table in front of the closed curtains. The room looked fine to Norman: it had a queen-sized bed and a single one, covers and a carpet that didn't appear dirty, and a nice set of dressers, counters and mirrors. The TV was raised in the middle of the unit, where it could probably be seen well from either bed. He glimpsed a counter and a sink in the nook at the other end of the room. The door to the bathroom was probably over to the right, hidden by the wall that ran out past the end of the far bed.

Not a luxury room, but not a dump, either. It would be a good place to spend the night. *My God, am I really gonna do it?* Norman's heart hammered. *I can just stay,* he told himself, *and mind my own business and keep away from Boots.*

'Ain't it a peach?' Boots asked. Grinning, she raised her arms and twirled around like an awkward, stocky ballerina. *From Dance of the Sugar-Plum Hog.* As she completed her twirl, she flopped backward onto the queen-sized bed. She lay sprawled there, her arms out, her legs dangling off the end with the corner of the mattress between her parted knees. Her thick thighs filled the leg holes of her cut-offs, so Norman couldn't see in. Her tank top had drifted up, baring her midriff.

Boots squirmed slowly and moaned. Raising her head, she looked from Duke to Norman. 'I'm ready when you are. What say we get the show on the road?'

Norman faced Duke, his mouth dry. 'You go first.'

Duke lifted his eyebrows.

'I'll . . . I can watch television. Or . . . I know, I can take a shower while you're . . . you know, busy. Unless you'd rather have me leave. I could go for a walk, I guess. Come back in, what, an hour?'

'Up to you, honcho,' Duke said. 'All the same to me. You can stay and join in, if it don't matter to Boots.'

She pushed herself up on her elbows and gave Norman a lazy smile. 'Don't you *dare* go running off.'

'But . . .'

Sitting up, Boots crossed her arms over her belly, clutched the tank top, pulled it up and over her head and off. She tossed it aside. It fell to the floor between the beds. Flopping onto her back again, she flung out her arms. 'Somebody wanna finish the job?' she asked, raising one of her booted feet.

'Happy to oblige you, ma'am,' Duke said. He stepped forward. When he tugged the boot off, the girl's whole body jerked. Her breasts hopped, wobbled, jiggled.

I've gotta get out of here, Norman told himself. *Before it's too late.* He took a step closer for a better view. In the lamp light he could see the pink of Boots's sunburn. The color was solid and even, except on her breasts. Her breasts were pale but had pink speckles where the sun had entered through the webbing of yarn. Her nipples were standing up straight. Both the tips looked ruddy, and Norman recalled how they'd been sticking out through the small holes in her bikini.

Her breasts lurched and swayed when Duke tugged off the other boot.

But after the boot was off, they didn't stop. They bobbed, swung and jumped, and Norman realized that Boots was wiggling slightly to make them do it. She grinned up at him.

'Take these jeans off me, Norman.'

'Uh . . .'

'You been wanting to all day.'

'Go for it, Normy,' Duke said. 'Peel her nice and slow, huh?

'I don't know. I really . . . I'm not sure we should be . . . you know, doing any of this.'

Pushing her heels against the floor, Boots raised her pelvis. 'Come on, Norman.'

Don't, he told himself. *Excuse yourself. Go out to the Jeep. Get in and drive away.*

Last call. Scram now, or forever hold your peace. He stared at the brass button at the waistband of her cutoffs. A couple of inches below her belly button.

And what's a couple of inches below this button? Oh man, oh man, oh man!

'Come on, Norman,' Boots repeated. Smiling up at him, she squirmed. 'Don't be yellow all your life.'

Duke told him, 'Come on, do what the lady asks.'

Heart slamming, mouth dry, Norman stepped between her knees. His own knees trembled. So did both his hands as he reached down to the brass button.

He unfastened it. *Oh my God.*

The denim edges spread, showing sun-pink skin.

With the thumb and forefinger of his right hand he pinched the zipper tab. He lost his grip on it twice but finally got a good hold and slid it down.

Exposing a deep V of bare skin and tight, wispy golden curls.

When did she get rid of the bikini pants? Norman curled his hands under the slit sides of Boots's cutoffs, then took hold of the denim and pulled. The tight shorts hardly budged. He stepped backward until he was clear of her knees. She swung them together. Then he pulled again. This time, the shorts came free. He backed away quickly, yanking them swiftly down her legs, past her ankles and off over her feet.

Boots smiled up at him. 'That was easy, wasn't it?'

Norman nodded. He swallowed hard.

With that lazy smile on her face, she raised her arms and folded her hands underneath her head. Then she opened her legs wide – and squirmed.

'What're you aiming to do, boys?' she asked. 'Just stand there and gawp at me all night? *Come and get it.*'

Chapter Fifteen

Norman thought: *My first time ever!*

His mind whirled. *And it's an orgy. Maybe something like this doesn't count as an orgy – just a threesome – but it sure seems like it ought to count.*

He supposed they'd been at it for an hour. Maybe longer. All three of them naked and sweaty and breathless on the bed, grappling, caressing, humping.

It seemed unreal.

Like some sort of exotic, erotic dream.

The way Boots had done him with her mouth right at the start of things.

Later, the funny stuff with the condom. How he'd unrolled the damn thing, then tried to pull it on like a sock – hilarious for Boots and Duke, embarrassing for him.

Then Boots showing him how it was done. Demonstrating. Taking a fresh one and ripping its wrapper open, then rolling it onto him with slow, gliding fingers and finally pulling him down on top of her and guiding him inside for his very first actual time. *I'm fucking her!* Norman had thought, astonished. *I'm really doing it! I shouldn't be doing it, but I am . . . anyway, it's all right, using a condom just like you're supposed to . . . hope it doesn't come off or break . . . Sure wish it wasn't so tight. Gotta be tight. But, shit, it hurts.* He'd used up three of the damn things so far – including the one he'd ruined by unrolling it – and now he was on his knees at the end of the bed, ripping open a fourth. His hands shook badly. Not from nerves – from exhaustion.

He plucked the condom out of its wrapper. It was prelubricated: slippery as a snail.

109

He started to put it on.

He could hardly believe that he was ready to go again. *My God, look at me.*

Though his penis stood up stout, it was shiny and red, and ringed with marks left by the other condoms. Just as if rubber bands had been wrapped tightly around it.

Why the hell do they make 'em so tight?

So they don't fall off, asshole.

Like Duke's had fallen off. His second one had come off while he was in her. They'd both laughed as if they thought it was hysterical. Norman hadn't thought it was funny – until he watched them struggle to fish it out. 'So much for safe sex,' Duke had said.

'I ain't got nothing you can catch,' Boots had said. After that, Duke hadn't bothered with any more condoms. He was on his back now, moaning and writhing. Boots, on her hands and knees between his parted legs, was using her mouth on him.

Norman fumbled and dropped the condom. It fell onto the sheet. When he tried to pick it up, it slipped out of his fingers.

Duke isn't even using one.

The hell with it, he thought.

He edged forward on his knees, running his hands along Boots's calves. They were thick, slippery, prickly with whiskers, but the backs of her thighs felt smooth. So did her rump. The crack between her buttocks felt clammy. Lower, though, she was wet and slick. Norman fingered her there to be sure that he had the right place – the front one, as Duke had called it – then moved forward and in.

In her for real, skin to skin, for the first time, and she was all heat and slickness.

He couldn't believe the feel of it.

I'm probably gonna die now, but who cares?

It's so wonderful.

So great. Better than anything. So what if it kills me?

What if I get AIDS from this? Or the clap? What if I wake up tomorrow and I'm whizzing blood and pus? My God, I must be out of my mind.

But it probably wouldn't happen, anyway, and it was too late now to stop. Norman was on his knees, thrusting in as Boots took her weight on her hands and knees, his lap making slapping sounds against her buttocks, his arms underneath her, hands on her breasts – squeezing them as he slid in and out, smacking against her rump as she sucked on Duke and Duke gasped and groaned . . .

. . . And a movement where there shouldn't be movement caught Norman's eye. He turned his head. Peered over the edge of the mattress. Saw a man squirming out from under the bed, belly-crawling, face-down. Something wrong with the back of his head. Hair pasted down with blood.

Shoulders furry. *Shit! Got a werewolf under the bed.*

Only dimly aware that he was still embedded in Boots and clutching her breasts, Norman gazed over the side of the bed and watched.

Not a werewolf. A desk clerk?

The guy kept squirming out from under the bed, apparently unaware that he was being observed.

Neither Boots nor Duke had seen him. Not yet. They weren't likely to spot him, either. Not unless Duke sat up on the bed, or Boots slid her mouth off him and looked over her shoulder.

The guy was wearing black knitted bikini pants.

'Boots?' Norman asked.

'Mmm?'

'Who's the guy under the bed?'

Her mouth made a quick slurpy, smacking sound. Then she said, 'What?' She sounded alarmed.

'What's going on?' Duke asked.

The man suddenly scurried across the floor.

Boots pushed herself up, turned her head. 'Shit! Get him!'

'Quick!'

Not me!

But Norman was on Boots and Boots was on Duke. *Me or nobody!*

'Get him!' Boots cried out again.

Norman let go of her breasts. He backed up, pulled out. The man was clear of the bed and crawling across the carpet toward the door.

He looked stupid in the bikini pants.

Stupid and disgusting, Norman thought, *like a pervert in some sort of crummy porno movie.*

How come he doesn't get up and run?

'Stop him!'

Norman leaped off the bed. He hit the floor and rushed forward. He knew he ought to jump on the guy. A great flying leap. But this

111

fellow really *was* repulsive to look at – all hairy and pale, shiny with sweat, his ass showing through the web of the knitted pants.

Don't wanna touch him!

Besides, Norman told himself, *it might be a crime to jump on him. Assault and battery, something like that. Dressed like that it might come down as a sex crime.* What would Norman's family say if they read about it in the newspapers?

So he dashed past the man.

Got to the door just ahead of him.

Whirled around and planted his back against it.

The man raised his head. Blinking sweat out of his eyes, he gazed up at Norman. He looked confused and about ready to cry.

Like a disappointed kid. A skinny forty-year-old kid in bikini pants who'd just had Santa take away his only Christmas gift.

Boots made a running dive. Her body slapped down on the man's back. He gave a grunt. His elbows folded, and his face thudded against the carpet. Boots hugged him tightly around the waist. She twisted and writhed as if trying to throw him over. 'Help!' she gasped. 'Come on!'

Norman stood and watched.

So did Duke. He'd hurled himself off the bed a moment after Boots and now he stood behind her, hands on hips, staring down at the struggle, an odd look on his face as if he couldn't make up his mind whether to scowl or grin.

'Guys!'

'You're doing fine,' Duke told her.

'Gimme a hand!'

'Who is he?'

'He's s'posed to be dead, the dirty fucker.'

'This guy your desk clerk?' Duke asked.

'Ain't no clerk.'

Duke's scowl lost the struggle. Smirking, he chuckled a few times. 'Don't tell me,' he said. 'You just came over and knocked on this guy's door, right? Picked yourself some poor sucker, came in, put your moves on him, then bonked him on the head.'

'Yeah, sure.' Boots sounded annoyed. 'So sue me. Why the fuck ain't he dead?'

'Didn't hit him hard enough.'

'I *strangled* him, too.'

'Didn't strangle him hard enough.'

'Don't hurt me,' the guy pleaded from underneath her. 'Please?'

'This is *his* room?' Norman asked.

'Help me out,' Boots said.

Duke grinned. 'Seeing you wrestle the guy naked's turning me on.'

'W-we'd better let him go,' Norman stammered. 'You'd better get off him, Boots.'

'No way.'

'Come on. This is crazy. We don't need his room. We can go someplace else. God Almighty. Tell her, Duke.'

'Tell her, Duke,' the guy underneath Boots repeated desperately. 'Please. You . . . you can *have* my room. Just let me go. Please? I won't tell. I promise.'

'He sounds like a friendly sort of guy to me,' Duke said. 'What do you aim to do with him, darling?'

'Kill his ass.'

'Oh, God. No, please. Help . . .' The man's voice stopped as Boots finally got her leverage right and flipped him over sideways. Keeping hold around his waist, she rolled onto her back.

The man had a bloody nose. Whimpering, he tried to unlock Boots's hands from around his middle. He twisted and squirmed and kicked at the air. Norman could see through the small holes of the bikini pants.

He's the only guy around here without a hard-on, Norman thought. *Seeing him and Boots grapple is a kinda turn-on.*

Course, he's the one she's trying to kill.

Boots swung her legs up on both sides of the man. She brought them inward and down, bending her knees, driving her feet down between his legs, trapping him.

'Good going,' Duke said. 'Now what? Gonna squeeze him to death?'

'If you'd just help . . .'

The man yelled, 'HELP!' at the top of his lungs. 'SOMEBODY HELLL—'

Norman dropped to his knees and clamped both hands over the man's mouth. 'Shut up!'

The guy snapped his teeth at Norman's palm.

Norman jerked his hand away.

The man yelled, 'HELLLL—'

Norman pounded his fist down like a hammer on the man's nose. The nose squished. Blood squirted from its nostrils. 'Now shut up!'

Clutching his face, the man whimpered and gasped for air.

'Thanks,' Boots gasped. 'Wanna get him off me?'

Norman pulled while Boots rolled. As the man started to fall sideways she let go of him.

He flopped facedown.

'Gimme back my bikini bottom,' Boots said. Kneeling, she untied the yarn sides of the bikini pants. She tugged the garment out from under her victim and flung it out of the way. Then she sat on his rump, dropped forward and shoved her right arm underneath his neck. She caught his throat in the crook of her arm. With her left hand she clutched the man's forehead.

'What're you doing?' Norman asked.

'Gonna choke his ass.'

'You're at the wrong end,' Duke pointed out.

'Ha ha. Lotsa help *you* been.' Boots's body started to shudder as she strained.

'You don't wanna do that,' Norman told her.

She grunted.

'Hey, come on.'

The man began twitching and flopping.

She is *trying to kill him*, Norman realized. He wondered if he should step in and stop things.

Better, he thought. *Can't just stand here and watch her murder the—*

Somebody pounded on the door. Norman jumped and gasped. The heavy blows felt as if they were striking him in the chest.

'Yeah?' Duke called. His voice sounded very calm. He winked at Norman.

'This is the manager.' A man's voice. 'What's going on in there?'

'Everything's fine,' Duke told him.

'Like fun. Open up the door and let me see, or I'll have to call the police.'

'No *problemo*,' Duke said. 'Hang on a second, I haven't got nothing on.' His jeans were a heap on the floor. He stepped over to them, crouched and picked them up.

Boots acted as if she didn't even care that the manager had come to the door. Her arm was still clamped around the man's neck, shaking as she applied pressure to his throat.

The guy no longer thrashed about. Lay still.

Norman suddenly felt as if an icicle had been shoved into his guts.

Dead? The guy's dead and somebody's at the door and she isn't even trying to hide the body or anything and Duke's walking toward the door just as if he actually plans to open it and he hasn't even got his jeans on, must've dropped them . . .

Backing away, Norman stumbled against the edge of the bed. The slight impact collapsed his shaky legs. He sat down hard on the mattress. Duke swung the door open wide, then held up both his empty hands and shook his head.

'Sorry about the noise,' he said.

'Thought you was gonna put some clothes on.'

'Sorry,' Duke said.

The manager looked him up and down, sneering and shaking his head. 'The weirdos are taking over the world.'

'Yep,' Duke said.

He had an opened pocketknife behind him, clamped tight between his buttocks.

Must've got it from his jeans, Norman thought.

'I never rented this room to you,' the manager said.

'My brother took care of it,' Duke said.

'Stand out of my way. I wanna see him.' The guy looked tough. Old, but tough. Maybe sixty. Thick in the chest, thick in the neck, with a broad red face. Bushy gray eyebrows. Hair the color of steel, short and brushed up. As he entered the room, he shoved Duke aside. 'Put some pants on.'

Stumbling out of the way, Duke reached behind his rump just in time to catch the falling knife. The manager glanced at Norman, then noticed Boots on the floor on top of the dead man.

'What kinda goddamn *orgy* we got goin' on in here?'

Guess it does count as an orgy, Norman thought.

'All of you, get your clothes on and get the hell out of my motel before I call the—'

Duke made his move.

Look out! Norman yelled. But only in his mind. He didn't say a word. Just watched.

Duke stabbed the manager in the back so hard that the blow knocked him forward a couple of steps. Mouth wide open, eyes bulging, the old guy stood very stiff and reached over his shoulder. Apparently, he wanted to find the knife and pull it out.

Duke beat him to the punch.

Pulled it out and stuck it in again. The big old guy dropped to his knees.

He started to cry out, so Norman hurried forward and kicked him in the stomach. That quieted him. And doubled him over. Duke, knife in hand, ambled over to the door.

He stepped outside. Looked slowly to the left and right.

Then turned around, entered the room again, and closed the door. He flipped his knife into the air. It twirled. He caught it by the handle.

'The night's sure got off to an interesting start,' Duke said. 'What's anyone fancy doing next?'

Chapter Sixteen

'Mosby's trailer,' Lauren announced, then opened the door.

It's not locked, Pamela thought. *But then, who in their right mind would drive all the way out into the desert to Pits, pop. 6, to steal a TV?*

If they even get TV broadcasts out here. There's no TV aerials I can see. Before entering the big old aluminum trailer she glanced back. *No telephone lines, come to that.*

Grimacing at the pain in her injured feet, she followed Lauren inside. The cuts and abrasions on her soles when she'd run barefoot from Rodney weren't serious but they *were* sore.

'Home sweet home,' Lauren announced, twirling, arms outstretched. 'Stay as long as you want. You're among friends now.'

A tear burned in Pamela's eye. 'Thank you.' She whistled. 'Gee, this is a big, big trailer.'

'A monster, isn't it?'

'A veritable behemoth.' Pamela gave a tired smile.

'You've got a shower. Three bedrooms. Lounge. Kitchen through there. Oh, Sharpe put some beers and cold cuts in the refrigerator.'

'Sharpe's a hero.'

Lauren's eyes went misty and faraway. 'Isn't he just?'

'I don't know how I can ever repay you.'

'Don't even think of it. Sharpe believes in helping people who are down on their luck. We all do.' Lauren took a breath. 'Now, the trailer's hardly this year's model. But it's clean.'

'And it belongs to . . .' Pamela recalled the name. 'Moby?'

'Mosby.'

'Won't he mind?'

'No . . . as a matter of fact he won't be requiring it any more.'

'Oh.'

'Now, that's my trailer next to this one. If you need anything, just holler. Right?'

'Right.'

'Way to go, girl. Okay, I'll leave you to yourself.' Lauren paused. 'If you need some me-time, that is. Otherwise I'll be happy to stay.'

'No. I'm fine.' Pamela appraised the comfortable furnishings. A huge puffy sofa looked as if it could swallow her whole. *Maybe that's where I'll find Mosby. Twenty fathoms deep behind the cushions.* 'It'd be kinda nice just to lie still in the quiet.'

'You've got it. There's no air-con but there's a couple of fans. Besides, when the sun's gone down it soon gets cool in the desert.'

Lauren made small talk for a while before she left. Pamela figured that the woman in her flowing hippie clothes had a warm hippie heart. She was concerned for Pamela.

Didn't want to leave her dwelling on what had happened just twenty hours ago.

Husband murdered.

House burnt.

Abducted by disgusting Rodney Pinkham.

He'd threatened to abuse her in such a vile, degrading way.

Twenty hours. Seems a lifetime ago.

On sore feet Pamela made a tour of the trailer. It was spotlessly clean. She drank cold water from a pitcher in the refrigerator. A row of Bud bottles faced her on the top shelf, left there by her bus-driver savior. Sharpe was the kindest man she knew. No wonder Lauren wanted to marry him. Course, he was weird, though, driving round in the bus with the dummy passengers.

But what's best in this world? Rational and mean, or eccentric and kind? Give me the benevolent oddball any day.

The lounge had the lovely soft sofa, comfortable chairs, plastic apples and bananas in a bowl; on a wall hung a framed photograph of an old man standing beside a marlin that had been strung up by its tail. The fish was as long as the man. Both seemed to be smiling. Mosby?

Where are you now, Mosby?

In the pit . . . in the pit!

Pamela closed off the sinister thought. *Old Mosby might simply have*

retired to Palm Springs. Or the Florida Keys, where even now he's sharp-
ening a fish hook to catch his biggest marlin yet. The old man and the sea.

Apart from the photo there was no personal stuff like clothes or
photos or car keys, or letters addressed 'Dear Mr. Mosby ...' This
was an old trailer. Clean. Comfortable. An ideal retreat from the world
for those hurt in body and spirit.

A tap sounded on the door.

They've come for you, Pamela. The pit awaits ...

'Aw, shut up,' she told her runaway imagination. She opened the
trailer door to find Nicki standing there with a basket under one arm
– the kind that might contain complimentary fruit. She still wore the
white pullover and red shorts, but the apron must be on the hook until
the cafe opened its doors tomorrow.

'I just thought I'd drop by.'

Pamela smiled. 'Come on in.'

'Not if you're doing anything?'

'No, I figured on turning in early.'

'Oh, I thought I heard voices.'

'Voices.' Pamela gave a soft laugh despite her exhaustion. 'No. That
was me.'

'Uh?'

'Talking to myself. I guess what happened today has sent me ...
you know ...' She gave a shrug of her shoulder. 'Nuts.' For a moment
she thought she'd start crying again. Fighting it back, she gave a wider
smile. 'Come right on in.'

Nicki slipped in through the doorway. Her slim body must be the
envy of every woman for miles. And the source of hot thoughts for
every man. The blond hair turned her head into a golden glow in the
electric light. A Nordic goddess. Complete with a ponytail. She could
braid that into a long Rapunzel-like plait.

'I've been thinking about your feet,' Nicki said.

'Me, too. Every time I stand on them. Ouch.' She grimaced. 'I guess
fear and all that shit made for a natural anesthetic. Now that I'm safe
my feet are reminding me what they've been through, too.'

'Hurts bad?'

'It's starting to kick in.'

'Go through into the lounge and lie on the sofa.'

'Well, I—'

'Please. Let me do this for you, Pamela. I've brought things to make you feel good.' Nicki moved the basket from under her arm.

Instead of fruit it contained jars of silvery powder and bottles of amber oil.

'I don't have any money. I'm sorry that—'

'No. I don't want you to pay.' A pink color flamed under Nicki's tanned skin. 'Please, never mention money again. We're like sisters. We help each other.'

'Sorry, I'm so tired. I'm not thinking properly.'

'Of course you're not. You went through hell today. Here, lie down. Let me take care of you. I'll just slip this towel under your feet. There. Good girl. First, I'll apply an embrocating oil with healing properties.'

Nicki smoothed out the fluffy white towel under Pamela's throbbing feet. Pamela relaxed back onto the sofa with a sigh, lying flat out.

Uh. This sofa's as soft as it looks.

'You just relax,' Nicki told Pamela. 'Close your eyes while I work some of this in for you. It'll feel good. It contains a natural antiseptic, too.' She smiled. 'Don't worry, I'll be gentle.'

'Thank you. I don't know how I'll—'

'Ah, ah.' Nicki held up her finger. 'Lie back, close your eyes. Nicki's taking care of business now.'

Pamela smiled, then eased her head back onto the cushion. Lying on her back on the sofa she looked up at the trailer ceiling that had been covered with a paper that bore a wood pattern in imitation pine. Very 1970s; it reminded her of her grandmother's house. There was something reassuring about the old-fashioned feel. It took her back to her childhood. Nicki knelt on the floor at the other end of the sofa so that she could work on Pamela's feet.

Pamela heard a bottle being unstoppered.

Then felt the flow of liquid along the top of her feet.

Cold.

'I keep it in the refrigerator,' Nicki said. 'Not too cold, is it?'

'No . . . wonderful.' Drowsy now, Pamela still gazed at the ceiling. 'It's putting the fires out.'

'Good. You just wait till I've done. You'll feel as if you're walking on air.'

'Ohhh.'

'Feel good?'

'Outta this world.'

And it did. Using gentle circular strokes Nicki massaged the cold oil into the top of Pamela's foot, then worked the embrocating fluid round the injured soles.

'Hmm,' Pamela whispered. 'Peppermint. I can smell peppermint.'

'Oil of peppermint's good for skin as well as for the digestion. There . . . let me know if it stings.'

'No . . . perfect . . .'

This is heaven, Pamela thought. *After the hell of last night I'm in heaven today. This foot massage is truly out of this world.* The oil cooled her burning feet. The sting left the grazes. That feeling of well-being spread through her body, releasing tension in the muscles in her back and face. She felt as if she'd been like a rubber band twisted so tightly that it had bunched into hard knots. Now she was unwinding, her muscles softening.

And all the time Nicki's gentle fingers flowed from Pamela's Achilles tendon along her heel to the arch of her sole, to the ball of her foot then smoothed away the hurt in her toes.

Pamela's eyes closed. A sliding motion moved through her that told her she was falling asleep. Her arms twitched a couple of times but Nicki breathed gentle reassurances that she was safe, that she was going to be okay. And all the time that cool slippery caress of fingers against her feet. Peppermint scented the air. A tingling freshness that flowed through her nostrils into her bloodstream.

A flurry of dream images drifted through Pamela's mind. Home. Jim sitting on the porch swing. Rodney tumbling into the pit. Sharpe driving the bus. The dummies sitting in their seats. The old-timer, Hank. Walking into the cafe. This time Pamela looked more closely at the diners in their booths. They were all shop mannequins. Even so, their plastic heads turned on stiff necks to stare at her. She looked at where Nicki and Lauren stood. They'd turned into mannequins, too. The Lauren effigy wore her hippie dress, while the Nicki figure wore the white pullover and red shorts. In the dream Sharpe loomed over her. She saw herself reflected in his sunglasses.

'They all came as regular people. But they all turned plastic, too.' He grinned. 'Same's happening to you. How's those stiff little feet of yours?'

Pamela looked down and saw that her feet had turned into the creamy plastic of a mannequin with fused toes.

Her eyes snapped open. The trailer was in near-darkness. Peppermint scented the air. Her feet were still being massaged, only . . .

Only differently now. Raising her head a little, Pamela looked down the length of her body. Nicki still knelt by the sofa. She'd removed her sweater. Holding Pamela's feet by the ankles she was rubbing her big soft breasts against the soles of the other girl's feet. The nipples felt like fingertips.

Nicki had freed her hair. It tumbled loose in blond waves down her naked back. Her face was raised to the ceiling, eyes closed. She moaned with pleasure.

I must be dreaming this, Pamela told herself. *Nicki couldn't be rubbing her bare breasts against my feet. It doesn't make sense. I am dreaming. Have to be.*

She forced herself to close her eyes while repeating to herself, *It's a dream. I'm dreaming. I'm dreaming . . .*

Chapter Seventeen

Norman drove. He didn't know where he drove . . . *Shoot!* Where the FUCK he drove.

Only needed to drive. *Gotta drive. Gotta get away.*

'Norman?'

'Shaddup!'

'Hey,' Duke sounded hurt. 'I only wanted—'

'Shaddup!'

'Normy, Normy,' Boots cooed. 'Gotta put your lights on, Normy. It's too dark to drive like this.'

Lights! Yeah, lights are good but—

But all of a sudden Norman was shouting. 'What did you have to kill those two guys for? Jesus H. Christ! Boots, you just – just stran-gled a guy.'

'Yeah, strangled him bare-assed,' Duke chuckled. 'Spose there are worse ways to depart the world.'

'And you, Duke!'

'Normy, slow down. Pleezy-weezy.'

Not gonna slow down. Never gonna slow down. But what the fuck am I doing with these two murderers in the car? Should have left them at the motel to meet and greet the cops. Not driving with the gruesome twosome that are going to end up broiling on Old Sparky.

Aw, shit.

Get them outta the car, Norman. Get 'em out!

'Now that's hardly fair, Norman.' Duke unwrapped a stick of gum. 'Sure, Boots strangled the pervert. Sure, I stabbed the old guy. But you, Norman, old buddy, you kicked him in the nut nest.'

'Nut nest? Nut nest!'

'Switch on your lights.' Boots sat in the back, rubbing Norman's shoulder as he drove.

Norman didn't see dark roads at midnight, he only saw the world streaked with bright red blood. 'Nut nest! I didn't kick him in the balls. I kicked him in the . . . ugh.'

Oh no.

Did kick him.

But that's not murder.

'Sure you kicked him.' Duke sounded calm. 'But you were helping your buddies. Here, let me get those lights for you. Don't want to run into a tree, do we now?'

Boots cooed. 'Where you taking us, Norman?'

To the cops! Those were the words he wanted to yell. But he'd have to be canny. Find a police precinct. Make some excuse. Dash inside. Tell the first cop he saw, 'Hey, I've got two murderers in my car.' *That'd make sense, wouldn't it? Get rid of these two bozos.* Hey, he might even get a citation for heroism. He could see the headlines in his hometown newspaper now.

First, find the precinct.

'Drive nice and legal,' Duke told him. 'If you don't ease offa that gas you're gonna draw attention to ourselves.'

Boots rubbed Norman's shoulder. 'Don't wanna get stopped by the cops, do we, Normy?'

Wanna bet?

Won't be me getting all gelled up for Old Sparky. Won't be me biting my tongue in two when they unleash fifty thousand volts through my bod.

'Normy, please. Slow down. We've still got some loving to finish up, haven't we?'

'Yeah,' Duke said. 'Sure can't pleasure the gal if we wind up in jail.'

'Remember what it felt like, Norman?'

Jesus. He remembered. The way her titties jiggled as he thrust his cock up inside her. The way she'd sucked him; the way she'd run her tongue around the big old purple bell while moaning with pleasure.

Made him moan, too.

His first time.

Fucking this fleshy woman . . . fleshy pig-woman. Then watching in horror as she wrestled naked with a guy that she thought she'd already killed. *Dear God. Dear God in heaven.*

Shaking his head, Norman eased off the gas pedal. The needle dropped to thirty-five.

'Adda boy, Norman!' Duke slapped his thigh. 'I like to burn rubber as much as the next guy but we need to lie low until this blows over.'

'Blows over? You two *killed* people tonight. Human beings.'

'Human beings. Huh.'

Boots confessed, 'You shoulda seen what the pervert did to me, Norman. He didn't get no hard-on. So he put things inside of me. Light bulbs. Shampoo bottles. Then he got a soda bottle. I thought I was gonna cry when he shoved the—'

'Okay, okay!' Norman took a right at random. 'But you still shouldn't have strangled him.'

'Nice way to go though, eh, Norman?' Duke's teeth gleamed like a vampire's in the dashboard lights. 'Boots's wet pussy in the small of your back, titties tickling you as she puts the squeeze on your neck.'

'And *you* stabbed an old man,' Norman protested. 'He didn't do nothing to you.'

'Would've called in the cops.'

'You stabbed him in the back. Twice!'

'You kicked him in the birdcage, Norman, old buddy.'

'That makes you . . .' Boots rooted for the phrase before whispering it in his ear. 'An accessory to murder.'

'I'm no murderer.' Norman knew what he was going to do now. He went over his earlier plan again. Find a police precinct. Stop the car. Dash inside. These two would be in jail within the hour. Then he'd be free to drive home. He repeated the words with conviction: 'I'm no murderer.'

'The cops won't see it like that,' Duke told him.

Boots whined, 'Yeah, you've got blood on your hands, too. Besides, you still like me, don't you, Norman? You're not gonna go all cold and law-abiding on me? After the nice things I did for you. I even sucked your—'

'Shit!'

'Nice and cool, Norman.'

'What's wrong?' Boots asked.

'Cops,' Duke said. 'Two of them. One cruiser. See the lights?'

'Oooh, yeah. Bright, aren't they?'

Norman stared ahead at the road lit by streetlights. He saw the police cruiser. A cop stood on the sidewalk, talking into his radio. The second cop stepped out, holding up his hand.

Oh, shit.

Suddenly, meeting a cop wasn't such a good idea. And another big SUDDENLY: Norman realized that the bodies had been found in the motel. Duke had wanted to leave them one piled on top of the other. 'That way it'll look as if they died fucking one another. Heart failure.' *Heart failure! Dear Christ.* One had been strangled while wearing Boots's black-knit bikini bottoms. The manager of the motel had been stabbed in the back. Twice. *That ain't natural causes. Not even to a cop with his eyes poked out and his ears filled with fucking candle wax.*

Now the APB had been made. The police must have been given a description of Norman's car. Probably another motel guest had seen the license plate.

The trooper took another step out into the road, hand still raised.

I'll be in the frame for murder, too. I'll wind up in the electric chair. Oh God, I don't believe this's happening to me. Please, if I can only turn back time. Just five hours. I'll be good. I'll go to church every week. I'll learn to love Jesus . . .

The cop stood facing Norman, feet apart, hand raised, palm out.

STOP.

The trooper wants me to stop.

Then the cuffs will go on.

I'm on my way to jail.

Norman screamed, '*No way!*'

Stomped on the gas pedal. The car surged forward.

Duke shouted, 'Norman! No. Don't—'

The car slammed into the cop. Norman saw the man's false teeth fly out of his mouth due to the force of the impact. Then the big guy folded over the hood, his face smashing against the steel frame of the windshield. Like a balloon bursting, the man's head shattered, splashing blood across the glass.

Norman accelerated. The body lay pasted against the windshield. Norman looked into the man's exploded head, the brain matter oozing on the glass. Then the body rolled sideways as Norman hauled a left. When it fell onto the road Norman didn't look back.

Duke was amazed. 'You just killed a cop. You just drove into him and *pow*! Wasted him. Did you see his brain coming out of the hole in his head? It was like his skull was taking a shit.'

Norman couldn't speak. He could only drive.

'Norman?' Boots was dumbfounded. 'Open season on perverts. But I don't know about killing the police. What d'ya think, Duke?'

'Whoa, don't matter what I think.' Duke looked back. 'Norman. The other cop's following.'

'*SHIT!*'

Norman glanced in the rearview mirror. The cruiser pounded up the road behind, lights whirling. He pushed the Jeep as hard as he could through the quiet – usually quiet – residential neighborhood. Its headlights flashed against trees, parked cars.

'Hey, dude,' Duke said. 'You're a real Viking, aren't you?'

Norman spat out the words: 'The police would have arrested us. They know what you two did to the guys in the motel.'

'Didn't look like that to me. Didn't you see potatoes in the road? They'd spilled from the back of a truck.'

Boots picked up the thread. 'So the police were only stopping us from running over the potatoes?'

'Looks that way.'

'Shoot.'

'But Norman here had got the killing fever on him.'

Norman groaned. The police didn't even know about the motel killings. He'd splattered the guy all over his car for no reason. Automatically, he flicked the wiper stalk to scrape away blood and brain matter from the windshield. It smeared real bad.

'Makes a pretty mess, huh, old buddy?'

Norman glanced at Duke. 'The other cop? Is he gaining?'

'Sure he is. You really think you can outrun a cruiser in this peewee?'

'I've gotta! I'm not going to jail.'

'I don't want to go to jail.' Boots sounded whiny again. 'I was born for lovin' and good times.'

Duke asked, 'What's the plan, Norman old buddy?'

'Shut up and lemme drive!'

Norman powered the car out of the residential neighborhood into open countryside. Now the road was surrounded by fields. And flanking the road were a pair of deep, deep culverts.

'Getting closer,' Duke warned. 'Soon the cruiser's gonna be bumping your ass.'

'Oh, God. This can't be happening to me!' Norman hunched over the wheel, teeth clenched, stare locked on a road lit by the blaze of headlights.

Duke thought for a while, then made an observation. 'Shouldn't be surprised if the cop doesn't try and shoot our tires out.'

'They'll bring in helicopters, too,' Boots said. 'I've seen it on TV.'

'Out here, Boots? They won't have no copters out here. No.' Duke nodded with the conviction of experience. 'They'll shoot our tires out. That – or try and get a shot at the driver's head.'

'Oh, Christ.' Norman wanted to go the lavatory badly. Very badly. He was panting. Sweat rolled down his face.

Now I'm going to take a bullet in the brain.

It's just not fair.

He glanced in the mirror. The cruiser was just a dozen yards behind his car. He saw the whirl of its lights. He could even see the grim face of the man whose buddy now lay smashed to crud in the road. The man leaned sideways through the driver's open window.

Norman thought: *Gun!*

That was when he brought both feet stomping down on the brake. The car screamed. Slid sideways. The driver in pursuit wrestled with his vehicle's wheel to stop from slamming into the back of Norman's car.

Norman watched as the police car roared past. The driver swung out to avoid Norman's vehicle that was still skidding sideways along the pavement.

Norman watched.

As the police car flipped out. Turning over into the culvert in a flurry of sparks and exhaust smoke. He even heard its engine scream as the vehicle became a ball of flame that raced along the water channel. The cruiser eventually slid to a stop, a burning ruin. Containing one dead police officer.

Norman's car came to a halt. Its engine idled. The sudden near-silence made Norman dizzy.

'Hey, man.' Duke was impressed. 'You're a cop-killing machine. I never knew you had it in you.'

Boots leaned forward, and put her arms around Norman from

behind and kissed his cheek. A wet kiss that felt cold as reptile spit against his burning skin. 'Norman. You're my hero.'

For a moment Norman watched the burning police cruiser send balls of oily black smoke into the night sky.

Then he said, 'We've got to go where they'll never find us.'

Light on the gas pedal now, Norman drove away from the burning police car.

Chapter Eighteen

Norman moaned.

Moaned as he drove.

Moaned as his sore eyes stared at what was revealed by the car's lights. Passing trees, road signs, roadkill, diners, gas stations, a lonesome truck hauling timber at two in the morning.

'Ohhh ... what have I done? Jesus, what have I done?'

'You've done two cops, that's what you've done,' Duke told him as he combed back his Elvis quiff.

'Did you see how the first guy's head burst – *pop!* – on the windshield?' Boots sounded excited rather than appalled.

I'm in a car with two crazies, Norman thought. *Two crazed killers. Gotta get out.*

But.

I'm a crazed killer, too. I just killed a pair of cops. But I'm pro Cop! I'm pro Law and Order.

'Oh my God,' he groaned. 'What have I done?'

'I can drive, old buddy.' Duke sounded concerned. 'You need to relax.'

'Yeah,' Boots cooed. 'Come and rest up in the back here with me.'

'No. I've gotta get away from here. The cops will be looking for us.'

'Yeah,' Boots breathed. 'You cracked one like a nut, then toasted the other.'

'Wicked.' Duke nodded.

'Oh ... oh ...' Boots suddenly pounded Norman's shoulder. She was breathless. She was on a high over the violence. 'Norman. Pull over. Pull over!'

'What?'

'Pull over just here. Oh . . .'

'What's wrong?'

'Nothing.'

'But we've gotta get away from here. Cops will be crawling over the roads. They'll shoot to kill.'

'Ain't that always the way?' Duke observed.

'But please, Norman. You've got to pull over. I've gotta do something, otherwise my panties will go pop.'

'You need to pee?'

'No.'

'The other thing?'

'No.'

Norman's mind swum as streetlights flicked past the car. *What's gotten into Boots? Crazy woman. Crazy pig-woman. With bulging thighs and heaving breasts. Christ, I think I'm going to faint . . .*

'Norman, pull over. *Please.*'

Duke said, 'Aren't you going to oblige the lady?'

Norman hardly knew what he was doing anymore. Guilt rolled over him in tidal waves. He could only think of the officers he'd killed. Their families? *Oh Christ, their families . . .*

The moment he stopped the car Boots almost threw herself out of the vehicle. The road was deserted. Here was countryside. No houses.

Maybe she needs to puke?

Wish I could puke. Get all this guilt out of me . . .

Duke said, 'Best kill the lights until she's done.'

Done what?

Norman turned as Boots dragged the driver's door open.

What on earth is she doing?

Norman stared at her as she stood panting. Her breasts jiggling as she inhaled mightily. 'Boots?' he asked.

'Duke?'

'Boots?'

'Duke. You watch or not. I don't care.'

'What ya planning, girl?'

Boots gasped like she'd run a marathon. 'Sweet Mary. I've never been so turned on. Watching Norman kill those cops and all. I got fire in my veins.'

Norman watched her in a daze. What was that woman on?

'Norman. You've gotta let me do this for you. You've gotta. I'll die if you don't.'

'Boots?'

She pounced as though she was ravenous and couldn't stop herself. Hands fumbling like crazy, she unbuckled Norman's belt, unzippered him. Then her hot hands gripped his penis and tugged it like she was strangling a snake.

'Not now,' Norman protested. 'Jesus. The cops will be . . . ah . . . ah!'

To his horror, despite the wholesale bloody mania of the last few hours, despite the craziness of Boots doing this at such a god-awful inappropriate time he felt himself stiffen beneath her stubby fingers as she worked at him.

'Oh, Norman,' Duke said, appreciatively. 'Reckon your birthday just came early.'

'Duke,' Boots panted. 'Be a gentleman. Shut yer eyes.'

'What? And miss the show? No way.'

'Suit yourself.' Then she went to work on Norman.

Norman drove. The night starless. The surrounding countryside just a blackness.

Empty.

Something strange happened to him inside. He could feel it working up through his stomach into his chest. Then it shot out from his mouth; he clenched his fists around the buckled steering wheel.

'Norman?' Duke looked at him from the passenger seat.

'You okay?' Boots asked from the backseat. She sounded anxious.

The noise coming out from his mouth was getting louder . . . LOUDER . . .

The noise was terrible. Electrifying. Some part of him recoiled in horror.

Then he knew what it was. He was whooping. A real cowboy yodel. Sheer exhilaration.

Exultation.

'Ya – hoo!' he hollered. 'We did it! We really did it!'

'Yeah.' Duke sounded puzzled. 'We did it, Norm.'

Norman whooped again and it turned into a laugh he'd never

laughed before. A full-blooded *manly* laugh. A laugh that belonged to football stars, lumberjacks, burly Marines, pro-wrestlers . . . you name it. Macho, macho, macho.

'I am a MAN!'

Boots and Duke must have been staring at him, wondering if he'd lost his mind.

'I'M A MAN!'

'Never doubted it,' Duke said.

'Tonight. For the first time: I've fucked a woman. I've killed two men.' Norman whooped again through the open driver's window. He felt stronger than Superman. Cooler than James Dean. Meaner than Satan. Cuter than Johnny Depp. 'I'M THE KING OF THE WORLD!'

He floored the gas pedal. The car roared into the night. And toward whatever waited tomorrow.

Chapter Nineteen

Pamela woke the next morning feeling full of life. The clock radio told her it was 10:34.

Slept late.

But then, sleep heals.

Not only had her feet quit hurting, she felt renewed emotionally. She knew that her husband was dead; she was a widow at twenty-three, but she no longer believed that she'd go insane with grief. She wasn't immune to that grief, but this was the time to start dealing with it.

Mosby's trailer looked good in the bright Californian sunlight pouring through the windows. Clean, comfortably furnished, it radiated a homely charm. She went to the closet. Instead of old-man clothes (surely Mosby was the old man pictured with the marlin), there were T-shirts in bright colors – a red, a blue, a green, a lemon. Also, there were clean pairs of shorts neatly folded on the shelf. New underwear, too.

Lauren or Nicki must have put them there . . . Nicki! Pamela suddenly remembered last night when Nicki had massaged the oil into her feet. She remembered the woman's slick fingers soothing her damaged skin. Then she'd fallen asleep.

And woken to see Nicki rubbing her naked breasts against Pamela's feet.

What do I say when I see Nicki? How do I look her in the eye?

Say nothing.

You dreamt it.

Had to have done.

Face it. You were exhausted. You'd nearly been killed. Jim had been

*murdered by the psycho Rodney. You were mixed up. You couldn't differen-
tiate between dreams and reality. Face it, girl, in those circumstances who
could?*

Quickly, she showered, using a fruit shampoo that smelt wonderfully of strawberries. Then she dressed in a lemon T-shirt and white
shorts. Whoever had thoughtfully provided the clothes had also left
pairs of sandals in the bottom of the closet. They were different sizes
but at last she chose some delicate brown leather sandals that had criss-
cross strapwork across her feet. These fitted just perfectly.

It's like Goldilocks and the three bears, Pamela thought. *Now all I need
to find are three bowls of porridge – one too salty, one too sweet, and one just
right.* She spent some time in front of a mirror, running a brush through
her hair. A solid silver one, hallmarked, and with the initials CJ elegantly
etched into the back. The brush felt so good that she lavished more
strokes on herself than she would normally. The light coming through
the window made her hair shine like gold.

I shouldn't look this good.

Shouldn't feel this good.

Not with Jim lying zippered in a body bag in a morgue. If there
was a body after the fire. If it wasn't reduced to—

Before the tsunami of tears came Pamela left the trailer at a run.

Immediately, she saw Hank.

He hailed her and lifted his richly stained hat. 'Mornin', ma'am. I
figure you might be rushing to see my Dillinger Death Car, but I've
bin told to point you in yonder direction.' He nodded toward the cafe.
'They've a nice plate of vittles waiting for ya.'

She blinked back the tears and smiled. 'Thank you. And good
morning to you. But I don't know if I'm hungry.'

'Good eating, my young lovely.'

'I never bother with much. Just toast and juice.'

'*Haw!* Breakfast's most important meal of the day.' He rubbed his
whiskery old-timer jaw. The red nose quivered like it had a life of its
own. 'Then lunch, dinner and supper come a close second.'

'I might rest up in the trailer for a while.'

'You got the Mosby place. Mighty fine trailer.'

'I like it.'

'He always took pride in the thing. He brought the sofa all the way
from Tucson.'

'I slept on it last night.'

'Work of art it is.'

'Don't let me keep you from your work.'

'Nothing that'll spoil for keepin'.' Hank settled the hat back on his head again. 'Don't forget that breakfast.'

'I'm not hungry.'

'If it's not food you're after, then there's good company.'

Pamela looked across at the cafe. A couple of trucks had been parked outside. She thought about Lauren and Nicki. She smiled.

'Yes, company would be fine right now. Thanks.'

'Don't mention it.'

As she started to walk through the hot desert sun to the cafe Hank called after her. 'Now, don't you go forgettin' the tour. See all of Pits with yours truly. There's plenty more to the place that meets the eye.'

Pamela walked into the cafe. Straight away the aromas of bacon and coffee hit her.

Oh boy, that does smell good. She realized she did have an appetite after all. The booths were empty but three guys in denim sat at the counter tucking into plates piled high with food. These had to be the truckers that belonged to the two vehicles outside. Well, two drivers plus mate. They were too busy eating for talking.

For a moment Pamela stood by a table, wondering if she'd blush when she saw Nicki. Instead Lauren breezed from the back. She wore a gypsy-style white blouse with embroidered lapels. To that she'd added a flowing skirt in cool cotton covered with a flower pattern. Definitely the fashion spirit of '69. Lauren smiled warmly when she saw Pamela.

'Good morning, Pamela. Sleep well?'

'Incredibly well. You must have something in this desert air.'

'Well, whatever it is, it's free.'

'Is Nicki here?'

'Sure. She's out back. Shall I call her for you?'

'Oh no, don't bother her if she's busy.'

'Right, first things first. What can I get you to eat?'

'Normally, for me it's toast and—'

'Not on my watch, buster.' Lauren smiled. 'Grab a table. Let me surprise you.'

'Thank you.'

'Coffee?'

'That'd be lovely.'

'I'll bring orange juice and water, too. You soon get a thirst in Pits.'

'Lauren?'

'Yes?'

'I have to tell the police what happened. About Rodney. And what he did to Jim.'

'Course you must, honey.'

'There's a telephone I can use?'

'Not in Pits, I'm afraid. We lost the cable in a rock fall a couple of months ago.'

'The phone company hasn't repaired it?'

'Low priority. We don't make enough calls to make it profitable.'

'But what happens when you need to make a call?'

Lauren paused as if the question surprised her. 'Really, I don't know. I guess none of us need to call anyone in the outside world. Funny, I just never thought about it.'

'The police must drop in here from time to time.'

'Oh, yes. We recharge them on coffee and doughnuts.' Lauren looked at Pamela seriously. 'But I know you need to report what happened to you. There's a town a couple of hours' drive from here. You can telephone from there. Now, make yourself comfortable. I'll get that breakfast.'

Pamela sat at the same table she'd sat at the day before. The one with the green Formica top. Through a window she could see Sharpe using a broom to sweep the dust from the side of the bus. He wore shades and despite the heat he looked as cool and as relaxed as the moment she'd met him. Just seconds after he'd shot Rodney.

The guy must have ice cream in his veins. I'd melt in that heat out there.

Lauren brought the coffee and ice-cold juice. The juice was heaven to Pamela's dry throat. *On a hot day like this, God lives in a cold drink,* she thought. She watched the truckers finish up, pay their check and then amble out to their waiting vehicles.

I could hitch a ride with them, she thought. *But then, what would they expect in return for transport out of here? A ride for a ride, as the old saying goes.*

No, I feel at peace here. Pits is restful.

Pits is a place where I don't have to confront the burnt ruin of my home.

Or meet Jim's grieving family. Or attend the funeral. Or start all over in a tiny apartment where I'd sit alone at night after a day's teaching in some bad neighborhood where the next kid you scold for chewing gum in class could pull a blade on you.

'Hi there, sweet pea.'

Pamela looked up. 'Hi.' It was Nicki, with her Nordic blond hair gleaming in the morning light. The hair was neatly braided. Once more she wore the knit pullover shirt and the bright red shorts. Over those she wore the blue apron with its pockets for the order pad. Her beautifully curved figure was the image of health and vitality.

Nicki engaged her in small talk. Pamela didn't blush. The memory of seeing Nicki rub her full breasts against Pamela's bare feet did have a dreamlike quality to it now. In the brilliance of a Mojave Desert morning such a thing seemed absurd.

Impossible.

Yeah – just a dream.

With no customers to serve, Nicki slid into one of the seats opposite. She chatted about the massage oils she hoped to sell to the diner's customers. 'It's important that Pits grows. We've got the beginnings of a real community here. It needs to start trading with the outside world. Then as Sharpe brings in more people we'll have a school one day. It would be lovely to hear children's voices again.'

'Sharpe's going to do that?'

'Sure.'

'But what makes people want to move to Pits?'

Nicki smiled. 'Look around you. There's space. It's clean. There's no crime.'

'But . . .' Pamela gave a little shrug, not wanting to dis Nicki's town. 'But it's kinda light on facilities, movie theaters, stores and the like.'

'True. But once you get used to it you love it.'

'And Sharpe just goes out and picks up people to come live here?'

'Not just like that. He *saves* people. Men and women who don't have a future in the outside world.'

Pamela took another swallow of juice. 'I do have a future. A career.'

Nicki smiled again. But this time the expression seemed disappointed, as if she was sad at the idea of Pamela leaving so soon. 'That's down to you, of course. You've got to make your own mind up about the future.'

Lauren appeared at that moment with a plate of bacon, scrambled eggs and steak, plus fried potatoes.

'Wow.' Pamela's mouth watered.

'Figured you could use the protein.'

'Figure I'll need to be moved round on a wheel after all this. It's a feast!'

'Enjoy.'

When Pamela had finished Lauren went back to the counter, then returned with a folded newspaper. 'I thought I'd let you finish up before I showed you this.'

Lauren sat down beside Nicki, opposite Pamela. She unfolded the newspaper and laid it flat on the table.

The moment Pamela saw the photograph on the front page her eyes blurred with tears. It showed a row of houses with a gap between a pair of them. She recognized the street. In the gap was a charred frame.

Gently, Lauren said, 'This isn't pretty but you might want to read it.'

'No.'

'It might help clarify your plans for the future.'

'No. Please . . .'

Lauren leaned forward and rested her hand on Pamela's forearm.

'There's something you should know, Pamela.'

Pamela used a napkin to dab her eyes. 'I know all there is to know. That bastard Rodney murdered my husband and burnt my home.'

'There is more. You don't have to read it now but it might be best if—'

'Okay.' Pamela took a deep breath. 'Get it over with.'

'We're here for you, Pamela,' Nicki said softly. 'We're going to help you any way we can.'

Pamela looked at the newspaper but her teary eyes blurred her vision so that the newsprint became black streaks.

'It's no good. I can't read it. My eyes are . . . uh . . .' She sniffed. 'You'd think I wouldn't have a tear left in me.'

'Don't worry. I'll give you the gist,' Lauren said. 'It says the fire-fighters found two skeletons in the debris. One male. One female.'

'Female?'

'Yes. Pamela, they believe the remains are yours.'

Pamela made a hiccup sound. Partway between a laugh and a cry. 'So in the eyes of the world, I don't even exist anymore.' She took a deep breath. 'Of course. It must have been Rodney. He killed another woman and brought her into the house before he kidnapped me. That way ...' She found her voice breaking. 'Th-that way, no one would come looking for me, because ... because the police would think husband and wife died together.'

Pamela looked from Lauren to Nicki. Both regarded her with deep sympathy. They were willing her to be strong.

'S'easy,' Pamela said. 'I go to the police. Once they see me they'll know I'm alive and ... and—'

'It's not as simple as that.' Lauren chose her words carefully. 'You see, Jim's wife flew in from New York.'

'No. You're mistaken. I'm his wife ... *widow*.'

Lauren shook her head. 'Jim was already married.'

'Impossible. I married him. We honeymooned in Maui.'

Lauren reached out to squeeze Pamela's hand. 'It looks as if Jim had married before. Only he ...'

'Neglected to mention it.' Pamela's voice hardened. She sat up straight. Stared out of the window. The rocky hills rose into the sky. Now they looked like teeth ready to chew a piece out of it. 'And never divorced. So it was a bigamous wedding.' She shook her head. 'My God. The day before yesterday, I was a wife. Yesterday, I was a widow.' A bitter laugh escaped her lips. 'Today, I'm neither.'

Chapter Twenty

Norman woke up and thought: *My God. The nightmare I've just had. Sex with a piglike woman called Boots. Murder. Me, slaying two cops. A bad, BAD dream* . . .

He opened his eyes. 'Oh, shit!'

A large face framed by short bleached hair looked down at him. Hell of a lot of makeup, too. He was lying in the backseat of his car with his head on her lap.

Heart pounding, he sat up.

Looked round.

Duke driving.

Boots smiling at him.

'You slept like a baby,' she was saying.

Duke glanced back. 'Sweet dreams, big feller?'

'Oh God . . . oh my God.' Norman shuffled his butt across the seat away from Boots, trying to cower in the corner with his hand over his mouth.

Repeating: 'Oh my God. Oh my God . . .'

Should've stayed asleep.

'Oh my God,' he said for the zillionth time. 'I thought I'd dreamt it all.'

Boots looked hurt. 'You thought you only dreamt making out with me?'

'Some wet dream, huh, Norm?' Duke drove one-handed, the other arm straight out across the back of the passenger seat.

'Oh, you mean you thought you dreamt all the other stuff? Zapping those cops. That *soooo* turned me on.'

141

'Yeah, you were awesome, man.' Duke gave the horn a couple of toots to celebrate his appreciation.

'You shouldn't do that, Duke,' Norman warned. 'Draws attention to us.'

'You mean cops? Shit, Norm, everything's dandy.'

'Yeah.' Boots waved her hands to point out of every window at once. 'No one about.'

Blinking against the bright sun, Norman looked out. The road ran through wooded hills. There were no buildings he could see.

'Bear-shit country,' Duke observed.

'I like cartoon bears. Don't think I'd like to meet the real thing.'

'No bear would dare tangle with you, Bootsy-girl.' Duke laughed.

Boots laughed along, then: 'Anyone hungry?'

'We've got soda and some leftovers from the beach picnic.' Duke sounded matter-of-fact.

Matter-of-fact like Jesus H. Christ we never killed four people yesterday. Norman was stunned.

Couldn't speak.

Kept thinking what his father would say.

'Mr. Wiscoff. Your son, Norman, is a cop-killer. He'll get fifty thousand volts for the crime.' Norman could hear the lawyer's words right now. *What's worse? The murders? Or the shame that I'll bring on my family?*

He didn't know.

What was it that Oliver Hardy said when his and Stan's plans went awry and they were up Shit Creek *sans* paddle? *'Oh, Gabriel, blow your horn.'*

Ollie was inviting the archangel to bring the world to an end so he wouldn't have to suffer the consequences of whatever mess the twosome had gotten into.

'Oh Gabriel, blow your horn.'

'What you say back there, bud?'

Norman sighed. 'Nothing.'

'Sure am hungry.' Boots said. 'Anyone else hungry?'

'I just told you, girl, we've got leftovers.'

'I don't want no picnic leftovers. I want real food. On a plate. With steam coming off of it.'

Norman sat up straight. 'If you think you can pull up at a diner, think again. The police will be looking for this car.'

'The man's right,' Duke said. 'A red Jeep Cherokee with cop brain stuck to the windshield. Dead giveaway.' Then he said something that appalled Norman. 'We're going to ditch the car.'

'Ditch it?' Norman gasped. 'It's my dad's car. He'll be livid.'

'Livid? Maybe the fact his loving son's a cop-slayer will take his mind off losing the car.'

'Besides.' Boots patted her hair in place. 'If it's your daddy's car then you won't have had the sweat of paying for it.'

'We can't just *leave* it.'

'Dead straight, Norm. Don't want to walk everywhere, do we?'

'Not me,' Boots said. 'Makes the skin on my heels hard.'

Norman glanced down at her thick sunburnt thighs. Those feet had to ship some heavy-duty meat for a living.

'So, this is the plan.' Duke glanced back. 'We find another car. Dump this one where the cops don't find it in a hurry. Then—'

'Then get some chow,' Boots stressed.

'Get some chow,' Duke agreed.

'I'm never gonna eat ever again,' Norman announced with feeling.

'Then we drive due south.'

'South?' Norman would have preferred to exit to another galaxy. Cops had a long reach.

'South,' Duke repeated. 'Get out into wilderness country where we can lay low.'

Norman glanced back through the window at the receding road. At any second he expected to see police cruisers appear with their lights flashing.

'Don't sweat it,' Duke said. 'We're three hundred miles from the motel. You know the one?'

'Yeah, I know the one.'

'The one where Norman stopped being a virgin.'

Boots smirked. 'Maybe they'll put up a plaque one day. *Norman popped his cherry here.*'

'Or rename the motel,' Duke speculated. 'Norman's First Hump . . . or how about this? The Cockwell Inn.'

Duke and Boots laughed.

Norman groaned, 'Oh my God.'

Then Duke nodded at a dirt track that led from the road. 'This is where we pick up our brand new conveyance.'

Norman began to understand the implications of the plan. 'Jesus. We're going to steal one?'

'No,' Duke snorted. 'We're going to stop the car. Get out. Get down on our knees, then pray to the Almighty that He should deliver a hot BMW straight from Heaven.'

Boots and Duke laughed again while Norman's heart sank into the dark pit of his stomach.

The house. Two stories. Shingle roof. Barn. Workshop. Despite the heat of the sun-filled day blue smoke rose from the chimney.

'They gotta car,' Boots whispered as Duke stopped the Jeep in the shade of a tree.

'Check out the pickup truck.' Duke pointed to where the Ford pickup was partly hidden by the barn. 'That's gonna have more poke than the old rice-boiler.'

Though it was close on a hundred yards away Norman could make out that the car parked outside the front door of the house was an aged Datsun.

'What ya gonna do, Duke?' Boots asked.

'I'm going backwards, that's what I'm gonna do, Bootsy-girl.'

'Careful,' Norman said. 'There's a lake behind us.'

'Perfect. Once we have the pickup, Norman, you roll the car into the lake.'

'Into the lake? My dad's car?'

'Yeah. Gonna be no use to us now.'

'More use to the cops,' Boots added. 'Fingerprints and stuff.'

Norman took a deep breath. 'Okay, let's do it.'

Duke switched off the motor and turned round, a surprised expression beneath his Elvis quiff.

'Aren't you forgettin' something, Norman?'

'Forgetting what?'

'Forgettin' to say shit like, "Are you sure about this? Aren't we breaking the law? Won't we get into trouble? What if we get found out? What if we get our asses busted?"'

'That's what you say normally, Norm.' Boots snickered. 'Hey, did you hear what I said? Normally, Norm? That's kinda—'

'We heard.' Duke opened the door, then said to Norman, 'That guilt thing ain't eating you no more.'

Boots leaned sideways on the backseat to squeeze Norman's knee. 'He's becoming one of us.'

They approached the house under cover of the bushes at the side. About a hundred wind chimes from the porch roof, eaves, house walls and tree branches. Under the hot sun there wasn't much wind, but there was enough.

The chimes turned.

Tinkled.

Chinked.

Sang.

A robot chorus of tinny voices.

I'm going through with this. Norman told himself. *And I don't feel bad. I'm not wanting to retch with guilt.*

That's because you've done worse than steal a car.

Cop-killer.

'Oh, Poppa,' he breathed. 'If you could see me now.'

Duke had led the way through the bushes to the house. Now he held his finger to his lips. 'You two stay put. Come forward to the porch when I whistle.'

Norman whispered, 'You going to hot-wire the truck?'

'I figured using an ignition key would make life easier.'

'Where you gonna find the key?'

'Where do you think?'

'Leave him to it,' Boots whispered. 'Duke knows what he's doin'.'

Duke winked. 'Duke sure does, baby.'

With that he stood up. Then, in plain view, not skulking, not looking shifty, he strolled up to the house, giving the Datsun just the barest sidelong glance.

'Norman?'

'Huh.'

'Kind of sexy here under the bushes.'

'Don't start that now, Boots.'

'Normy, Normy, Normy.'

'Quit touching.'

'Betcha I can get you hard.'

'Not now.'

Norman tried to watch Duke's progress. Especially as Duke was walking with the knife gripped in his hand so that it stayed behind the back of his thigh, where it wouldn't be seen from the house.

'Norman . . .'

'What?' He turned to Boots who tried to look coy, one of her thick fingers resting against her fleshy lips. Even in the dappling of shadow and sunlight under the bushes she looked broad. A heavy blend of muscle and fat. Her bare arms were thick and were colored a patchy red with sunburn from yesterday, while her elbows had scabbed from carpet burn.

Must be from when we made love yesterday.

Made love?

Sheesh. We screwed her plain and simple.

But there was something about her smile and her take-me-I'm-yours eye contact that sent a shivery tingle up his spine.

'Remember what I did for you in the car yesterday, Norman?'

'Uh-huh.'

'Wanna do it again?'

'Now?'

She nodded. 'Here.'

For a heavy girl she moves fast. Boots pushed Norman so that he sat on his butt, taking his weight on straight arms, his hands planted just behind him. She got down on her knees, unzipped him.

'Boots . . . ah, ah, you sure pick your times . . .'

''S good, 's nice . . .' She slurped.

The girl has to be crazy.

Getting horny at a time like this.

Stealing a truck.

Duke knocking on the door.

Oh . . . but it feels so good.

Boots's bleached hair bobbed up and down in the shadow. Norman's heart thudded. Blood roared through the veins of his neck.

His head swiveled from watching Boots . . .

. . . to watching Duke. The man's body masked the knife. He looked cool as James Dean standing there. Oiled blond quiff shining in the sunlight. He tapped on the screen frame with his free hand.

Cooing, whispering, Boots did incredible things with her mouth.

Holy shit.

That's good.

That's the best.
Boots is good at this.
Must have had practise aplenty.

Dizzy with the erotic thrill of it all, Norman watched a thin guy in dungarees step into the doorway while holding the screen open.

Couldn't hear much. But Duke was talking to the guy. A guy of around sixty in a red cap.

Duke pointed at something away in the trees. The guy stepped out onto the porch to look, shielding his eyes against the glare of the sun. Duke smiled pleasantly. Came across as chatty. The bony guy in the cap appeared relaxed. The young stranger turning up at his door hadn't made him suspicious.

Boots moaned. She was aroused, too. With one hand she opened her blouse, flipped her bra to expose a jiggling white boob.

Norman moaned. 'Uh . . .' This was too much.

Pleasure overload.

But he had to see what Duke did next.

Duke was still talking to the guy, circling round to stand beside him, still pointing.

Saying what?

'Hey, mister, you don't know me but I've just seen a truck come off of the road yonder. Driver's hurt bad.'

Or:

'Is that a helicopter that's crashed in the trees?'

Or:

'Just seen the Mayor buck naked in the lake. He's swimming there with the Chief of Police and the High School principal.'

Whatever.

It worked.

The old guy stared good and hard toward a line of trees.

Duke moved.

Raised his knife hand.

Blade catching the sun, a hard quicksilver glitter.

Boots sucked harder.

The old guy shouted.

Norman shouted.

Boots had worked her crazy erotic magic on him all over again.

Chapter Twenty-one

'You've really got to educate yourself not to shout out when I'm taking care of business.'

Duke finished rolling the body under the crawl space of the house, then let down the trellis flap to hide it.

Boots wiped her mouth, smearing her lipstick a little. 'My fault. I got Norman all carried away.'

'Gotta get smart, otherwise the cops will be snapping on the cuffs in no time at all.' Duke plucked his knife from a porch timber where he'd planted it for safekeeping. He wiped the blood off on the grass. 'Like I say, I don't do jail.'

Boots fluttered her eyelids and in her breathy way cooed, 'Sorry, Mister Duke.'

'Aw, shit. Who could stay mad at you?'

Norman looked up at the house. Close up it wasn't looking too healthy with its paint cracking and peeling up and its missing shingles.

'Say. Anyone else at home?'

'Nah. Only old Mister Brundle.' Checking that the blade was clean, Duke slid the knife into his motorcycle boot. 'And his wife.'

'*His wife?*'

'Don't have a cow, Norman. She's not going to beat us up.'

Boots growled. 'I'd like to see any woman *try* and beat me up.'

'Ain't our Bootsy-girl formidable?'

'Yeah,' Norman agreed.

Half woman; half sow.

Only . . .

She was *kinda exciting.*

He remembered the look of joy on her face as he'd squirted his twin-pack into her sucking mouth.

Maybe, I'm becoming more like Duke, he thought. *I'm seeing the world differently. Seeing babes differently.*

'Anyone hungry?' Duke asked.

'You betcha. Could eat a hairy-assed goat.' Boots licked her lips. 'What we gonna do with the guy's wife?'

Duke shrugged. He didn't care. 'Mister said she couldn't move around by herself these days.'

'Probably tucked up in bed,' Boots observed. Then a thought occurred that pleased her. 'Hey, guys. There might be a spare bedroom. We could grab some shut-eye.'

'And anything else that comes our way.' Duke winked. 'What say you, Norm?'

'I've gotta eat first.' Boots crossed the porch to the door.

'An army marches on its stomach.' Duke gave a little bow to Norman. 'After you, bud.'

'The guy's wife must be upstairs,' Norman said as they helped themselves to beers from the refrigerator in the kitchen.

'Go tuck her in if you like.' Duke took a slug of beer.

'Probably an invalid. My grandma was an invalid,' Boots said. 'Welfare paid us money to keep her, but you know after a while she got—'

This is a story I don't want to hear, Norman told himself. 'Hey, there's a bunch of steaks in the refrigerator.'

'Great choice, Norman.' Duke checked out a shelf. 'Gotta skillet. Bound to be some grease for frying hereabouts. Ah, tomatoes in the basket.'

'I got the bread.' Boots held up a loaf.

'I thought I heard something.'

'Probably the old lady turning over in bed.'

'Or coming downstairs.' Norman wondered what the tough guy would do to the dead man's wife.

Duke bit into a bright red tomato. 'Say, Norm, check out the freezer for French fries. I'm as hungry as a horse.'

Norman went to the big chest freezer in the corner. Flipped up the lid.

'Holy shit!'

'No French fries?'

Norman backed off, staring into the cavernous interior as freezer mist rolled out into the warm air.

'What's wrong, babe?' Boots sauntered across, her white footwear clicking on the boards.

'We gotta get out of here,' Norman spluttered.

'Oooh-ee. The old guy was right about his wife being not much of a walker.'

'Hey.' Duke smirked. 'He put the old lady on ice.'

Norman stared at the frozen body of an old woman with blue-rinsed hair. The eyes were open.

One peered left.

The other stared right.

Her lips were as gray as her skin. She looked as if she'd snuck into the freezer for a nap.

'Wonder why he froze her up like that?' Boots poked the old woman in the eye with her finger. The eyeball looked as hard as glass.

Duke pursed his lips, considering. 'Sentimental attachment.'

'Or Necro-fuller,' Boots suggested, giving the nose an experimental prod.

'Phrase is Necro-filler,' Duke corrected her.

Necrophilia! Norman would have shouted the word but seeing Boots prodding the rock-solid corpse made his insides feel strange.

'Close the lid.' Norman swallowed. 'Now.'

'Guy's right. There's no French fries I can see. Boots, peel some potatoes.'

'Like fun I will.'

'I'll peel the potatoes,' Norman said. Gratefully he released a lung full of air when Boots closed the lid.

'Ain't he a gent?' Duke patted Boots's rump. 'He doesn't want to see the lady spoil her nails.'

Boots looked round at the kitchen. 'We should check the house over. Might be money. We're gonna need cash.'

'Smart as well as sexy,' Duke said appreciatively. 'Ain't she a catch?'

'You betcha, Duke.' Norman turned his eyes away from the freezer-cum-casket with an effort.

Went to the sink. Ran water. Started peeling potatoes. He did it mechanically.

The Glory Bus

Wonder what it's like to kiss a frozen corpse on the lips?

Shit. His imagination supplied the sensations. *Like pressing ice to your mouth.*

'We're gonna take a look round,' Duke said. Then to Boots: 'Coming?'

'Only in yer dreams, buster.'

Then, giggling girlishly (the giggles punctuated by swinish snorts), she ran from the kitchen with Duke slapping her heavy rump. Norman heard their footsteps go clumping upstairs. Presently, he heard Boots giggling in a breathy kind of way. That was pretty muffled.

Unlike the *squeak-squeak* of bedsprings: he could hear the noise coming through the ceiling.

Norman forced himself to concentrate on peeling the potatoes. But every so often thoughts intruded.

Old boy dead under the crawl space.

Wife frozen like a pea in the freezer.

Dear Lord.

What kind of nightmare have I fallen into?

As he carved the skins from the potatoes, nicked out eyes with the point of the blade, he heard the creak of the bed.

Sometimes it sounded like the opening of the deep-freeze lid.

Then his head would twist round so fast that his neck muscles would hurt.

She's climbing out the deep freeze.

Gonna get you, Normy boy.

Each time Norman looked he was convinced that he'd see the old girl's gray face, with its gray lips, with eyes that looked out to the sides like those of a fish. He'd see her peeping out at him with the appliance's half-open lid resting on her blue-rinse hair.

'Come join me in the deep freeze, sweetheart.' He could almost hear the whispered invitation. 'Come cuddle up with old Mother Brundle. It's safe and dark in here.'

Shut up!

The *creak-creak* of bedsprings sang down through the ceiling at him. Duke and Boots would be naked up there. Duke'd be boring into the pig-girl like he planned to come out clean through on the other side.

Then there was the old ice maiden. Norman was sure that he could hear movement in the deep freeze.

Maybe he should check on her? Make sure she was dead.

Maybe he should go upstairs. Make up a threesome.

Maybe he should grab the Datsun's keys. Make dust.

The thought caught Norman by surprise. He looked across the kitchen to where a wooden board had been fixed to the wall. Beneath a picture of a German Shepherd were the words: LET ME GUARD YOUR KEYS.

Beneath that caption were little metal hooks where bunches of keys hung. Some were car keys.

In five seconds he'd have the keys in his hands.

Would need to go close to the deep freeze with its ice maiden, though.

Worth the risk.

Because in twenty seconds he could be driving away from here.

Alone.

Duke would still be humping Boots.

Never know he'd gone.

Until it was too late.

Sweet.

Where would I go?

Who cares, as long as I've dumped the crazy duo.

Norman put the knife and a part-peeled potato in the sink, dried his hands on a towel, then moved slowly toward the keys that glinted in the light bouncing through the windows. Outside, it was still in the isolated valley. The sun shone down on the trees. In the distance the open road beckoned.

Gonna be free of Duke and Boots. No more madness. No more killing.

Be away from the deep-freeze lady, too. I'm sure I can hear her running her fingernails across the metal sides in there.

He reached the key-keep. Yeah, there were the car keys. One had the word *Datsun* impressed on its plastic fob. He could be driving away from here within the next few moments.

Norman reached out. Touched the keys.

'*Hey.*'

The shock nearly blew his heart clean out of his chest. He spun, expecting to see the old lady standing up in the deep freeze, hands on hips, demanding to know what the game was.

Instead, he turned to see Duke standing in the doorway with a rifle in his hands. The man was butt naked.

'What you got there, Norm?'

'Uh?'

'Those the keys?'

'Uh . . . sure. Just checking them out.'

'Good move,' Duke said brightly. 'You never know when we might have to shoot out of here. Grab this.'

He threw the rifle to Norman.

Norman caught it. Its weight nearly dislocated his fingers.

'Found this upstairs. Thought it might come in useful if you get any surprise visitors.'

'Thanks.'

'How long until chow time?'

'Not long.'

'Just give us a yell when you serve up. That Boots is insatiable, you know?'

'I know.'

With his legs shaking, his belly full of watery sensations, Norman went back to peeling the potatoes.

Upstairs the bed once more began its creak . . . creak . . . creak . . .

Okay, okay, I could just go right now.

Grab the keys.

Race the Datsun down the track to the road.

But he couldn't do it. He'd realized when he went to get the keys just before Duke showed up in the kitchen doorway that his heart just wasn't in it.

Have they gotten some kind of hold over me? he wondered.

Maybe it's Boots. A sexual magnetism.

Or maybe I need Duke's instinct for survival to protect me.

I'm a cop-killer. If I'm busted then it's the end of everything for me.

No future.

Not even a heartbeat.

Norman thought about the dead woman lying in her ice tomb. *No. Not me. I don't do death.*

Chapter Twenty-two

Duke said, 'That was a great steak, Normy. Just how I like it.'

Boots patted his knee. 'Yeah – so rare that a good doctor could get it breathin' again.'

'Thanks.'

Norman had been driving two hours. The house was a long ways back in the isolated valley.

Along with . . .

The old guy stabbed by Duke.

The old gal in the deep freeze.

And . . .

Ouch!

His red Jeep Cherokee.

Duke'd released the brake so that it'd coasted down the slope into the lake where it had disappeared with a gurgle. In minutes all that remained were a few bubbles and spreading blooms of oil on the water, painting iridescent rainbow colors.

Shit.

Loved that car, man. Really loved it.

Only they'd had to ditch it and replace it with the pickup truck that had belonged to the old guy, who now lay in the crawl space with only spiders for company.

The Ford pickup was a dull blue. Ten years old. But ran well.

The old-timer must have lavished attention on it. Loved it, just like I loved my little red Jeep.

Norman imagined the old guy checking the oil, or inflating the tires with an old hand-pump, while his wife baked apple pie in the kitchen. Then one day the guy had gone indoors to find his wife dead.

Couldn't bear to say good-bye.

So he'd emptied the deep freeze. Plonked her inside.

Norman shivered despite the heat.

The road ahead was clear of traffic and sunlit.

Now all three of the amigos sat in the single row of seats in the front of the truck, Duke nonchalantly resting his elbow on the door frame with the window rolled down inside the shell. He chewed gum, wore shades, looked cool.

Boots sat beside him, legs apart, dirty white footwear gleaming under the dash. She hummed. There was no tune. Could have been a crappy old refrigerator-motor sound for all Norman knew, or cared.

Hmmm . . . hmmm . . . hmmm . . .

Duke grinned. 'Hey, that's one of my favorite songs.'

Favorite song? Christ. That noise is as flat and as tuneless as you can get!

Duke started to sing the Elvis classic 'Are You Lonesome Tonight?'.

Boots could change the words to sing 'Are You LOATHSOME Tonight?'.

Yeah, that's the woman's own personal anthem for sure.

Duke sang most of the song. He was pretty good. Maybe he could have made it as a bar singer with his cool bad-boy looks. He'd never be an Elvis impersonator, though. Norman was sure that Duke would figure that as being too cheesy, too uncool. Duke probably worshipped Elvis as a god. Though he probably wouldn't admit that, either.

'What we get?' The breeze zithered Duke's hair.

Boots paused her hum. 'Back at the old boy's house?'

'Yeah.'

'Got some homemade jerky, cookies, soda—'

'No, Bootsy-babe. The gold that folds.'

'Uh . . . oh . . . six hundred . . . and eight dollars.'

'Not bad.'

Yeah, so we robbed the house, too.

Add it to the charge sheet, why don't you?

In the light of me killing two cops that's kid stuff. Bring it on, Joe Blow . . .

Norman drove one-handed. His window was down. He could smell the grass in the fields as well as the asphalt of one hot road that rolled due south. Here the countryside was flatter. There were cows. Farms. Small, drowsy towns with diners, barbers' shops, convenience stores.

I'm turning into Duke, he thought. *Here I am, driving with my elbow out the window, wearing shades, chewing gum. For the first time in my life a girl might look at me and think, 'Hey, that guy's cool.'*

Norman smiled.

Yeah, what I've done in the last twenty-four hours has buried NORMAL NORMAN. Meet the new guy: Norm, prince of cool.

'I got something else, too,' Boots said. She was rooting something out of a brown paper grocery bag. 'Normy, you think you could get these off for me?'

Norman glanced down.

The Prince of Cool saw a pale hand with slender fingers.

Boots had short stubby fingers. Like thick pegs. Chewed nails.

This hand had a speckled back. Thin fingers. Gold wedding band. A diamond ring on the middle finger.

A fingertip touched Norman's bare forearm.

'Holy shit!'

He braked so hard that the pickup screamed through three-sixty. A smell of burning rubber polluted an otherwise finely scented day.

'Shit, shit, shit!' He threw open the truck door. Jumped out.

Danced.

Shouted, 'Shit, shit, shit!' While wiping at that cold sensation on his arm where the finger had made contact.

'I didn't mean to startle you, Normy,' Boots said, looking out through the door. Her eyes were all innocent-looking.

'You broke off the old woman's hand? You broke it off? You brought it with you!' He was shouting the words. 'I don't believe you'd do such a—'

He held his breath. *Jesus Christ. That's just it. I DO believe she'd do such a thing. Boots is capable of anything. She'd choke the Pope if she took a fancy to his robes.*

'Jesus, Mary and Joseph.' He had to remove his sunglasses as a fear-sweat ran down his face. 'You could have waited until I'd stopped the car.'

Duke laughed. 'Just a little Boots joke. Ain't that right, Boots?'

'Yeah, I thought you'd see the funny side.' She held up the hand so that she could see how the diamonds caught the light. 'I like these sparklers, though.'

'You keep it, Boots,' Duke told her. 'You're worth a tub full of diamonds. Isn't that right, Norman?'

Norman managed to grunt, 'You betcha.'

'Here's your present, Boots.'

'Oh! Thank you, Duke.'

Norman watched the pair in the truck. She kissed Duke's cheek. She was overjoyed. Tearful.

'No one's never given me a diamond ring before. I'm just so happy to hang out with you two. You're the best.'

'Don't mention it, girl.' Duke broke off the frozen finger. Threw the snapped digit out of the cab. Norman danced to avoid the white sticklike thing as it bounced on the road near his feet.

'There you go, beautiful.' The ring wouldn't even make it over the first joint of Boots's stubby middle finger. With some spit and shoving Duke got it onto her pinkie.

Boots gushed with a mixture of tears and smiles. 'Oh, thank you, guys. I'm never gonna take it off. Never ever.'

'You deserve it. Ain't that so, Norm?'

'You sure do.' Norman backed away as Duke broke off the third finger.

Know what's coming next.

Duke slid off the wedding band. Then threw the severed finger out of the truck where it bounced onto the road-tar near Norman's feet. In the hot sun the fluid content of the digit began to melt. Liquid blood began to ooze from veins that trailed like soggy noodles from the raw end of the finger. Duke hurled the rest of the hand. It sailed close by Norman's ear.

Thumped down into the long grass at the side of the road.

'Something for the coyotes to snack on,' Duke said. Then, 'Hey, Norman, you gonna start driving?'

An eighteen-wheeler swept by. The driver laid into the horn as their pickup still blocked half the road sideways on.

Boots complained, 'You don't want to see us get killed out here, do you, Norman, honey?'

Hold that beautiful thought.

As Norman returned to the pickup a police cruiser glided to a halt beside it.

The cop rolled down his window. 'You guys in trouble?'

Norman thought he'd crap his pants. But to his surprise his reply was cool as milk. 'We just spun out there, officer.'

'Yeah?'

'My fault,' Norman said. 'A bee flew into the cab. Tried to sting me.'

'You don't say.'

'Guess I just panicked.'

'Sorry, officer,' Duke called from the pickup. 'Our friend's a bit of a wuss.'

'Looks like that to me, too,' the officer observed. 'Y'know bees don't bother you unless you bother them.'

'I'll remember that, officer,' Norman said. 'Sorry to trouble you.'

'No trouble for me, son. You best be on your way before another big rig comes this way, otherwise your vehicle's gonna end up tinfoil.'

'Yes, sir.'

Norman smiled. Waved. Climbed into the driver's seat.

Just hope that the cop doesn't glance down on the road and see those deep-frozen fingers melting there on the road-tar.

Norman keyed the ignition. The engine clunked, rolled, whirred. Didn't start.

'Sure you're not having any trouble?' the cop called from his car.

'No, sir. We're fine.'

Fine, fine, fine. Oh God, please don't let him recognize us. We've ditched the red Jeep but surely every cop in the state has been radioed our descriptions.

'Come on, truck,' Norman muttered. 'Start. In the name of God, please start.'

He turned the key again.

Click. Whirr. No go.

'Take it easy,' Duke said coolly. 'Just try a little more gas.'

Norman tried again. The engine fired.

He waved at the cop to say everything was okay.

Yeah, as if . . .

The cop nodded, his face impassive.

Oh God, maybe he's remembering the APB. Two guys and a girl in white boots. Cop-killers.

The cop pulled a wad of gum from his mouth, rolled it between thumb and forefinger. Then flicked it through his car's open window.

The Glory Bus

Norman watched the gob of gray drop beside the old woman's wedding finger *sans* its gold band.

Oh, Christ on an ass.

The cop stared impassively at Norman in the truck.

Norman's artificial smile took on huge proportions.

Stop grinning, you ape, he told himself. *That kind of grimace screams guilt.*

Any second the cop's gonna pull his revolver. Maybe loose off a couple of rounds into my chest for good measure.

Then the cop gave a nod, eased the cruiser past the pickup. Norman pressed the gas pedal. Not hard, so he pulled away in a smooth, law-abiding way.

No wheel spin.

No fugitive dash.

'That's it,' Duke purred. 'Drive away nice and slow. Don't give Mister Police Officer any cause for suspicion.'

'Norman's turning into one cool customer.' Boots rubbed his inner thigh. 'I like Normy more with every hour that passes. I'm gonna treat him to somethin' nice tonight.'

Norman gently accelerated along the road. He glanced back in the mirror.

The police cruiser was pulling away, too, in the opposite direction. Norman expected at any second that its lights would start whirling and the cop would pull a tight U in the road and chase them.

But the cop had other things on his mind.

He eased his big black-and-white along the highway, receding all the time.

Norman let out a sigh and a half. 'Phew-ee. I did okay, didn't I?'

'You did just fine, Norman, old bud. Just fine.'

As the sun started to set, Norman was figuring that they'd done six hundred miles in the pickup.

Still aiming the Ford's nose due south.

Duke said, 'We need to eat. We need to sleep.'

'I'm thirsty, too,' said a drowsy Boots.

'We've plenty of cash so we'll stop at the next motel.'

'Ooh-ee,' Boots sighed. 'My skin's itchy. Could use a shower, then a big, big soft bed.'

'You've got it, babe.'

Boots ran her fingers up Norman's thigh. 'Could you use a nice clean motel room?'

In a laid-back way, Norman shrugged. 'Yeah, cool.'

Inside, his heart lurched.

Oh my God. A motel room. Here we go all over again.

Chapter Twenty-three

Pamela's life had been exploded.

Demolished.

Torn asunder, as the old phrase goes, she thought. *Marriage was the foundation I'd built my life on. Rodney was a murderer who killed my husband and made me a widow. Now I've learnt that Jim was still married when he went through the wedding ceremony with me. He's a bigamist.*

A dead bigamist.

Rodney killed him. Burnt him.

But who's the bigger rat? Rodney or Jim?

Pamela had walked out into the desert to be alone. She'd climbed into the rocky hills that seemed to glow like fire beneath the afternoon sun. Now she stood on the edge of a rock that ended in a fifty-foot drop. Below her and quarter of a mile away was Pits. She could see the diner, the old house, the line of trailers, vehicles. Even Sharpe as he crossed the road to climb into his bus full of mannequins.

Sharpe saves, she told herself. *Saves people who are so down on their luck that even the bottom of a well would be a long way up for them. And then some . . .*

I could end it here. Just requires one step forward. Then a fall of a few seconds through hot dry air to even hotter rocks at the bottom of this cliff.

No more hurt. No more misery.

Just the perfect forgetfulness of oblivion.

Takes one step, Pamela . . . that's all . . .

Pamela's head spun. Heat rising up from the white rock had the intensity of a furnace. In the desert stood saguaro cacti. Like a whole army of people stood watching her. Waiting for her to fall.

161

Waiting for the crunch of her flesh and bone on rocks. The hiss of her blood leaking onto stones that were thirsty after a hundred years of drought. Above. Clear blue sky. Vultures whirled.

Yup. They knew what she was gonna do.

Seen suicide before. Knew the signs.

Knew the sweet taste of self-killed flesh.

Pamela's knees turned watery. She leaned forward. When she looked down now it was all the waaaayyy down . . .

'There's a better way than that, miss.'

'Sharpe?'

Pamela squinted into the brilliant sunlight. There was Sharpe in silhouette. Easy to make out his flat-top haircut, the glint of his shades reflecting two perfect images of her face with the cluster of buildings that was Pits behind her.

'This is only a fifty-foot drop,' he said. 'If you go across yonder you can drop into the mine pits themselves. Don't know how deep they are.'

'How'd you know I was gonna—'

'Kill yourself? Know the signs. When someone has that defeated look in their eyes that's so deeply rooted it goes all the way through into their soul. That's when I know.'

'You know what my husband did?'

'Bigamy? Sure.'

'I could face being a widow. Not this.'

'Ashamed?'

'Wouldn't you be?'

'It's your fault?'

'I was gullible. I should have—'

'Gullible don't make you guilty. Anyways, I don't see how you could have known. Married men don't come with the word tattooed on their chests.'

Pamela looked up at Sharpe's face but could see no expression on it because the dazzling presence of the sun was directly behind him. 'This is just *so* not fair.'

'Not fair isn't a self-execution offence, is it?'

A tear squeezed onto her cheek where the fierce sun stole the moisture in a second. 'I just want to stop thinking about what Jim did . . . hell, what Rodney did, too. It hurts, Sharpe.'

'Sure it does. And if you want to stop the hurt there's the pit.'

'Where is it?'

'Back that way. It's a long drop but it'll do the job.'

'Show me, will you?'

'So long that you might fall all the way to China.'

Despite her misery, Pamela laughed. 'China. Yeah, China's just about far enough away.' A smile had found its way to her face. She raised her head to show Sharpe that maybe she wasn't as deeply depressed as she'd first seemed.

There was no Sharpe.

She looked down at Pits again. Sharpe was stowing cartons into the hold of the bus.

Hey, Sharpe . . . how come you got back down there so quick?

That's impossible.

Can't be two places at once. Not even Sharpe.

But then he found me just as Rodney was going to shoot me. Right time, right place.

'Gee, Sharpe, you've gotta be an angel in disguise.'

Just for a moment, the shadows falling on Sharpe from the bus's luggage-compartment doors fell across his shoulders. Dizzy, her vision blurred, Pamela saw the shadows as wings unfurling from Sharpe's back. He straightened after stowing a box.

Even from this distance he seemed to be looking at her.

Looking directly at her through those shades of his.

Impossible.

Can't see me way up here. Not properly, anyway.

But Sharpe is special. 'Sharpe, you *are* an angel,' she whispered.

Light-headed from the heat Pamela tottered forward. Below, the rocks at the bottom of the cliff seemed to leap at her. Quickly, she stumbled back to safer ground.

She shouted: 'NO!'

I'm not going to kill myself. Rodney was a murdering rat. Jim was a lying rat.

Both rats are now dead.

And there's no reason why you, Pamela, need join them.

'I'm going to live,' she told herself, her head held high. 'I'm going to make my home in Pits. And I'm not going to let Rodney or Jim, and what they did to me, ruin my life.' She called out to the sky. 'This is Pamela Wright. This is my declaration of independence. From this moment on I am a free woman. And I am going to live my life exactly how I please. And do exactly what I want! Whenever I want!'

The echoes died away. At that moment Sharpe looked in her direction again. She fancied that she saw him nod in agreement with her statement, even though he couldn't possibly have heard from this distance.

Angel Sharpe.

Then he climbed on the bus, started the motor, and drove away along the desert road.

Chapter Twenty-four

'Motel Ha-Ha.' Boots read the sign as Norman stopped the truck fifty yards from the motel's reception office.

From the truck's cab Norman scanned the place. It consisted of individual pine cabins standing on a gravel track that ran out into a field before looping back to the parking lot. Beyond the motel the landscape consisted of cornfields.

Not much else.

Seems like a quiet place. No cops . . .

Duke said, 'You planning on us walking everywhere, Norm?'

'Uh?'

Boots slid her fingers inside the top of her tank top to pluck it away from her breasts. 'It's too warm to walk.'

The duo sat beside him. Their faces were flushed with heat. That and too many miles on the road.

Norman was doubtful. 'Yeah, but . . .'

'But what?'

'The cops are going to be looking for two guys and a girl with short bl—' He was going to say bleached hair but you didn't mess with Boots; he neatly morphed the words into '*Blond* hair.'

Duke shrugged. 'We're not in a red Jeep Cherokee. All the clerk will see are three ordinary folk in a truck.'

'Yeah, going to visit our white-haired grandmother.' Boots snickered.

'Drive us in, Norm.' Duke slid him a tough-guy look. 'Don't make me ask twice.'

'I just thought—'

'Just thought shit, Norm. It's been a long day. The lady needs to bathe her beautiful bod. Okay?'

'Okay.'

Norman clunked the gears. The truck lurched forward onto the Motel Ha-Ha driveway.

Boots leaned forward, fanning her fat throat with her hand.

Trotter hands, Norman thought. *How can anyone be attracted to the pig-faced woman?*

But you *are, aren't you, Norm?*

Shit, damn straight. That's it with sexual lust. Sometimes – most times! – you just can't control it.

And out the window goes your better judgment.

'Motel Ha-Ha,' Boots repeated, seeing the sign standing proud of the reception office roof. 'Funny name.'

Duke nodded. 'You mean funny ha-ha?'

Good joke. Norman laughed.

'What's so funny, Norm boy?' Duke sounded irritated for some reason.

'The joke.'

'What joke?'

'Motel Ha-Ha. Funny ha-ha.'

'Are you pulling my rod, Norm?'

'No.'

'Better toe the line, Normy boy. You gotta show some respect.'

'Okay, guys. Argue when we're in the room. I'm so close to that shower now I can almost feel it on my boobies. Norman, check in.'

'Me, check in?'

Duke reached over Boots to flick Norman's shoulder with the back of his hand. The gesture was aggressive, ill tempered rather than friendly.

What's eating Duke?

'Okay, okay,' Norman said. He wanted to avoid a confrontation.

'Oooh, you're a hero,' Boots said, stretching luxuriously. 'Sooner I get out of these dirty clothes the better. My feet feel like two oven-baked chickens. My fanny's just cooked, too.'

Duke said to Norman, 'Step on it, bud.'

'I'll need cash. The cops will be able to trace us through my MasterCard.'

Boots pushed back her sweat-damp hair before handing him the wad of notes that they'd taken from the old guy, who was now sleeping the sleep of eternity in his dusty crawl space. Relieved to get out of the cab and away from the gruesome twosome, Norman trotted across the dusty driveway to the timber office. An accommodation tariff sat on a table just inside the window alongside a vase of purple flowers. The place was far from modern but it looked clean.

The prices were reasonable, too.

Norman pushed open the door. A guy of around forty sat at the desk. More of the purple flowers stood in vases on the desk. The room smelt of pine and flowers.

A good place, Norman thought and wished he was here by himself. *Or with a girl.*

Any girl but Boots.

The clerk looked up with a bright, welcoming smile. 'Hello there. Cabin for one?'

'Three.'

'No problem, sir.' The guy was smartly dressed, albeit in black pants and a black roll-neck sweater. Even his hair was an intense black that matched the clothes. Could have been a dance instructor with that slim build and air of poise.

'If I could ask you to complete the registration card. Vehicle license. Home address. Names of occupants. Etcetera, etcetera.'

'Sure.' Norman was getting his cool back now that he was away from grumpy ol' Duke. He wrote fictitious details in the boxes on the form, though he glanced back and wrote the license-plate number – the actual number. That was one detail that the registration clerk could check out there and then.

The clerk said, 'My name is Darren. If you need anything just call. Would you prefer a two-bedroom cabin or a three?'

'A three-bedroom's great,' Norman said.

Jeez, he thought. *A room of my own. I could use some private time right now. Killing two cops takes a while to absorb.*

The rest of the registration procedure went smoothly. Norman paid cash for one night. As he finished up counting the notes he glanced at the timber wall behind the desk. There were five picture frames. Each one contained the cover of a TV guide. A couple featured single-person portrait photographs of a handsome Hispanic-looking guy. The others were of a posed group of men and women in white coats.

Norman looked from the photograph of the dark-haired guy to Darren the clerk as he counted the cash out into a drawer. Darren glanced up. He smiled when he saw where Norman was looking.

'Yeah, this office also doubles as the altar to my ego.' He smiled again. 'Or Altar Ego, as it were.'

Norman blinked. 'You're Doctor Sanchez Guido?'

'In another life.' Darren tapped the printed card standing upright in a holder on the desk. 'Now Darren Klein, dispensing rooms in the Motel Ha-Ha.'

'Shit! Uh, excuse my language.'

'No problem. I love the word. Must do, the times I use it.'

'But shit, man. *Intensive Care*? I used to love that show.'

'No shitting?' The clerk studied him with those handsome brown eyes. 'I guess you caught the reruns. You'd have been too young to see it first time out.'

'You played the doctor who all the nurses fell in love with. Hey, even my sister had the *Intensive Care* cast poster on her bedroom wall.'

'We looked good back then. A long time ago, though.'

'Just wait until I tell her.'

Then his stomach dropped. *If I ever see Sis again. Cop killers don't just go home whenever they feel like it. I'm on the run now.*

'*Intensive Care* was good to us,' Darren said as he lifted a key from a board that held a bunch of others. It had a bright yellow fob the size of a flattened table-tennis ball. 'My first pro acting job, and it ran for six series. But – let me think – the last episode aired ten years ago to the month.' He shrugged as he handed Norman the key. 'Time moves on. Different places. Different roles.'

'You quit TV?'

'I prefer live work.' He winked. 'I'm playing a motel clerk now.'

'It's . . . different.'

'Yeah, different is a good word. Not too judgmental. There you go, sir. Cabin twenty-one. It's at the far end of the lot. Have a nice stay.'

'Thanks.'

'Say.' Darren had an idea. 'We're having a barbecue tonight. A few beers, that kind of thing. Why don't you join us?'

'Us?'

'Yeah, I'm in partnership with some of the guys from the show. Nurses Lowe and Petri. Guti the paramedic. And Doctors Rennin, Brown and Pearman.'

'Doctor Pearman? But he was the guy who gave your fiancée the insulin overdose, then tried to embezzle the children's charity.'

'It was just a show, sir.'

'Ah, of course.'

'They're really nice people.'

'I'm staying here with a couple of friends.'

'Bring them. More the merrier.'

'Sure. Thanks.'

But Norman thought: *No way. Not those two lowlifes. I'll slip out myself. Just think. To meet the cast of* Intensive Care. *These people were household names!*

Then why did they vanish from the show-business radar?

'There's a patio area round the back,' Darren said. 'Amble up between eight and nine. We're as informal as you can get round here.'

'Great, thanks.' Norman was pleased. 'I'll see you later.'

'Ciao.'

'Took your own sweet time,' Duke said.

'We were baking in here. It's like an oven.'

Boots sat sideways in the driver's seat of the truck so that her plump legs dangled out. The heels of her dirty white boots thumped against the vehicle's metalwork as she swung her feet from side to side.

Norman was more than ready to fire back an irritated: '*Why didn't you get outta the truck and sit in the shade?*' But Duke had been antsy. He wasn't the kind of guy you got angry.

Remember the knife he keeps in his *boots?*

Norman remembered. Wasn't in a hurry to feel that blade part his ribs.

Instead: 'I got us registered. We've gotta be discreet so I didn't want to rush it and make the clerk suspicious.'

'Yeah, like we walk in terror of the big bad motel clerk. He'll be a wuss faggot boy like you, Norm, old buddy.'

What's eating you? Norman wondered.

Boots swung her legs into the cab as Norman climbed in behind her.

169

'I got the key,' he said holding it up by its bright yellow fob.

'Wuppy-do, wuss. Now if it ain't too much trouble, boy, drive us to the room.'

The pine cabin was roomy with three bedrooms, a lounge area boasting a kitchen in the corner, and a good-sized bathroom. The sun was low in the sky as Norman closed the door behind him and locked it.

'Afraid someone's gonna steal you from us, Normy?' Duke lit a cigarette, then lay back on the sofa, gazing up at the ceiling.

Boots closed the blinds. 'Don't want anyone lookin' for free.' She peeled off her tank top to expose her jiggling breasts. They looked too small for that wide-shouldered body of hers. 'Norman?'

'Yeah?'

'Wanna soap my back in the shower?'

Jeez, not at this moment. I want to lie down in my own room, just be alone and still, and not have to think or talk or listen to the gruesome twosome articulate their same old shit.

'I might grab some sleep.'

'You sure you ain't no faggot?' Duke blew smoke toward the ceiling.

'Please, Normy. Come and cover me in bubbles.'

'That's an offer no red-blooded man can refuse, bud.'

Norman forced a smile. 'Sure. I'll be right in.'

Boots said, 'I'll just drop my bag in my room.' She smiled. 'I'm getting naked in there, so no peeking when I come out.' She laughed.

Duke didn't laugh. His face was grim.

Norman thought: *Best grin and bear it. Duke's acting so weird. He's got a dangerous look about him.*

Boots slipped through one of the pine doors. Norman heard her 'oooh' and 'aaah' over clean sheets and a soft bed. More purple flowers in pink vases adorned every room. Norman thought of saying something to Duke to placate him.

Can't think of anything.

Come to that, anything I say might enrage the man. He's unpredictable. Dangerous.

Crazy dangerous.

Norman left Duke smoking. He went into his bedroom where he peeled himself out of his dusty threads. Ah, it felt good to be out of the clothes. To feel that cool, air-con atmosphere taking the heat out of his skin. The bed looked so clean that he longed to lie down on it right away. Then—

'Normy . . . oh, Normy . . . you ready to shower?'

Norman sighed when he heard the voice. Then he took a breath, puffed out his chest.

Show-time. Here goes . . .

Keeping his voice pleasant, he sang out, 'Coming.'

There were clean folded towels on the bed so he wrapped one round his hips. Then he left the bedroom, walked by the supine Duke. Still smoking. Still staring ceilingward.

As he passed Duke the man stretched out his arm and gripped Norman by the wrist. The grip was the fiercest that Norman had ever felt.

'Don't ever shit me, Norman. If you ever get me angry, I'm gonna . . .'

He grunted, then let go of Norman's arm, breaking eye contact at the same time to resume his ceiling stare.

Norman shuddered.

Yeah. He was reading the warning signs. *A volcanic anger's brewing in the guy.* Making Duke's eyes meaner than ever.

'Oh, Normy . . .' Boots's voice wailed from the bathroom. 'Normy, Normy, Normy.'

Norman walked into the bathroom. He was wary now. He expected to feel the point of Duke's blade between his shoulder blades at any moment. He closed the door behind him, feeling thankful for the barrier it put between Duke and himself.

Already the room was filled with steam. Water hissed into the shower stall.

Behind a semitransparent plastic curtain a figure moved.

She's rubbing shower gel into her breasts, he told himself. *Then she's working down over the swell of her stomach.*

Down, down . . .

Into that enticing area between her legs.

Norman groaned.

Ten seconds ago he'd been worried about what Duke was winding himself up to do.

Now . . .

He groaned again. Boots – ugly, unlovable Boots. She worked the voodoo on him.

He looked down as his body betrayed him.

The front of his towel had formed itself into a pyramid.

'Hmm, Norman. You come right in here and let me bathe you, honey.' Boots moaned with pleasure as her silhouette soaped itself.

God, he was so aroused.

So aroused that it hurt. Norman let the towel fall from him, then he slid aside the shower curtain and stepped into the stall with Boots.

Chapter Twenty-five

Norman finished making whoopee with Boots in the shower by seven o'clock that evening. She swathed herself in towels, not to mention dreamy smiles, then disappeared into her room.

Norman dried himself. Shaved.

His knees still shook after what he'd done to her.

She'd loved it. Had begged for more.

When Norman left the bathroom he found Duke asleep on the sofa. The cigarette had burned itself out. Now the dead butt poked from his lips.

Norman didn't wake him.

Didn't relish arousing the tough guy's wrath.

He went to his own room, slipped on a pair of clean undershorts. Then he lay down on the bed. The clock radio scrolled over to 7.18. Outside it was still bright but there was an orange tint to the sunlight now.

When Norman closed his eyes he thought: *I'll just rest here for five minutes.*

When Norman opened his eyes again the clock radio told him it was 8.53.

'Shoot,' he murmured. 'Barbecue time.'

Darren had told him to turn up to the barbecue between eight and nine. *Sweet Jesus* – despite everything, all the crud, the sex with Boots, the slayings, he wanted to meet up with the cast of *Intensive Care*. There had to be a pretty cool story about how half a dozen actors from one of the most popular TV shows of its decade had wound up out in the middle of Nowhereville. And running a motel, to boot.

What about Duke and Boots? They'll want to come.

Boots will wet herself when she hears that there are famous actors having a barbecue just a minute's walk from the cabin. This will be paradise for a backwoods girl like her.

Shit. Make something up.

Tell them you're just going for a walk.

But that was the kind of thing that Duke didn't want to hear. *Might piss the big guy off.* The notion of Norman just walking for the pleasure of it could prove to be a major source of irritation.

'Oh well, nothing ventured,' Norman grunted.

In ten seconds flat he'd pulled on a clean white T-Shirt, stone-hued chinos and sandals. No doubt Duke would have something smart to say about Norman's choice of clothes, too.

Norman popped his head round the bedroom door to the living room. It was gloomy now. But to his relief – major, MAJOR relief – Duke was still asleep on the sofa. The butt of the unlit cigarette looked to have taken root in his surly mouth. When he realized there was no sound coming from Boots's room either he checked in on her.

She lay bare, ass up.

Dead to the world, too.

Yeah, come to that she even looked like a freshly killed porker. Now that her muscles had gone slack as she snored softly, her face looked as if it was in the process of melting. The features drooped, then slid sideways as gravity pulled them down to the pillow where part of her face pooled.

Norman looked at her wide rear. The crack between her ass-cheeks had become a deep gully that you could lose a moose in. And deep down in the center was the intimate place that one of his friends called 'the old Jap's eye.'

Norman grinned. *Wow.* If he'd had a firecracker right then he didn't think he could have stopped himself.

The gruesome twosome were both sleeping royally. He could slip out without having to answer any questions.

Stealthily, he exited Boots's room, crossed the living room to the cabin door. He glanced back.

Hell.

Those two didn't even seem like regular sleepers. There was

something of the corpse about them. They slept like they were rehearsing for the biggest sleep of all.

The sun was low over the cornfields when Norman headed up toward the motel office. From here he could see the reverse of the name sign that was lit already as dusk fell. Motel Ha-Ha.

A friendly kind of name, Norman figured. *In a funny kinda way.*

Behind the motel office a tall, thick hedge enclosed an area of land. He saw that an arch had been cut into the vegetation to form a narrow gateway. He heard conversation, the sound of a cork being pulled.

This's gotta be it, Normy.

Now he caught the aroma of flame-seared meat. His mouth watered. He stepped through over the threshold into an enclosed lawn area. And there they were. The cast of *Intensive Care.*

Norman goggled, even though they weren't in the uniforms he'd gotten to know so well after watching close on a hundred episodes. The nurses had worn surgical green tops and pants. *Sex-eee!* The doctors had worn pristine white coats. He saw Nurses Lowe and Petri. Petri was the male nurse, Guti the Native American paramedic. There was Doctor Sanchez Guido (aka Darren, motel clerk) flipping burgers at the barbecue grill. Then Doctor Rennin, a glamorous redheaded woman of around forty-five, sipping a cocktail. Nearby were Doctors Brown and Pearman, their hair now graying as they jogged through life into their fifties.

Holy shit.

The cast of *Intensive Care.* Despite the passing of the years their glamour still shone brightly.

Doctor Sanchez (aka Darren) noticed Norman.

'Hey, sir. Good of you to show.'

'This I wouldn't miss,' Norman said with feeling.

Darren waved him closer. 'Come and meet our troupe of players.' He laid a steak on the barbecue. Instantly it began to sizzle with the heat. Puffs of flame jumped up from the coals. 'Everyone . . . hey, guys. This is one of our customers. Mister—'

Norman jumped in. 'Norman. Call me Norman.'

'Welcome aboard, Norman.' The guy who played the evil Doctor Pearman smiled. He looked like such a warm and friendly guy. Nothing like his screen persona.

Norman smiled back and hello'd and hi'd his way round the group.

Shook hands. The redheaded woman held his hand longer than the rest and fixed him with her green-eyed gaze as she greeted him.

Darren said, 'Norman. Give me a hand with these burgers, won't you? They're just about done.'

'Sure.'

'Plates are there on the shelf under the table.'

'Got them.'

'If I pile the burgers onto the plate you can hand them to Gillian over there, although you'll know her better as Nurse Lowe. She's been slicing tomato and cheese for the buns.'

'Great.' Norman was in awe.

Here I am, mingling with the famous beneath open skies. It's like a Hollywood party.

Evil Doctor Pearman handed him a bottle of beer. *Gee, he really is a nice guy.*

Not like his on-screen character who blocked IV tubes or deliberately withheld anesthetic during surgery, so that the patient woke up screaming with their guts spilling out of their stomachs.

In real life this guy wouldn't tread on an ant. Never mind sew up the lips of the kid in series three. Norman could even recall the dialogue word for word.

'Now you can't tell the police what you've just seen,' the Doctor had intoned as he pushed the suture needle through the kid's top lip. 'What's that you say, child? You want anesthetic? Let me tell you, young sir, there'll be no pain relief on my *watch.'*

Oh boy, oh boy. What an episode. What a series!

'You happy with your cabin?' Doctor Sanchez – oops, Darren – asked.

'Fine,' Norman enthused. 'Really comfortable.'

'And your friends?'

'Oh, they couldn't come. They're catching up on some sleep.'

'No, I mean do they like their accommodation?'

'Oh, sure. Say, Darren?'

'Yes?'

'What was the real reason for canceling the series?'

'The real reason?' Darren raised his dark eyebrows.

'Man, that show could still be running. It was how a medic drama should be.'

'It was a good show. But the real reason it was canceled was it got too expensive.'

'But it had millions of viewers.'

Darren shrugged. 'If a show stops being profitable – even if it's watched by everyone plus the President's mother – they'll pull the plug.'

'That's not fair.'

'Tell me about it. Here, the steak's done if you like it rare. Grab a plate. The cutlery's on the tray.'

Norman gratefully received the sizzling steak onto his plate. It looked so inviting but he didn't want to stop talking to Darren. 'Surely they could have trimmed the budget and kept the series running.'

'They did.'

'Uh?'

'*LA ICU.*'

'*LA ICU?*' Norman shook his head, puzzled.

'Exactly. No one remembers it. They sacked the cast of *Intensive Care*, then applied the format to a new show with new actors – low-cost actors – and set it in an intensive care unit in LA.'

'Hence the name.'

Doctor Pearman joined them. 'And, dear boy, did you ever hear of such a diabolical title for a show? *LA ICU?* I ask you. Who knew what it even meant?'

'So here we are ten years later. Hey, Norman, sit to the table there so you can eat your steak. We'll join you.'

Norman sat at a picnic table with Darren and Doctor Pearman sitting opposite.

So I know it's not really Doctor Pearman. But then, I don't know his real name.

Don't like to ask.

Hell, it's cool to think of him as Doctor Pearman. The baby-butcher of Ward Thirteen. Heh-heh-heh ...

Norman grinned. 'Sorry. I can't stop smiling.'

Doctor Pearman smiled back. 'No problem, my boy. We like happy people round here, don't we, Darren?'

'Sure do.'

Norman cut into this steak. Luscious red blood flowed from its near-raw center. 'It's just that I remember the episode from the last season when the college student was admitted onto the ward.'

'How I hated college students.' The white-haired man grinned. 'At least, my character did.'

'Then you insisted on performing an emergency circumcision on the guy.' Norman sliced another piece of bloody beef from the fillet. 'And as you picked up your scalpel, ready to slice off the foreskin, the student cries out: "Anesthetic! Give me anesthetic!" and you say, cool as ice—' Norman paused, giving the actor an opportunity to speak his catch-phrase line.

'"Let me tell you, young sir, there'll be no pain relief on my watch." Ah . . . Circumcision, where is thy sting? As the immortal bard might have penned.' Doctor Pearman smiled. 'Of course, every episode required me to utter the notorious phrase at least once: "There'll be no pain relief on my watch."'

'It's a great line.'

'I wish I had a dollar for every time I've declaimed it since that final season.'

Norman swallowed a mouthful of the delicious steak. Refreshing himself with a chug of beer he asked, 'But why did you guys quit acting, and . . .' He didn't finish the sentence, merely gestured in the direction of the motel office with his beer bottle.

'Buy a motel?' Darren shrugged.

'You were still famous.'

'Yeah, but ask even famous actors how secure their career really is.'

Doctor Pearman nodded his agreement. 'Parts come and go. Shows open and close. But motels are here to stay. A poet might wax lyrical on their constancy in the American way of life.'

'So we pooled what was left of our paychecks and the Motel Ha-Ha was ours.'

Norman swallowed a piece of steak. 'Motel Ha-Ha. It's an unusual name.'

Darren answered, 'Some people come here thinking there's a Native American connection.'

Doctor Pearman gave a theatrical wave of his hand. 'But the truth is a little more prosaic, my dear boy.'

'When I floated the idea with the cast that we pool our resources and invest in the motel business their response was . . .' Darren nodded a cue to Doctor Pearman.

'Ha-ha.'

'They all scoffed. At first. But I ran the numbers for them.'

'And here we are this beautiful evening.' Doctor Pearman sipped his wine. 'Prosperous businessmen and women. In the appropriately named Motel Ha-Ha, a reminder of our initial doubts.'

'And . . .' Darren worked his way through his hamburger. 'It's working out so well we're planning on expanding, buying a couple of motels nearer to town.'

'And expanding the units we have here,' Doctor Pearman added.

Norman thought back to his arrival at Motel Ha-Ha. 'But it doesn't seem that busy. There weren't many cars parked at the cabins. In fact, I can't remember seeing—'

'No, dear boy, there weren't. That's because passing trade isn't our main business. Conventions are the thing.'

'Conventions?'

'Yes.' Doctor Pearman warmed to his theme. 'We take mass bookings for the entire motel. Last week we had a hundred Baptists on a Scripture-interpretation course.'

'Next week we have a bunch of horror writers coming from all over the world. That'll be one whole week, fully catered, and pre-paid bar. Those horror writers drink like fishes. Just their beer bill's gonna pay for the upkeep of this place for six months.'

'Motel business is a great business to be in, my boy.' Doctor Pearman stroked back his silver hair. 'Many people prefer our homely environment to those of the big hotels.' He gave a theatrical shudder. 'Soulless things, my dear boy. Soulless.'

Darren looked at Norman thoughtfully for a moment.

'You know . . . I shouldn't be saying this, Norman. But you seem to me to be a decent and honest young man.'

'I am, sir,' Norman said brightly. Then he thought: *If you disregard killing a pair of cops.*

Darren appeared to be wrestling with some dilemma. 'So I wondered if—'

'Darren, Darren.' Doctor Pearman shook his head. 'This young man wouldn't be interested in what we have to offer.'

Norman's curiosity was tickled. 'Interested in what?'

'Well, Norman. You see we're looking for . . . Actively looking for, but . . .' He quickly shook his head. 'No, my partner's right. It's not for you.'

179

'It might be,' Norman said eagerly. Not having an inkling what the two former actors were talking about but passionately craving to be part of whatever it was they were discussing.

'Investors, Norman.'

'Investors?'

Doctor Pearman nodded wisely. 'We're inviting people we can trust to invest in our motels.'

'But we have to be careful,' Darren added. 'Our investors must be discreet. They mustn't talk about the business.'

'Why?'

'The return is so great that we fear a gold rush.'

'You see, Norman, we're breaking new ground by catering for conventions at motels. If our competitors were to learn what kind of profits – huge, huge profits – we're reaping they'd rush to copy us.'

Norman breathed out, seeing dollar signs float in front of his eyes. 'I understand.'

'So, you appreciate, dear boy, we have to be selective. We only chose individuals who we know are discreet.'

'Absolutely.'

'So . . .' Darren rested his cold beer bottle down on the table. 'Are you interested?'

'Very, but – uh, how much?'

'As much as you care to invest, dear boy. Speaking for Darren, I think we know a man of integrity and vision when we see one.'

'Thank you, sir,' Norman gushed.

'We've pegged the minimum investment at five.'

'Five hundred dollars?' Norman ran calculations through his mind. 'I might be able to manage that, if you give me a few days.'

'Norman.' Doctor Pearman looked pained. The same flinch he'd perfected in his days in the medic drama when his professional integrity was questioned. 'Norman. Norman. Dear boy, we are talking in thousands here.'

'Five thousand dollars?'

'A trifling sum, when all's said and done, but it is symbolic of your faith in our business acumen.'

'Oh, sure, sure.' Norman nodded, trying to appear wise. 'Five thousand dollars.'

'Does that sound reasonable?'

'Oh, yes. Completely reasonable.'

Maybe I can raise the five thou on MasterCard? Or maybe I can rob a bank? After all, after killing a couple of cops armed robbery is no great shakes.

Doctor Pearman raised his glass. 'Then may I propose a toast to our new business partner. And I have never seen such a wise head on such young shoulders. If I—'

'You rogues! You damn rogues!'

Startled by the sound of a female voice in an outbreak of sheer fury, Norman turned to see a young woman in a white nurse's uniform come striding through the entrance to the enclosed lawn.

Norman goggled. The woman was curvaceous in the nurse's outfit. Her dark hair was cut short. Somehow angular, too. The effect, combined with her flashing eyes, was formidable.

She advanced on the table where Norman was sitting with the two men.

'So,' she said, looking at Norman, 'who's this pathetic bastard?' She gave a contemptuous toss of her head. 'The next poor lamb to the slaughter?'

Chapter Twenty-six

The moment the woman began advancing across the grass, everyone stopped talking.

Stared.

Bubble burst.

Party pooped.

Norman had been starstruck in the company of these still-glamorous actors and actresses. Now—

BINGO!

What was I doing, agreeing to invest money in a motel?

The guy who played Doctor Pearman gave a charming smile. 'Dee-Dee.'

'Don't Dee-Dee me.'

Jesus. This nurse – was she a real nurse? – was formidable.

Norman thought: *I'm in love.*

His stare swept over the nurse's figure in the tight-fitting uniform. How old was she? Twenty-three? Twenty-five?

Her short-cut hair was immaculate.

Dark.

Glossy.

Uh, not like Boots. Not bleached. Not spiky.

This was beautiful hair.

The nurse strode up, her gaze scanning the food and drink on the tables.

'Dee-Dee, honey,' Doctor Pearman purred. 'Sit down; have a glass of wine.'

'Oh Dad, you promised you wouldn't do this,' the woman called Dee-Dee groaned.

Darren tried a disarming smile.

It looked on the thin side.

'We're only entertaining one of our guests,' Darren said.

'Of course,' Doctor Pearman agreed. 'We thought a little barbecue. A pleasant interlude.'

'Interlude, my eye,' Dee-Dee stormed. When she spoke it was directed at everyone on the lawn. 'You've all decided to put on one of your shows again, so you can fleece the first no-brained sap that comes your way.'

'Hey,' Norman said, stung by her insult.

She turned to Doctor Pearman again. 'Dad. We can't save all this by defrauding our guests.'

Norman stared at the woman in the nurse's uniform.

She stared back.

'You oughta go,' she told him.

'You were in the show?' Norman asked, puzzled. 'I don't remember –'

'No, I wasn't in *Intensive Care*.' The woman sounded as if she'd explained this so many times that it bored her to repeat it again. 'I'm too young for that pile of crap. Besides, I'm no actor. I'm the only one here with medical qualifications. I'm a nurse at St. Jude's Hospital downtown. A *real* nurse.'

She looked real enough.

Look good through and through.

Norman noticed that the zipper on the uniform that was all glacial whiteness in the light of the setting sun ran from her throat all the way down to the pit of her stomach.

Now that's a zipper worth unzipping, he thought as he watched the angry rise and fall of her breasts.

'Sir,' she said in a softer voice. 'You won't report this to the police, will you?'

'Uh, no, of course not, but—'

'But you're wondering what's going on?'

Norman nodded.

Dee-Dee walked round the assembled cast of ex-actors and former actresses. They had that glassy-eyed expression of people who know that they're in the wrong. As she walked she explained.

'They've probably told you . . . uhm?'

'Norman.'

'They'll have explained, Norman, how after the show was canceled because they'd all demanded huge hikes in salary they bought the motel?'

Norman made with the nod again, concealing his previous ignorance of the real reason for the cancellation of Intensive Care.

'They didn't explain that they were so inept, and so lacking in business acumen, that they bought a motel that wasn't on a major highway?'

'No, they said it was thriving.'

'Thriving, huh? We're lucky to have a dozen paying guests a week. Isn't that right, Dad?'

Doctor Pearman nodded.

'Isn't that so, Darren?'

Uncomfortable, Darren nodded, too.

'So this bunch of retired thespians live in the motel, taking it in turns to play the roles of chalet cleaners, motel clerks, groundskeepers.'

Doctor Pearman looked pained. 'This young man doesn't want to hear all this . . . this *fact*. Facts are the weighted boots of reality. Facts, my dear, make the world miserably trudge when it should be dancing.'

'Dad, you can't charm people out of their money. That's a painful fact of reality that you've got to learn.' Dee-Dee shook her head sadly.

Norman got up to speed. 'You mean there are no conventions? No horror writers turning up next week?'

'Alas, no, dear boy.'

'And we couldn't even give the place away,' Dee-Dee told Norman. 'So it's my nurse's paycheck that feeds these scoundrels. It meets the loan payments, too – *just* – and this is how the damned ingrates repay me.'

'Are you sure you wouldn't like a nice glass of chilled white wine?' Darren asked.

'Maybe I should, seeing as I've paid for all this.' She glared at Darren. 'What happened to the list I gave you for the groceries?'

'Well, eh, we—'

'I don't recall putting wine and T-bone steaks on the list.'

'No. Dee-Dee, we're sorry, we thought—'

'Thought? That's it, you never *do* think. Dad, you could go to jail for trying to pull a stunt like this.'

Norman watched Doctor Pearman swallow. This was getting too much for him.

'I don't think they really meant any harm by it,' Norman told her.

'That's just it.' She sounded weary. 'They are harmless. They're ineffectual, too. They cook up grand schemes over martinis, and they're all just daydreams. I gave Darren a hundred dollars to buy the groceries on my list. A list budgeted so tightly because we don't have any money in the bank. And look, they've spent it all on beer, wine, fancy steaks. Shit . . . I don't think I can carry on anymore.'

'Darling, darling,' Doctor Pearman cooed. 'We can work something out.'

'No, you can't,' she said. 'None of you can.'

Norman winced at the expressions on the faces around him.

Sorrow. Guilt. Remorse.

Dee-Dee continued, 'When it comes to remembering your lines and pretending to be someone else you're great. When you try and live in the real world you're . . .' She shrugged. 'Oh, what's the point?'

There was a pause while no one spoke. No one moved.

Insects hovered on the air as day turned into night. Somewhere a sensor activated floodlights that lit the lawn a garish green. A hamburger that had been forgotten on the barbecue gave a pop. It started to burn with a greasy yellow flame.

Phew, what a night.

Sure is cool to hang out with the cast of Intensive Care, *though. Even if they are a bunch of conmen.*

Not very good conmen.

Now this girl called Dee-Dee shows up, the daughter of Doctor Pearman.

Probably just in time before he, Norman, went out to rob a liquor store for the five thou.

It was the kind of pause that could be filled by anything.

More remonstrations from the formidable though sexy Dee-Dee?

A tearful breakdown by Doctor Pearman? Leastways, by the guy who played him.

But:

Three figures stepped through the gateway in the hedge.

Two burly guys. And a rugged woman of around thirty.

They wore police uniforms.

Dared he hope that these were actors, too? Three tired players from a cop drama wanting a room for the night.

Dee-Dee groaned. 'See, Dad? One of your victims has reported you.'

'Oh my,' he breathed. 'I don't think jail is my preferred venue.'

Darren paled.

The rest of the has-been actors and actresses looked as if they'd faint.

'The game's up,' Doctor Pearman muttered.

Dee-Dee took a step toward the three officers. 'Please. I can explain. My father is an actor. He tends to live in a fantasy world.'

'Dee-Dee?' Doctor Pearman looked pained.

'Whatever my father and his friends have done I'm sure we can resolve it.'

The three cops slipped revolvers from their holsters.

Aimed them across the table laden with wine bottles and potato salad.

'My dear sirs, madam.' Doctor Pearman rose to his feet. 'There is no need for weaponry. I shall not resist arrest.'

The oldest cop spoke. 'Wiscoff. Norman Wiscoff. I have a warrant for your arrest.'

Now all stares swept toward Norman as the three police officers closed in, aiming their handguns at his chest.

Norman swallowed a lump the size of Tennessee in his throat.

Tried to.

Failed.

His heart thudded against his chest.

The female officer reached down to pull out a pair of handcuffs from her utility belt.

Still kept her stare and the gun bead on him, though.

Norman raised his hands.

'Okay, okay.' His voice came as a rasp. 'You've caught me.'

That was when it all became too much for Darren.

'Oh my God.'

He fainted. His head hit the tabletop with a forceful *clunk*.

All three officers glanced at him.

This is your one and only chance, Normy, old buddy. Uncannily, it could have been Duke's voice in his ear.

Gotta take it.

Don't wanna shake and bake in The Chair.

Norman stood with his back to the hedge. Its branches were densely woven. It was taller than him.

If he could only . . .

He turned.

Ran hard at the hedge.

'Stop!'

Those were the cops' commands.

Don'tcha know what's gonna come next?

He was right.

Gunfire.

Bullets smacked into branches at either side of Norman, tearing holes through the greenery as he ran into the hedge. His weight and speed carried him through.

He busted out the other side. Then ran in zigzags to spoil the cops' aim. In the darkness he saw the bullets fly past him like spits of red fire.

Am I hit? I don't know. Can't feel anything.

But then, they say that if you're shot you don't feel anything.

At least, not at first.

Natural anesthetic.

In his mind he heard Doctor Pearman's chilling TV persona. *'What's that you say, child? You want anesthetic? Let me tell you, young sir, there'll be no pain relief on* my *watch.'*

Norman ran like crazy across the motel site. He weaved round cabins. Didn't know where he was going. Only knew that he had to get away from the cops.

A figure glided toward him from his right. In this near-darkness it looked like a ghost.

'Run straight down to the bottom of the plot.'

'Dee-Dee?'

'Keep running. They're right behind you!'

Glanced back.

No shit.

Flashlights.

Gotta run faster.

Beside him the slender nurse ran.

'Dee-Dee. What are you doing here?' he panted.

She flashed him a wild grin. 'Figured it was time I ran, too.'

They climbed over the fence. Dee-Dee hauled Norman by the arm, guiding him to a narrow track that ran between cornfields. A vehicle approached from behind.

'We can't outrun them,' he gasped.

'I don't wanna go back. I don't wanna keep working to keep those old has-beens in booze.'

Now wasn't the time to stop and discuss her folly. Norman sprinted.

The vehicle drew closer along the dirt track. Norman expected cruiser lights to whirl at any moment. Maybe the report of a twelve-gauge before the buckshot chewed his back to mincemeat.

The car pulled alongside them. From an open window came a voice:

'You two gonna jog all the way to Mexico?'

'Duke!'

He glanced sideways through the driver's open window.

Sure enough. Duke. Beside him, in the passenger seat, Boots.

'Get in,' Duke told them. He stopped the car.

Norman dragged open the rear door of the car. Dee-Dee bundled herself across the seat, her skirt rising up over her thighs.

Norman followed into the backseat, slammed the door shut behind him.

'Nice uniform,' Duke said to Dee-Dee.

Then he floored the gas pedal. The car roared away along the dirt track.

Chapter Twenty-seven

'I'm enjoying this,' Pamela told Lauren as she collected dirty dishes from the cafe table.

'Really?' Lauren smiled.

'First time I've waited tables in a restaurant.'

Lauren's smile broadened. 'You might find that the glamour wears off after a while.'

'It's good honest labor.'

'It is that. Filling an empty stomach is God's work.'

Pamela glanced askance at the other woman.

Lauren shook her head. 'No, I'm not particularly religious. But it *is* satisfying to put full plates of hot, tasty food in front of hungry customers. Oh, table seven needs more coffee, I'll just—'

'No, no,' Pamela insisted. 'I'll get it.'

'Who'd have thought it? Nine o'clock in the evening and we get a bus full of pool players.'

'They're good tippers, too.' Pamela smiled. 'I'll keep that coffee flowing.'

'You're a hero. I don't know what I'd have done without you.'

'No worries. Like I said, I'm loving it.'

'Say.' Lauren touched Pamela's arm as she turned to grab the coffee pot from the counter. 'You know you could make this a permanent arrangement?'

'Lauren? You're offering me a job here?'

'You like the work. I like how you handle customers. Kind of go together, don't they?'

'Jeez . . . I don't really know . . .'

'I'm not rushing you. Sleep on it tonight. Okay, looks as if those guys are ready for my apple pie and whipped cream.'

Man, the cafe was buzzing tonight. Pamela didn't have the uniform but she wore a dinky white cotton apron with pockets for her order pad and pen. Quickly she sashayed across the cafe to refill the coffee cups of four guys in white shirts. They were appreciative of the attention and made friendly comments. She'd expected some bawdy remarks but then she noticed the badge on the team shirts. *Shearville Pentecostal Chapel Pool Team.*

All the booths and tables were full to capacity. There must have been forty people on the team bus. But there'd be no rebel-rousing from these guys. They had plenty of appetite for steaks, lasagne, meatballs, pizza, even a Pits Burger or two, but no appetite for cussing or slapping the waitresses' butts.

The love of the Good Lord was intoxicating enough for them. They were happy with their sodas and coffee.

Pamela moved from table to table. Her offers of a refill were accepted with polite thanks.

She glanced back to see Lauren serving massive wedges of apple pie, topped with a gleaming mountain of whipped cream. Terry worked the griddle. He'd probably cooked more steaks tonight than he had in a week.

When Pamela returned to the counter with the coffeepots Terry glanced back at her. He was a slim, good-looking guy in his twenties, with a red-brown fringe that hung down to his eyebrows. Young-looking for his age. He could have passed for a high-school student with a wisp of dark hairs on his chin.

Probably only had to shave once a week.

He was perspiring hard. His was hot work.

Above the buzz of diners' conversation Pamela heard the sizzle of beef turning a succulent brown over the lick of flame.

'Pamela?'

'Yes, Terry?'

'A car full of people has just turned up. I'm running low on steak – would you bring more from the refrigerator, please?'

'Sure.'

'Refrigerator ain't in the kitchen. It's further out back in the utility.'

'Okay.' Lightly, she made her way round the back of the counter.

This was the first time that she'd actually been into the back of the cafe. It was all new.

Hope I don't walk into a closet by mistake.

Or the john.

Sight of the grizzled old-timer Hank sitting on the lavatory bowl while chewing a plug of baccy and dumping a fresh load wouldn't be the prettiest sight of the evening.

The kitchen was clean. It smelled of fresh herbs. There were gleaming stainless steel fixtures complemented by white-tiled walls. On shelves were catering-size cans of cooking oil, vegetables, coffee. Tubs of flour, sugar, salt, spices. Racks of cutlery, copper pans, tableware – a real working cafe kitchen. With Terry cooking behind the counter and Lauren serving apple pie to customers Pamela was alone back here.

Humming to herself, happy to be busy, she breezed through the kitchen.

Ahead lay a door.

She read a sign. UTILITY.

This's got to be it.

She pushed open the door. It was gloomy inside but she entered nonetheless. Terry needed to start grilling those steaks. The door swung back behind her. With it being night outside suddenly it was absolutely dark in the utility room.

Come to that, there might be no windows anyway.

She reached out to one side where the light switch should be. Groping for a switch in an unfamiliar room isn't easy.

Should have held open the door to the kitchen before switching on the light.

Goofball.

Might wind up tripping over a pail.

After all you've been through, to fall and kill your fool self in a culinary-related accident would be stupid beyond belief.

Unable to see anything but a glimmer of light in the crack of the kitchen door, Pamela set to work, searching with both hands. Her fingers found the wall. They ranged over it like a pair of five-legged spiders.

Though she could still see squat.

A shelf. Maybe the switch was above that.

She ran her hands across it.

Something sharp. Angular.

A plastic tub?

Something soft?

Cloths?

More objects. Cylindrical. Aerosols?

Just don't touch anything warm and furry.

Fondling mice in the dark isn't my thing.

She wasn't frightened. She even chuckled at the thought of it.

Yeah, mice. Right. Like I'd be scared of a little rodent after Rodney nearly killed me.

'Shit.'

She'd run her fingers round the obstacles in search of the elusive light switch when she knocked a flat surface with her knuckle. Whatever it was slipped off the shelf to make a light clattering sound on the floor.

Ooops. Hope that wasn't an antique clock.

After all, it's good here in Pits. I don't want to do anything that sours my relationship with a bunch of nice people.

'Oh, light switch,' Pamela breathed, 'where are you?'

Got it.

No.

A nail in the wall. Probably where Terry hangs his apron.

Ah!

Bingo!

Found switch – and—

Click.

The lights burst from the darkness with a brilliant intensity.

Pamela blinked.

Then looked down in the hope that a precious Swiss clock wasn't lying on the concrete floor in a mass of cogs.

Nope.

Just a shoebox and a bunch of . . .

'Uh, that's odd.'

She stared in surprise at what had spilled from the box.

False teeth. Spectacles. Wristwatches.

She bent down. There must have been five or six of each. Those sets of false teeth didn't look too tasty.

Some stained. Nicotine. Coffee. Red wine.

One bottom set of dentures still had a little green fleck of broccoli stuck between incisors.

The watches.

Mostly cheap everyday watches with plastic casings. A couple worked. Then a bunch of spectacles that could have been worn by a mix of young and old.

Pamela grimaced as she put the spilled contents back into their box. 'Ooo-eee.'

Handling a stranger's eyeglasses was a little on the icky side. Handling a stranger's false teeth was a supper-raiser. As she quickly picked up the pink and white dentures she gulped down the taste of the chili that she'd eaten earlier. When she'd scooped them all up she quickly rose to her feet.

Returned the box to the shelf that was at her shoulder height.

The things you find.

What's worse? Stranger's dentures? Or a used condom?

Pamela pushed the box back onto the shelf. The shelf was a deep one with kitchen-cleaning products lining its front. Concealed behind the regular domestic stuff were another two shoeboxes without lids. One contained sets of car keys. They'd been there long enough to have a spider's web spun across them to create a dusty membrane over the box.

Saw the keys clearly enough.

Some with personalized key rings.

DAD'S KEYS . . . SOUVENIR OF MIAMI . . . I GOT OUT OF ALCATRAZ . . . As well as those with messages there was a novelty skull fob, a mini plastic hamburger, a red plastic heart.

'House keys, too.'

Strange.

The next box contained a dusty array of pens, asthma puffers, cigarette lighters, button badges (JESUS SAVES, MILWAUKEE CANINE LEAGUE, I BELIEVE, PEACE), penknives, a pencil sharpener, one of those little pocket diaries that were smaller than a carton of cigarettes. Pamela could see that was three years old from the gold numerals embossed on a black leather cover.

Curious.

Must be lost property. But can customers misplace so many sets of dentures?

193

Surely it's the kind of thing you notice is missing?

Can't be easy to gum through a pork chop, can it?

Car keys, too. Soon as you got back in your car after leaving the cafe you'd realize they'd gone.

She plucked the diary from the box.

Opened it.

Benny Loscoff, age 10 (and last will and testy mint).

Pamela turned over the dinky little page; the next one was crammed with a child's handwriting in pencil.

My name is Benny. This is what happened to me and my bud, Gyp, when we ran away from—

Footsteps on tiled floor.

Pamela heard the noise. Suddenly she was flustered; not wanting to be discovered here in the utility room, reading this child's diary from the box full of lost possessions.

She stared at the door to the kitchen.

Heard approaching feet.

Any second the door would fly open and—

Shit.

Hands moving lightning fast, she plucked her order book from the pocket of her apron and threw it on the floor. Then she slipped the tiny diary into the pocket just as—

Just as the door swung open.

'Lauren, hi.'

I'm blushing. I know I'm blushing.

'Pamela? Is there a problem?'

'No . . . no.' She grinned in an attempt to look relaxed.

'Terry said you'd come to collect the steak.'

'Oh, I was just about to get it, and . . . and I dropped my order book.'

'Pamela. It's there on the floor.'

'Oh.'

'Behind you.'

'Right. Great. Thanks. Can't see for looking, can I?' She picked it up. Stuffed it into the apron pocket. Felt the hard oblong of the diary beneath it.

Hope its shape doesn't show through the cotton apron.

'I'll get the steak,' Pamela told Lauren, backing across the utility room to three large refrigerators. One was marked DAIRY. The second MEAT. The third OTHER.

'No, don't, Pamela.' Lauren's expression was suddenly hard.

'Pardon me?'

'*I'll* bring the steak.'

'But I was just—'

'No, don't worry. The refrigerator door sticks.' Lauren smiled. It looked forced. 'Got a mind of its own, that door has.'

'Oh, right.'

'Will you attend table three? They're ready for ice cream.'

'Yeah, sure. Uh ...' Pamela was going to add something inconsequential so as not to appear to have been acting suspiciously, but decided that to say any more *would* look suspicious. Smiling, she turned to walk away. She noticed that Lauren didn't make a move to open the refrigerator door while Pamela was still in the room.

She went to serve the ice cream.

The pool players were cheerful. Delighted with a great meal.

Terry was flipping burgers for another bunch of diners who'd just taken a booth.

Pits Burgers for three. Two middle-aged women and an older man with red pimples on his bald head. He wore purple spectacles that reminded her of divers' goggles.

Pamela was troubled.

Why are those keys and personal effects in the shoeboxes?

What made me take the boy's diary?

A little voice in the back of her head said: *There's a story in that diary. It's got facts about Pits. About Lauren, Sharpe and the rest.*

Facts you don't know.

Pamela couldn't wait until the cafe closed up for the night.

Then she could return to her trailer.

Read the diary.

A gut feeling told her that it was important.

Chapter Twenty-eight

'Where'd you get the car?' Norman asked as Duke drove along the dirt track that ran between cornfields. Duke and Boots rode up front. Dee-Dee and Norman sat – bounced, rather – in the backseat.

'It's Darren's car.' Dee-Dee leaned forward in her tight nurse's uniform. Even in the near-darkness Norman saw the curve of her back.

Sexy curve.

Sexy white uniform in cool, crisp cotton. She smelt good, too. *Soap scents, maybe.*

'Darren who?' Boots asked. She sat in the front passenger seat with her feet resting casually on the dash, like she was ready to take a nap.

Not being pursued by cops.

Norman remembered the way the bullets had flashed like shooting stars past his head.

Man, close call.

'Who the fuck cares who?' Duke growled. 'We got a car. That's the main thing.' As he drove he looked back. 'We saved your ass, bud.'

'Thanks.' Norman meant it, too. *God knows what would have happened if the cops had arrested me.*

I'm a cop-killer. If they hadn't shot me they'd have pistol-whipped me. Maced me.

Maybe kicked my jonglies black and blue.

The same jonglies that Boots had kissed and 'Ahhed' over . . .

Now they were in a sedan tearing through country fields.

'Are we being followed?' Norman asked, keeping his head down.

'Take a look, wuss-boy. Do you see any lights?'

Norman glanced back through the rear window. Saw nothing but darkness.

'Speaking of lights,' Dee-Dee asked. 'You *do* know you're driving at night without headlights?'

'Who's the stripper?' Duke asked.

'Hey, I'm no stripper.' Dee-Dee sounded stung.

Boots looked back at Dee-Dee as she sat in the back seat. 'Looks like a stripper. That ain't a real nurse's uniform.'

'It is. I am a qualified nurse.'

'That qualifies you to query my driving methods, miss?' Duke asked in a sarcastic-respectful voice.

'If you don't switch on the headlights we'll wind up smeared over a tree trunk.'

'Get her,' Boots said.

'Preferred mode of driving,' Duke added.

'At least the cops won't be able to see us in the dark without lights.' Norman risked another peek back.

'Give the kid a doughnut.' Duke casually teased a cigarette from a pack with his teeth. 'Hey, miss?'

'The name's Dee-Dee.'

'Miss Dee-Dee. Do you know where these tracks are headed?'

'They run for miles. Only people who use them are farmers.'

'You don't say.'

'I'm trying to help, you lummox.'

'Lummox.' Duke grinned back at Norman. An alarming action since he wasn't looking where he was driving. 'You've picked up a live one there, boy.'

Dee-Dee fumed. 'He didn't pick me up!'

'Say, he's not boned you yet?'

'No!'

Boots turned round to smirk. 'He will soon enough. Normy can't get enough. The guy's a fucking love machine.'

Duke laughed. 'That's cos he's been saving it up for years.'

'Hey.' Norman didn't like this kind of talk in front of Dee-Dee. *Too personal. Too revealing.*

Too damn embarrassing.

She was beautiful. Sexy. Best girl I've ever seen.

No, no, no! Don't want Boots and Duke, the gruesome twosome, ruining any chance of romance.

But:

Boots turned round so that she could look at Dee-Dee properly. Then she whispered, 'Did you know that until two nights ago Norman here was a virgin?'

'That's none of my business.'

'None of my business.' Duke guffawed. 'What's your business hitching a ride with us?'

'Yeah,' Boots said. 'We don't know you. You might be a weirdo or something.'

'Dear God, that's rich.' Norman couldn't stop the words coming out.

'Hey, what's that supposed to mean?' Boots was hurt.

Duke snarled, 'You gotta show respect to your girlfriend, man.'

'Boots isn't my girlfriend.'

'Coulda fooled me. The way you were stickin' it in her the other night I thought you two were on your honeymoon.'

'Shut the fuck up, Duke,' Norman snapped.

He stared at the big guy's silhouette as he drove. Then Duke did something that made both Dee-Dee and Norman shout out.

Duke floored the gas pedal. The car roared along the track in total darkness. Couldn't see nothing but flitting shapes in the starlight at either side.

Then Duke took his hands off the wheel. Placed them behind his head.

Gazed forward just like *he* was the passenger.

Not the driver of this budget sedan hurtling along a dirt road.

That was when Dee-Dee and Norman shouted.

'Hey, what you think you're doing!'

'You'll kill us all!'

'Duke, get your hands back on the wheel!'

'You crazy fuck!'

Boots turned back to laugh at the pair in the back seat. 'Serves you right for being rude to me.'

'Boots, make him steer!'

Both Duke and Boots laughed and whooped. They slapped the car roof with their hands. Duke switched on the car radio.

The Glory Bus

A country-and-western song jangled out.

Shit, Norman thought. *That's the song I'm gonna hear as I die.*
I hate country and western.

Boots and Duke sang along, adding cowboy yodels.

The mad fucks.

Dee-Dee moaned.

Fainted.

Leaning sideways against Norman.

'Duke! You mad sonofabitch!'

Duke swiveled back so that both of his hands rested on the top of his seat. 'Norman. Your lack of faith disappoints. Ain't that right, Boots?'

'Right, Duke.'

'Yah think you've got me down as this cretin.' The car sped on. *Sixty? Seventy miles an hour?*

And here was Duke, acting like the car was on autopilot or something.

'You underestimate me, Normy, old buddy. That makes me sad. Cos I've done so much to educate you in the ways of the world. To change the boy to a man.'

'Duke, steer the fucking car. Please, Duke.'

Norman felt like fainting, too. Dee-Dee was a dead weight against him.

'Now here's another fact,' Duke told him. 'Dirt tracks like this always have deep ruts from where tractors and combine harvesters have gone backward, forward, backward, forward for years—'

'Duke. In the name of God, please put your hands back on the steering wheel.'

'—So they act like rails on a railroad. The car's wheels lock into the ruts. The ruts steer the car. *Comprende, amigo?*'

Norman could only stare at Duke's grinning face there in the gloom.

Any second the car's gonna flip out.

Then we'll be dead.

Norman sweated.

Sweated rivers of perspiration down his chest.

And all he could see was Duke grinning at him like a demon.

'I trust Duke, Normy. He won't crash us into nothin'. See? The car's running like God's steerin' it.'

After what seemed a long, long time, Duke shook his head. Then, still smiling, he turned back to the business of driving the car. He slowed it. Put his hands on the steering wheel.

Norman sagged down in the backseat with a massive sigh. His muscles were locked hard with tension.

It would take a while to relax.

A *long* while.

Duke said matter-of-factly, 'I've lost the cops. It's time we found a highway.'

Chapter Twenty-nine

'Midnight,' Lauren said as she locked the cafe door.

'The witching hour.' Pamela stood with her hands in her apron pockets, making sure that no one saw the oblong bulge of the diary.

'Couldn't have put it better,' Lauren said. 'Oooh, look at the sky. You know, you don't appreciate how bright the stars are until you see them out in the desert.'

Pamela looked up at the display of shining stars. 'Awesome,' she agreed. 'And it's so wonderfully cool after being in the diner.'

'It was sizzling today. And you did marvelously.'

'My pleasure.' Pamela smiled.

'Remember, if you want that waitressing job it's yours.'

Pamela opened her mouth to speak.

'No, don't decide now. Let me know in the morning.'

'Thanks.'

'We did real good business today. I'll see you get your share of the tips come Saturday.'

'Oh, there's no—'

'Hush. You've earned it. The place was a furnace tonight.' Lauren walked alongside Pamela as they strolled across the parking lot. The chill desert air was as refreshing as a glass of cold champagne. 'And if you decide to join us we'll agree a fair wage. You get accommodation, too.'

'That's a generous package. I really do mean it.'

'What we're short of is glamorous night life. What we're *not* short of is peace and plenty of quiet.' Lauren paused, looking down the road that appeared as a gray strip in the starlight. In this eerie ghost light her face, which was bony and hollow-cheeked at the best of times, could have been the face of an ancient Red Indian warrior.

'Lauren, what's wrong?'

'I was just wondering about Sharpe.'

'He drove out in his bus today, didn't he?'

'Hmm, looking for more people to save.'

'How long will he be gone?'

'You never know with Sharpe. Days. A week.'

'You miss him, don't you?'

Lauren sighed. 'Sure do. But that's the nature of Walter Sharpe.'

'His mission?'

'Yeah . . .' Lauren's forest-green eyes were far away. Then: 'Come on, it's getting late.'

They walked across the lot by the assortment of cars, trucks, vans and a motorcycle or two.

Never struck me as being so odd, Pamela thought. *That parade of abandoned vehicles.*

But in the light of those shoeboxes in the utility room. Crammed with pens, spectacles, false teeth, car keys . . .

Where did all those cars come from?

In the meager light they looked like sleeping beasts.

How easy is it to lose your car keys and eyeglasses?

Surely a darn sight easier than losing your truck?

You don't simply forget to climb in and drive away after eating a Pits Burger, do you now? You don't walk off along that desert road thinking: 'I'm sure I've forgotten something important.'

At Pamela's trailer she and Lauren said their good nights, then went their separate ways. Pamela let herself into the trailer. It still held the heat of the day. She was grateful to bathe in the warm air. Outside it had suddenly seemed too cold.

Too chilling.

Rodney's just walked over my grave.

Not funny.

She closed the door behind her. Drew a bolt. Then pulled the diary from her apron pocket. She had a feeling that the contents of the little book wouldn't be funny either.

* * *

Pamela showered, relishing the pummeling jets of warm water. After the fried-meat smells of the diner the scent of the strawberry shampoo felt pretty good, too. After drying herself she slipped on a long T-shirt that she was using as a nightshirt.

Then she went into the trailer's kitchen where she poured herself a glass of cold milk and took it into the lounge where she'd left the boy's diary on the coffee table.

She remembered the words in a child's hand on the first page: *Benny Loscoff, age 10 (and last will and testy mint).*

Testy mint.

Clearly, he meant 'testament.' But why would a child write their will in a diary?

Does this form part of the equation when you add in the boxes of personal effects in the utility room, plus the row of vehicles – new as well as old – abandoned in the cafe's lot?

Pamela took a sip of milk. Cold and creamy, just how she liked it.

Settling down into the sofa, she opened up the diary and began to read.

My name is Benny. This is what happened to me and my bud, Gyp, when we ran away from summer camp.

As she took another sip of milk she heard the gasp of air brakes. Opening the drapes by a fraction of an inch she took a peek out. Sharpe's bus had pulled into the lot. The door opened. Out stepped what appeared to be a young guy with a mass of curly hair.

Too dark to see properly. But he seemed hunched forward.

Tired? Hurt?

Pamela didn't know.

Sharpe left the bus next. He always walked upright. Almost like a Marine, proud of his uniform and his flag, ready for parade. He closed the bus's door behind him, said something to the curly-haired guy who nodded. Then they both went round the far side of the diner.

She watched for a moment; they didn't come back.

Pamela let the drapes fall back into place. Took a moment to make sure that there were no chinks through which anyone on the outside could peer in.

I'm getting paranoid.

No one'll care if they see me reading a kid's diary.

Or am I developing a heightened sense of self-preservation?

203

Shoot.

She shivered. Opened the diary.

Began to read.

My name is Benny Loscoff. This is what happened to me and my bud, Gyp, when we ran away from summer camp. Mabley and his gang was going to pound us because we told Mr. Taylor about what they did with the snake. We snuck out before sunup and took the bus to Vegas. Only the bus broke down, so me and Gyp ran into the desert because the driver said we didn't look old enough to be traveling by ourselves to Vegas, which he called Sin City. And that there were women downtown that kiss guys for money.

Anyway me and Gyp ducked off into the desert so we couldn't be taken back to summer camp.

Pamela took a swallow of milk. It stroked a cold pathway down her throat. She glanced at the next pages of the diary. Benny Loscoff talked a lot about trying to catch birds to eat – with no success. And getting thirstier and thirstier until they couldn't walk any further.

That was when the bus pulled up on the desert road.

A bus full of mannequins.

A bus driven by Sharpe.

The diary continued with an account of the two boys staying in a trailer in Pits. How they helped out at the diner and played in the abandoned cars in the lot. And that an old guy who looked like a prospector was going to show them the old mine workings. They were looking forward to that.

Then the diary came to an abrupt end.

Pamela read the words scrawled across the page. Words scrawled in a hurry.

THEY MADE GYP BURGERS! AND THE OLD GUY SAID THEY'RE GOING TO MAKE SAUSAGE OUT OF ME!

Chapter Thirty

Duke was still driving at sunup.

Driving south. When you need to flee, he'd told them, flee south. So he pushed the sedan hard along Oregon's roads in the direction of California.

'California?' Dee-Dee had said as she woke up in the backseat to the sight of a passing road sign. 'LA or San Francisco?'

'Neither,' Duke said. 'When you lie low you take yourself off to wilderness country.'

'I thought you said you should drive south?' Norman asked from the backseat of the car.

'Yup. South into wilderness country.'

Boots awoke with a stretch and a yawn in the front passenger seat. 'Gee, I'm hungry and thirsty.'

'We're gonna refuel soon,' Duke said. 'Us and the car.'

'The cops will be looking for a gray sedan,' Dee-Dee pointed out. 'They'll have the license plate.'

'No sweat.' Duke drove one-handed, scratching his stubbled chin. 'We ditch the car, pick up a new one.'

'Oh, shit,' Norman said remembering the last time.

He saw that Boots was looking back at Dee-Dee. Probably getting a good look at the nurse's uniform for the first time in the daylight.

That uniform.

Oh, boy. Still looked cool, crisp and very sexy to Norman.

Maybe Boots is finding it sexy, too.

She's hinted that she's seduced women, hasn't she?

Dee-Dee was very beautiful in a dark, pixie way. *Come to think of it, that sharply defined hairstyle is short as a boy's, so maybe—*

'Quit staring at Dee-Dee's boobs, Normy.'

Norman flushed. 'I wasn't.'

'You were, too,' Duke said. 'Saw you in the mirror.'

'And we can all guess what you were thinkin', too,' Boots said with a smirk.

'Ah ha. Busted, Normy boy.'

'Norman wouldn't be the first man to stare at a woman in a nurse's uniform,' Dee-Dee said with a smile that was somehow prim and sexy all at the same time.

What happens if we stop at a motel again? Dee-Dee and Boots lying side by side in a big motel bed. Giggling. Inviting me to join them.

Uh . . . Something stirred in Norman's underpants.

'You look uncomfortable there, bud.'

Norman noticed Duke watching him in the rearview.

'I'm fine,' Norman grunted.

'Don't look that way to me. Looks like you're sitting on something hard.'

'Just keep watching the road, huh?'

'Ohhh, Normy boy, that's no way to speak to your best bud.'

Norman folded his arms and looked out at the passing scenery. There were hills. Forests. A lake beneath a perfect blue sky.

Felt hotter. Maybe they weren't far from California now?

The air smelt of pine.

Boots shuffled her butt until she sat almost looking back at Dee-Dee. Her piggy eyes kept sweeping up and down Dee-Dee's slender bod.

'Had enough of nursing?' Boots asked.

'Not really.'

'Why come with us, then?'

'Heat of the moment.'

'Must have been a hot moment.'

'I was sick of the motel. It was my salary that kept it going.'

'Sounds like a major responsibility,' Duke observed.

'It was.'

'So you decided to skip?'

'Yes.'

Duke glanced back at her. 'How do you propose to pay for the ride?'

'Pay?'

'Gas don't come free, y'know.'

'You stole the car in the first place.'

''S mine now.'

'There's a kind of logic there,' Dee-Dee said with a sigh.

'So how you gonna pay your fare?'

'You've got something in mind?'

'Sure do.'

'Okay, then. Let's get it over with.' Dee-Dee sighed again and rolled her eyes. 'Here will do.'

'Hey . . .' Norman protested. 'She can ride with us if she wants.'

'Course she can,' Boots said. 'Gotta pay the driver, though. It's only right.'

Duke pulled over to the side of the road, then ran the car onto the dirt and under some overhanging bushes.

'Shit,' Norman said. 'I don't believe this.'

'Jealous, Norm?'

'No, but—'

Dee-Dee hissed, 'Deal with it. I've been screwed over the motel for years.' Norman saw impatience in her eyes at his slowness when she added a weary 'Figuratively.'

'Oh.'

'So taking a porking in return for my freedom from a whole heap of debt isn't going to hurt, is it now?'

'Oh, I . . . Ah . . .' Norman didn't know what to say.

They were out of sight of any passing traffic here. Duke opened the driver's door.

'My apologies, ma'am, for there not bein' a bed or nothin'.'

'It's okay by me.'

Norman felt his face burning as he opened the back door.

'Where ya goin', Normy?'

'I thought you . . . well . . . thought you might want to make use of the backseat.'

'Very considerate of you, Norman,' Duke said politely. 'But we haven't got time for that.'

'Your call,' Dee-Dee said. 'You're doing me a favor taking me to a new life, so name your pleasure.'

Dear God, Norman thought. *Dee-Dee's beautiful. It should have been me.*

Duke unbuckled his belt. 'You just pop yourself round here. No time for a regular screwin' so I thought you could practice your microphone technique.'

Norman frowned. *Microphone technique? Oh, my dear Lord. Does Duke mean what I think he means?*

Norman watched Dee-Dee get out of the car. She smoothed the crisp uniform down over the swell of her breasts and her hips.

Jeez, that dress is short.

He looked at her slender bare legs. *Wow* . . . her delicate fingers. The swanlike neck.

Boots leaned forward. Her piggy face was a picture of excitement. She was gonna watch?

Duke was gonna *let* her watch?

Norman gave a polite cough. 'Uh, Boots. Maybe we should step out of the car and give these two some privacy.'

'Shit, man.' Duke shook his head. 'No time for that. If the pair of you wanna watch, then watch. Don't bother me.'

Boots's eyes flashed as an erotic burn flamed through her. 'Hey, Norman, lean forward next to me. You can see better.'

'I don't want to see better.' His voice rose in a protesting squeal.

Norman closed his eyes and clamped the palms of his hands over his ears. *See nothing. Hear nothing.*

Norman felt sick.

Am I revolted that Duke's demanded sex for driving Dee-Dee to California? Or am I sick with jealousy?

He loosened his hands a little . . . just enough to hear Boots breathe, 'Normy. You gotta watch this. You won't believe your eyes.'

Norman couldn't bear it. He pressed his hands back so hard against his ears that all he could hear was the sound of his own blood pumping through the arteries to his brain.

He tried not to picture what Dee-Dee might be doing to Duke. Even so . . .

Norman had to adjust himself. His shorts were binding. His heart beat faster.

Then, moments later . . .

The whole car shuddered.

'*Sweet Lord on high!*' Duke's sudden shout made it through Norman's hands clamped against his ears. *Dear God, what's happened there in the front seat?*

It was a while before Norman could bring himself to uncover his ears, open his eyes.

Dazed, Norman saw that Dee-Dee was now standing by the car. Her skin was flushed.

'Thank you, ma'am.' Duke zippered up.

'Pleasure's all mine.' She licked her lips. 'I could use a drink of soda.'

'Sure didn't look like thirsty work,' Boots said, grinning.

Dee-Dee ran her tongue round inside her mouth as if checking that her teeth were all still in place. Then she said, 'All the same, a drink would be nice.'

Duke pulled his door shut, then nodded back through the open window. 'There's some sodas in the trunk. Grab one before we go.'

He pulled the trunk-release lever. Watched Dee-Dee in the rearview mirror as she pulled out a can of orangeade. She slammed down the trunk lid.

That was when Duke started the motor. Floored the pedal.

Left Dee-Dee staring at a cloud of dust preceded by a departing sedan.

'Hey!' Norman shouted. 'Wait! What're you leaving her behind for?'

Boots laughed a wet gurgling laugh.

Duke made one shoulder shrug. 'Didn't she look wacky to you?'

'No!'

Boots was still laughing as she looked back through the rear window at the diminishing figure of Dee-Dee. 'Aw, no fair. I thought she'd try and run after us.'

Norman glanced back to catch one last look at Dee-Dee as she stood there with a can of orange soda in her hand.

'Cooee! Bye-bye, Dee-Dee!' Boots waved.

Duke said, 'Good mouth.'

Norman groaned, 'Oh, God.'

An hour later they traded the sedan for a yellow SUV. Driving along a twisting backwoods road, they came across a solitary guy fishing by a lake. The SUV sat a few yards behind him on a swathe of dry earth.

No other traffic.

No people.

Duke pulled up. Sauntered across to the fisherman who didn't even look up as he dozed in the hot sun.

Duke slipped the blade into the back of the man's neck. Norman climbed out of the sedan with Boots who ran forward to throw the guy's rods and tackle into the lake. Duke rolled the body across the ground with his foot until gravity took hold and the corpse tumbled down the bank into the lake.

Ripples spread across calm water.

A red stain started spreading, too.

Norman heard Boots say, 'As the guy rolled into the lake he farted.'

Duke was disgusted. 'In front of a lady, too. Some people've got no manners.'

Norman said, 'You *did* remember to take the car keys out of the guy's pocket?'

'Shoot.'

'Duke, what a dumbfuck thing to do.'

'Best get them before he drifts too far out, Normy.'

'No way!'

Norman watched the stabbed corpse. It farted again, bloody bubbles popping up between the guy's legs.

'Norman. We need the keys. Go fetch.'

'No way! I'm fucking sick of you giving me orders!'

Boots stuck out her bottom lip. She looked as if she was going to cry. 'Don't get mad at Duke. He's been drivin' all night. He's wore out.'

'Wore out? Pumped out, more like. I mean, what the hell did you leave Dee-Dee behind for, Duke? What kind of dumbfuck trick was that?'

'I told you. She was a flake.'

'Jesus H. Christ.'

'Best get the keys, Normy. If the guy keeps blowin' gas like that he's gonna lose buoyancy.'

'I'm not going in there, Duke. It's your fucking idiot mistake. *You* get the keys!'

'Are you disprectin' me, bud?'

'Disrespecting you! Of course I am, you dumb fuck.'

'Please, Norman.' Boots's eyes watered. 'Don't fight with Duke.'

'If he used that brain of his for once, he—'

Duke struck.

And, boy, did he know how to strike.

The blow landed under Norman's chin. This was pain the like of which he'd never felt before. He went spinning to land on his butt.

Duke, there's no need to fight. We can resolve our differences by discussing them.

The words that Norman planned to say drowned in the blood that filled his mouth. He climbed to his feet but stayed bent over at the waist. He marveled at the pretty patterns the spots of red were making on the dry earth.

'Oh, poor Norman,' Boots cooed.

Duke walked smartly forward. Then rained more punches into Norman's face. This time Norman crashed backward like falling timber. Once more he started to climb to his feet.

Only made it as far as his knees.

Boots wiped away a tear. 'Poor Normy. What a pickle you've gotten yourself into.'

Pickle!

Duke stepped up to the line again. This time he delivered a savage kick that sent Norman rolling as far as the road like a soccer ball.

Norman was past speaking.

Nevertheless he held up his hand.

Enough already.

I've had enough.

Norman figured the hand gesture would be clear enough to anyone. Groggy with pain he looked up.

Duke looked down.

Face impassive. Stone-like. Eyes hard.

Then Duke swung back his motorcycle boot.

Norman groaned.

This time the full-blooded kick slammed into the side of Norman's head. That was the mother of all pain.

The sky turned black.

Then the whole world.

Dimly, far away, Norman heard his mother's voice. 'Norman? Didn't I always tell you not to give lifts to strangers?'

211

No shit.

Was this his moment of dying?

What he'd done over the last forty-eight hours would take some explaining to God. But then He'd have seen everything already, wouldn't he?

The sex with Boots.

The cop-slaying.

The old guy at the house with the wife in the deep-freeze.

Shit. Those dead cops would be waiting for him in heaven. Even being dead wouldn't save him from having the crap kicked out of him. He could imagine them smiling as they pulled out their batons. They were gonna kick his sorry ass all over heaven.

Heaven?

Hell!

Satan wants me for a moonbeam.

Norman's thoughts disintegrated as his mind sank deeper into unconsciousness.

Maybe gonna sink so deep I'm never coming back up . . .

Chapter Thirty-one

When Norman woke he was being hit all over again.

No fists.

Brilliant sunlight that felt like a steel spike was being driven into each eye.

Uh . . .

Least I'm not dead.

Yet.

But that light alone was punchy enough to hurt.

'Lie still.'

That was Boots.

'Lie still, will you? I'm putting a sticking plaster on your eye.'

'Uh. I'm sore.' Norman winced. 'All over.'

'You should see yourself. Your face is a mess.'

'Thanks. I feel better for knowing that.'

'Duke broke you up real bad.'

Norman squinted up at Boots as she leaned over him. Couldn't see much more than her porky silhouette. The sun blazed behind her head.

'Where is Duke?'

Norman was suddenly aware of unpleasant possibilities.

Duke's digging a shallow grave?

Boots shrugged, then spoke in that vague (and more than a little stupid) voice of hers. 'Oh. Around.'

'The fisherman. We need to get away from the lake.'

'We *are* away from the lake.'

'Uh?'

'Sit up, Normy, take a look-see.'

Sitting was hurting. Royal hurting.

'If you see a lake I'll somersault bare-assed for you.'

Norman realized that he was lying in the back of a pickup truck on bales of newspaper that formed a mattress. A tarp had been pulled to one side.

Something tells me I've been riding in the back all covered up like a baby.

Maybe Duke doesn't want to kill me after all. Or maybe he's just saving me to hurt for fun later.

Duke's the kind of guy who really knows how to inflict pain.

Boots kneeled beside Norman on the bales. As she leaned forward he saw the sway of her breasts inside her top.

She saw that he was looking.

'From the way you're looking at my boo-boos it shows that Duke hasn't busted your eyeballs.'

'Sorry.'

'I'm the one who's gonna be sorry when men stop admiring my goodies. Well?'

'Well, what?'

'Are you gonna sit up or just lie there?'

'I'm trying. It hurts like hell.'

With a sigh as if she was being inconvenienced like you wouldn't believe, Boots helped Norman to sit.

'Ah, my fucking back!'

'A twinge?'

Norman grunted. 'No, I just like screaming out names of body parts for the hell of it.'

'Who's woke up in a grumpy mood, then?'

'I took a wee bit of damage, you know?'

Boots fluffed her spiky bleached hair. 'None of it's lasting. And before you ask, I checked your John Thomas and his two sons. They're all fine.'

'Thanks.' He grimaced.

The idea of Boots fiddling with his genitals while he was unconscious . . .

Dear God.

At last Norman managed to sit upright in the back of the truck.

'What happened to the SUV?'

'We've traded in a couple of times since then. The cops are hunting hard for us, you know. We heard it on the radio.'

'Oh, Christ.'

'Duke phoned them to tell them they're wasting their time. He says the only time a cop will lay a finger on him is when he's breathed his last.'

'Oh, Jesus Christ.' Norman managed to focus on his surroundings. '*Holy shit.*'

'Yeah.' Boots looked round. 'Looks kinda funny, don't it?'

'Where in hell are we?'

For the first time since he woke he forgot about the orchestra of pain playing the Agony Overture all over his body.

'This is desert . . . fucking desert!'

He blinked. A blazing sun beat down on sand dunes. A straight desert road stretched ahead and behind.

No vehicles.

Heat haze rippled Joshua trees so that they looked like drunken men dancing. Beyond sand, desert shrubs and mesquite trees lay a ridge of strangely red mountains.

And the heat, this fucking heat . . .

'The motherfucker's brought us to Death Valley.'

'Don't be silly, Normy. This ain't Death Valley.'

'Damn well looks like it.'

'We've already driven *through* Death Valley. This is Furnace Creek.'

'We're in California?'

Boots nodded, smiling. 'After your disagreement with Duke you slept all the way.'

'Slept? Beaten unconscious. Half fucking dead.'

'Norman, that's all in the past now. Besides, Duke got all upset about what happened.'

'I wasn't in a fit of giggles over it, either.'

'Duke's – you know – sensitive.'

'Just hides it well, huh?'

Norman stood up in the back of the truck. The newspaper bales shifted under his feet. Worse was the sudden wave of nausea.

Then vertigo.

He took a deep breath.

He must have slept for days as Duke drove them south through

Oregon, on into Northern California, then probably through the High Sierras – wilderness country, not too many cops – before picking up Highway 190 into the Death Valley National Park and then winding up here in the sand dunes of Furnace Creek in the Mojave Desert.

Was there ever such an unforgiving place?

Snakes, coyotes, kangaroo rats, ghost towns.

But at least no cops.

'I sure could use a meal and a cool shower.' Boots fanned her face with a chubby hand.

'Hell, *I* could just use some *shade*.' Norman shielded his eyes.

No houses. Certainly no welcoming diner.

Nothing.

Nothing but god-awful wilderness. Arid wilderness. Snake-filled wilderness.

'So where's Duke gone?' Norman asked again.

'He just took himself for a walk.'

'A walk?' *Crazy guy.* 'Boots, you don't stroll aimlessly through the Mojave Desert. This is the kind of place you carry a snake-bite kit.'

'You'll allow it looks kinda peaceful, Norman.'

'Peaceful, huh? There's also the Edwards Air Force base out here along with the China Lake Weapons Center where they test the biggest, baddest bombs known to humanity.'

'Gee, I ain't seen no soldiers.'

Norman sighed. 'We should sit in the shade of the truck.'

'I'm working on my tan.'

'Your tan? In this heat you'll fry.'

Norman climbed off the truck. His legs didn't work too good.

Stiff from lying on newspapers for days.

He caught sight of his reflection in a side window.

'Uh, I don't look too pretty.' Bruises, contusions. A cut through his right eyebrow that Boots had taped shut with a Band-Aid.

'I've had worse,' she said lightly. 'You'll soon heal up nice.'

'I hope—'

'Norman, catch me.'

She jumped off the back of the truck. Norman did his best.

'Shit!'

Like catching a sow.

My arms! My back!

Grunting, he fell back with her in his arms. They landed sprawling in desert sand.

'Norman. You were supposed to catch me.'

'I think you've snapped my spinal column.'

'Don't joke. Just 'cos I carry an extra couple of pounds.'

'Couple of pounds? Jeez.'

As Norman disentangled himself from the chunky Boots a shadow fell across the pair of them.

Norman looked up.

Duke.

Oh, shit.

Norman climbed to his feet while beating clouds of dust from his clothes. Damn desert grit was in his mouth, too.

He looked up at Duke. The other man's blond, greasy hair was still swept high. His blue eyes were hidden by a pair of mirror-shades that reflected the black and green bruises on Norman's face.

Bruises that Duke had made with those rock-hard fists of his.

The face was impassive. He was staring at Norman.

Maybe figuring to finish the job with his knife. In minutes I could be lying in the desert with blood squirting from my throat.

Norman waited for Duke to speak. It was like waiting for the outbreak of war.

Tension built in Norman's stomach.

I feel sick.

Boots watched without talking. Waiting for Duke's first move.

Duke raised his arms at either side of his head. His biceps bulged.

Norman flinched.

Duke stepped forward to inflict a massive bear hug. It reminded Norman how sore his ribs were.

This is it. The monster's gonna crush me to death.

Duke kept squeezing.

'Norman?'

'Uh . . . Duke?' he managed to say with his face pressed into the hard muscle of Duke's chest.

'That was a bad thing that happened between us, Norman. We've got to stand together like brothers. Never let it happen again. D'ya hear? Never again.'

'Gnnaa . . . sure. Never again.'

Duke released his grip.

Norman breathed.

That's a good feeling.

'But you made mistakes, Norman, old bud. I had to correct them. It broke me up inside but I had to show you what you mean to me.'

Boots chipped in. 'All friends now. That's the main thing.'

'Sure we're all friends now.' Duke beamed, then slapped Norman on the back. It was a friendly slap; the force of it nearly made Norman swallow his tongue.

'What you say, bud?'

Norman forced a weak smile. 'Sure. Best friends.'

'More than friends,' Duke told him. 'We're *family* now. We stick together to the end.'

Now that part of the reconciliation didn't thrill Norman.

Together to the end? No way.

For a few minutes Duke and Boots chatted to Norman. They checked his face. They reassured him that he'd be fine.

After that, Duke opened a can of Pepsi, took a swallow, handed it to Boots. Boots took a slug, then handed it to Norman.

Uckk.

Warm.

'We've got three of those left,' Duke said nodding at the can in Norman's hand.

'I'd give a hundred bucks for a cold beer right now.'

Duke guffawed. 'You and me both, big fella.'

Norman shielded his eyes against the raging sun. Beneath a clear sky the dunes wobbled in the heat haze. Further away layers of hot air just above the road surface created phantom pools of blue water.

'Not much of a road,' Norman ventured.

'No, sir.'

Boots added. 'At least it's quiet.'

'Sure doesn't look like a regular desert highway.'

'Yup,' Duke agreed. 'The pavement's all broke up.'

Norman had learned that disagreeing with Duke, or even questioning his decisions, could have pretty bad side effects. So his tone was cautious when he said, 'Boots said we were close to Furnace Creek. Is this Highway one-ninety?'

'Hell, no, bud. Where you find highways you find cops.'

'So this is an offshoot from the highway?'

'Yup.'

'I see.' Norman took a breath as he judged once more the risk of suggesting the obvious to Duke. 'It's just that the last time I was down here in the Mojave we were warned to stick to the main highways.' Norman shrugged as if what he said next was someone else's observation. Not his. 'Some people say it's dangerous to leave the main desert routes.'

Boots held her hands above her head to create a little shade for her face. 'Wusses always say things like that, ain't that so, Duke?'

'No shortage of wusses, babe. The shortage is in real men like me and Norm here.'

'Damn straight,' Norman agreed.

There was a pause. Duke stared out over the dunes at nothing in particular. Boots stood with her hands still above her head, smiling at Norman.

Norman knew he'd another obvious question to ask (especially as he'd just seen a rattlesnake poke its head out of a burrow at the side of the road).

Not a good sign when the local wildlife starts to get interested. He glanced up.

Black specks circled in the sky. The local bird population was taking a gander, too.

All we need now is a pack of coyotes along with a few of their bobcat friends and everything will be dandy.

When moments had passed with no movement from Boots and Duke, Norman posed the question.

I just hope that Duke doesn't take offense. The last thing I need right now is another beating.

'Duke?'

'Huh?'

'How about that cold beer?'

'I don't think you're gonna find any out here, bud.'

'No. I thought we could drive further . . . Maybe find a store?'

'Can't do that.'

'Oh?'

Duke nodded at the truck. 'Motor's busted.'

'You mean we're stranded here? *In the desert?*'

Richard Laymon

Boots said, 'Darn thing just went BOOM under the hood.'

Duke looked at Boots. 'Didn't you mention to Norm that we'd broken down?'

'Ooops. Must've slipped my mind. Sorry, Normy.'

Norman said, 'Shit happens.'

But he would've liked to yell at the pair. Another beating wouldn't help, though.

'Yeah, shit happens,' Boots agreed.

Norman looked up at the circling birds.

Vultures. Now I know why they're so interested in us. Forget beef jerky. In this heat we'll dehydrate so fast we'll soon be human jerky.

Those desert critters are gonna have themselves some tasty snacks.

Again, Norman had to voice his view of their situation. 'I guess you could say, technically, we're stranded in the desert.'

Duke nodded. 'Technically, I guess you could say exactly that.'

'We've got some soda left,' Boots said optimistically.

'Two cans.' Norman nodded, digesting the situation that faced them. 'I just wondered . . . has anyone any idea what we do next?'

Chapter Thirty-two

Pamela was crossing the desert with only a glass of water and a little bread; the glass wouldn't even last her an hour. Maybe the bread would last longer than Pamela . . .

She half dozed on the couch with the fan streaming air over her. In the heat of the afternoon it felt so good to lie here in the trailer. She let thoughts drift through her head.

Thoughts of escaping across the desert. But she was right about the bread lasting longer than her.

This time of year the heat's a killer.

Walk out of here?

Might as well put a gun to my head.

Then do I want to escape?

My liar husband is dead.

Got no home.

No future.

Pits is a good place.

Only a weird place. There were the shoeboxes full of people's personal possessions. Dentures. Asthma puffers. Spectacles. And why are there so many new cars left to gather dust in the cafe's parking lot?

Only too well, Pamela remembered the last entry in the kid's diary that she'd found in the cafe's utility room. It ran: 'They made Gyp burgers. And the old guy said they were going to make sausage out of me!'

'So you're concluding,' she murmured to herself, feeling the rush of cooling air on her face, 'you're concluding that two young boys came to Pits as runaways after being rescued by Sharpe. And that the

221

boy called Gyp was murdered by Lauren, or by someone who lives in Pits, and they fed the boy into the meat-grinder and turned him into hamburger meat. And then the "old guy" – Hank? – told the kid who wrote the diary that they were going to make him into sausage.' She rubbed her forehead as troubling thoughts circled behind her eyes. 'Does that sound genuine? Maybe the kid wrote that stuff in the diary for a joke.'

She cast her mind back to last night when Sharpe had arrived on the bus with a curly-headed guy.

Had they killed him, too?

The other night Lauren didn't want me opening the refrigerator door. Maybe I'd find heads on the shelves with open staring eyes. Maybe a tag stapled to an ear that read BEST BEFORE MAY 23.

'Shit,' Pamela breathed. She liked Pits and everyone in it.

Sharpe had saved her life.

An over-active imagination was poisoning her enjoyment of the place.

'Here be cannibals?' she mused. 'As if.'

Even so, she had to get the ridiculous notion out of her head. The one that suggested that Pits was turning passersby into Pits Burgers, then leaving their cars in the lot.

Pamela was due to start work at the cafe in an hour.

Gonna lay this ghost.

I'll open the refrigerator door. Take a good long look inside.

All there'll be will be burgers, chops, steaks – just regular food you find in any diner.

There won't be human heads waiting to become soup. There won't be butt fillet steak. There'll be no truck-driver oven-cooked ribs, or schoolteacher burritos, or student Dim Sum.

Pamela headed to the shower, peeling her clothes off as she went.

Time to freshen up.

Change into the uniform of a knit pullover shirt in white with 'Pamela' stitched in red thread above the left breast. Bottom half: red shorts – bright red! Last on is the blue apron with pockets for order pad and tips.

Cute as a squirrel's nut, as the old saying goes.

Then take a little walk to the cafe's utility room and open that refrigerator door.

Prove that Pits is no cannibal town.

* * *

Pamela left the trailer. She saw the old-timer Hank with a shovel over his shoulder. He seemed to be walking back from the cemetery. He was too far away to hail her.

Gave her a casual salute nonetheless.

The sun was sinking toward the rocky hills now. Beyond the town of Pits the desert burned.

Arid. Implacable. Snake-infested.

Not your average walking country.

God take pity on any poor soul stranded out there.

Pamela gazed across the sandy terrain to the road. It was empty tonight. Feeling the heat rising from the desert ground she headed across the parking lot, passed the parked cars in front of the cafe.

She noticed a motorcycle parked near the front door. It was a big purple Honda with silvery tassels hanging down from the ends of the handlebars. Painted in profile on the gas tank was the head of a howling wolf.

My, what big teeth you've got . . .

Pamela moved toward the front door.

Then she remembered her mission.

I've got to do it, she thought. *I've got to prove to myself that Lauren, Sharpe and the rest aren't cannibals.*

That what the kid wrote in the diary was probably just a joke.

Hell, I remember a kid at school who always wrote his 'What I did on my vacation' essay about flying round the solar system.

The schoolteacher always told him he'd wind up in jail.

Kid proved them wrong.

Went into politics instead.

So the diary she'd read about the couple of child runaways – it was probably just fantasy.

But gotta be sure.

I need to know that they aren't turning customers into salami back there.

Round the back, girl.

Be brave.

So, instead of entering through the cafe's door, Pamela turned and followed the line of the wall. It took her to the back of the building. It was awful quiet. No sign of Sharpe's bus with its mannequin riders.

Nor of Wes's old pickup.

The only people in the diner were probably Nicki, Lauren and Terry. Oh, and a customer. The biker, possibly a pillion rider as well.

But won't they have seen me when I headed for the front door? They'll wonder why I'm skulking round the back.

A suspicion-tickler or what?

No.

When she'd approached the cafe the window blinds had been closed to shield the interior from the full force of the sun. Now it was low in the sky.

Still sizzling hot, though.

So no one would have seen Pamela.

So far, so good.

She headed for the rear of the cafe. Here there were trashcans.

And flies . . .

Man, oh man, the flies.

Millions of desert flies had flown in to enjoy the cafe's cuisine.

They've found the curly-headed man in the dumpster. Or what's left of him.

'Gee,' Pamela whispered to herself. 'Sure does smell raunchy.'

The trashcan that was playing host to the flies stood some distance from the back door. That was the one that contained discarded food.

Maybe even the offal of a passerby.

Suddenly gritting her teeth she strode forward, gripped the lid of the trashcan. Held her breath.

Boy, the stink and the flies.

Then she lifted the lid.

Gonna see a curly head with a bloody face staring out at me.

Chicken carcasses. Maybe six of them.

That was all.

No young guy's giblets.

Unless they had uses for all parts of the body. Maybe Lauren uses his butt-hole as a penholder?

Relief at not seeing human remains there in the trash made Pamela so giddy that she laughed to herself.

But you're not done yet, she told herself.

Gotta check those refrigerators.

As she moved toward the rear door of the cafe, the setting sun cast a red light on the walls. A blood red.

The Glory Bus

It looked as if someone had thrown a pail of gore against the stonework.

Ominous, Pamela thought.

Then, steeling herself, she eased open the door and stepped into the utility room.

Well . . . just like it was before. A windowless room lit by fluorescent strips in a hard white light. On the walls were shelf after shelf of stores. Big catering cans of vegetables, cooking oil. Bottles of ketchup. Jars of creamy white mayonnaise. There were boxes of crockery. Spare cruet sets. Hefty bales of napkins. Spare kitchenware.

Pamela spied the shoeboxes full of stuff that customers had left behind.

Whatever had happened to them.

The boxes had been pushed to the back of the shelves. Partly concealed by packs of dried foodstuff. She could even see a pair of dentures grinning at her from the gloom.

What happened to the owner of those?

Sliced.

Diced.

Stir-fried in peanut oil. Served with grilled polenta and zucchini.

Black beans are fine. Baked beans are dandy. But nothing compares to human beings.

Now that's sweet eating for sure.

'Shush.' Pamela scolded her runaway imagination in a whisper. 'Just take a look round. Reassure yourself that nothing weird's happening. Then walk in through the front door with a friendly "hi" as if nothing's happened.'

Goddammit. I like Pits.

Pamela realized that she was seriously thinking about staying on.

So check the refrigerators. If it's regular food: Fine.

If not . . .

Then she couldn't stick around.

No, sir.

Hell, I might be coated in breadcrumbs to be served up as dish of the day.

Before checking the contents of the refrigerators she listened at the closed door that led through into the cafe's kitchen.

I don't want anyone to walk in on me, do I now?

Then I really would be up shit creek.

Holding her breath, Pamela listened. Nothing but the thud of her own heartbeat. With only a couple of diners at the most Lauren, Nicki and Terry might be taking a break themselves.

No smells of cooking either. Just a faint aroma of coffee. Perhaps the biker and his chum had just called in for a caffeine fix.

Now, speed up the investigation, girl. You're due to start work in seven minutes. Don't want to be late.

She moved quickly along the narrow room toward the two refrigerators and massive deep freeze set against the end wall.

Clang!

Her elbow caught a roasting tray that had been hung on a hook from a shelf. The big metal tray flipped up from the hook, turned over, and then gravity took hold. It fell toward the concrete floor.

Where it would make a hell of a crash.

Which would bring people running in here.

Asking awkward questions. As a waitress Pamela had no reason to be in here.

So why sneak in through the back door, they'd be asking.

As the heavy tray sped downward she knew she couldn't catch it. *Deaden its fall.* Like lightning she kicked her foot under it.

Slam!

The tray hit edge-on into the top of her foot. She was only wearing pumps so that steel edge felt like a guillotine blade.

No metallic clang.

But the agony . . .

Pamela pushed her knuckle into her mouth to stop herself screaming out. That would have brought the staff running just as surely as the metallic clang of the tray striking concrete. Tears oozed from her eyes. The stifled scream came out as a gasp of pure pain. The tray toppled off her foot to hit a carton of paper towels.

The only sound it made was a very soft thud. With an effort of sheer will to stop her blubbing with pain Pamela returned the tray to its hook. Then she hobbled to the end of the room. There she checked for damage.

An angry red line ran across the top of her foot just below the ankle. It felt like red-hot pincers were crimping the flesh. Luckily it wasn't bleeding. Probably nothing was fractured.

But that mother would swell.

'Come on,' Pamela hissed. 'Finish this.'

She opened the refrigerator marked with the word *Dairy*. That sign didn't lie. Inside she found a respectable stock of butter, cheese, milk, cream and yogurt, along with a tub of guacamole.

Of course, if there were going to be any butchered people here they were going to be in the refrigerator labeled *Meat*. Its door was as big as a house's. Someone had welded a couple of steel loops where its edge met the appliance's frame.

The kind of loops that would hold a hefty padlock.

Lauren liked to keep this refrigerator locked.

Only it was open now. Pamela's gaze roved to the left. On a steel shelf full of pans she spied an open padlock.

Saves having to gnaw the thing off, she thought, trying to mask her anxiety with flippancy.

'Okay, here goes . . .'

Door opens.

Chill mist rolls out.

Pamela stared until it felt as though the desert heat had sucked the moisture from her eyes.

'Okay: inventory,' she murmured.

The interior of the appliance was pristine aluminum. Stacked on its shelves was meat galore, from T-bone steaks to burgers to pork chops.

Severed human hands?

Eyeballs in cut-glass bowls?

Face-meat kebabs?

Nope.

Not a sign.

Sheesh. Just paranoia on her part. Stoked a little by some kid who'd been fooling around with an old diary. Pamela checked the deep freeze. A moment's perusal revealed that this contained frozen foods that you'd find in any diner food-store.

Still, there *was* a cut of meat suggestive of a human thigh. Gingerly, she lifted it out.

The cold was biting. She saw the bloody marrow in the sawn-through bone at the joint's end. The whole thing was wrapped in clear plastic with a mass-printed label attached that read PORK. DEFROST AND COOKING INSTRUCTIONS.

This definitely wasn't the curly-haired guy's upper leg. This came from a beast with four legs and snout.

Voices. She heard a clamor from the kitchen area. Someone was hurrying this way.

Someone knows I'm here, Pamela thought, panicking.

Any moment now they were going to burst through the door from the kitchen. Find her standing here by the open deep freeze with a good fifteen inches of frozen swine leg in her hands.

They'd dismiss her as a nut.

Or a thief.

She shut the appliance door. *Great, you idiot, you were supposed to put the frozen meat back first.*

Voices – louder and louder.

The door to the kitchen banged open. Gasping, Pamela wedged herself in the gap between the deep freeze and the shelves where two walls of the room met.

Fine. The shelves were piled so high with packs of flour, sugar and dried pulses that no one would be able to see her.

Unless they've come to grab something from the freezer.

Explain your way out of this one, Pamela.

Suddenly there seemed to be a lot of movement in the utility room, even though she could see nothing from where she was crouching. Voices. Loud ones. Feet scuffing the floor.

Lauren's voice first: 'Just leave her here with us! She's not going to say anything.'

Talking about me?

But then: 'I'm not coming back with you, Zak.'

'The fuck you are!' A man's voice she didn't recognize. Rough-sounding.

Violent-sounding.

The man bellowed again. 'Think you can just run out on me, Nicki? Didn't ya think I wouldn't find ya? Ya dumb bitch.'

Sound of a smack. Nicki cried out.

So they're not talking about me.

Pamela raised her head a little to peep out through a crack between two giant packs of dried rice. In the harsh light of the fluorescent strips she saw Nicki and Lauren standing side-by-side with their backs to the kitchen door. Fear blazed in their eyes.

The Glory Bus

And standing with his back to Pamela was a youngish guy in leather pants and a hide jacket that gleamed with metal studs. He wore a red bandanna. The biker. She remembered the Honda she'd seen parked outside the cafe.

Most of all she saw what was in his hand. A revolver. He was pointing it in Nicki's face.

'You're my bitch, ya don't walk out on me,' he snarled. 'So ya get two choices. Ride back with me. Or kneel down and start prayin'.'

Chapter Thirty-three

Pamela watched in horror from behind the shelves. The guy pulled back the hammer of the handgun with his thumb. He pointed the muzzle at the center of Nicki's face.

Both Lauren and Nicki stared transfixed. Eyes wide open.

'Nicki was my best whore,' the leather-clad guy said. 'Earned five hundred bucks a trick.'

'I'm not going back to do that again, Zak,' she whispered. 'It nearly killed me.'

'I gave you grade-A smack, ya bitch. Ya could be fucked by a mule on that stuff and not feel squat.'

'I'm clean now, Zak.'

'You'll never be clean. Not as long as ya live.'

'She's not going back, mister.' Lauren faced him, defiant. 'She lives here now.'

'With you bums? Shit . . . Pits? What a dump.'

'It's her home. We're her family now. Nicki's not going back with you.'

'Okay.' The pimp nodded as if this didn't faze him. 'Her decision. But I'm just going to deliver her severance pay.'

Even from here Pamela could see the guy's posture alter when he tensed as a prelude to shooting Nicki.

'I'm popping you, too, sweetheart,' he told Lauren. 'Ya've seen too much of my face. Okay, Nicki, say a little prayer . . .'

Pamela looked down at her hand. It had stopped hurting from the cold now. The ten-pound hunk of frozen pork had numbed it.

The hunk of meat. Hard as concrete.

Then she stepped silently from behind the shelves. With all her strength she swung the frozen joint.

Down on the punk's red bandanna. The ice-bound meat made a soft clunking sound as it struck punk head-bone.

'Uh.' He dropped down to his knees.

Still kept a grip on the pistol. Began to raise it to shoot Nicki.

This time Pamela wielded the frozen pig leg like an executioner's axe. Gripping it with both hands, she swung down.

This time no thudding sound.

A sharp snap instead. Bone had broken. Pamela doubted that it was the pig's leg bone that had just busted.

Nope.

The pimp lay sprawled on the concrete floor. Blood seeped out of one his ears. His eyes were open but they were darting round like he was trying to lock onto a dancing hornet. His breathing sounded funny, too.

Sort of snorting. Irregular.

Pamela let the frozen pork joint slip from her fingers to the floor.

She looked up at Lauren and Nicki.

And swallowed. 'I think we ought to get an ambulance.'

'Forget that,' Lauren said firmly. 'Nicki, get me the meat cleaver.'

Pamela stared at Lauren who returned her gaze coolly.

'Pamela. Once I'm through here we need to talk.'

Lauren closed the diner early that day. She told Pamela that she had work to do in the kitchen. Probably something centering on the big old butcher's block on the table. Hank, Wes and Terry helped out, too. She guessed that Sharpe would have worked alongside them as well if he hadn't been out on the road in his bus.

Nicki asked Pamela to sit with her in her trailer.

Pamela obliged. She felt kinship with these people.

As Nicki showered Pamela fixed her a sandwich and a cold drink.

Nicki emerged, toweling dry her long blond hair. Despite the shit that she'd been through today she still looked like a Viking goddess. A Viking goddess in a white cotton nightshirt, that was.

'Oh, tuna and tomato,' she said, beaming as she sat on the sofa. 'I love that combination. Cool and refreshing. And soda. Thanks.'

Pamela set the tray bearing the plate and soda on the girl's lap. 'Don't mention it. After what you've done for me the last few days it's the least I could do.' Pamela didn't mention what had happened earlier. About Zak. About the frozen pork knocking the daylights out of him.

Nicki talked freely, though.

'And thanks for what you did earlier.' She sipped her drink and said 'Hmm' appreciatively. Then she looked Pamela in the eye. 'He really would have killed me, you know.'

'He looked the type.'

'Once I saw him cut the throat of one of his girls because she kept back some money to buy her baby some formula.'

'Gee. The guy's a little shit.'

'Yeah.' Nicki nodded, her eyes misting. 'Shittiest guy I've ever met. And I've met a few.'

'Was Zak your . . .'

'Pimp? Yeah.' Nicki took a bite of her sandwich. There was a look of recollection in her eyes as she chewed. 'I was at college, and I went and fell for a bad boy. I thought it was so cool that he'd pick me up on the motorcycle. The leathers were a turn-on, too. A real turn-on. Shoot . . . he was my first real love, you know? The first guy who I let . . .' She shrugged. 'Well, I thought he loved me for myself, only then he started to spin this line that he owed some gang members money and that they'd kill him if he didn't repay it.'

'So he asked you to help him out?'

Nicki delicately nibbled a slice of tomato. 'Yeah . . . I thought I was helping the guy I loved. And I was convinced that Zak loved me. But he spun the same line to lots of different girls. He didn't owe any money, he was just preying on our naiveté to earn himself some easy cash.'

'That's horrible.'

'He fixed me up with a room. Painted purple it was, with purple drapes and purple sheets on the bed. I'd turn up at nine in the morning and guys would come to the room to fuck me until midnight, then I'd go home.'

'Oh, Nicki.' Pamela felt a lump in her throat. 'That has to be the worst thing.'

'Oh, there are worse things. Like you saw today. Anyway, I stuck it for fifteen months. During that time I learned that Zak had other girls doing the same thing in other rooms in the building. Guys screwed us girls for cash, and Zak collected at the door.' She grimaced. 'He beat up girls when they didn't perform like they should. And he supplied the heroin. The drugs kept us going.' Nicki blinked as if the mental images had gotten too vivid. 'Stopped the hurt, too.'

'But you got away in the end.'

'Sure. One morning Zak gave me the address of a hotel and told me I was going into corporate entertainment. A Peruvian sales team was in town. They wanted to pass round a blonde for the morning before they went to the conference in the afternoon.'

'The guy was a monster.'

'Anyway, he gave me enough money for a cab to the hotel. Only I walked to the bus station. I didn't have a destination in mind so I bought a Greyhound ticket that would get me the furthest away from Zak.'

'And wound up here.'

Nicki smoothed back her still-damp blond hair. 'Yeah. After another five weeks' worth of adventures.'

'Sharpe found you?'

'Yeah. I was renting out old pussy here to a bunch of soldiers who'd gone AWOL down in Victorville. They'd taken some bad acid and were planning to drag me behind their truck on a wire. They said they wanted to see how fast I could run. Even took bets on what speed I'd reach before I lost my balance.'

'And *he* showed up just in time.'

'That's Sharpe's trademark.' Nicki sipped her drink. 'It's uncanny, but he's always there just at the right time.'

'Like an angel.'

'I'll say. Anyway . . . Sharpe took care of the guys.'

'And you rode back on his bus full of mannequins.'

'Absolutely.' Nicki smiled. 'That was two years ago this spring. They welcomed me here in Pits like a long-lost daughter. For a spell I did a lot of cold turkey; the heroin addiction took some shifting. But Lauren and the rest were there for me. Night and day.'

'Sounds like you went through hell, Nicki.'

'And then some.' Nicki smiled warmly. 'But I'm in heaven right now.'

'That explains a lot,' Pamela said. 'But when I knocked Zak cold Lauren had no plans to turn him over to the cops, had she?'

'You popped a blood vessel in his brain anyway.'

Pamela recoiled. 'You mean I killed him?'

'He deserved it. The rat.'

'But the police will accuse me of homicide.'

Nicki shook her head. 'Pamela, listen to me. The cops will never know.'

'They're gonna get rid of the body? Just like Sharpe did with Rodney, the guy who tried to kill me?'

'Oh, they'll dispose of it properly. He'll even make a valuable contribution to our little town's economy.'

'You're going to eat him, aren't you?'

'You'd best wait until you hear what Lauren has to say.' Nicki took another bite of her tuna sandwich.

Lauren turned up at the trailer at eleven o'clock. Outside there was that perfect desert darkness. Plus absolute silence. Beautifully cool, too. Lauren looked exhausted.

But she looked satisfied as well.

'A job well done,' she told the other two girls as she eased herself down into one of the trailer's armchairs in the lounge. She gave a huge sigh that came all the way from the straps of her sandals.

Pamela asked, 'Could you use a cold beer?'

Lauren nodded. 'Oh yes, please, that'd be wonderful.'

When Pamela returned with a bottle, white with refrigerator frost, Lauren gave a little moan of pleasure. 'Oh, that looks *good*.'

Nicki smiled. 'As you always say, on nights such as these God lives in a cold drink.'

'Hear, hear.' After Lauren had taken a good, deep swallow of amber liquid she nodded to Pamela as she stood by the doorway. 'Best rest your bones. I've got a story to tell.'

Pamela sat down beside Nicki on the couch.

Okay, she thought. *Lauren has hippie looks, but she does things no hippie ever would. Something tells me she's going to tell me that Pits is a cannibal town after all.*

Pamela had a sense that her world would change once again as she sat there in the trailer with Lauren and Nicki.

'Well,' Lauren began. 'The first news is that we're going to have some new specials on the cafe menu. We'll be featuring the Pits Burger

Largesse, that's a double meat patty in a bun. We'll also be offering double pork steak for the price of a single.'

'Zak?' Pamela ventured.

'After using Nicki here for so long, we get to use bad boy Zak for at least the next few days.'

Pamela couldn't believe her ears. 'You mean we're *eating* the guy?'

'It's not compulsory for us,' Lauren said in a no-nonsense way. 'But we're serving him to the cafe's customers.'

'Although Hank likes to make his own-recipe blood sausage,' Nicki said. 'He calls it his vampire bait. Sorry, Pamela. This is all a bit new to you, isn't it?'

Pamela gulped. 'Just a tad.'

I'm glad it isn't suppertime. And I don't want to even think how the old-timer makes blood sausage . . .

'Okay.' Lauren set her beer bottle on the table. 'Let's begin at the beginning. Back in the 1960s Pits was a ghost town. Years ago they used to mine borax here. It was a rootin'-tootin' son-of-a-gun kind of place.' Lauren smiled. 'A real Wild West town with shoot-outs at the saloon. There was a population of more than five hundred. Then by 1920 the borax was all mined out; people drifted away. Soon it was deserted. Then in 1970 a man settled here. They called him Priest.'

'He was the town's only inhabitant?' Pamela asked. 'Sounds more like a hermit than a priest.'

'I guess you could say his was a spiritual calling,' Lauren continued. 'You see, he'd come from a family that was rich in money but poor in love. He believed that building a society where people cared for one another was more important than owning lots of possessions. Priest had drifted round the hippie communes of San Francisco – summer of love and all that. Only he was anti-drug, so the communes weren't for him. Also they – the people who claimed they were dropping out of society – still wanted to live in the big cities. Priest hankered for wilderness country.'

'So he found Pits.'

'Indeed he did,' Lauren said. 'He moved into the big house near the cemetery. Of course, it was long abandoned by then. First he fixed it up. Then he went out on the road, looking for society's casualties. The men and women who'd fallen through the cracks due either to drink, drugs, poverty or mental illness. One by one, he started bringing them in. Some left after a while, some stayed on and found a healing in this place.'

'Hank must have been one of the first,' Pamela said. 'He told me he came here in 1972.'

Lauren nodded. 'Hank was the ninth person that Priest saved.'

'Just like Sharpe saves people now?'

'Sharpe stepped into Priest's shoes when Priest couldn't continue anymore.'

'What's Hank's story?'

'That's for Hank to tell. If he chooses. But it's enough to say that modern life didn't suit Hank. He opted for something that suits his nature.'

'I see.'

'Here in Pits we're all refugees from the modern world – in some shape or form.'

Nicki added, 'Pamela knows what happened to me. And about Zak.'

'And good riddance to *him*,' Lauren said with feeling. 'At least he's going to bring some money into the neighborhood. And as for me . . . I suffered anxiety attacks. It got so I couldn't ride a bus or walk down a street. Never mind visit a store. I just got it into my head one day four years ago that if I camped out in the desert by myself everything would be fine. Of course, city girls don't come to a place like the Mojave and pitch their tent under a cactus and everything turns out hunky-dory. I got sunstroke, drank bad water from a spring, got dehydrated, delirious – then, to round off a hell of a month, a snake bit me. I was laid on a sand dune waiting to die when I saw a bus on the road way in the distance.'

'Sharpe?'

'Yup. Guardian angel Sharpe. My future husband.' Lauren gave a weak smile. 'If he'll marry me.'

'He will.' Nicki leaned forward to squeeze Lauren's knee. 'Just give him time.'

Lauren blinked away a tear. 'How Sharpe saw me from that distance I'll never know. But I remember lying there being burnt to cinders by the sun and seeing this giant with a flat-top haircut walking right through the heat haze toward me. There were times I'd swear his feet never even touched the ground as he walked.' She smiled. 'Or maybe I'm being too romantic for my own good. Anyway, he brought me to

Pits. Together we fixed up the cafe. It was just a ruin in those days. Opened it up; we've been doing nice business ever since. And some way along the line I stopped being anxious about the world. The panic attacks just vanished.'

Pamela had to broach a difficult subject. 'I understand *what* you're going to do with the guy I walloped with the frozen pork joint. But I don't understand *why* you took to eating people.'

'Priest started it before we all came here. He told us that eating human flesh is like a magic rite.'

'*Magic?* Lauren, Nicki, that's *cannibalism*. Cannibalism is barbaric.'

'It's misunderstood.' Lauren took a deep breath as she explained. 'Rites of eating human flesh have been commonplace in human history. It empowers people. Eating human flesh cured us of our anxiety attacks, our drink and drug addictions. It even cures people of low self-esteem. You see, if you eat a person's flesh you absorb their power.'

'So all those abandoned cars out in the lot belong to people you've eaten?'

'Mostly from a long time ago. Priest told us that society chews good people up and spits them out; therefore, we had every right to chew society up.'

'Only we didn't spit – we swallowed,' Nicki added.

'My God.'

'That's how Priest was able to buy the things that Pits needed. He even had the dirt road through here paved with the proceeds of the jewelry and cars he could sell.'

'But you preyed on innocent travelers,' Pamela protested. 'You murdered people. Stole their belongings. Ate their flesh!'

'I guess we came to that conclusion, too. You have to understand that Priest was a visionary. He had this charisma. Everything he told us we believed. Then, though, maybe his cure for us worked better than he could have dreamed. We realized that we shouldn't murder travelers and devour them. So we stopped. And –' she sighed '– Priest had to go.'

'And Zak?'

'Every rule has its exceptions.' Lauren picked up her beer. 'If someone like Zak comes here intending to do us harm, then they're gonna end up on the menu.'

Nicki said, 'And we sell their possessions to add to community

237

funds. Zak'll have enough gold in his fillings and jewelry to buy us another trailer.'

'But what about the guy I saw last night?' Pamela asked.

'Ah, Marvin White?'

'I don't know his name. A curly-headed guy. Sharpe brought him in on the bus.'

'That was Mr. White.'

'Are we eating him, too?'

'No.' Lauren laughed as if the idea was ridiculous. 'Mr. White is a geologist. He got lost in the hills. Sharpe found him. He figured it best to bring him here to spend the night. Then in the morning he drove him back to find his car.'

'So he didn't wind up as dish of the day?'

'No, of course not. Mr. White is a perfect gentleman with a career and a family. So he didn't need saving in the sense that we needed saving when we couldn't live in regular society. And he certainly wasn't planning to do us harm. So we offered him hospitality like any civilized human beings would. Now he'll be safely back home in Barstow.'

'Hmm.'

'You don't believe me?'

'Well, I did see all those shoeboxes in the utility room, full of spectacles and dentures and stuff.'

'Oh, they're years old.'

'Back from when Priest was in charge,' Nicki said.

Pamela remembered what she'd found in one of those boxes of personal belongings.

'But there was a diary. Two boys who'd run away from summer camp. They wound up here . . . one claimed that you'd eaten his friend and planned to eat the other one later.'

'Oh, that'll be Benny Loscoff.'

'Loscoff. That's the one.'

'Back then, Priest told Benny that was what had happened to his friend Gyp, and that we planned to munch on Benny too. In truth, Priest was getting a little soft in the head. Sharpe drove the boys home.' Nicki smiled. 'We've got a letter of thanks from the mothers for saving their sons – we can show it to you if you don't believe us.'

'What happened to Priest?'

'Priest's no longer here.' Lauren didn't add any more about the mysterious guru. Instead, she said, 'In fact, Mr. White said he planned to drive out here with his wife and family at the weekend to have lunch at the cafe.'

'Okay, Lauren, Nicki, I believe you. Eating people is a strange notion, but . . .' Pamela shrugged. 'Like they say, it's a dog-eat-dog world.'

'Ain't that a fact.'

For a second all three stared at each other. Then Pamela gave a snort . . . followed by another snort. A second later she had a fit of giggles.

Lauren looked at Nicki.

They were relieved. Pamela knew what they were thinking.

Pamela's all right. She's one of us now.

They started smiling.

Smiles turned into laughter. Soon all three women were rocking to and fro because they were laughing so hard.

At last Pamela could catch her breath.

Grinning, she asked. 'Is it true? Do people really taste like pork?'

None of them could answer. Laughter had them in fits again.

Chapter Thirty-four

The same moment that Pamela, Lauren and Nicki were laughing in the trailer until tears rolled down their eyes, Boots, Duke and Norman were warming themselves round a campfire.

'Midnight,' Norman told them as he looked at his wristwatch.

'Is that a fact?' Duke was nonchalant. He lay on his side, smoking a cigarette. He was at ease with the place.

Boots sat with a jacket round her broad shoulders. 'Sure gets cold in the desert at night.'

'Sure does,' Duke agreed.

'I guess tomorrow we'll have to find some way of getting to the nearest habitation.' Norman poked the fire with a stick. Sparks flew into the night sky.

Duke yawned. 'Sure. We need to pick up a new set of wheels.'

'And something to eat and drink.' Norman thought about sizzling steaks, cold beer, ice cream.

And all we've got left is one lousy can of soda.

'Could use a shower,' Boots told them. 'I'm itchy like I got ants in ma pants.'

'Ain't that a picture to conjure with, Normy?'

Norman grimaced. 'Ain't it just.'

Hell. The pair irritated the bejesus out of him.

Only it's not wise to criticize Duke. I sure don't want another beating from the guy.

Next time it might not be fists.

Tough guy might decide to use the knife.

'Know what feels good?' Duke asked them.

'Clean sheets?' Norman ventured.

'Nope. Better than that.'

Boots said, 'Making whoopee in clean sheets.'

'Nope.' Duke sat up. 'Being with your best buds. Just like now.'

'Gee, I don't know what to say.' Boots's piggy eyes filled with senti-mental tears.

Norman groaned inwardly. *Don't blow it, Norman*, he told himself.

'I couldn't agree with you more,' he said, with a cheesy smile

'I'm kinda thinking it's like my honeymoon,' Boots told them, with a gulp. 'Only I got two husbands for the price of one.'

Oh Christ, woman . . .

'Maybe the King is up there watching over us.' Duke's face was solemn. 'You know, I think he brought us together like this for some . . .' He rooted around inside his brain for the apt word. '. . . For some higher purpose.'

Norman bit his lip.

I wanna laugh.

But if I laugh in his face I'm a dead man.

But the idea of it: Elvis Presley looked down from heaven and decided that the three of us should meet? For crying out loud.

Norman had to bite his lip harder, then put his head down as he sat in front of the fire, his knees pulled up toward his chest.

'What's the matter, Norman?'

Oh, Jesus. Duke had seen him choking back the laughter.

Norman kept his eyes closed but he knew his shoulders were shaking as a peal of laughter tried to escape from his body.

He put one hand over his eyes. Duke would be reaching for knife.

Then something red and wet was going to smear the pristine desert floor.

Then Boots said in a low voice, 'Poor Normy. Look at him, Duke.'

'I'm looking.' An ominous tone.

'The poor pet lamb is crying.'

'Crying?' Duke sounded surprised.

'Poor Normy can't have had no close friends like us before, Duke. He's getting all emotional.'

A lifeline!

This I gotta grab.

Now it was suddenly easy to change genuine laughter into fake sobs.

Boots shuffled round to him on her backside to hug him in a mothering kind of way. 'Don't worry, Normy. We're here for you. We're proper friends – just like that TV show. Here, let me kiss those tears away for you.'

She kissed his eyes.

Felt more like the lips of a hog snuffling wetly over his eyelids.

Dear God, I've gotta get outta this place!

When Duke spoke next his tone was surprisingly caring. 'This kind of thing's hard on a college boy. But we'll take care of him. He's one of us now.'

Holy shit. I'm stranded in the desert with a pair of crazies. Them telling me I'm one of them *isn't what the doctor ordered.*

Gotta get away from them somehow. Otherwise they're going to be the death of me.

Chapter Thirty-five

Norman woke with the morning sun shining into his face.

First thing he saw:

Boots taking a pee behind a cactus. Then—

Oh no – it's not a pee *she's having!*

Norman turned over. His bed for the night had been desert sand. Surprisingly soft.

Duke stood by the truck, smoking a cigarette. Sleeping rough had left his dirty blond hair even spikier. Even though he'd been staring out across the barren lands, with nothing but dunes, rocks and cactus in sight, he seemed to know that Norman was looking at him.

Without turning, Duke intoned, 'Gonna have to move out today, bud.'

'Sounds good to me.'

'We're gonna have to do it on foot.'

Norman was going to point out that he knew the truck's motor was busted, thank you very much. But he'd learned to be wary of Duke's mood swings.

Duke said, 'We should find a motel before long. We'll check in. Rest a while.'

Motel? Out here? On a Mojave Desert back road? The guy's gotta be out of his frigging mind.

But Norman wasn't going to risk yanking the hard man's chain. 'Yeah, we should find one before long.'

'All finished,' Boots called out brightly. 'You boys can look now.'

'Uh, sorry.' Norman looked too quickly. He saw her hoisting her denim cutoffs up over a creamy expanse of skin interrupted only by a strip of dark hair.

She giggled. 'Oh, you boys. Betcha you were peeping at me all along.'

'No, ma'am,' Duke said. 'I wouldn't watch a lady squirting her nuggets.'

'Nor me,' Norman added with genuine feeling.

'Well, maybe I believe you, maybe I don't.' She finished tugging up the zipper. 'Only don't go walking near this cactus here or you might step in some twoses.'

With that Boots came walking toward them with what she must have imagined was her dainty walk. Her grubby white boots chugged through the hot sand.

Man, how those boots must be cooking her feet.

'Okay,' Duke said. 'Grab your belongings from the truck. Time to hit the road.'

'I'll show some leg and get us a ride.' Boots raised one of her thick legs.

Norman saw white skin through the slit in her cutoffs.

Ugh, what makes her so deluded? Only guy who's gonna give her a ride will either have to be a pervert or desperate for a poke.

Yeah, just like me, Norman thought. *You do crazy things when you're desperate for a woman.*

'What're you scowling at me for, Normy?' Boots asked.

Jeez. He must have been pulling a sour face when she'd been talking about how eager a guy would be to stop for her.

'Yeah, what you so unhappy about?' That annoyed tone crept back into Duke's voice.

Norman thought fast. 'Boots is wearing a tank top.'

'You gotta problem with that?'

Boots puckered her lips in a hurt little-girl expression. 'I like it. Don't *you* like it, Normy?'

Duke grunted. 'You weren't complaining when you were aiming to catch a look at her titties.'

Norman forced a smile. 'No. Course I like her top. It's just she's got bare shoulders and that sun's going to get pretty hot today.'

Duke nodded. 'You gotta point, Norman. See, Boots? He just had your interests at heart.'

'Oh Normy, you're always taking care of me.' Delighted, she kissed him on the cheek.

'Don't want that bootiful skin to burn,' Duke said. 'Best cover up your shoulders before we start marching.'

'I've got just the thing.' Boots delved into her big denim bag. She pulled out a huge white T-Shirt. 'I bought this for bedtimes.' Beaming, she gave a shrug of her shoulders. 'But since I sleep naked as a jay in the summer it's gonna work fine as a shawl.' She draped it round her shoulders.

'Don't forget your bag, Norman.' Duke reached into the truck and hauled out Norman's rucksack.

'Thanks, Duke.' Norman hoisted it onto his shoulders.

'Okay.' Duke slipped on his shades. 'Let's roll.'

They started walking. Behind them the useless truck receded into the heat haze. In front of them the road shimmered as it cut a line through the wilderness to a distant horizon.

Nothing but cactus and sand.

Man, I'm thirsty, Norman told himself. *If we don't get fluid soon we're going to die out here. That is if a rattlesnake doesn't strike first.*

From the clumps of cactus at the roadside he heard the rustle of desert critters. No doubt beady eyes were watching the three humans pass by.

Gonna be a tasty snack for all those carrion-eaters out there.

Norman glanced up.

Vultures circled.

Great.

Just great.

If only I hadn't stopped at that particular gas station Duke wouldn't have climbed into my car. Would never have met Boots, either.

Or killed those two cops.

I'd have been at home with my parents right now.

Not on the run. Holy shit, we're not even on the run *now. We're* walking *through the third circle of hell. We're gonna dehydrate, then die in the dust at the side of the road.*

Gonna have some ugly lizard nibbling on my eyeballs by sunset.

'Hear that?' Duke stopped to scan the arid scenery.

'Let me know if you hear a motor,' Boots said. 'Then I'll start flashing some leg.'

There's not going to be any vehicles out here, Norman told himself. *We're way off the highways.*

'Sounds like diesel,' Duke said with confidence. He nodded. 'Bus or a truck.'

Norman could hear squat. Nevertheless he joined the other two to scan the terrain. They held their hands above their eyes to shield them against the unforgiving sun.

'Not a new motor,' Duke told them with the absolute confidence of someone who knew engines. 'But well maintained. New muffler, too.'

Norman wasn't going to disagree.

Boots whined, 'I don't see shit out there. Only sand and rocks and things.'

Norman looked hard. Heat haze made the whole world ripple like it was soft plastic. He saw Joshua trees that looked like men waving at him. Then—

'Hey,' Norman crowed. 'I see something!'

Boots saw nothing. 'Sure it ain't one of those mirror jars?'

'Pardon me?'

'You know – *mirror jars*. When you think you see rivers in the desert but they aren't there.'

'A mirage? No, it's real.'

'I see it,' Duke said. 'Way over there to your left.'

'I can hear it as well.' Norman was pleased.

Salvation!

Norman stared through the distorting effect of hot desert air at a long vehicle perhaps a mile away from them. Dust billowed high behind it as if it was some old-time locomotive throwing out smoke and steam.

'It's a truck,' he said.

'Nope,' Duke corrected him. 'A bus.'

'Coo-ee,' Boots sang out. She waved both hands over her head.

The bus driver won't see you. It's too far away, you dimwit. Norman would have liked to spit the words out at her. Then he figured that Duke would disapprove.

He choked back the insult.

Duke said, 'Still heading east.'

'The road will bend round,' Boots said, hopeful.

Duke shook his head. 'These roads are straight.'

'You mean it's not headed this way?' Norman was appalled.

'Damn right.'

'Oh, shit. We're never gonna be saved.'

'Don't give up hope.' Boots rubbed his back.

'Never give up hope,' Duke said. 'Unless you wake up dead in your casket.'

Boots laughed at the joke. Norman thought: *Oh, Christ. Gallows humor I don't need.*

I've gotta get a drink.

Gotta rest in some shade.

Duke said, 'Come on. Start walking.'

They continued along the dirt road. Cactus. Sunlight. Dust. Dunes. Mountains. Plenty of those. But no diners, no houses. No proper freaking road.

Shit. Do I want to die out here?

Not with the gruesome twosome I don't.

Duke must have read the pessimistic expression on Norman's face.

'Don't fret, bud. That bus was running along a regular highway. You can bet your last dollar that this back road plugs right into it.'

'A ride would be good.'

'I could sure use a little air-conditioning right now,' Boots said, with a sigh.

Duke grinned, the desert reflecting in his sunglasses. 'In a couple of hours from now we'll be in a motel room and Norman will be soaping your bazooms in the bathtub.'

She perked up. 'I'll hold Norman to that.'

Norman pulled a tight smile. 'The pleasure'll be all mine.'

Duke tapped his finger against his nose. 'But I reckon it'll be only right if Boots sucks my cream-pump dry first. After getting us out of trouble I reckon I've earned it.'

'Sure you've earned it, Dukey honey. I don't mind blowin' you right here.'

Duke considered. 'Later.'

Then all three continued walking.

An hour later saw them at the junction. Now a paved two-lane road ran east and west. In the heat of the midday sun there was no traffic. Not at first . . .

Then Duke tilted his head. 'Here she comes again.'

'Uh?' Boots's face was red with sunburn. 'Here comes who again?'

'Same vehicle,' Duke told them. 'Big old diesel motor. Purring sweet as honey.'

They peered to the east.

Like a ghost manifesting itself from the ether came a large, shining object. It rippled. Was distorted.

Eerie-looking, Norman thought.

A ghost bus.

Here it comes.

The bus surged by with a blast of hot air and dust.

Kept on rolling.

Boots let out a whistle of surprise. 'You see that?'

'Yeah,' Norman said mournfully. 'It went right on by without stopping.'

'It's an old school bus,' Duke said.

'But not painted yellow,' Boots pointed out. 'It was a funny-looking gray. And did you see the drapes covering *all* the windows? They were bright yellow.'

Duke nodded. 'Boy, that motor was running sweet. Someone loves the old girl.'

'It didn't stop,' Norman reminded them. 'It went on by.'

Bastard.

Must've seen us. Two guys and a gal.

Drying out under a murdering sun.

'Bastard saw us and left us out to here to die.' Norman didn't stint on words now. 'He'll have been fucking laughing at us as he drove by.'

'You can't be sure of that,' Duke said.

Norman's throat felt raw but he still yelled. 'The bastard knew we were here. He's fucking laughing at us. Murdering bastard!'

'You might want to revise your opinion of said bus driver,' Duke said.

'Why's that?'

'Check out the bus. It's coming back.'

Chapter Thirty-six

The bus's door opened with a hiss.

Norman was ready to fall on his knees.

Thank God!

Thank Beelzebub, Stalin and the IRS man, come to that.

Anyone who brought the bus – the miracle bus! – along the road is all righty by me.

He stood beside Boots and Duke who gazed through the open door at the driver. It was hard to see against the glare of sunlight but he looked like a young guy in sunglasses, boasting a flat-top haircut. A suggestion of lean and fit.

'Your call,' the driver said in a controlled voice after a pause. 'Ride with me or walk, either's okay with me.'

'Riding's my bag. Thank you, sir,' Boots enthused. She dashed up the steps.

Duke nodded an understated 'thank you' at the driver. Then climbed the steps.

Norman followed, half stumbling in his eagerness to get on board. The strap of his backpack caught on the door mechanism, yanked him back.

Could be a sign?

Could be a demon driver.

But he struggled free. Three seconds later he stood in the aisle with his two amigos. They blinked.

In the dull yellow light sat rows of passengers.

'Not a lively bunch, are they?' Duke observed.

'Please take a seat,' the driver told them. 'Company rules. No standing while the bus is in motion. No smoking. No talking to the driver.'

'You're the boss,' Duke said.

'You're a nice man, too,' Boots cooed. 'I sure am grateful. Really, really grateful. Know what I mean?'

'Thank you, thank you. Oh, Jesus. I thought we were gonna die out there.' Norman was close to babbling. 'Thank you.'

'Take a seat, sir.' The driver was scrupulously polite. 'You, too, ma'am.'

Norman sat alongside Duke and Boots who had taken the long bench seat behind the driver. The sort that faced the aisle.

'Nice drapes,' Boots said, waving her arm to take in the yellow fabric covering the windows. 'After blue, yellow's my favorite color.'

The driver said nothing. Merely released the air brakes. With a whooshing hiss the bus rumbled away. The throb of the well-maintained motor rose smoothly in volume as the bus picked up speed. Duke nodded. He knew a healthy internal combustion engine when he heard one.

Norman leaned forward to try to catch a better glimpse of their driver. *There's something steely about him. Something kinda righteous like a preacher or* . . . Norman gulped at his next thought.

A cop.

All he lacked was an officer's hat. His black hair was cut short close to his head at the back and sides. On top, it stuck up as stiff as bristles on a brush. Norman looked at the man's reflection in the rearview mirror. The eyes covered by shades revealed nothing.

Nothing, that was, but an aura of steely determination.

The face possessed that aura, too. The features were lean, a little rough-looking. Yet the guy had shaved his strong jaw so expertly that the skin had a glossy smoothness to it.

Yeah, something of steel in that, too.

Wonder who would win if bus-driver man and Duke went head-to-head in a battle royal?

An elbow dug into Norman's side. He glanced back at Boots. She was making eyes at him.

Not here, woman.

Norman smiled. Nodded.

Then Boots nudged him in his ribs again and made little indicating movements with her head.

She was gesturing to Norman to notice what was happening in the main seating area of the bus. Norman looked back into the hazy yellow glow.

Odd.

Scratch odd.

Weird.

The yellow drapes appeared to be rugs that had been fastened with silvery strips of duct tape to the frames of the bus's windows.

Whooah, Mister Bus-driver Man takes his passengers' eyesight seriously. He's not exposing these suckers to the old retina-searing Mojave sun.

But what kind of passengers are these, anyway?

Norman frowned. Old people. Middle-aged. A young couple in tennis wear. A kid of around eight in a baseball cap, jeans and a T-shirt. There was a slogan there, half-hidden by the strap of a safety belt.

Odd.

'*I've been to Pits,*' it read. '*It Is the Pits. Pits—*' Something or other – he couldn't read the rest.

And why did everyone sit so upright and so still? No one tried to peek out the covered windows. No one sneezed.

Coughed.

Not a fidget amongst them. And you always have at least one fidgeter on a bus.

Norman was still working out the freaky nature of the passengers when Boots piped up.

'Sir . . . Oh, sir? Did you know that you got yourself a bus full of dummies?'

The driver didn't turn back. He kept his attention on the road.

Boots persisted. 'Sir, there's dummies sitting on the seats.'

'No talking to the driver while the bus is in motion, ma'am. Company policy.'

Boots scrunched her shoulders with a smile of apology on her piglike face. 'Oh, gee. I'm sorry. Just thought you should know, that's all.'

'Boots, the guy's gonna know, isn't he?' Duke growled. 'His bus, his business who rides in it.'

'I guess.' She fanned her face with a thick-fingered hand to cool it. 'Looks kinda peculiar, don't it, Normy?'

Agree with Boots, and disagree with Duke?

Norman shrugged. 'At least they're not throwing peanuts at us.'

Duke nodded as if those were wise words.

Boots chuckled and said, 'I guess.'

Norman's eyes had all but recovered from the hell-glare of the desert sun. In the murky golden gloom of the old school bus he now began to make out its inanimate passengers a little more clearly. Dummies. All of them. Like the kind you'd find in clothes stores. Most modeled casual wear. Knit pullovers, Bermuda shorts, T-shirts (including one 'girl' mannequin who wore a white T-shirt with the slogan I ATE A PITSBURGER AND LIVED TO TELL THE TALE). There was one mannequin dressed in a pinstriped suit and tie. He even wore gold-rimmed spectacles to make him look like a well-heeled executive.

'Make great conversation, don't they?' Norman observed.

The driver said nothing. Neither did Duke. To him this was a ride. That was all that mattered. Could have been chimpanzees back there dressed in Hawaiian shirts and tennis shorts. Wouldn't have bothered him.

A ride is a ride, you dig?

Lowering her voice, Boots said to Norman: 'They give me the willies.'

Norman couldn't resist saying, in a spooky whisper, 'I see plastic people.'

'Oooh.' Boots elbowed him and gave a girly laugh. 'You're making me all goosefleshy.' She pointed at her breasts. 'Just look at that. My nipples have gone all hard.'

Her breasts jiggled under the tank top as the bus went over bumps in the road. Then Boots slipped her hand onto the inside of Norman's thigh. She smiled up at him with what experienced people called, 'Come-to-bed eyes.'

Oh, no . . .

Norman felt himself getting hard against the confining fabric of his underpants.

Man, she's so ugly. So piglike. Only she's got a certain something that fires me up inside.

A cool, air-conditioned motel room would be pretty damn wonderful right now. Nude Boots. Lying on a bed. Stroking her stomach. Teasing strokes that worked down toward that magic zone of crisp hair and moist—

'Ten more minutes,' the driver announced. 'Then you folks can get yourselves some vittles.'

He didn't turn round. Didn't say any more.

Norman turned away from hot, sweaty thoughts of a hot, sweaty (and naked) Boots to the view through the bus's windshield. Still brush, mesquite and cacti. But more ravines and jagged piles of rock and mountains. Just as desolate as the desert. In fact, even more remote-seeming. The granddaddy of wilderness country.

Then, straight up ahead, a sign:

MAKE A PIT STOP AT PITS
IT'S REALLY THE PITS
PITS, CA, pop. 6

The T-shirt on the kid. Norman looked. The slogan blazoned across the chest read in part: I'VE BEEN TO PITS.

Norman thought: *Looks like we're heading to Pits, too.*

Hell of a name. He ran his tongue over his lips.

Hell of a name.

Chapter Thirty-seven

That Friday afternoon was a busy one. Pamela had been waiting tables since noon. The weekend traffic had started early. Now there were plenty of people with appetites to satisfy and thirsts to quench. Everyone from truckers to vacationers.

Phew-ee. Hot work.

Yet satisfying, Pamela thought, as she served ice cream to a young couple with a child in a high chair. The two year old sat munching on a French fry. Once he'd yelled out loud. The little tyke had bitten into his own finger instead of the golden sliver of fried potato.

He was happy now, though. Already he had a dribble of strawberry ice cream on his chin.

At the counter Pamela met up with Nicki.

'The Pitsburger Largesse is really flying today,' she said.

Nicki smiled warmly. 'Yeah, and to think I never thought Zak had a tender side.'

From the griddle Terry sang out, 'Three Pitsburgers for table five.'

'This job's going to keep me slim,' Pamela murmured. 'I must walk five miles a day waiting tables.'

'You think you're gonna stay?' Nicki's expression was hopeful.

'Just try and drag me away.' Pamela winked at her, then moved to where Terry had set three massive plates on the counter. Double meat patties turned the hamburgers into mini-skyscrapers. Surrounding those were fries, coleslaw, potato salad.

Even though I know what the dish of the day consists of I'm starting to feel hungry myself. Pamela lifted the plates onto the tray, then whisked them across to three guys in shirts and ties. They waited with eager

254

anticipation for the delicious feast that was gliding their way in the hands of a beautiful girl.

There was a great tip coming her way. She could sense it.

As she took their appetizer dishes away Lauren intercepted her, a serious look in her eye.

'Pamela,' she whispered by the counter. 'Sharpe's brought some people in.'

Pamela experienced a sudden thrill. 'He *saved* them?'

Lauren nodded. 'Look like teenagers. Two men and girl.'

'They're okay?'

'They were stranded in the desert when their truck broke down. They're tired. Very dehydrated.'

'Looks as if they could use some cold drinks.'

'And then some.'

'You want me to prepare a table?'

'The empty booth. I'll need to talk to them when they eat. Find out their story, that kind of thing.'

Pamela sensed a dizzying swirl of flashback. *Just a few days ago it was me being brought to Pits. Saved from psycho Rodney by Sharpe.*

'You okay?' Lauren asked, concerned.

'Oh, me? I'm fine. It's just all so new.' She looked up at Lauren. 'Do you think they've been in trouble?'

'They look pretty tired. Sharpe figures they're running from something.' Lauren shrugged. 'All they'll say is that they were heading down to Las Vegas when they got lost, then their truck died from under them.'

'You think they might be lying?'

'Judge not, lest ye be judged.' Lauren gave a little smile. 'That's what the Good Book says, doesn't it?'

'Wise words.' Pamela nodded.

'We always take people as they are. It's how they act and what they say now that defines their character. Not what they did to people or what people did to them in the past.' Lauren handed a menu to a plump old guy in a baseball cap. Clearly, in Lauren's eyes, he looked like a man ready for dessert. 'We've got a real nice fresh-baked apple pie,' she told the man.

'Sounds sweet to me, ma'am.'

'Large slice, sir?'

'Absolutely.'

'Cream or ice cream?'

'Yes, please.'

'Apple pie, cream and ice cream.' Lauren wrote the order down on her pad. 'Table seven. Be right with you in a moment, sir.'

'Thank you, ma'am. And let me tell you, I've never eaten a hamburger like I've eaten here. Flavor's out of this world.'

'Why, thank you, sir. I appreciate your feedback.'

'How d'you make 'em taste so good? Kinda sweet and savory at the same time.'

'Oh, our secret recipe, sir.'

'Secret, eh?' He chuckled. 'You can tell an old man, my dear.'

Lauren leaned over to whisper into the man's ear. 'If I told you, I'd have to kill you and serve you to the customers.'

The man threw back his head and laughed. 'Ah, that's rich,' he said, wiping his eyes. 'Just you keep griddling up hamburgers like that, sweetheart, and I'll keep coming back.'

'And you're welcome anytime, sir.' Lauren beamed. 'Now, I'll get that apple pie.'

'And cream and ice cream.'

'Shan't forget those, sir.'

Lauren and Pamela left the man chuckling to himself.

'Another happy Pits visitor,' Pamela observed.

'And speaking of which,' Lauren nodded toward the cafe door, 'here comes Sharpe with his three lost lambs.'

Pamela turned to look at the trio as they walked through the doors.

Lost lambs?

Sharpe held the door open for them as they sauntered in, covered in desert dust and radiating a certain aura that Pamela found somehow disturbing.

She looked at each in turn.

First in: A girl of around eighteen but she looked a lot older. She had a wide face. Blunt features. Broad shoulders and hips. Short bleached hair. Clothes consisted of cutoff jeans with slits up the side that exposed a dimpled white skin that contrasted with sunburnt lower legs. Her bare shoulders were exposed by a tight – over-tight – tank top. Her makeup needed refreshing. Looked on the heavy side, too. She carried a bulky denim bag.

What was most striking about her were the boots that she wore. Dirty white high-heeled, pointy-toed cowgirl boots from which a pair of stocky legs emerged.

Second in: A college boy for sure. Late teens. Looked unkempt, as if a nice, tidy kid had been sleeping in a field for week. He'd got nasty-looking bruises on his face.

Sheesh, what was his *story?*

Third in: A swaggering tough guy. Could have passed for a young Elvis. Beneath his blond, greasy swept-high hair a pair of shades rested on the bridge of his nose. Age? Might be a teen; certainly no more than twenty-one, Pamela guessed. He wore a muscle-hugging T-shirt that would have brought appreciative gasps from girls and jealous glances from guys. On his bottom half, oh-so-tight blue jeans that had faded in a kind of interesting way round the crotch and buttocks. Below the cuffs of the jeans she saw a pair of black motor-cycle boots. Metal side-buckles winked at her in the late afternoon light.

Sweet Jesus, this is the template for a bad boy. The kind that good girls fall for.

The kind that girls' dads hate.

That their moms secretly fancy.

But three lambs?

Hardly.

This threesome looked like trouble to Pamela.

But Pits policy, Lauren had said, was to treat everyone as if they were as innocent as newborn babes. Until they did something bad, that was.

Sharpe followed the trio in, then directed them to one of the booths along the wall. Nicki had got pitchers of iced water waiting on the counter ready. Pamela picked up a couple and weaved through the tables of customers to where the 'three lost lambs' had taken their seats. The girl and the college boy looked round at their surround-ings.

The bad boy didn't give a damn. He just stared at his fingernails. He was used to people coming to him with respect written large on their faces.

Sharpe remained standing by the table.

As Pamela walked up Sharpe indicated the three people with a gesture of his hand. 'Pamela,' he said. 'Allow me to introduce you to three new guests of ours.' He nodded at each in turn as he recited their names. 'Boots, Norman, Duke.'

Pamela didn't get much of an opportunity to talk to them. They downed pitcher after pitcher of ice-cold water. Lauren took a seat beside the college boy. He was called Norman. Duke and the oddly named Boots sat opposite them at the booth table. Lauren chatted to them, then signaled to Pamela to take the order.

'You must be hungry,' Pamela said. 'What can I get you guys?'

'What's good to eat here?' the bad boy called Duke asked, nonchalant as James Dean.

'We've got a special today. Pitsburger Largesse. It comes with all the trimmings.'

'Oooh,' the girl with the boots called Boots cooed. 'Sounds scrummy-diddly to me. What say you, boys?'

'I'll have the Pitsburger Largesse, please. Thank you.' Norman was the polite, well-spoken one.

'Got any beer?' Duke asked.

'Bud.'

'Bud's cool. Three Buds for me and my buds.'

Pamela gave a polite laugh to indicate that she'd noticed the guy's play on words.

But he didn't laugh back. Did he even realize that he'd punned?

This one needs watching. He might be bad news for Pits.

Norman downed another glass of water, then said, 'I'm afraid we don't have much cash on us. And I lost my MasterCard when I—'

Lauren waved her hand as if to waft away his words. 'Don't worry about money. You've obviously been through an ordeal. This is our treat.'

'You don't want us to pay?' Boots sounded dumbfounded.

'No.'

'But you'll want something in return?'

'Nothing. It's the least we can do.'

'Mighty Christian of you,' Duke said.

'Yeah,' Boots said. 'Last so-called free meal I got left me with a bloody butt and pube lice.'

Pamela saw that even Lauren gaped at the coarse confession.

'Just shows,' Boots said, then sipped her water. 'Not all preachers are gentlemen.'

'You can rest assured,' Lauren said firmly, 'there'll be nothing like *that* happening to you in Pits.'

Boots shrugged. 'I wouldn't have minded but the preacher promised me that God would—'

'Boots,' Duke interrupted. 'Let the lady take the orders. She's too busy to hear the life story of your fanny.'

Boots clammed up, looking hurt. Her face had the look of a badly wronged sow's.

Pamela noticed that Norman looked uncomfortable, as if these two weren't his companions of choice.

Talk about an odd couple.

These were an odd *trio*.

Pamela smiled her professional waitress smile. 'So that's three Pitsburgers Largesse and three beers.'

Duke touched his eyebrow by way of salute. 'Thank you, ma'am.'

Pamela went to pass the order on to Terry. Then Nicki joined her at the counter.

Nicki whispered, 'Three more for Pitsburgers?'

'Yup.'

'Looks as if Zak finally did something useful in life. Well . . .' She smiled. 'You know what I mean.'

'Yeah, for everyone else it's the grave that's inevitable. Zak wound up in the gravy.' Then Pamela became serious. 'Nicki?'

'Uh-huh?'

'Those three that Sharpe brought in.'

'Oh, yeah, I haven't had a chance to say hello yet.'

'I don't want to put three strangers down, but . . .' Pamela shrugged. 'There's something kinda unsettling about them.'

'Believe me, Pamela, there was something *unsettling* about all of us when we first arrived here. I screamed for a fix for three weeks solid.'

'Yeah, but these guys are—'

'Shh, honey. Don't fret. They'll be fine.'

Nicki hurried away to refill a diner's coffee cup.

Under her breath Pamela muttered, 'Gee, I *hope* they'll be fine. Something tells me there ain't a cop for miles around.'

Moments later, Terry was flipping some more of those pink Pitsburgers on the skillet.

Human flesh sizzles just like a cow's, Pamela told herself. *If only the three strangers knew what – or whom – they were eating.*

From deep down came an additional thought: *Somehow, looking at those three, I don't think they'd give a damn.*

Chapter Thirty-eight

'Who'd they say this trailer belonged to?' Boots asked as she walked into the lounge area with a huge fluffy white towel round her body and another swathing her head.

Duke shrugged. 'Who cares?' He lit a cigarette and sprawled back on the sofa.

Blew smoke at the ceiling.

Thinking.

I get uneasy when Duke starts thinking, Norman told himself. *The guy's planning something.*

Illegal.

Lethal?

Boots took her ease in a black leather armchair. It was old. Worn. Still comfortable, though. Norman sat in its twin by a picture window that looked out toward a cemetery. A real Boot Hill.

Probably a few outlaws sleeping with their boots on up there.

And speaking of boots . . .

Boots frowned. 'Didn't Lauren say this trailer belonged to someone by the name of Valeria?'

'Valdemar,' Norman corrected her. 'Lauren said it belonged to a Gregor Valdemar but he moved on two years ago.'

'Shoot. Leave a lovely place like this? I could make my home here, couldn't you, Duke?'

'I don't take root in any one spot. I move around.'

'I've moved around too much,' Boots said.

'Well, I guess we *need* to keep moving,' Norman said. He watched as Boots bent forward from where she sat on the sofa. She examined a small blister on her little toe where her beloved footwear had rubbed.

Bending had loosened the towel.

Norman saw soft white cleavage.

Hmmm . . .

Those old thoughts were coming back.

'I'm all for moving on,' Duke said, then blew a smoke ring at the ceiling. 'Eventually.'

'Oh Dukey, that sounds good to me. We can rest here awhiles.'

'But the cops—' Norman began.

'You worry too much, bud.'

'Besides, I can't see no cops coming to a little place like this.' Boots examined her other foot. One of her boobs flopped out. 'Oops, 'scuse me, fellas.'

Duke grinned. 'Our pleasure.'

'You guys ready to shower? That water's awful nice after days on the road.'

'Sounds good to me.' Duke stood up, with a yawn. 'Might hit the sack soon, too.'

Boots pulled at the towel to make sure she was covered. 'Wasn't it nice of these folks to give us the trailer home? It's so big. And there's a refrigerator and a stove and everything.'

'They seem like good folks,' Duke said. 'We should stick around and make sure we show our appreciation.'

Duke made the remark seem ominous.

'Okay, shower time.' He left the lounge area.

Boots removed the towel from her head and then rubbed her jaw with it, moaning a little with pleasure at its softness.

Norman looked out the window.

Didn't want to make it seem like he was looking at her bare legs. That towel only just covered her broad rump.

Some rump, too.

His heart beat faster.

Those moaning sounds. She made those when I reamed her.

Oh, boy.

Duke's in the shower.

Now we're alone again. She's making those sounds. Oh no.

I'm getting a hardy.

Any second she's going to notice. How come part of me finds her repulsive, piglike? But then another part, a part getting bigger by the second, finds her soooo sexy . . . Soooo desirable . . .

Norman was suspicious at the way his emotions made these crazy swings from lust to disgust.

He stared out the window like he was enjoying the sunset. His eyes focused on the cemetery on the rise of land. At the top was a freaky-looking house. Just like the Bates house that overlooked the *Psycho* motel. Kind of place that had ghosts in the attic.

Vampires in the cellar.

Zombies in between.

Then, behind the house, glowing with a deep and bloody red, was a range of rocky hills.

Gee, funny little place. Pits. Population six. Lauren looked like a hippie. Sharpe, the guy who drove them in on the freak bus full of store dummies, could have passed for a cop on his day off, or even a Marine on leave. Then there were the waitresses at the cafe. Pamela and Nicki. They were a toothsome twosome.

Sexy.

Briefly Norman imagined himself in bed with the pair of them.

Oh, yes . . .

He shifted in the leather armchair as the blood ran hot in his veins.

How about a nice sandwich with those two?

With me as the salami filling.

More meat than you can eat, girls.

Blood surged into his groin. It ached.

'Normy?'

'Yes?'

Boots's eyes sparkled. 'I know whatcha thinking about.'

'You do?'

'You're thinking hot, sexy thoughts.'

'I am?'

'And you're thinking 'em about me.'

Norman looked at her. After the shower she did look good, he had to admit that. Her short hair was fluffed. Her skin was clean. A fresh smell filled the lounge from her recently showered body.

'Duke's gonna be some time in the shower yet.'

'I guess.'

'Norman, you've been really sweet to me. You've taken care of me.'

'I do my best.'

'You're not like other guys.'

Well, you could take that two ways. But Norman took it as a compliment.

'Thank you. Just doing my job, ma'am.'

'Now you sound like a cop.'

'That's me, ma'am. Officer Norman Wiscoff, reporting for duty.'

'Is that a fact?' Boots scrunched up her shoulders.

Yup, no doubting it.

Her smile was sexy.

Norman let his stare roam over her bare legs to where they vanished beneath the fluffy towel.

Hmm . . . she did look good.

'I think the sofa looks more comfortable.' She went to it.

Lay back flat. Her head was raised on cushions.

Norman stood up. Walked toward her. Some little bit of him found her sexually exciting. And that little bit was growing all the time.

He stood over her.

Boots made a pretend sad face. 'You're not here to arrest me, are you, officer?'

'I think you might be carrying a concealed weapon, ma'am.'

'Then you oughta do your duty, officer.'

Reaching down, Norman whipped open her towel.

Exposed.

A milky expanse of body. Her breasts had firmed. Nipples hard, pointing.

He groaned under his breath. He was so aroused that it hurt.

So he unzipped.

Unbelted.

Undressed.

Oh God, here I am again. Naked with Boots. I think mean thoughts about her but when we're naked together . . . I can't stop myself. This is lust. I've gotta have her.

Norman knelt down on the floor beside the sofa. He buried his face between her breasts. Began kissing her nipples. Tonguing them.

Then he made love to her.

Five minutes later, Duke walked into the lounge area. Shower-wet hair. Wearing nothing but blue jeans.

He gazed down at the pair of them locked together. His face was expressionless.

Norman looked up at him over his shoulder. Boots looked up at him from her supine position.

Norman knew that it seemed kinda absurd to be still pumping away at Boots.

But both of them were on the cusp of orgasm. He couldn't stop himself. So he went for the finishing line, thrusting harder and harder, faster and faster into Boots's warm, moist slickness. Her body convulsed.

Then both of them climaxed in a rucking, bumping, grinding chorus of squeals from Boots and panted '*YESSES!*' from Norman.

Duke still stared down at them as they stopped moving and their cries subsided to post-climactic panting sounds.

'I've gotta plan,' Duke told them, just as if he'd found Boots and Norman doing nothing more than reading magazines. 'This place Pits . . . we're gonna make it ours.'

Chapter Thirty-nine

Lauren showed the three newcomers around. Pamela went along too, at Lauren's request.

'It'll be dark soon,' Lauren told them. 'So it's gonna be a short tour, I'm afraid.'

'That's just fine,' Boots said. 'I'm about all done walking.'

'Thank you for showing us strangers your hometown.' This was the bad boy, Duke. He spoke respectfully.

A little too respectfully for Pamela's liking.

Or am I just naturally suspicious now?

Hardly surprising after a guy marries you – and he's already married. Then a creep you know from school kills your pseudo-husband, burns down your home, then tries to kill you.

Those life experiences make a girl sorta wary.

Lauren walked a little ahead while Pamela walked with the three strangers past the sprawl of trailer homes. Boots had an odd quality. Naive yet worldly at the same time. She wore lots of makeup but took a childlike delight in the things she saw.

Norman had a hunted look in his eye. He had education. Probably came from a wealthy family, too. His casual clothes and footwear looked expensive.

Duke swaggered like the young Elvis. He was cool, confident. Possessed an air of danger. Pamela guessed that nothing fazed him.

Seen all, done all. Still got a taste for more.

He lit a cigarette with a flourish.

Guy acts like he owns the world.

Lauren pointed. 'This is Pits's cemetery.'

'Looks like something out of a Wild West show,' Boots commented.

'This was a frontier town in its heyday. Folk moved out when the mines closed.' Lauren nodded at two acres of dust where old wooden crosses leaned this way and that with tumbleweed and cacti for company. 'No one's been buried in there for years. Except dogs and monkeys, that is.'

'Monkeys?' Norman echoed.

'Owner of the house up there used to own a whole menagerie of monkeys.'

Duke gazed through the gathering dusk at the old house with its decaying shutters. 'Who lives there now?'

'Oh, no one.'

'Big house. Looks as if it could be valuable.'

'I guess,' Lauren said. 'If you were prepared to sink a whole hill of cash into restoring it.'

'So, no monkeys there now?' Boots sounded disappointed.

'Not one. Well, no live ones, that is. Hank tells me there's still a couple of stuffed ones up there in the attic.'

'Cool,' Norman said.

'Who's Hank?' Duke asked.

'The mayor of Pits,' Pamela answered. 'He's around somewhere.'

Duke's eyes narrowed. 'And you say there's only seven people who live in Pits?'

'Yup,' Lauren said, with a smile. 'That's if we include Pamela, and she might be just passing through. But we're optimistic about our population growing.'

'I hope it does, ma'am.' Duke nodded. 'Looks a nice town.'

'We like it.'

They walked to the cemetery but stopped short of continuing on to the old house on the hill. Then they backtracked to the cafe.

Lauren opened the door for them. 'While we've no customers at the moment we might as well grab the opportunity of meeting the Pits people under one roof.'

They filed in.

'Looks like the whole town turned out to meet us, guys,' Boots said. She was beaming at the younger men – Terry and Wes – and especially at Sharpe. Sharpe was as smartly dressed as ever in a crisp white shirt and chinos. He was clean-shaven.

Then there was the old-timer, Hank. He didn't get a second glance from Boots in his weather-beaten clothes and stained hat.

Boots stroked her hair.

Fiddled with the strap of her tank top.

Drawing attention to her unfettered breasts beneath the fabric.

Got an eye for the men, haven't you, girl?

All of Pits was there – all seven of them. The guys sat on stools with their backs to the counter so that they faced the new folk in town. With the exception of Sharpe, they drank bottles of Bud.

Sharpe hefted a glass of water.

He had his Mission. There was no place for alcohol in his life.

Nicki sat at the table nearest the counter.

Lauren introduced the three. 'Ladies and gentlemen of Pits, I'd like to introduce you to Boots.'

Boots gave a little curtsy.

Elegant it wasn't.

'And these are Duke and Norman.'

The Pits people said 'Hi,' 'Pleased to meet you' and so forth. They were friendly, smiled. They were genuinely pleased to have visitors, Pamela realized.

Lauren indicated Hank, in his prospector's clothes and with a face shriveled like a sun-dried plum. 'And this is Hank. Mayor of Pits.'

'Pleased to meetcha. You look like real fine people.' He winked at Boots. 'Especially you, mademoiselle. A real peach, if I might say so?'

Boots fluttered her hand in front of her face as if it was a fan and she was a southern belle being courted by an old-money gentleman. 'Why, thank you.'

Lauren said, 'Seeing as it's near to closing time anyway, what say you we have ourselves a little reception party for our new guests? Nicki, will you get the drinks? I'll set out some snacks. Oh, Pamela?'

'Yes?'

'Would you turn off the cafe sign and lock the door?'

'I'm right on it.'

Soon everyone was chugging down bottles of beer.

Except Sharpe.

He still favored water.

If anything, he was the only one who retained his cool reserve. Everyone else was smiling. Lauren stood real close to Sharpe several times.

Showing Boots that they were a couple.

So hands off. He's mine.

Norman looked a little tipsy on the beer. He smiled a lot at Nicki. Her blonde Nordic beauty had caught his eye. She smiled back politely.

But I see Terry, who has got the hots for Nicki, starting to show signs of jealousy.

Then, Nicki never showed any interest in boys.

And Duke's standing almost toe-to-toe with Sharpe as he talks to him.

No aggression whatsoever.

But I get the feeling that Duke is sizing Sharpe up. As if he's assessing the guy's physique and demeanor just in case he needs to fight him one day.

As Pamela helped Lauren to hand out plates of cold cuts, potato chips, dips, nachos and sourdough bread, she felt that unsettling tug of paranoia again.

Is it really paranoia, she thought, *or am I reading a whole heap of sinister body language here in the guy who calls himself Duke?*

Then there's the hunted expression that haunts Norman's face.

Then Boots – strange, strange Boots.

It's cruel to label another human being dysfunctional without really knowing them. But then, Boots is odd. Sort of not connecting with the rest of the human race.

But maybe Pamela was a minority of one.

What happens if I go to Lauren and Sharpe and say 'Hey, those three strangers. I don't trust them. They're up to something'? Maybe they'll think I'm the weird one.

Maybe ask me to leave.

And that's what I don't want to do. I like Pits. I like the people here (except the Gang of Three). I want to stay here. I really do.

Chapter Forty

Norman explored. Though he hadn't shared his emotions with anybody, just like Pamela he was uneasy, too.

Duke's got plans for Pits.

Duke hadn't explained anything in detail. His line had been, 'We're gonna make this place our own.' Duke'd repeated the statement often. But he still hadn't described how it would work.

Now, at eight o'clock in the morning, Norman had decided on a stroll to clear his mind before the heat of the day took the desert and everyone in it prisoner.

But Jeez, had he slept well. No wonder. They'd been on the run for days, he'd been knocked unconscious by Duke, then they'd hiked through the desert and damn near died of thirst.

Would have, too.

If it hadn't been for Sharpe.

Now there's a man who's a mystery wrapped in an enigma. Why does he cruise the desert roads in that old bus full of mannequins?

Some religious conviction?

Some psychotic impulse?

But Sharpe had brought them to a quiet cop-free place. A place with good food. A place with a mobile home that had soft beds.

So Norman had slept the sleep of the dead. Never heard a thing.

Even so, he'd been disappointed that Boots had chosen to share Duke's bed rather than his. Boots was peculiar. Irritating. Had weird piggy looks.

But Norman couldn't get enough of boning her. He loved it when she sucked his cock. Or when she hunkered down onto all fours with a smiling invitation to screw her dog-oh.

Loved to see her skin blotch as sexual excitement kicked in when he reamed her. The way her titties jiggled with the force of his groin pounding against hers.

Norman's heart began to beat harder. A tingle started in his penis.

Ohhh . . . just the thought of Boots naked set him on the path of hot erotic thoughts.

But instead of being able to satisfy these urges, last night in his bedroom as he'd undressed for bed he'd heard the pair moaning with pleasure. The thin walls of the trailer had held nothing back. He had even been able to hear the *squelch* as Duke had pumped his rock-hard cock into Boots's wet 'n' happy valley.

Lucky bastard.

He clicked his tongue. 'Leave it, Norman. Do some sightseeing.'

And at least the noise hadn't stopped him falling asleep the second he'd closed his eyes.

Norman sauntered across the cafe's parking lot. On one side was the straggling line of trailer homes. On the other a bunch of cars that seemed abandoned.

Some were real wrecks. So old that Henry Ford himself could have personally pumped the tires before they rolled out of the workshop. Then, and this piqued Norman's curiosity a lot, there were newer cars.

Several in good shape.

Despite the dust.

Could see someone step into one, start it up, then drive off in a swirl of dust.

But they clearly hadn't been driven anywhere in a couple of years. Tires part-deflated. Windshields thick with dust. One silver Pontiac boasted a big green lizard sunning itself on the hood. Who'd leave cars like this at a desert cafe?

'Someone who couldn't pay the tab,' Norman mused aloud. 'But would you exchange a new Toyota Land Cruiser for a couple of pizzas?'

No dice.

Not buying that, Tonto.

There was even luggage in the vehicles' cargo spaces. Wind-borne sand had seeped in through the door seals to leave a yellow film on the baggage. He walked along the line of cars, trucks, vans, and a pair of motorcycles. A couple of cars were rusted shells. One even had bullet holes in it.

Someone tries to run without paying for the Pits Burger. Lauren or the sexy Pamela rakes the car with machine-gun fire. The silly train of thought amused Norman. He chuckled.

Then the chuckle dried.

This line of abandoned cars is weird, though.

Hey! Who's that strolling up through the cemetery?

Shielding his eyes against the sun rising over barren hills, he stared hard. *Looks like Boots and the blonde girl. The Swedish-looking girl. Nicki? Yeah, Nicki. Man, is she a sexy piece of work. Cool as glacial runoff but, boy, would I like to scale her snowy peaks.*

They were over a hundred yards away. Both seemed to be talking to each other in an earnest kind of way.

'Sharing secrets, girls?' Norman wondered. Only there was one secret about himself he didn't want spilling. And no, not the one about him being a virgin until a few days ago.

Killed two cops, didn't I?

Word of that gets out, I'm gonna fry in The Chair.

The Mojave heat had been climbing steadily since sunup. Only now Norman felt a distinct chill creep up his backbone.

He whispered to himself, 'I've got to hear what you're telling her, Boots. Don't want you revealing any confidences about me.'

Glancing round to make sure that no one was watching him, Norman strolled back through the line of trailers to the cemetery gates. Behind him the desert road was empty. He could see no one. A little blue haze rose from the cafe flue where Terry must have been frying bacon and eggs. *Hmm, breakfast . . .*

'S gonna have to wait. I need to find out what these two are talking about.

So here goes . . . walking through the cemetery gates . . . following the path up the center.

Brush, dry grasses, cacti; they'd infiltrated the cemetery to grow around old tombstones, wooden crosses. Iron plaques spelt out names, dates, and invitations to RIP. Sometimes an epitaph: 'Long was his race, longer will be his rest.' 'Little Jimmy tried his best, only his best weren't good enough. Died weeping for his Momma.' Then there were some real old stones that had been almost weathered out.

Norman paused to read one out loud to himself. '"Eli Crabber. Shot by Sheriff Dunbar, Christmas Day, 1878." Holy shit. A real-life shoot-out.'

The Glory Bus

He looked back at Pits. It still had a look of a frontier town. It was an island standing in a whole ocean of sand. Across the road from the cafe he could make out rectangular depressions in the earth where buildings had once stood. Probably the town's jail alongside the saloon and maybe a brothel or two. All rotted, then blown away by the Mojave winds.

He squinted against the glare of the hot sun.

Boots and Nicki were still walking uphill. They'd left the cemetery now.

Heading up toward the abandoned house on the hill.

Probably this was the only original house from Pits's glory days as a working mine. Must have belonged to the richest guy in town. The guy who owned the bank, maybe.

Or, more likely, the owner of the mine. Back then, a guy like that would have had the power of life and death over the people of Pits.

His mine.

His town.

In Norman's mind he could see a big man of around fifty dressed in a suit and stovepipe hat. He'd have had big, bushy side-whiskers and would've stood up there on his porch with one of those old-time pocket watches in his hand.

Gotta make sure that the miners aren't late for work.

And when they were all down in the pits, hacking rock faces with their picks, Mister Big would stroll down through *his* town until one of the miners' women caught his eye. Then he'd order her up to his house to wash. Once she was freshened up he'd exercise his rights as employer to the max.

Oh boy, oh boy. Norman sure wished he were that mine-owner.

The fantasy was so pleasurable that he nearly had an accident in his underpants.

Pausing, he took a few steadying breaths. Up ahead the two women had almost reached the house. Boots could have asked Nicki to show her the stuffed monkeys.

Yeah, whatever floats your canoe.

Just hope she doesn't bring one back to the trailer as a souvenir. Don't want to share the place alongside a fusty chimpanzee with glass eyes staring at me all the time. Give anyone the creeps.

Even as Norman walked the last few yards through the cemetery, he saw rows of newer headstones that were in a different style to the rest. These had just a single name painted on them. 'Jango.' 'M'pallar.' 'Mansize.' 'Rebo.'

Never ever owned a monkey, he thought, *but these sure look as if they could be names for baboons and shit.*

He headed for the cemetery exit. The path continued to wind up the hillside. Here it was pretty much barren. Although off to his right Norman could see a thicket of cottonwood trees where there might have been some moisture oozing up from the rocks below ground.

Beyond that the land rose to more arid terrain. All he could see were greenish swatches of cholla cacti. From here their 'fingers' looked fluffy and soft but he knew that they bristled with sharp spines.

From a clump of dry plants near a tombstone with 'Stoker' written on it came the ominous rattle of one of the desert's bad guys.

Norman hastened on.

Soon he was through the rickety fence. Just in time to see the pair of women disappear into the house.

If Boots blabs about the way I killed the police officers Nicki's gonna race out of the house and come running down through the cemetery to the cafe where she's gonna dial nine one one.

You can bet your bottom dollar that's not gonna happen. 'Cos I can't let it happen.

Wild thoughts rose in Norman's mind. Of him beating down on Nicki's head with one of the broken tombstones. Then burying her.

Best place to bury the person you murdered is in a cemetery. Place is full of stiffs anyway.

He licked his suddenly dry lips.

Course, Normy, before you murder the beautiful blonde woman you must make use of her facilities first.

Oh my God. He stopped. His own thoughts startled him. *Am I really starting to think like Duke now? That people are like gum. Chew 'em up, then when the flavor's gone spit 'em out.*

Although it was now even hotter, his bones felt even colder.

Still, it was his survival he was thinking about now.

Gotta put numero uno first. Me, myself, I is the important one.

Even if that means the delicious Nicki winds up lying in the ground with monkeys.

Norman walked faster to the house now that the pair had gone inside. On reaching it, he immediately tiptoed round the side, rather than up to the front door through which Boots and friend had entered.

His heart beat faster.

Palms sweated.

Afraid?

Yes.

Excited?

Definitely.

Norman wondered if one way or the other he'd wind up leaving a mess in his pants after all.

He circled round the back of the house. Shutters sagged from hinges. Sandstorms had long ago taken the paint off the woodwork. They'd even begun to sculpt window and door frames into weird shapes. But all the glass in the windows was in place.

Maybe a modicum of care had been given to the building. Perhaps by that old-timer who looked like a mule skinner. Hank probably came up here to keep the building secure.

So does that mean there's something of value in there?

Norman reached the far side of the house. There was no yard to speak of. It looked as if the whole house had been picked up from someplace else and then plonked down here onto the hilltop. Surrounding the house was nothing but loose dry earth and stones. A tumbleweed had rolled up to rest against a basement window. At the back of the house, craggy yellow hills. The place was an advertisement for wilderness. It was as barren as the dark side of the moon.

For a moment he stood eyeballing the two-story house with its spooky crooked roof from which poked an even more crooked chimney stack.

No sounds from inside.

Boots was chuckling over the stuffed monkeys, no doubt.

Better that than telling Nicki about their adventures on the drive south from Oregon.

No one from the cafe or the trailers could see Norman at this side of the house so he didn't have to be furtive anymore. He strolled forward to take a gander through the window. Through the dusty glass he saw red-checkered drapes that were part-open. Between the gap he saw an old-fashioned kitchen with a big iron stove. A kitchen table and chairs, too. On the table were a couple of china plates.

Not quite the wreck that Norman had expected.

Not quite a home from home, either.

Probably a snake or two curled up under the john in the bathroom. Just waiting for the unwary to slip down their pants as a prelude to a dump, then—

Wham!

A pair of poison fangs right in the butt.

Hell, who in this place would suck out the poison? Norman thought about the full lips of Pamela. *She'd be first on my list.* But as so often happened with imagination it shot images into his head that were just plain unwelcome.

As he smiled to himself, picturing Pamela walking toward him saying, 'Best get out of those clothes, Norman. I've got to suck out every last drop of that venom,' the unwholesome image snuck in. This time it was of old Hank in the prospector's hat that looked as if a mule and his best friend had shit in it for luck.

Norman couldn't stop the imaginary episode kicking in.

Poor Norman running back into Pits yelling that a snake had bit his right buttock. Then Hank licking his scabbed lips that in turn revealed his gums that were barely interrupted by a few brown, twisted teeth. And surrounding the mouth from hell was the thick mustache and beard.

The man's bloodshot eyes would gleam in anticipation. 'Looks like ya got yerself an ass full of venom there, feller.'

Norman would say he'd be just fine.

Only old Hank would hitch up his belt, all the time shaking his head. 'Nope. Nothin' fer it, I'm gonna have to suck out the poison meself.' Pause to spit out a plug of tobacco in a stream of yellow saliva. 'Yup, you drop them college-boy panties, then I'll suck out that rattler juice before it rots your tricky-dicky right off of you.'

'No, I'll be fine, thank you.'

'Don't want to go through life whizzing like a dame, do you?'

Then the indignity. Dropping his pants in front of Hank. Then bending over, waiting for the wet mouth to batten on his buttock. Then the slurping, sucking – followed by spitting – as Hank drew out the snake venom.

Of course, as Norman bent over bare-assed, Hank would say something like, 'Now, young feller, I'll be saving your life so don't you go doin' a number two in my face, all right?'

A cry.

Norman jerked himself out of his imagined scenario. *Jeez.* He'd have to learn to stop his imagination running away with him. Thoughts of Hank sucking on his butt like a baby sucking on its mother's breast weren't pretty. Not even when the image was plug-fuck imagined.

Norman looked up at the storm-scarred walls of the house. *Shit. Where did the cry come from?*

And who cried out?

Nicki?

Boots?

Could be Nicki. Boots killed the guy in the motel. Murder's no stranger to her. Maybe the stuffed monkeys weren't to Boots's taste. Now she was extracting suffering from the beautiful blonde waitress.

Shit. No fair.

Norman wanted a peek at Nicki's goodies first. He ran to the next window.

Peered in.

Some kind of office. A typewriter on a desk. Racks of files.

He hurried to the next window just as another cry sounded. This one higher. What the hell was Boots doing to hurt that blonde goddess? *Probably hammering a nail into her forehead.*

The cry had that kind of quality. Made Norman's hair stand up on the back of his neck.

Next window.

Norman thrust his face to the grimy pane. Stared in. And saw . . .

And saw . . .

Holy moly!

Couldn't believe his eyes.

Boots had done all kinds of things, but he couldn't believe she'd do *that.*

What's French for sixty-nine?

Norman's mouth dried. His heart hammered. Blood whooshed through his neck to swirl around his brain so forcefully that vertigo nearly tipped him backward onto the ground. His eyes bugged. He couldn't stop watching.

Hell! Don't want *to stop watching!*

Couldn't stop watching if I tried. Nicki and Boots. Both naked. They were in a room empty of everything but a large rug that covered half the floor. Boots's short, stocky body was a hell of a contrast to Nicki's long, slim bod with firm breasts that were in perfect proportion to the rest of her frame.

Unlike Boots's small soft breasts that were set on a broad-shouldered torso.

Man oh man. Norman looked at the women, trying to work out who was doing what to whom. Nicki was on all fours with Boots lying underneath her. It was the classic sixty-nine position.

Right now, Nicki wasn't doing anything with her tongue. She held her head up. Her blond hair cascaded softly around her shoulders. Her eyes were closed, her lips were partly open. She was smiling.

And she was the one crying out.

Cries of pleasure.

Norman turned his attention to Boots. She lay with her head under Nicki's groin, with Nicki's knees planted on the rug either side of Boots's head.

But what was Boots doing to Nicki? He could see the blond spiky hair bob as Boots moved her head up and down. Only he hadn't bargained on—

Damn!

Norman's breath had gotten so hot that it had steamed up the windowpane. Now all he could see were misted blobs. He raised his hand to wipe the glass. Decided against it.

The *squeak-squeak* of his sweating fingers on the glass would betray him.

And, Jeez, this I gotta see, he told himself, panting. Groin aching.

Instead, Norman had to move his head to a different pane of glass in the window. Then find part of that which wasn't too obscured by dust.

'C'mon, c'mon, you're missing all the action,' he hissed to himself.

Then he found another area of the glass that had a heaven-blessed clarity.

Thank God!

Oh, now he could see. Could see real good.

So this was how it went.

Boots lay flat on her back with her head raised by a pillow. *Great!*

Only this was unusual: what was Boots doing with her hand?

Nicki cried out in pleasure. Almost howling. Boots grunted, too. A snuffling sound that Norman could hear through the window glass.

Norman was gasping as well. His knees shook.

His breath misted the window again.

Oh no . . . missing the action, missing the action!

He found another clear area of pane.

Looked in. Saw that both women were moving faster in their excitement.

Both sweating.

Both flushed with exertion.

Both panting.

And Norman was panting, too.

Then his breath went and misted the window yet again. He found another pane. Only this one was obscured by a spider's web. All he could see were two pale shapes jigging around in there. It looked good. It looked real fine . . . but he couldn't make out any detail.

And he realized that he did need detail. Plenty of it. He found a clean corner of glass. All he could see were Nicki's bare feet. The way she scrunched up her toes in ecstasy excited him more than words could say.

Uh . . . Norman didn't know if he could take anymore of this.

'Oh yes, oh yes!' That was Nicki!

Norman darted his face to another corner of the window. Now he could see Nicki from the shoulders up. *Damn.* He couldn't make out the rest of her bod, nor Boots's. Nicki cried out the words again while twisting her head from side to side so wildly that her long blond hair flew. Norman marveled at it. He'd never seen hair as beautiful as this. Like summer cornfields and gold dust all rolled into one.

But Norman had to see *all* the action. Had to witness what those two sex-crazed women were doing to each other.

He risked wiping a misted section of glass with the tip of his finger. It squeaked a little but he figured that the two girls were making enough noise to drown out a mule braying, never mind the faint rubbing sound of his sweaty fingertip.

He saw naked bodies but . . . *Oh God, no.* The glass was still blurred with grime. All he could make out were two indistinct shapes. Even so, he knew they were female. They were Boots and Nicki going for broke.

Faster ... faster, faster, faster ...

The pair cried out as they climaxed in body-shaking judders.

Moments later they lay side by side on the rug, panting. Sucking in air so that their breasts rose and fell.

At last Norman found that he could move back from the window.

Oh no – I don't believe it.

Norman realized that the clean underwear he'd slipped on just an hour ago was no longer in a condition of which he could be proud.

He decided to go back to the trailer. To swab away the 'night custard,' as one of his high-school buddies had called it. Change into a fresh pair of boxers.

Norman had just turned the corner of the house when he noticed something else. At the bottom of the slope at the far end of the cemetery was a shallow gully.

Duke was there.

He was engaged in strange behavior as well.

Chapter Forty-one

Norman stared.

Duke walked backward in the dusty gully. He walked backward because he was hauling a sausage-shaped object that was wrapped in a tarpaulin.

In dry grass by the cemetery fence a creature that Norman couldn't see chattered to itself. It could have been chattering over and over: 'Oh no, here we go again.'

Because Norman could see what the shape in the tarp looked like. Other than a sausage, that was. Because it would have had to be a *big* sausage. A big, guy-sized sausage. And Duke was having to dig his heels into the dirt so hard to find purchase that he was kicking up a whole fog of yellow dust.

Norman glanced down toward the cafe. No one could see Duke from there but they might see the dust cloud. Then they'd start wondering what was happening near the cemetery.

Maybe some kind of resurrection action. *That's gotta tug their curiosity string.* Or maybe they'd picture a funky zombie-monkey scenario. *Long-dead baboon's coming back to life, clawing its way to the surface . . .*

Oh shit. Norman reckoned he'd have to do something about his maverick imagination.

He turned back to the big old house. Boots and Nicki would still be busy exploring each other's bods. *Too busy for Nicki to see what Duke's doing.*

At that moment Duke looked back over his shoulder. 'Hey,' he called. 'Come here and give me a hand.'

Shit, I'm involved again. Another of Duke's adventures.

281

This's all gonna end in tears one day soon.

Norman shot glances down at the cafe as he picked his way across the stone-covered ground. He still hadn't forgotten the rattlesnake/Hank scenario that his imagination had treated him to. So he trod carefully toward Duke.

Can't give those snakes a free shot at my rear.

Luckily, it was still early. No one seemed minded to stroll around Pits at this hour. Sharpe's bus with the yellow drapes still sat in the lot alongside various abandoned vehicles.

Norman descended into the gully. It was a small one. Little more than a slit in the earth between the rise of the hill and the boundary of the cemetery. Its sides only rose as high as Norman's ears.

'Wanna take a peek at Sleeping Beauty here?' Duke asked. Then whipped back a flap of the tarp.

'Terry?'

'Yeah, he kept staring at me – so I figured I had to teach the kid a lesson.'

I remember the lesson Duke taught me.

Norman looked down at Terry's blood-covered face. More blood matted his red-brown fringe.

'Kid put up a fight?' Norman asked.

'None that you'd notice.'

'I guess Pits is gonna have to find another cook for its cafe.'

'You guess right, Normy.'

'Uh . . . where you plan on taking him, Duke?'

'Back there into the scrub. They'll bury him later.'

'They?'

'Sharpe and the rest.'

'You don't think they might be . . . uh, upset that you've killed one of their townsfolk?'

'They'll learn to get over it.'

'I know, but they might have been fond of the guy, Duke. He could have been a—'

'Norman, are you going to stand there chinnin' me to death? Grab a corner of the tarp – start pulling.'

Norman grabbed a corner. Arguing with Duke wasn't healthy.

Hell, even *looking* at Duke wrong wasn't a beneficial option.

'Jesus. This is harder than it looks,' Norman panted.

'You need to work on those muscles, bud. Girls like 'em, guys respect 'em.'

'Some guys like 'em, too.'

'You faggin' out on me, Norman?'

'No . . . uh . . . just making an observation.'

'You make with pulling Sleeping Beauty here. Leave the observing to me.'

'Sure, Duke.'

Pulling a corpse over uneven ground was hard work. Norman's back ached. His arms hurt. He thought his shoulder might dislocate pretty damn soon.

Sweat started.

Not a moistening of the temples. But a salty river running down the inside of his shirt.

And that sun . . .

Damn hot. Damn, damn hot.

They both tugged what could have been an oversize dim sum. Only this roll wasn't stuffed with fish or animal meat: it contained one hundred and sixty pounds of what the Good Book reckoned had been made in God's image.

Namely the cadaver of Terry, late of Pits.

Duke hardly sweated a bead of moisture. Still cool under pressure.

Norman perspired like he was in a Turkish bath.

Glanced back. Saw the roll of tarp with its heavy cargo sliding through the dust, stones rolling under it, flattening a small cactus here, a tuft of grass there. At one point Terry's bare arm flopped out. Duke told Norman to ignore it. Keep hauling.

Norman kept hauling.

Ached like crazy, though. Sweated like a pig that'd learnt the truth about bacon.

Oh, Lord. And he still hadn't gotten to change his underwear after his accident watching Boots and Nicki make out.

'Don't worry, Norman. I've got it all planned.'

After a series of grunts as they hauled Terry over a rocky outcrop Norman managed to echo, 'Planned?'

'Yeah,' Duke said. 'This place. We're taking it over.'

'Oh . . . right.'

'I'm gonna be mayor instead of the old guy.'

'Sounds a good move.' Norman decided to humor Duke.

For obvious reasons.

'You and Boots will be my deputies.'

Isn't there a fundamental flaw here? What about Sharpe (a tough guy in his own right) and the rest?

'Once we've taught them a lesson they won't forget they'll do as we say.' Duke was confident as ever.

'Sure,' Norman agreed. 'Like dogs need discipline, we can discipline them.'

'See, Norman, that's the value of a college education. You grasp the concept. That's why I like you. You think like me.'

Norman had to pause for a minute to catch his breath. Also to wipe his sweating palms on the legs of his pants.

Duke put his hands on his hips, then looked round like he already owned the place. 'We'll share out the town between us. Cars and trailers and stuff.'

'That'll be great.'

'And—' He fixed Norman with a steely look in the eye. 'And we'll share the women out, too.'

Norman almost doubled up as if winded. Now Duke's plan really did appeal.

The women!

'I'm gonna have Lauren and Pamela,' Duke told him. 'You can have Nicki.'

'Oh, right!' Norman couldn't stop himself letting out a howl of excitement.

'I've got eyes.' Duke allowed himself one of his coolest smiles. 'I saw you'd got the hots for the dame.'

'Oh, thanks, Duke. You're the best!'

'You earned it, Normy. You're my number two.'

'Uhm, but what about Boots?'

'Aw, Boots is special, ain't she?'

'She sure is.

'A real peach.'

'Top-drawer, Duke.'

'Right. So I decided we'll share her between ourselves. You take her weekends, I'll have her weekdays.'

'Thanks, Duke. That's a great idea.'

'See, Norman, you gotta plan ahead.' Duke spat on his hands. 'Okay, time to lose stiff boy.'

Norman shielded his eyes against the rising sun. If he lifted his head he could see down through the haphazard mass of tombstones to the cafe. A truck carrying lumber was just pulling into the lot in a swirl of dust. First customer of the day.

'Wonder who's gonna cook the trucker's breakfast now?' Norman wondered.

'Guy ain't gonna pull himself, Normy.'

Norman and Duke started again to haul the body along the dry-as-bones gully.

Norman felt he was in as poor a shape as Terry by the time Duke said, 'This'll do.'

They'd dragged the body into a stand of cholla cacti.

'No paths nearby,' Duke said. 'No one will see any dead bastard in here.'

'Coyotes'll probably start work on him soon enough.'

Duke chuckled. 'Well, that ain't no skin off of *my* nose.'

Norman dropped the corner of the tarp, then stretched his arms up, arching his back. *Dragging the corpse this far has nearly been the death of me, too,* he thought sourly.

Duke bent down to grip the edge of the tarp where the corpse's head would be. 'You wanna give him a good-night kiss, Normy?'

'I'll pass.'

'Wuss.'

'Duke?' Norman swallowed as an unpleasant taste came into his mouth. 'You're not gonna . . .'

'You prejudiced against a different sorta love?'

'Holy shit.' Norman looked down in horror as Duke began to lift the tarpaulin away from the dead face. 'Duke . . . I – I don't know . . .' *Oh God, the guy's out of his mind; is he really gonna—*

Duke grinned. 'Relax, buddy. Ain't you ever been on the receiving end of a wind-up before?'

'You mean you don't want to . . . to . . .'

'Boy oh boy, Norman.'

'It's just that when you asked if I wanted to give Terry a good-night kiss, I – I—'

'Joke, Norman. Just a laugh, okay?'

'But what're you doing with—'

'Don't worry, I'm not gonna make you touch him.' Duke opened up the tarpaulin to expose Terry's body. The corpse was wearing a chef's apron over his clothes.

Bloody clothes.

Man, Duke knows how to use those fists of his with killing effect.

Duke explained. 'You don't just dump a body without checking it for stuff. Might be gold rings. Cash in pockets. A nice Rolex.'

'Anything?'

'Plastic watch. Not worth taking it off. Thirty bucks in the shirt pocket. Lousy cheap shitter.'

Even a victim being dead didn't soften the wrath of a guy like Duke. He punched the corpse in the family jewels.

The corpse screamed. Norman screamed louder.

'So the guy's not dead,' Duke remarked. 'What do you think I am, a brain surgeon?'

Terry sat bolt upright. He was gasping. Blinking weirdly in the bright sunlight.

Duke pulled the knife from his boot.

'Norman, pull his head back so I can get at his throat.'

'Oh, shit.' Norman's knees felt about as stiff as ice cream on a summer's day.

'Don't take all day about it. We've got work to do.'

Norman pounced on Terry. The young guy fought back like a crazed puma. Slashing at Norman with his hands. Snarling.

Suddenly he was on top of Norman, pushing him against a cactus. Sharp spines stabbed Norman's arm. He cried out.

And all the time Terry's bloodied wild-eyed face was jammed up close to his.

Eyeball to eyeball.

Blood from the guy's bleeding lips sprayed against Norman's face.

Duke remained patient. 'Norman. *You* were supposed to be holding *him.*'

Norman managed to put the heel of his palm against Terry's forehead. He pushed hard. Shoving the head back.

'Way to go, Norman.'

With the guy's throat exposed Duke reached round with the knife.

Then drew it slow and deep across the throat just below the bobbing Adam's apple.

Immediately, Terry lost all interest in wrestling with Norman. Instead, he became preoccupied with holding the gash closed with both his hands. Even so, blood streamed through his fingers.

Norman rolled sideways, stood up and watched in horror. The guy made like a goldfish with his mouth opening and shutting. He was trying to gulp in air but none was going down into his lungs. Blood covered his hands so he looked as if he'd been mashing raw strawberries with his fists.

Fingers, hands, wrists – all a slick crimson.

Terry stared at Norman. Eyes pleading with him.

Norman stared back.

Then Terry began to make a strange mule-like screaming.

'Blunt knife,' Duke explained. 'Didn't cut all the way through.'

'Duke, do something.'

'He'll quieten down soon enough.'

Only he didn't. He kept that weird braying sound going – louder and louder, too.

Christ, I can't take this anymore. He's going to bring everyone running.

Norman dropped down into a squat, found a hunk of stone the size of a football. Then he stood back up. Heaved the rock up high over his head until his arms were straight, elbows locked.

Terry still hee-hawed. Still stared at him.

Duke stood, coolly watching what Norman did next.

I've gotta do this, Norman thought. *I've no choice. Gotta stop him yelling out like that.*

Gotta stop him staring at me.

Freaking me out.

The huge hunk of stone that Norman had lifted straight above his head in his two hands must've weighed at least twenty pounds. His elbows quivered. *Can't hold it much longer.*

Gritting his teeth, Norman brought it down hard onto Terry's head. The top of the guy's skull caved in.

One eye popped clear of its socket.

Terry went down.

Lay twitching.

Feet kicking up a swirl of dust.

The mindless hee-hawing stopped. Norman thought the silence was beautiful.

Duke was impressed. 'Nice work, Norman.' He gave the body a casual kick with the toe of his motorcycle boot. 'He won't wake from that one.'

'I killed him.' Norman wasn't sure if that was a statement or a question.

'Yeah, and how. You know, you're getting some bloodlust on you.' Duke grinned. 'You've become a killing machine. A real term-in-a-tuh.'

'I'd like to go back to the trailer now.'

'Sure. You need to clean up. That damp patch in your crotch is unsightly, you know? You're supposed to leave that in a woman's pussy, not in your shorts.'

Norman could only nod. Half staggering, he turned and then walked back toward the trailer.

Duke called after him. 'I'll be there in half an hour. It's time we started work.'

Chapter Forty-two

'Anyone seen Terry?' Pamela asked Hank, who was dragging a plastic sack full of trash from the kitchen toward the utility room.

One of the old-timer's chores. Part-time mayor, part-time tour guide, part-time trashman.

'I ain't seen Terry but I got an eyeful of you.' He winked that old-lecher wink of his. His scabbed lips stretched into a wide grin. The grin put his gums on display again with their half a dozen yellow teeth. 'Yer a beauty, that's God's honest truth.'

'Thank you, Hank.' Pamela smiled. She was used to his ways by now. 'There's customers waiting for food and I can't find Terry. Do you know where he might be?'

'I don't rightly know.' Hank scratched his white whiskers. 'He's always here by nine.'

Pamela colored a little as she said, 'You don't think he might be with Nicki? In her trailer?'

'I knows he's taken with Nicki, but that ain't reciprocated.'

'Terry's nice, she might have . . . you know . . . warmed to him.'

'Oh, don't get me wrong, ma'am. Nicki likes Terry but not in that kinda way.'

'What makes you say that?'

'I've bin on God's Earth long enough to know a thing or two. If you ask me, Nicki plays for the other bowling team, if you see what I mean?' Hank winked his bloodshot eye again.

'Hank, that's not nice; you shouldn't speculate about things like that.'

'It's not just speculatin'.' Again the crusty wink. 'I've got two eyes in m' head. I seen Nicki entertainin' ladies in her trailer 'fore now.'

'Oh Hank, you shouldn't spy on people.'

'So I seen Nicki on the old beaver hunt, if ya catch my drift.'

'I catch it all right.'

'Seen her do the scissor-sister thing. Watched her drink from the hairy cup. Saw her plow a fresh furrow. Took a gander as she—'

'Okay, okay, Hank, I get the picture.'

'Me, too.' Hank's purple tongue licked his lips. 'A nice clear picture.' He patted his chest. 'Makes the old ticker step up a beat, too.'

From the cafe behind Pamela came the sound of someone pounding a fist on the counter.

'Hello! We gonna get any service in this dump?'

Hank resumed dragging the sack of trash in the direction of the rear door. 'If you could use some advice, ma'am, it's not smart to keep a hungry feller from his vittles.'

'Oh, great.' Pamela simmered.

I can't find Terry. I'm alone in the cafe. And there's a trucker and his buddy grumping for food.

'Catch ya later, sugar pie.'

Pamela glowered at Hank. 'Thanks a bunch. If you see—'

'Terry. Sure, sure. I'll tell him ya can't live without him. Tee-hee.' He cackled with laughter.

'Hey! Anyone home?' The trucker calling out again.

Pamela made sure her best professional waitress smile was on her face, then walked back into the cafe.

The trucker and his friend sat at the counter. They rested their muscular bare arms on the counter top and glared at her. They both wore white T-shirts with a stylized brown log running across the nipple zone. Beneath that were the words 'We Love Lumber, Too.' Then a telephone number.

Company uniform.

Came with regulation sweat circles in the armpits, too.

The two guys were in their forties. One wore a baseball cap. The other had a mass of curly hair that must have added three inches to his height.

'Ain't our money any good here?' said the one in the cap.

The other added, 'Yeah, or do you only take Iraqi pesos?'

'I think you'll find it's the Iraqi dinar.'

'Uh?'

'The currency of Iraq,' Pamela said, smiling. 'It's dinar, not peso. Coffee?'

'Oh, a smart waitress, eh?' The one with the curly hair said this with a sneer. 'You got a university degree or just in love with an Iraqi guy?'

'I know what she has got ...' This came from the trucker in the cap. 'She's got long legs that go all the way up to her fanny.'

'Yeah, and what a fanny.' The curly-haired one smirked. 'Nice titties, too. Make a nice soft pillow for a workin' man.'

'You're dead right. Won't you pass me my X-ray glasses, Frank?'

The one called Frank slipped a pair of Elvis-style shades with large aluminum frames from his pocket and held them out to his buddy.

The trucker slipped them on, then looked Pamela up and down and gave an appreciative whistle. 'Best thing we ever bought, Frank, these X-ray spectacles.'

'Oh, very droll,' Pamela said. She plucked her order book from her apron pocket.

'Lovely breasts. The right one has a freckle. Nice flat stomach. And man, oh man, you should see her—'

'Okay.' Pamela plucked the cap from the trucker's head. 'Either you quit the commentary or I'll fry your hat alongside your eggs.'

'At least you'll be fryin' somethin',' the curly one said with feeling.

'Yeah, and you can give me my bitchin' hat back.'

Pamela's patience was running low. 'What're ya going to do if I don't give it back? *Sir*.'

'I'll come round there and give your sweet fanny the slappin' it deserves.' He nudged his buddy.

Both of them laughed.

Maybe they're thinking I'm all alone here.

They're getting ideas.

That dessert might not come in a bowl.

Oh, where are you, Terry? Where's anyone? Lauren? Nicki?

'Okay, you're both hungry. I'm a waitress. What can I get you?' Pamela stood with her pen poised over the pad, ready to write.

The one called Frank had a look in his eye now that needed no explanation. 'Oh, I know exactly what I want. How about you, Joe?'

'Sure. Something hot and spicy.' Both of them laughed again.

Pamela sighed. 'Are you two going to keep up this dazzling repartee all day or are you going to give me your order *for food*, so I can fix you something?'

'Give me some tasty rump, followed by—'

Pamela's schoolteaching experience kicked in. 'Okay, you two. I've just about had enough of this.' Her voice was a perfect balance of ice and steel. 'Either you order your food now or you can go hungry for the rest of the day.'

'Hey, listen, we—'

'No, *you* listen to *me*, buster.' Pamela slammed her hand down on the counter. 'The next diner is four hours' drive from here. So it's your choice. Eat here or hit the road.'

'I—'

'And if you eat here I expect a modicum of civilized behavior.'

The two men looked at each other. One handed the sunglasses back to the other.

'Now, do either of you wish to say anything?' Pamela shot them her best steel-eyed look. The kind she'd reserved for the hoodlum kids in class.

'Yes, ma'am.' The trucker sagged visibly under the impact of her formidable stare.

'Well? I'm waiting.'

'Please may I have my cap back, ma'am?'

She handed it back to him.

'Now,' she said briskly. 'Coffee?'

The two guys nodded and were quick to say their 'pleases' and 'thank yous'.

'That's better. So, gentlemen. What would you like to eat?'

Respectful now, they gave their order.

With Terry a no-show I'm going to have to cook, Pamela thought. *But no big deal. I can fix bacon, fried eggs and the usual breakfast extras.*

As she turned away she heard one of the men whisper to the other, 'Time of the month.'

She smiled to herself. They couldn't resist reassuring themselves that they'd lost the battle to the superior biological force of menstruation. They couldn't admit to themselves that a waitress had stood up to them. When confronted with the period thing most men yielded like a vampire cringing from a crucifix.

Without turning to them as she laid rashers of bacon on the hot

292

skillet, Pamela couldn't resist saying, 'Bathroom's over there. You might want to wash your hands before you eat.'

She turned to smile at them as they looked at their grubby fingers in surprise. As if washing their hands before eating was alien to them.

Which it probably was.

They nodded. The one in the cap touched the peak. A respectful gesture.

'Good idea, ma'am.'

The pair scuttled toward the bathroom.

Game, set and match.

'Nice work.' Pamela spun to her right.

Duke stood in the kitchen doorway.

'Oh,' she said, 'I didn't see you there.'

'You soon got the upper hand with those two,' he said. 'I'm impressed.'

'Just a little firmness.'

'Worked, too. You're some gal.'

'Thank you.' She cracked eggs onto the hot metal. The clear liquid turned a sizzling white around the yellow yolk.

Duke slipped a stick of gum into his mouth. He gave Pamela an appraising look as he chewed.

'You're not a waitress.'

'I'm both waitress and cook now.'

'I mean you've not been in this line of work long.'

'No, I used to be a schoolteacher.'

'How come you wound up in Pits?'

'Long story.'

'Sharpe bring you in?'

'Uh-huh.' Pamela flipped the bacon rashers over. Bubbles of oil seemed to dance on the cooking meat. Even though she kept her eyes on the food she was aware of the guy studying her.

Yeah, he's good looking in a bad-boy way. Blue eyes, blond hair. Tattoo. Narrow waist. Broad shoulders.

Course, a guy like that's gotta be trouble.

'You could set two plates out here for me.'

She guessed Duke didn't take orders from anyone.

But he gave a little nod. As if what he saw in Pamela he approved of. So he was prepared to give a little help.

Oh God, I hope he doesn't have any romantic intentions. I'm not ready for that yet.

And especially not for a guy like Duke. He looks as if he's running away from a whole heap of trouble.

Could have broken out of jail.

Or poisoned his grandmother for her life savings.

The two guys returned from the bathroom. They looked cheerful and relaxed now that she'd laid down some ground rules.

They both held their hands up, palms facing Pamela.

'Nice and clean, miss,' said the one in the hat.

'You'll pass muster. Grab a seat, breakfast's ready.'

Pamela glanced to see how Duke had reacted to her handling of the customers.

Duke had already vanished.

Like he's got somewhere important to go.

The shiver that ran down her spine wasn't lost on her.

Someone just walked over my grave.

And as Pamela served up the bacon and egg, hoping that Terry wouldn't be long in returning from wherever he'd taken himself to, she didn't know that the cafe's cook was lying under a cactus with ants busily crawling across the unholy mess of his crushed skull.

Chapter Forty-three

Norman sat drinking cold, sweet water from a glass. He was back in the trailer.

Changed his underpants before his jism dried and formed a crust. His mind was full of all kinds of shit.

Boots and Nicki making naked whoopee in the old house.

Duke hauling Terry in the tarp.

Norman killing Terry with a rock.

Oh Christ, I'm a killing machine.

Three men in less than a week.

Norman shook his head. He let his head rest against the back of the sofa. The fan blew air to cool his face. But that desert heat was seeping into the living room of the trailer.

Gonna be hot today.

Have a feeling it's gonna get hotter than hell yet. In more ways than one.

Norman swallowed another mouthful of water.

Felt good, that cold liquid sliding down his throat.

I wish I could stay like this for the next zillion days. Do nothing but feel the fan on my face. Drink cold water.

'Cos every time I move from one place to another I wind up killing someone. Or nearly getting killed myself.

Dangerous times, Norman. So stay in the trailer. Hey, stay on the fucking couch. That way no one gets hurt. Least of all me.

A tap sounded on the door.

Now you've got a dilemma, Norman told himself. *Either answer the door. Or stay here. If you answer the door it'll be someone trying to kill you. Or you'll trip on the mat and head-butt them to death by accident.*

Oh, shit.

The tap came again. This time followed by a croaking voice. 'Young 'un. You in there?'

Holy cow. The old-timer. What's his name?

Hank. Yeah, Hank.

Only old Hank. Should be no danger.

To the old mule skinner or to Norman.

Norman headed to the door. Then suddenly paused.

Maybe Hank had heard that Norman had been bitten by a venomous snake.

I haven't, of course, but that might not stop the guy wanting to suck out the poison. Norman couldn't stop himself remembering the mind movie that his imagination had made for him. Of Norman being struck by a rattlesnake that had planted its fangs in his fanny. Then lurid mental images of toothless old Hank with the cracked lips and bushy whiskers taking his own sweet time in sucking out the poison.

Shit.

What an imagination. Why did it have to torture him 24/7?

'Huloooo!' More tapping.

Norman went to the door.

He opened it. The sunlight hit him in the eye like a couple of pistol rounds. He recoiled, blinking at its brilliance.

'Had a mind you were in there, young feller. An' I was right.'

'Good morning,' Norman said politely, wondering why the hell the old guy'd shown up at his door.

Hank stood in the dust at the bottom of the trailer steps. He looked up at Norman. His eyes were puckered into folds of skin to stop the sunlight dazzling him. His nose showed through a foliage of bristles. It was as red a strawberry. An overripe, stood-upon strawberry. The coot could have been an old-time prospector in those clothes. Even in this heat he wore a plaid flannel shirt that had long sleeves. Below that were blue jeans. On his feet were dusty black cowboy boots. Good scorpion-stomping footwear, those.

Norman saw that the old man was grinning. He was holding that filthy hat of his that was probably held together by nothing more than dust and the old coot's sweat.

'Figured you might want to take a look-see in my hat.'

'Look in your hat?'

'Yessiree.'

My God, why do I want to stand here admiring the inside of the old shit-shoveller's hat? What's the man thinking of?

'See what I got fer ya and yer two buddies.'

Norman peered into the shadowy interior of the hat. Were those poop stains on the brim?

Come to think of it, toilet tissue could be in short supply when you're walking out in the desert.

And the brim of a hat's got to be softer than cactus leaf.

Norman began, 'I don't quite see . . .'

'Right there in the bottom.'

'Oh. Eggs.'

'Damn straight. Fresh today.'

'Thanks, but we've got some in the refrigerator.'

Hank's lopsided grin broadened. 'No, these ain't come from no hen's tush.'

'They're not hen's eggs?' *Duck, goose, quail?*

'These eggs are the best ya'll ever taste.' Hank smacked his lips. 'Rattler eggs.'

Norman's jaw sagged. 'Snake eggs!'

'Sure they're snake eggs. You never tasted 'em afore?'

'Never.'

Never likely to, either.

'Fresh rattlesnake eggs are good fer whatever ails ya.'

'I don't think that—'

'Just pick 'em up, like so.' Hank took a round white egg from his hat. 'See, they're soft. Ya can squish 'em.' Hank squeezed gently. 'Ya can pickle 'em, or boil 'em in milk.' He winked at Norman. 'But ya can't beat 'em just as God made 'em. Just like this . . . now you watch, young feller.' He chewed on one with the remains of his yellow teeth. 'Gotta tough outer membrane. But you stick with it, you'll bite a hole clean through. Now tilt yer head back, open yer mouth. And squeeze.'

Hank followed his own instructions. Norman watched in a kind of horrified fascination as the old coot squirted the contents of the rattlesnake's egg into his mouth. It shot from the hole in the membrane like a ball of green mucus streaked red with blood.

'Ah . . .' Hank crowed with relish at such a delicious morsel. 'Betcha ya'll have tasted nothing like it!'

'I bet you're right.' Norman swallowed. His mouth tasted of bile. His palms were sweating.

Dear God, that looked just awful.

Hank held out the hat so that Norman could see the cluster of glistening white eggs nested in there. 'Want me to get one started fer ya?'

'No, thanks. I'm a . . . I'm a . . .' Norman's stomach twitched. 'I'm a vegetarian.'

'Shit, is that so? I'm a Libra.'

Norman muttered something about leaving the shower running, then closed the door on the grinning man standing there with his hatful of snake eggs.

Norman went back to lie on the sofa. Air played on his face from the fan.

He had to work hard not to recall the image of Hank gulping down with gusto the slimy green contents of the snake egg.

Had to work very hard.

Ten minutes later he realized he wasn't going to puke after all.

But it was a close-run thing.

And just when Norman began to think that life was looking better the trailer door opened. In stepped Boots and Duke.

They had guns in their hands.

'Norman. Time to start the show.' Duke sat down in the armchair opposite him.

Boots chose to park her butt on the arm of the sofa.

Norman remembered how a naked Boots had made love to a willowy naked Nicki. The thought made him warm.

Made it hard to look Boots in the eye as well.

But then, the guns they carried had their own magnetic attraction for his attention. Boots carried a revolver. Looked like a .38 home-protection model. Duke carried a .357 Magnum in his right hand and in his left a Glock automatic. It was gold-plated, too. A rich man's toy.

Norman had to ask an obvious question. 'Where'd you get the guns?'

Boots said, 'While you were sleepin' on the ride down here we got them from a guy driving a motor home.'

'Guess he didn't complain.' Norman wore his fixed smile, so as not to rile Duke.

'Boots worked the ol' Boots magic,' Duke said. 'While he was on top of Boots pluggin' her water hole like their lives depended on it I—' He made a clicking sound as he ran his thumb across his throat, miming a knife slicing a trachea. 'I relieved him of these beauties that he'd got stowed away.'

'Nice work,' Norman said, nodding.

'Boots is the gal who gets all the praise.'

'Oh, I did nothin',' she simpered. 'Just smiled and opened my legs.'

'Like I said,' Duke told him. 'The old Boots magic.'

'They look like formidable pieces.' Norman eyed the guns. 'Know your way around them?'

'Sure we do.' Boots spun the ammo cylinder of her revolver. It made a clicking sound. 'While you were sleeping we got some practise in, too.'

While I was sleeping? While I was unconscious, more like. After the beating Duke gave me it's a miracle I woke up at all.

'Here's your piece, Normy.' Duke handed him the Glock automatic.

'But I don't know anything about—'

'Nothing to it. It's an auto, a Model 20. Just point and pull the trigger. It's a ten-millimeter. A fucking cannon. Course, you gotta remember to take the safety off first. It's this little doohickey here.' Duke showed him how to slide the safety catch across.

'But we're not actually gonna shoot anybody?'

'I guess not.' Boots sounded disappointed.

'These are to back up our suggestion that we take over the running of the town,' Duke said.

'They'll be powerful persuaders,' Norman allowed as he felt the weight of the gun in his hand. And when he remembered what Duke had told him, about Nicki being his when the plan was complete, he began to smile.

Duke asked, 'What're you smiling about, bud?'

'I'm just thinking about the future. About how much we're going to enjoy ourselves.'

'Damn straight.' Duke smiled, too. 'Okay, if you guys are ready.' His smile became a leer. 'Let's do this crazy thing.'

Chapter Forty-four

'Cafe first,' Duke told them.

Holy shit. This is like a Wild West showdown.

And we're the Jesse James gang.

Mean, dangerous, armed.

The time was nearing high noon. Norman walked to the right of Duke, Boots to the left. They walked purposefully across the parking lot, their feet raising puffs of dust with every step. Boots wore her white cowgirl boots. Duke strode manfully in his motorcycle boots. Norman wore sneakers. The sun burned down from directly above, hardly casting a shadow.

Deserted.

Not a sound.

No vehicles on the road.

No people.

No birdsong.

Only a death silence. Like the grim reaper had put his bony finger to fleshless lips and breathed, 'Shhhh . . .'

Old Mister Death knew what was going down.

He'd seen it happen before in Pits. This was frontier country. A hundred years ago there'd been plenty of shoot-outs. Some gambler, maybe, who'd slipped an ace from his cuff once too often. Or two guys arguing over a burlesque dancer.

Story's the same.

Out come the guns.

Blam! Blam! Blam!

Then comes the solemn procession behind the long pine box up to the desert cemetery.

Norman felt terrified.

Felt excited.

Now, this is a hunk of history repeating itself.

The three of us walking in a line with guns in our hands. Three desperados.

Gonna make this town of Pits our own.

They'd chosen their time. Waiting for a lull in customers.

Duke squinted against the sun. 'Sharpe's gone,' he said.

'One less to worry about,' Boots added.

'Yup.'

They crossed the furrows in the dust left by Sharpe's bus. He'd gone out 'saving people' again. Ahead lay the line of abandoned trucks and cars. Then the cafe itself.

'In through the back way?' Norman asked.

'Nope. The front door. We own this place now.' Duke spat into the dust.

Above them vultures glided in circles.

Norman nodded. 'Okay.'

They circled round the front. There were customers after all. Two big Harleys stood by the front door.

'I never saw those arrive,' Boots said.

'It's not a problem. Come on.'

Duke shoved open the cafe door. They followed him in.

Inside were two bikers. Chunky guys in black leather. They were a couple of hard-asses. They sat at the counter.

Waiting tables was Pamela. Cooking the food was Lauren.

Norman ran the mental file. That meant Wes, Hank and Nicki were absent.

'Cafe's closed,' Duke announced.

'Hey,' one of the bikers snarled. 'We ain't eaten yet.'

Duke raised the hand that held the Magnum. Its six-inch barrel in blue steel looked wicked beyond belief.

'Take that fucking gun out of my face,' the biker warned. 'Like I said, we ain't eaten yet.'

'Steak's off but here's your dessert.' Duke fired. The heavy round smacked into the biker's forehead. He flopped back like a dead seal. Rubbery. Heavy. What was left of his head made a loud smacking sound as it hit the floor.

'It's cool,' the other biker said. 'I don't want no—'

Boots fired. A cock shot. The biker squealed and clamped both hands between his legs.

Duke nodded at Norman. 'Finish him.'

Norman fired the Glock automatic. The big cartridge filled the cafe with an ear-splitting noise. A glass on the table beside him shattered, the report was so loud.

The ten-millimeter round struck the guy dead center in the chest. He went down, pumping blood.

Duke shook his head. 'You should have listened to me first time around. I said the cafe is closed.'

Norman saw Pamela and Lauren staring at the three 'desperados' in horror.

Duke touched his eyebrow in salute. 'Let it be known that . . .' He hunted for the phrase.

Norman supplied it. 'From henceforth.'

'Thank you, Norman. Let it be known from henceforth that I am the master of Pits. Boots and Norman here are my deputies. My word is law. Okay?'

Lauren opened her mouth, ready to protest.

Norman stepped in. 'Just relax, take it easy. Everything's going to be fine.'

Boots sang out. 'We're gonna have a great time. This is the start of a real good friendship.'

Norman glanced at her. She smiled. But there was an emptiness to her brown eyes. As if a whole chunk of her vision was directed inward to some dark recess of her mind. Not outward to the people in the cafe.

'That's right,' Duke agreed. 'A real close friendship. And we're gonna make this town a cool place to be. More girls. More fun.'

'All right,' Norman enthused. He stared at Pamela in her figure-hugging sweater and shorts. He liked the dinky waitress outfit.

Kinda sexy. Shame that Duke has laid claim to her.

Duke was still pointing his handgun but he used his free hand to reach into his shirt pocket, pull out a carton of cigarettes and slip one long white cylinder from the pack, using his lips. After returning the pack to his pocket he lit a match one-handed too, then inhaled deeply.

'We regret the mess those two guys made.' He nodded at the dead bikers.

Hot shit. Duke's blaming the two guys for bleeding all over the frigging floor. It's as if shooting them had nothing to do with it.

Norman went along with Duke's line. 'We'll get it cleaned up in no time.'

'Don't worry,' Lauren said. 'We've handled plenty of dead meat before.'

Norman noticed the little glance that Pamela shot her friend. As if there was more meaning loaded into those few words than was at first apparent.

'Question is,' Boots wiggled her finger against the trigger of her revolver as if her skin was getting itchy, 'what are we going to do with you two?'

'Lock them up,' Norman said quickly before Boots decided to dispatch the two babes.

'Here?' Boots wrinkled her snout-like nose. 'They'd escape easy.'

'No,' Norman said.

'Trailers are no good either,' Duke observed.

'The house on the hill. Bound to be a cellar or something,' Norman said.

'Sounds good to me, Norman, old buddy.'

Boots moved so that she could look through the door into the kitchen. 'Where are the others?'

Probably wondering where beautiful blonde Nicki is, Norman thought. *After I saw Boots making love to Nicki this morning she might be wanting to stake her claim.*

No fair.

Duke promised Nicki to me.

Norman began to wonder if there was a way of getting rid of Boots somewhere down the line. Those dead brown eyes gave him the creeps. Watching that girl-on-girl action had been fun but he didn't want Boots hogging all the good times with Nicki.

Lauren looked at Pamela, then said, 'I don't know where they are.'

'You sure you ain't seen Nicki?'

See! Norman's face flushed. *Boots wants a second helping.*

303

Boy oh boy, does Boots have to go.

'And when you expectin' Sharpe back?' Duke asked.

'He can be gone for days,' Lauren answered.

'Where are the others likely to be? Wes and the old-timer?'

'Around.' Pamela shrugged.

Lauren added, 'They've all got their chores.'

'Okay.' Duke slipped his gun into the belt of his pants. 'You ladies aren't gonna give us no trouble, are you?'

'What do you think?' Pamela's shock was being replaced by anger. 'You three have got the guns.'

'Feisty. I like it.' Duke was pleased.

'I'll give you feisty,' Pamela snarled.

Boots raised her gun again. 'And we can give you a tit full of lead, so don't get antsy.'

Norman played the diplomacy bit. 'Remember? Nice and easy, then no one's gonna get hurt.'

Duke nodded. 'Norman's got brain. Take his advice, okay?' His stare hardened. *'Okay?'*

Both Lauren and Pamela nodded. Norman noticed the fire still burning in Pamela's gaze. She wanted to take a swing at Boots.

Norman wondered if she ever would.

Catfight.

Could be fun.

Could be a way of getting Boots out of the picture.

'Now we're all being sweet with one another let's take that walk up to the house. Norman, lock the door to the cafe. Put up the closed sign.'

'I'm onto it.'

'Ladies.' Duke nodded toward the kitchen door. 'Promenade time. We'll head out back, then up to the house. If we see any of the others don't do anything bitchin' stupid like shouting out warnings or shit like that. You follow?'

They both nodded.

'Sweet. Lead the way, ladies.'

They worked their way up through the cemetery. Past the tombs of guys who'd lost gunfights a hundred years ago. Then by the tombs of the monkeys. The house shimmered in heat haze in front of them.

Lauren and Pamela led the way. Their bare legs looked captivating to Norman.

Boots complained about the heat.

Complained that Nicki was nowhere to be seen.

Duke walked in silence. Cool as ever.

They didn't see any of the remaining inhabitants of Pits.

As they climbed onto the porch of the house Nicki was just step-ping through the front door.

'Makes three,' Boots said brightly.

'Now to locate Wes and Hank,' Duke said.

'What's happening?' Nicki asked. The sight of the guns startled her.

'Nothing to worry about, ma'am. We're taking charge of Pits for your own protection.'

'Our own protection?' Nicki echoed. 'We don't need—'

'Nicki,' Lauren said calmly. 'Do as they say.'

Nicki watched Boots with a pained look in her eyes. Norman figured that she was recalling the sweet, sweet tongue-loving she'd had from Boots this morning and was feeling hurt by the betrayal.

'Boots, why are you doing this to me? I thought we—'

'It's getting mighty hot out here. If I don't get some coolness soon I won't be able to stop myself pulling this trigger.'

'Okay, okay,' Pamela placated the pig-girl. 'Don't worry. We're doing as you say. Nicki, go back into the house please.'

'But—'

'They've promised they're not going to hurt us.'

Nicki nodded. Her blue eyes were watchful as she pushed her long blond hair back behind her shoulder.

Clearly doesn't trust us an inch, Norman thought.

The interior of the house was as dark as a cave. Norman hoped that it would be as cool as one, too.

But no.

He followed everyone into the gloomy hallway. It was hot, with a musty atmosphere. Still, at least they were out of the fierce sunlight.

Duke said, 'We need to find somewhere comfortable for the ladies.' He opened a door at random.

Norman nearly told him not to bother with that one. It was the big empty room with no furniture where Boots and Nicki had got throbbingly naked with each other.

Norman decided against saying anything.

Don't want to give myself away, reveal that I was watching them. I don't want them thinking I'm some kind of pervmeister, do I?

'Empty room,' Duke told them.

Boots said, 'Has it got windows? It's no good if it's got windows.'

Rather than the sweet, simple-minded character that Norman had first encountered, Boots'd become edgy of late. Instead of being easy-going, her nerves now had a brittle quality.

Wish she'd put the fucking gun away.

Norman began to sweat.

Anxiety sweat. Nothing to do with the heat.

Duke checked the downstairs rooms. 'All got windows,' he announced. 'Too easy to break out of.'

'There's gotta be a basement,' Boots said, hopeful.

'I don't doubt,' Duke replied. 'But a basement's no place for a lady.'

'They'll live,' Boots said. Then she added, 'Or we could tie 'em up.'

'These are our friends. You don't tie up people who're your friends.'

Norman decided that a contribution from him was needed. 'An upstairs room. They're not gonna jump out of a bedroom window and risk busting a leg.'

'Good thinking, Normy.' Duke glanced up at the grand stairway that ran in a long curve to the next floor.

Norman looked up, too. It was a huge void full of shadows.

Spooky.

Duke put his boot on the first step.

The step creaked.

That creak went echoing up the staircase like the footsteps of a ghost.

At last Nicki blurted out, 'You can't go up there.'

'Can't?'

'No.'

'Why?'

'You just can't.' Nicki was gasping with fear.

'Oh, can't I?' Duke pulled the Magnum from his belt. 'Wes up there?'

'No.'

'The old-timer?'

'He's away dumping trash.'

'What's so important up there that you don't want your bud Duke to see?'

Nicki blurted again, 'You can't go up there.'

'Oh? See anyone trying to stop me?'

'No,' said Lauren. 'You mustn't.'

Pamela joined in. 'You can see it's not safe. The timbers are rotted.'

'Looks sound.'

'Too much weight could bring the whole house down on top of us.' Pamela nodded at the walls. 'See the state it's in.'

'Just looks like peeling wallpaper to me.'

'They're shitting you, Duke,' Boots told him. 'Slap the bitches up. Teach 'em respect.'

Duke raised his eyebrows. 'I just might do that. If they give me just cause.' He stood back and raised the gun. 'After you, ladies.'

Lauren repeated, 'It's really not safe up there.'

A slow smile spread across Duke's face. 'Now you've really got my curiosity in gear.'

In the near-dark of the old house they climbed the stairs. Norman glanced at the three women. Both Nicki and Lauren looked wired with anxiety. Pamela seemed puzzled.

She genuinely doesn't know why the two women are so nervous about us going upstairs.

But there must be something up there.

Any minute now we're going to find out what it is.

Chapter Forty-five

They reached the landing. Light filtered through a corn-flour sack that had been nailed over the landing window. Little needle-sharp rays scattered points of radiance on the floor.

Clean floor, Norman noted.

Someone's maintaining the property upstairs.

Six doors led off the landing. All but one had been boarded up. The single functional door lay at the end of the passageway in near-darkness.

'Okay, Normy,' Duke said in a low voice. 'Go ahead and check the status of the room.'

'Status?'

'Yeah, check whether there's anyone in there. Of course, if you're too much of a wuss . . .'

'No. I'll check.' Norman smiled to show that he wasn't afraid. 'Probably only old Hank in the bathtub or something.'

'Or Hank and Wes in bed playing bury the salami.'

'Boots,' Duke said disapprovingly, 'guys don't do that to other guys. They do it to girls.'

Norman noticed that Pamela shot a glance at Lauren as if to ask, 'Is this guy for real?'

Oh, Duke's for real all right. Something tells me you're gonna get to know all his little quirks real well.

'What're you waiting for, Norm?'

'It's cool, Duke. I'm going. I was, uh, just checking that the safety was off.'

Norman advanced slowly along the passageway. He held the Glock

308

automatic out at arm's length. Its gold plating was the brightest thing here. He licked his lips. They were dry. Dusty. He didn't like the look of the sealed doors. They made him think of the entrances to tombs.

God alone knew what lay behind them.

Open one of those doors, Norman, you're gonna die screaming.

'Shut up.' Norman addressed this to his rebel imagination that was forever skimming troubling scenarios across his mind.

'You say anything, Norman?'

'No, nothing, Duke. Just clearing my throat.'

'You don't want to take all afternoon opening a bitchin' door. We've work to do.'

Norman reached the door, keeping the gun at arm's length and pointing it at the woodwork.

Just in case Wes steamed out brandishing a knife.

He reached out his other hand. Found the doorknob in the gloom. Turned it.

Creak.

The mechanism was old.

Hinges were old, too. The door opened with a wailing squeal.

Inside.

Dark. Very dark.

Holy moly. Smelt funny, too. Like they'd kept a sick dog in here.

Kind of an animal smell . . . a shitty smell.

Norman advanced through the open doorway. He couldn't even see his arm in the near-dark but the gun glittered in what light filtered through heavily draped windows.

What's that sound? Norman asked himself.

The sound of scratching? It brought to mind an image of a sick dog pawing the bars of a cage.

Or is it the sound of breathing?

Breathing!

No sooner had Norman thought the word than a wet *something* folded around the hand that carried the gun.

'Jesus,' he gasped. The gasp became a yell.

Pain flashed through his hand. He cried out again.

Duke dashed through the door. In the gloom Norman saw only his silhouette. The man raced to the window. Grabbed the drapes in his two hands. Dragged them down.

Sunlight blasted in. Its brilliance made Norman close his eyes even though some monster was chewing on his hand.

Hell – must be an alligator, or a puma, or a wolf, or—

He opened his eyes.

Or a man! Norman stood blinking in the bright light and watched as an old coot in a wheelchair gnawed at the back of his hand.

'Get him fucking offa me!' Norman yelled.

Suddenly everyone seemed to be in the room.

Nicki cried, 'Please don't hurt him!'

Pamela gaped. 'Who the hell is that?'

Duke aimed the gun.

The old guy in the wheelchair looked around ninety. He had no hair on the top of his skull, but he had plenty round the bottom of his head and around his jaw so that it formed a snowy-white collar. The eyes were glistening slits surrounded by red skin. Arching over them were fuzzy eyebrows of white hair.

'He's biting my fucking hand!' Norman wailed.

'Stand back,' Duke told him. 'I'll blow his face off.'

'No way, Duke! My hand's in his mouth!'

Nicki and Lauren pleaded with them not to hurt the guy.

'He's breaking skin, he's breaking skin!' Norman wailed louder.

Boots angled her gun to shoot the guy in the stomach.

'Don't you dare, you'll wind up hitting me,' Norman warned. Then he said 'Here!' and handed her his gun.

Now, with his hand free, he could do something about the biter. He jammed his thumb into one of the slitty eyes. Warm, soft. Norman pushed harder. At last, with a yell, the old guy quit biting.

Duke scolded Nicki. 'Hey, you got a grandpa, you gotta feed him now and again.'

Nicki rushed forward to the old man. 'You better not have hurt him!'

'What about me?' Norman asked, pained. 'The bastard drew blood. Look!'

He showed her his hand with puncture wounds in the skin. Wincing, he clamped his handkerchief to it. 'And see his teeth? The old coot's got fangs.'

'Hey, Norm's right,' Duke said, impressed. 'Just look at those pointy teeth.'

Pamela stared, too. 'They've been filed down to points.' She glanced at Lauren. 'Did he do this to his own teeth?'

Norman was maybe the only one not impressed by the old guy's mouthful of canine-looking teeth. Despite the oldster being a physical wreck his teeth were perfectly white and healthy. Perfectly sharp, too. Red splotches soaked through Norman's handkerchief.

'I should get a tetanus shot,' Norman told them. 'And one for rabies.'

Duke nodded at Lauren. 'So who's Father Time?'

'They call him Priest.'

'Priest. Hey, Priest, meet Duke.' Duke held out his hand.

Priest looked at it with interest through his slit eyes. They seeped a syrupy stickiness. Especially the one to which Norman had delivered a damn good thumbing. Then the old dude spoke.

A dry, cracking voice. Like desert brush being disturbed. 'You want me to eat all of them? Now?'

'No, Priest,' Nicki soothed. She stroked the old guy's forearm while crouching beside the wheelchair.

Priest didn't seem to hear her. 'Ya know you gotta kill 'em and cook 'em before I eat 'em. That's why I wrote out all those recipes for ya.'

'This is Priest?' Pamela said in disbelief. 'I thought you said he was dead!'

'Not dead. I didn't say that,' Lauren explained. 'I meant no longer in charge.'

'Ya can fry these guys' balls,' Priest was saying. 'Grind fresh pepper on 'em, then serve 'em on a bed of lettuce.'

Duke said to Lauren, 'Mebbe you need to do some explaining. Who's the old guy?'

'Like I said. His name is Priest.' Lauren made a gesture that seemed to encompass the town. 'He rediscovered Pits more than forty years ago. He brought it back to life.'

'But what's this about eating us?'

'He's old, Duke. He's getting confused.'

'Confused, hell!' Priest protested. 'Got the appetite of a young man, I have. See the girl there?' He pointed a wrinkled finger at Boots. 'I'd wager I could down four pounds of her flesh in ten minutes and still have room for her tongue.' He smacked his lips. 'Stir-fried with garlic.'

'Hey . . .' Boots was unhappy at the man discussing her culinary possibilities. 'No one's eating any of me.'

Duke chuckled. 'You weren't complainin' when old Normy-boy here was munchin' on yer glory hole.'

Boots turned all sullen. If anything, her brown eyes looked even more dead now. There wasn't even a spark of anger there.

To Norman that seemed more dangerous somehow.

Norman took the opportunity during the conversation to look over the room. This one was furnished. Heavy velvet drapes had covered the windows. There was a bed in the corner of the room. Neatly made. Nicki, he guessed, had been doing the housekeeping. There was also a table, a wind-up gramophone. Cases of old books.

Cookbooks stuffed with recipes.

Then Norman took a gander at the man who'd taken a snap at his hand.

The white whiskers and strip of hair round the back of his head formed a hairy collar. The top of the head was bald and pretty much ruinous-looking with cracked skin, pimples and scabs that resembled about fifty Rice Crispies stuck to his bare scalp.

He wore a dark pullover and dark pants. He might have been confined to the wheelchair for many reasons but a very obvious one was that he had only one leg.

The vacant leg of his pants had been doubled over so that the turnup could be pinned to where the knee should have been. On his remaining foot he wore a white sock. Oddly, it was a *dazzling* white.

But then, he never walked on it.

Figures.

'You're not going to hurt Priest, are you?' Nicki asked. She was so anxious that Norman wanted to take her in his arms.

Comfort her.

Take her mind off the here and now.

He remembered Duke's promise. His groin began to ache.

'What do you take us for?' Duke appeared mildly shocked by the implication. 'Course we're not going to hurt him.'

'You already have,' Priest said with feeling. He gripped the chair's wheels with his hands to spin it round. 'College boy there tried to poke out my frickin' eye with his thumb.'

'You were biting me.'

'I thought you were lunch.'

'Lunch!'

'Don't worry,' Priest said, wrinkling his nose. 'Don't care for rare meat anyway. I'd have sent you back.'

'Old-timer's certainly got a thing about eating folk,' Duke observed.

'He's confused,' Lauren said.

'Stop saying that,' Priest snapped. 'My mind's gin-clear. Why, I remember—'

'Priest. Shush now, please.' Lauren looked uncomfortable.

'I remember when we all sat down round the table. You and Sharpe and Wes and Hank. Course, you weren't there, Nicki.' He smiled fondly as he remembered.

'Please don't say anything, Priest. These people are from out of town.'

'And we all sat at that table at Thanksgiving,' Priest said proudly. 'And—' He slapped the leg stump in his pants. 'And you ate a whole quarter of me.'

Lauren groaned, realizing that she couldn't stop the flow of words.

'Foot, calf muscles, thigh. We ate the damn lot. Been simmering for a whole day in red wine and herbs.' A smile illuminated his face. 'Man meat. Once tasted, never forgotten. Food of the gods.' He made a gesture that could be described as priestly. Priest-like. 'My gift to my friends. My people of Pits. I gave them a piece of me.'

Norman glanced across at Pamela. She was surprised. But there was an expression of understanding, too. As if what the old man was telling them filled in gaps in her knowledge of Pits.

Boots said, 'No offense. But I think the guy might be loopy.'

Duke was impressed. 'Helluva story.'

Priest held up his finger again, his stare fixed on Duke's face. 'A true story, young man.'

Norman began to make sense of random clues. 'All those abandoned cars outside the cafe . . .'

'Manna from heaven,' Priest said. 'You know, there's an almighty prejudice against eating our fellow human beings.'

'Oh shit.' Lauren shook her head.

The cat's out of the bag?

Priest continued pontificating. 'Our ancestors knew it made good sense to eat not just their enemies but their own parents – when they died of natural causes, of course. It don't make no sense to waste valuable protein. Also, human flesh has a special, *special* quality. It's like a magic potion. Once you've eaten it, you'll know what I mean.'

313

'It does what to you, exactly?' Norman said. 'Eating human flesh?'

'Ah, young friend. I'm not going to spoil your first time. You'll find out the effect – the *extraordinary* effect – for yourself.'

Norman thought hard. *Are these really the ramblings of a senile old coot? The guy seems lucid enough to me.*

But eating people? Can we really have found a community of cannibals? Holy shit.

Boots wasn't impressed. 'We gonna stand and listen to his stories all day? We've gotta find Wes and Hank.'

'Sure thing, babe.' Duke motioned to Norman to follow him and Boots out of the room. 'I'm gonna lock you folks in here. Norman's gonna be right outside. So no shouting out the windows, do you hear?'

'Who is that young feller?' Priest asked. 'Reminds me of my first *real* meal.'

Norman followed the pair out onto the landing. Duke had plucked the key from the lock at the other side. Now he closed the door. Locked it.

He handed Norman the key.

'Keep it safe. We'll be right back.'

'Sure,' Norman said.

Pits, he thought. *A helluva town.*

Even with all that talk of cannibalism his mind still strayed to Nicki. Slender, blonde Nicki with the soft blue eyes.

He'd seen her naked.

Now he leaned back against the wall with his arms folded, his eyes closed, and pictured himself doing the same kind of things Boots had done to the Nordic beauty this morning.

Norman didn't have a long wait. In fact, his daydream of lounging back and watching Nicki straddle him bare-assed was just starting to warm up real nice when Boots and Duke came stomping back up the stairs.

They had Wes and Hank.

Hank, the old-timer, wheezed. 'I'm not used to steps. You'll have to let me take 'em slow.'

Boots jabbed the muzzle of her pistol in his spine to move him on.

'Ya can shoot me, miss,' Hank panted. 'But it ain't gonna make me move any faster.'

Wes said, 'All you had to do was *want* to stay. We'd have been happy to invite you folks in.'

Norman heard Duke say, 'We're stayin', all right, but from here on in we'll be in charge.'

They reached the top of the stairs. Norman unlocked the door, opened it. Then stood back to allow the two new captives through.

'Once we've got Sharpe we've got everybody,' Boots said.

Old Hank went through the door first. Then Wes.

Boots followed.

When they were all in the room Duke demanded, 'So, where will we find Sharpe?'

Lauren shrugged. 'He's out on the road.'

'Saving people,' Nicki added.

'He's sure got a thing about that, ain't he?' Duke rubbed his jaw, thinking.

Lauren said, 'We don't know how long he'll be gone.'

'Well, how I see it, if he brings back more people that's a good thing, especially dames. Norm and me have keen appetites in the whoopee department, don't we, Norm?'

Norman felt uncomfortable answering the question in front of Pamela who even now was shooting him an accusing stare. Instead, he changed the subject a little. 'What is it with Sharpe?'

'How do you mean?' Lauren asked.

'Why the mannequins? Why does he drive round with a bus full of them like they're real passengers?'

'They're kinda souvenirs,' Lauren said. 'They represent all the people he's saved out on the road.'

'Then you ate their asses.' Boots grinned.

'No, we did not eat *those* people.' Nicki sounded insulted. 'Sharpe rescued them. They were stranded in the desert when their vehicles broke down.'

Hank piped up. 'They woulda died of thirst if it weren't for Sharpe.'

Lauren added, 'Sharpe made sure they got safely home.' She took a deep breath as if explaining some quality of Sharpe's that she didn't fully understand. 'But it's important to Sharpe to keep the image of the people he saves.'

'Might be easier to take a photograph,' Duke pointed out.

'Sharpe is special. His ideas are unique. When he found an abandoned

315

truck full of store mannequins out in the hills he dressed them in the same kind of clothes as the people he saved, then put them on the bus. Of course, he gave them the names of the people he rescued as well.'

'Crazy.' Boots whistled.

'Makes sense to me,' Priest chipped in. 'I always kept a tooth from every single person I ate. Made a mighty fine necklace, I can tell you.'

Lauren strained to make her explanation of Sharpe's habit logical. 'What Sharpe does with the dummies is an art form as well as creating a remembrance.'

'Art?' Boots made a weird puffing noise to highlight her disdain. 'Who's gonna put a bunch of dummies in an art gallery? Sharpe's as crazy as a—'

That was the moment when Wes attacked. He spun round, pushed Boots hard. She crashed back into Duke.

Suddenly there was pandemonium. Folk shouting. Wes and Duke fighting.

Norman ran into the center of the room from where he could get a clear shot at Wes. Priest kicked out with his one remaining leg. Norman stumbled over it. His hand spasmed. He fired a bullet down into the floor. Hank lunged at him. Norman sidestepped; the old-timer fell flat on his belly. The impact was enough to make Hank fart with a loudness and a violence that Norman wouldn't have believed humanly possible.

Shit. Smells worse than a reptile house at the zoo.

Boots was picking herself up from her fall. She grunted, 'That's no way to treat a lady.' Her thick legs had been grazed during the rough 'n' tumble.

Wes was brave.

Wasn't enough.

Three swift punches from Duke knocked the guy cold.

Barely ruffled, Duke stood back in the doorway. He leveled the Magnum to cover the milling people in the room.

'Okay,' he called out. 'Everyone stand still.'

They saw the gun.

They stood still.

Lauren and Nicki were next to Priest. He shook his head and spat. 'Pah!'

Boots's piglike eyes scanned the room. 'Hey, where's Pamela?'

Duke turned to look back at the empty landing. 'She must have slipped out.'

'I'll go get her.' Boots cocked her pistol.

'No, you stay here with me,' Duke ordered. 'Norman, what're you waiting for? Go bring Pamela back before she calls the cops.'

The cops!

Norman had forgotten all about those guys.

'What're you waiting for, Normy?' Then Duke said something that electrified Norman. 'You find her, bud, you've got my authority to be the first to take her.'

'Don't worry, I'll find her.'

Norman jumped over the unconscious Wes, then ran along the landing to the stairs. He ran down those two at a time.

Pamela?

I get to take her first!

Oh boy, oh boy.

Chapter Forty-six

Pamela thought: *I've traveled back in time. It's happening to me again.*

Is it really Norman chasing me?

Or is it Rodney?

Back from the dead.

Zombie Rodney Pinkham. He'll do the bad things to me in death that he couldn't do in life.

Her mind-chatter went into overdrive as she ran from the old house on the hill. When Wes had attacked Duke in the bedroom she'd seen that Boots had landed on her fanny. The pig-girl had been in no position to fire her gun. The scary old guy, Priest, had tripped Norman.

So Pamela had taken her chance.

She'd fled.

Down the stairs. Through the door. Out into brilliant sunshine. Dazzled, she could barely see.

Didn't stop her running, though.

Unlike last time, when Rodney had pursued her, firing his pistol at her as he went, Pamela wasn't barefoot as she ran across the arid, stony ground of the Mojave. She wore new trainers that Lauren had given her for her waitress work. Clean white ones with a soft rubber sole.

Even so, those sharp stones made themselves felt as she ran.

But where am I going? she thought, dazed. *I'm running away from the cafe. I should be running toward it. Might be some would-be customers. One might have a cellphone, or they can drive me to the nearest town so I can tell the cops.*

Tell the cops what?

The Glory Bus

When they come to investigate the Duke Gang's armed takeover of Pits they'll also find that we've been killing and eating people.

Go figure.

Pamela's eyes were by now more accustomed to the sun's midday glare. Even so, the yellow rocks reflected a hell of a lot of rays. She had to squint to see.

Above her, the burning blue of the desert sky. In front of her, the ground rose up into rocky hills. These were sliced by brutal ravines. She saw the ruins of mine buildings. Rusty hunks of machines littered this side of the hill. There were the remains of iron rails, complete with a corroded ore hopper or two.

She could also see that she was being chased.

Norman had raced after her. She made out the golden gleam of the automatic in his hand.

Chasing her. Just like Rodney.

Only he hadn't fired yet, thank God.

As Pamela climbed the boulder-strewn hillside she glanced back. Norman must have been nearly a quarter of a mile away. He weaved between clumps of cacti. She'd gotten a good start. Was he gaining on her? She couldn't tell.

Could she hide?

No tree cover. No intact buildings.

Only rocks, sand, skeletal ruins. Not many options when it came to concealment.

Press on, she told herself. *You might find somewhere in the hills.*

So Pamela pressed on. She could almost see herself from a vulture's point of view. A young woman with blond hair. Dressed in the uniform of a Pits cafe waitress: knit sweater, bright red shorts, dinky apron, white sneakers. Still had her order book in the apron pocket.

Could do with a Luger. Or a machine gun. Then I could blow Norman away.

She huffed for air. Sweat ran in a salt river between her breasts. The sun burned the back of her head. She dodged a cluster of prickly pear. Then pushed for speed again: chin tucked down to her collar bones, back hunched, arms pumping, feet splashing dust.

'Pamela!'

Norman sees me all right, she told herself. *I must still be out of range, otherwise he'd have tried for a lucky shot . . .*

Pamela considered a change of direction. Making a run back to the cafe. Or even the highway in the hope that a passerby would pick her up. Whisk her to safety. Maybe even Sharpe again in his bus.

But to double back would take her too close to Norman.

Gotta keep running away from him. That means running in the opposite direction to the cafe, too.

'C'mon, Pamela,' she panted. 'You need a plan. You can't run all the way . . . way to Vegas.'

She was slowing. She knew it. Heat, exhaustion, running uphill. All conspired against her. Norman would catch up with her soon.

Or close the gap enough for him to fire a round or two off at her.

Pamela slowed her pace to a lope. Still she had to dodge cacti and mesquite. Only she knew she had to pump oxygen into her brain. *Gotta do some thinking.*

A plan. Need a plan.

What to do, Pamela?

Stop here? Fight him? Brain him with a piece of old iron from the mining equipment?

Iron bar versus automatic pistol? Think harder, Pamela.

Now she was almost walking. A stitch penetrated her side. Ahead, the hill split in two.

Can't keep climbing. Gotta take the easier route.

Pamela entered the V-shaped depression in the hillside. She soon realized that she was entering a small canyon. The ground beneath her began to run downhill. Still a lot of loose rubble underfoot. Sun beat at her from the canyon sides. But a little easier to make progress.

If she couldn't outrun Norman this might give her more time to consider a plan.

C'mon Pamela, think . . . think! What are you going to do to save your life?

Chapter Forty-seven

Norman was no athlete. But on the upside he was young. At college he jogged (mainly so that he could watch the female joggers jiggle pleasingly round the track).

Also, he had incentives.

Duke had given him permission to bone Pamela. His reward for catching her.

Course, there's a downside, too. Duke will beat seven yards of crap outta me if I don't catch her.

And if I don't catch her she'll call the cops.

I'm a cop-killer. Therefore the conclusion isn't hard to make.

I fry in the electric chair.

All that was enough to keep Norman running as hard as he could. Which wasn't that fast when it came to marathon standards. But not so terrible, either. He reckoned he was gaining on Pamela as he dodged cacti with their sharp spines or jumped over boulders. He even at one point sidestepped a snake that had red bands running along its body.

The gold Glock automatic in his hand grew a mite too heavy from time to time, so he'd pause to change hands.

Ahead, Pamela was running up the slope of the barren hill. Norman saw the flicker of her long, bare legs. Saw the sway of her butt clad in bright red shorts.

He wondered about claiming his prize.

Take her there and then on the hot ground? Or escort her down to the trailer where he could enjoy the comfort of a soft mattress?

Hell, she'll be my mattress.

Norman even began to wonder about afterward. If he pleasured her sweetly enough there might be a bond. Pamela might fall in love with him.

It'd be a shame to hand her over to Duke.

He paused for a second to wipe sweat from his eyes. Glancing back, he saw the lone house on the hill, the cemetery with its long-dead gunslingers and monkeys. Beyond that was the cafe beside the deserted highway.

Still quiet.

Quiet as a grave.

Norman pushed himself hard to run across the slabs of rock and past discarded mining machinery. At one point he had to leap over the skeleton of a mule. Perhaps three hundred yards ahead of him he glimpsed Pamela. The sight of her slim-waisted figure sent a fire running through his veins.

Man, was she beautiful.

Desirable.

He couldn't wait for that slippery moment of entry.

Squinting against the sun's fierce glare, he saw her hair fly out as she turned her head swiftly to look back at him. He couldn't see her face so he couldn't tell if she wore an expression of fear.

But being chased by a horny guy with a gun, how would you feel?

Feel shit-yer-pants-full scared, that's how you'd feel.

Norman grinned. This was a rare feeling of power, of being in control. He realized that he was enjoying himself. He even called out Pamela's name a couple of times. Never expected her to stop, but that was part of the chase game, wasn't it?

Let the victim know that you're hot on their trail.

He upped the pace. Now it was hot perspiration on his face that dried the second it beaded from his skin. Only his shirt became damp and itchy from sweat.

Once he'd tamed Pamela he'd put her to good use soaping his back in the shower. That would feel good.

Norman circled a patch of prickly bushes. Now he could see that a section of the hill ran into a gully. Pamela was headed along it.

She can't run forever, can she? I'm going to catch her soon. And then?

322

Chapter Forty-eight

Questions Pamela asked herself – whether her stamina would hold out, or whether she'd suddenly find she'd happened upon the main route to Las Vegas, crowded with vacation traffic – were suddenly answered for her.

'Damn.'

She gazed up at the rock face in front of her. The canyon had ended as suddenly as if someone had built a fifty-foot wall in front of her. Pamela looked left. Looked right. Looked forward. Sheer cliffs.

Only one way out.

That's back.

Back the way I came.

Right into the arms – and firearm – of Norman.

But Norman is no Rodney Pinkham. He looked like a college boy from a good family. He spoke politely. He didn't act like bad-boy Duke. And he certainly didn't seem a psycho like Rodney.

But who can tell a psychopath from a friendly, well-mannered guy? There's no knowing who's nice and who's a killer.

'Pamela!'

She looked back along the canyon. It was perhaps a hundred feet wide. Flat at the bottom and covered with a loose scree. Almost like the dried-out bed of a river.

'Pamela!'

The sun had passed its zenith now. A strip of deep shadow ran along the right-hand side of the canyon floor. She could still see Norman.

He had gained on her.

Now he was a hundred yards away.

323

'Pamela!' His voice echoed along the canyon walls.

Oh, God. She saw the glint of the gun, too. A gold brilliance.

After being nearly killed by Rodney she couldn't just stand there and wait for Norman to stroll up and shoot her.

'Pamela. There's nowhere to run.'

He didn't even seem to shout now. The narrow gap between the horizontal planes of rock amplified his voice. They channeled it to her as well. Lending it an eerie quality.

'So here you are, Pamela,' she hissed to herself. 'Caught like a rat in a trap. So . . . what ya gonna do? Stand and fight? Or walk toward him? Beg for mercy? Offer anything he wants?' She gulped. A tear came to her eye.

And when she wished for someone to save her it wasn't the man she once believed had loved her – her dead husband, Jim – it was Sharpe. Guardian angel of the freeway. Driver of the gray bus of salvation. The tear rolled down her cheek.

'Pamela.'

Norman was now maybe eighty yards away. He stepped over knee-high boulders. Sometimes he'd vanish into shadow then re-emerge closer.

Shockingly closer.

'No,' Pamela hissed. 'I'm not giving up!'

Her eyes scanning the rock face, she searched for something – anything! A cave. A niche to hide herself. A secret passageway.

The sunlit cliffs were featureless. Very nearly as smooth as a man-made wall.

Only now she took a closer look at the cliff that lay beneath a veil of dark shadow. *Ah ha.* This was different. More exposed to the west wind. She saw that the yellow rock had been weathered. There were fissures, hollows, recesses and protrusions. Not big ones.

But, God willing, big enough.

'Pamela!'

Closing out the voice, she ran across the stones that shifted beneath her feet. She stumbled. Almost fell. But sheer willpower kept her balance. Seconds later she reached the rock face.

Good-bye, fingernails. Hello, grazed knees. But needs must.

Pamela began to climb the vertical rock.

'Pamela. You're wasting your time.'

She didn't care. She climbed. A born-again rock monkey. Driven to scale a vertical wall of stone because her survival depended on it. Her eyes scanned the rock, locating handholds. Some were more like burrows in the cliff.

Pray God that there are no snakes in them.

Pamela's fingers probed hidden spaces. She expected the needle-sharp sting of fangs in the back of her hand at any moment. But her luck held. No snakes, no scorpions. Steadily she worked upward. Her back ached. She panted. Her fingertips were sore. One finger bled from the nail. Not a bite; just relentless wear and tear.

'Pamela. Don't risk it. You'll fall.'

'No, I won't.'

She glanced down. Thirty feet or more to the canyon floor. As she began to climb again she glimpsed Norman. He was perhaps forty yards away now. Close enough to fire on her.

Gritting her teeth against pain, gravity, exertion, Pamela drove herself higher. *Still a helluva way to the top.* She'd never make it before Norman reached the bottom of the cliff.

She glanced to her right. Almost level with her there was a protruding lip of rock. It formed a ledge a good five feet wide. Ten feet long. It didn't go anywhere. It was covered in boulders and loose stones that had dropped from above due to erosion over the years.

It had one thing she prized, though.

Sanctuary!

Not risking another look to see where her pursuer was (though she could hear his feet clattering over stones – he must have been close), Pamela shuffled sideways across the cliff face. Her body ached. Her muscles felt as though they were on fire. She'd grazed her chin because she'd hugged the vertical surface so closely. Fifteen seconds of shuffling like a human fly brought her to the lip of rock. Almost recklessly, she flipped sideways so that she could grip the ledge with her hands, while her feet were still wedged in a crevice on the rock face.

It was awkward. Her torso was twisted. Elbows locked straight, she took her body weight on the palms of her hands that were flat down against the horizontal surface of the ledge. Then, like someone climbing out of a swimming pool without using the steps, she hauled her body onto the platform of rock. A moment later she lay panting on a mattress of jagged stones.

As mattresses went it was uncomfortable. But right at that moment an exhausted Pamela thought it was the most beautiful place on the planet to rest.

A voice wailed from below. 'Pamela. There's no way out of here. Come on down.'

'Get lost.'

'I won't hurt you.'

'Yeah, like I believe that, Norman.'

She realized that her legs from the knees down still hung out over the edge of the ledge. A bullet in her shin wouldn't help matters so she wriggled forward. The dust that she raised made her sneeze. But when she glanced back she saw her entire body was laid flat on the rock.

Not even a heavy-duty handgun like the gold one Norman hefted could punch a slug through three feet of sandstone.

'Pamela,' Norman called. 'There's nowhere to go from there.'

'I'm not coming down.'

'Aw, don't be like that. Climb down here. We can talk.'

Pamela worked herself into a sitting position with her back to the cliff. She didn't risk glancing over the edge just in case Norman shot her in the head.

'Please, Pamela. I wouldn't hurt you for the world. Believe me.'

She called back. 'If you don't want to hurt me, prove it. Go back down to the cafe.'

'What? And leave you here?'

'Yes.'

'You'll call the cops.'

'How? The nearest telephone must be fifty miles away!'

'You might have a cellphone.'

'They don't work out here.'

'Pamela,' he pleaded.

'Go away, then I'll come down.'

'You know I can't do that.'

'Why not?'

'Orders. You saw what Duke's like. He'll rip me a new corn-chute.'

'Norman. Go away. I'm not coming down.'

'I'll come up and get you, then.'

A boulder as big as a basketball rested on the brink of the ledge. She pushed it off with the sole of her foot.

A crash. A loud one that echoed back as it struck home.

Silence.

Dear God. It hasn't hit him, has it?

Then came an aggrieved bleat. 'Hey, be careful! That nearly hit me.'

'If you try to climb up here I'll make sure the next one cracks your skull.'

'You wouldn't do that.'

Pamela folded her arms. 'Try me.'

She heard a more reflective Norman mutter, 'Shoot.'

For a few moments silence descended on the canyon. It would be too dangerous to expose her head by looking over the side of the rock ledge, but if she knelt up with her back to the cliff she could see the shadow creep across the scree floor. This'd become a waiting game now.

Waiting for dark ... What would Norman do then? Retreat? Or try to reach her under cover of darkness?

At last she heard Norman say, 'Looks as if we've got a dilemma.'

'I've got no dilemma,' Pamela retorted. 'I'm staying put.'

'You can't stay there forever without water. Not in this heat.'

'Neither can you, Norman.'

'One of the others will be along in a minute.'

'So you're a telepath. You can communicate with them and tell them that you're way up here in a hidden canyon?'

'Ugh.'

She heard the grunt as he realized the flaw in his thinking.

No one knew they were here. So no one would bring Norman a cool bottle of water to slake his thirst.

To sit it out in this arid channel of rock would be an endurance test. The one whose craving for liquid got the better of them would lose.

'I don't want you to die of thirst, Pamela.'

'Women survive longest without water, Norman. We've got a thicker layer of liquid-filled fat under our skin. Boobs are pretty much all fluid anyway. Y' know? Like camels' humps?'

When Norman spoke next Pamela realized that he was changing his strategy. 'Pamela? We're alike, you and me.'

'Don't think so, Norm.'

'We're educated. I can tell you are from the way you speak.'

'How observant, my dear Holmes.'

'Well read, too.'

'I saw the old Sherlock Holmes movies.'

'Yeah, Basil Rathbone, he was the greatest, wasn't he?'

'Norman, you're patronizing me.'

'Listen. We both know it's stupid for us to sit out here in a godforsaken canyon without water. If you come down here we can walk back to the cafe and talk all this through over a glass of cold white wine. How does that sound?'

'Sounds wonderful. But you'll shoot the fuck out of me the moment I start climbing down.'

'Pamela, I'm not a barbarian.'

'What about Duke and Boots? They psychotic or what?'

'Uhm . . . that's one of the subjects I need to discuss with you.'

'Say again?'

'You're intelligent. I need your advice. To be honest with you I'm in a bit of trouble. Well . . . more than a *bit* of trouble. A hell of a *lot* of trouble.'

Pamela realized that she needed to see Norman's face. His expression would indicate whether or not he was telling the truth. Come to that, the look in his eye would suggest whether or not he'd murder her in cold blood.

She inched toward the edge of the rock ledge. Just one glimpse down. One glimpse at his face would be enough.

That was when the shot rang out.

'Norman, you double-crossing son of a—'

'Pamela. Pamela!'

'You promised you wouldn't try and shoot me.'

'I didn't! I've just shot a rattlesnake. It struck out at me.'

'Like I'd believe you.' She hunkered back against the cliff. Out of sight.

'Pamela, you've got to believe me. I shot a snake. There's another thing . . .' His voice sounded troubled.

'What's that?'

'Pamela, you've got to help. The rattler bit me!'

Chapter Forty-nine

'You're shitting me, Norman.'

Norman looked up the cliff face. It was in shadow, but he could still make out where the rock ledge bulged out. Couldn't see Pamela, though. She must be hunkered back against the cliff, out of sight.

'Please, Pamela,' he called, his voice echoing from the canyon walls. 'There was a rattler. It really did bite me.'

'Yeah, and the second I poke my head out you blow a hole in it.'

'No.'

'Can't trust you, Norman.'

'It's starting to burn. It's the venom . . .'

'Where'd it bite?'

'My leg.'

'Where on your leg?'

'Come down, Pamela. See for yourself.'

'As if.'

'Please.'

'Are you sure it was a rattlesnake?'

'Take a look for yourself.'

'Put the gun on a rock – somewhere I can see it, but well away from yourself.'

'Yes, yes, anything. As long as you help me.'

Norman still couldn't see Pamela, so he walked twenty paces and laid the gold-plated handgun on a boulder. Then he returned to the bottom of the cliff.

But he noticed something.

Something bad.

He was limping now. The venom burned up through his veins as if hot wax was flowing there instead of blood. A moment ago he'd felt too hot – now cold shivers ran down his spine despite the heat in his veins.

Oh, God. All this and now I get chewed by a snake – a fucking rattler of all things . . .

His legs had become wobbly by the time he'd gotten himself back to the bottom of the cliff.

When he called out again, his voice had gone croaky.

Start of the death rattle?

'Pamela . . . I got rid of the gun . . . You're safe . . . Please . . . you gotta do something. I feel weird . . . I . . .'

'Okay, Norman. You've gotta stay calm. Breathe nice and slow.'

He looked up. The sky was a dazzling blue. This side of the canyon was dipped black in shadow now. But he could see her!

A lithe figure with blond hair. Long bare legs swinging over the ledge thirty feet above him. She moved fast.

Her hands and feet found small lodges and holes so that she could descend.

So she can save me!

Norman's heart pounded. An awful taste filled his mouth. The venom? Was it invading every part of his body in a tide of bitter poison?

Oh, God . . .

Norman closed his eyes. He only opened them when he heard a thump of feet. Pamela had jumped the last five feet to the ground.

'I really think it's kicking in.' His voice was weak-sounding. Hoarse.

'Where's the snake?' She sounded suspicious.

She doesn't believe me.

Swaying slightly, he pointed.

His finger had swollen.

Shit. That stuff acts fast. He was inflating like a balloon.

'There.'

He pointed to three feet of tube-shaped reptile lying in its own snake blood. His shot had blown most of the head away, leaving strands of skin and gristly bits of snake muscle.

'My God,' she breathed. 'That's a rattler, all right. Do you see the tail?'

'Saw the tail? Felt its teeth, too. Bery farp.'

'Say again?'

The Glory Bus

Norman moistened his swollen tongue, then took a run at the two words again. 'Very sharp. Rattlesnake bangs. Bery farp.'

'Here, sit down on this rock, Norman.'

'Bank yar.'

'It's affecting your speech, Norman. The venom's entering your bloodstream fast.'

'Uh . . .'

He felt like death.

Pamela cupped his face in her two hands. She looked into his eyes. He saw the anxiety there.

'Norman,' she said in a calm but firm voice. 'I need to get as much of the venom out of the wound as I can.'

'Uh-huh.' He grunted the affirmative. His hands felt cold as frost. Circulatory collapse. Toxic shock.

She spoke again. 'Norman, listen . . . no, stay awake for me, Norman. Where did the snake bite you?'

'Thigh.'

Pamela stepped back to see where he was pointing.

'Your inner thigh?'

'Uh.'

'Okay, Norman. Help me drop your pants. I'm going to have to suck out the poison.'

He'd wondered what Pamela's lips would feel like against his skin. Now he was going to find out.

But he hadn't anticipated these circumstances. Not for one minute.

With her help he slid his pants down. Then he sat on the boulder with his bare legs apart. They were awful pale-looking. Shaky, too.

'I see the bite mark, Norman.' She took a deep breath. 'Okay. Here goes.'

Norman felt Pamela's cool lips on the burning wound. The fangs had indeed punctured the skin on his inner thigh. Midway between knee and groin.

Now Pamela'd clamped her lips on the two bleeding holes.

Oh man, and how she sucks!

When she paused for breath she also spat. Despite Norman's dizziness he saw that her saliva was a bright pink with blood.

'Ya gonna apply . . . apply a tourniquet?' he croaked.

'Nope. Never apply a tourniquet to snake bites.' She wiped her lips with the back of her hand. 'Always make sure the patient is calm, keep the affected limb lower than the heart. With luck, the venom will localize and not spread through the body.'

'You really know what you're doing?'

'I should hope so,' Pamela told him. 'I'm a teacher. I took first-aid courses so I could take the little darlings on field trips. Of course, they never got bitten by snakes, stung by scorpions or chased by grizzly bears. Instead, they got drunk on beer or whacked out of their skulls on E. Here goes again.' Again she ducked her head down to suck his naked thigh.

Norman's mind was fuzzy to say the least. His hands were cold as ice. His leg was swelling. But he realized what this must look like to anyone watching the pair of them.

Here I am sitting on a rock with my pants down. Pamela is crouching in front of me. Her head is below my waistline. She's sucking away like crazy. Her head's twisting from side to side. I'm moaning.

Only not with pleasure.

Snakebites aren't fun. They hurt. Fucking hurt!

'Yee-ow!' he cried.

Pamela spat and wiped again. 'Hurting?'

'You could say.'

'I think I've got some of it.'

'I'm gonna die.'

'No, you're not.'

'If you felt the agony I felt you wouldn't say that.'

'Norman.' She was panting from the exertion. 'In this country more than eight thousand people are bitten by snakes in any one year. Less than one percent die.'

He grunted. 'One percent still sounds like scary odds to me.'

'*Less* than one percent. *Far* less. More people die from wasp and bee stings.'

'You've gotta get me some antidote.'

Pamela shook her head. 'You won't get any antivenom in fifty miles of here.'

'Aw, crap.'

'Besides, not a lot of doctors administer it for snakebites. Sometimes the side effects of the treatment are worse than the snake poison itself.'

'That doesn't make me feel any better.'

'Well, you *sound* better.' Pamela looked closely at his face. 'Your speech's improved. So has your color.'

Norman straightened up. Experimentally, he moved his arms, and then turned his head from side to side. 'Hey, I don't feel as bad as I did a few minutes ago. The dizzy spells are passing.'

She smiled. 'You'll live, then.'

'Yeah,' he said, pleased. 'I will, won't I?'

Pamela turned to look at the gun on the boulder twenty paces from them. 'You still going to shoot me, Norman?'

'No. I never planned on killing you, anyway.'

'But you're going to take me back to the house and lock me up with the others?'

Norman shook his head. 'I've decided. This madness has got to end.'

'Oh?'

'I'm gonna call the cops.' He paused. 'At some point.'

'Why at some point? Why not now?'

He grimaced. 'That's why I need to talk to you.'

'We'd be more comfortable talking down at the cafe.'

'With the dead guys there?' He shrugged. 'It's a bit of a mess, I'm afraid.'

'My trailer, then.'

'Okay.'

He stood up.

She looked at his legs. 'Norman?'

'Uh?'

'Your pants. Before you walk anywhere, best pull them up.'

Chapter Fifty

'So there it is,' Norman said. He took a swallow of ice-cold soda. He'd talked so much that his throat burned. 'Now you know everything that's happened to me in the last seven days.'

'You killed two police officers?' Pamela stared at him.

'Yes . . . but I didn't mean to. You've got to believe me.'

'Shoot.'

'It's being with Duke and Boots. It's like some kinda dope. You can't think straight. They make really crazy stuff seem like the most perfectly rational behavior in the world.'

'You mean like taking over Pits at gunpoint?'

Norman nodded. Then he glanced across the trailer lounge to a table where the gold-plated handgun gleamed in the afternoon light.

He winced as he shifted in the armchair. The snakebite still seared his thigh although it felt a little less painful than before. Pamela had washed the puncture marks with antiseptic and then had taped on a dressing. After shuffling to get comfortable he sat brooding.

At last, Norman said to Pamela: 'You must think I'm the worst.'

'I think maybe you've done some stupid things, but . . .'

He looked up at her. The change in her tone when she said 'but' suggested that something was weighing pretty heavily on her mind, too.

'But?' he echoed.

'But Pits isn't what you think.' Pamela went to the table where she'd left a pitcher of chilled water. She refilled her glass.

Pamela'd ditched the waitress apron.

334

Norman noted with some pleasure that its absence revealed more of her slim figure. She still wore the cafe's uniform. Bright red shorts, plus a white pullover shirt.

Boy, she looks good.

'S easy to get distracted when a babe looks that hot, Norman told himself. He took his mind off the curves of her bod, concentrated on what she was saying.

'Norman, I thought Pits was just a little desert community,' Pamela went on.

'Doesn't look much more than a ghost town to me,' he added.

'Just what I thought. It's only got the cafe, gas station and trailers. Those, and a population of six people.'

Five, Norman thought. He realized that Pamela couldn't know that Terry, the cook, was lying dead in a patch of cholla cacti. He let it pass. Such admissions now would complicate the situation with Pamela ... *Delicious Pamela.*

Pamela, he realized, was trying to explain certain facts. 'You remember what the old guy was saying earlier?'

'The one-legged guy?'

'Priest.' She nodded.

Norman shrugged. 'He's a crazy old coot, isn't he? All that talk of eating people. Has to be certifiable.'

'He's not crazy, Norman.' Pamela took a steadying breath. 'Here in Pits they really do eat people.'

Norman laughed out loud. Then clammed up.

Pamela ain't laughing.

'Jeez,' he hissed. 'You're not kidding me, are you?'

'Nope. That's how they funded the cafe refit and the trailers. You see, what they couldn't eat they sold. Jewelry, watches and stuff.'

'Holy moly.' He had to remember to close his jaw. His chin was nearly resting on his chest in amazement. 'And you've ... ?' He mimed gnawing his hand.

'I'm a newcomer. I haven't eaten anybody yet.'

'This is soooo far out.' He had to take a deep gulp of soda.

'But *you* have.'

'Me?'

Pamela nodded.

'Oh no, no.' Norman shook his head so hard that it made the

snakebite sting. 'I've killed people these last few days, sure. But I've never *ever* eaten anyone. Shit, as a kid I didn't even eat my own boogers.'

'Have to disagree, Norman,' Pamela told him matter-of-factly. 'When you first arrived you ate the Pitsburger. Lauren's special-recipe burger.'

'Christ on a motorcycle.' He swallowed as if he could taste human flesh.

Cannibals say that humans taste like pork. That's why they call their victim 'Long Pig'. Did those Pitsburgers taste of pork? They were kinda spicy.

He gulped. 'The person I ate . . . anyone you know?'

'Nicki's pimp.'

'Holy shit.'

'The guy rode out here to kill her for running out on him.'

Norman gave a bilious smile. 'I guess it couldn't have happened to a nicer guy.'

'If it helps . . . *I* killed him.'

'Wow.'

'I biffed him on the head.'

Norman's nausea passed. His smile broadened. 'Looks like we've got a regular killing spree here.'

'But you're right, Norman. The madness has got to stop.'

'Any ideas?'

Pamela stood up. 'I'm going to tell the cops.'

'The cops?' He shifted uncomfortably. Thoughts of the electric chair crackled into his mind.

'No time like the present, Norman. After all, we don't know what Duke and Boots are doing to my friends up at the house, do we?'

'No,' Norman replied. 'We don't.'

But knowing those two psychos I have a fair idea.

'Stay here,' Pamela told him. Her expression was businesslike. 'I'll be back as soon as I can.'

Norman got cold feet. 'Is it wise to telephone the cops? Maybe we should wait a while – Boots and Duke might just decide to take off.'

'There's no working telephone in Pits so we'll have to drive to the nearest pay phone. You sit and rest that leg.'

* * *

336

Fifteen minutes later, Pamela hurried into the trailer's living room.

She rattled a set of keys. 'We'll take Wes's truck. It's parked next to the gas station.'

'I don't know . . .'

'What ya mean, you don't know, Norman?'

'Where we gonna go?'

'To a pay phone. Or to the nearest town. Find the sheriff's office. Listen, Norman. My friends are in danger up at the house. If we don't bring help they're likely to wind up dead.'

Norman realized that Pamela could see the doubt on his face. Her nostrils flared with anger.

'Norman. Don't wuss out on me now. I saved your life, remember?'

'I know.'

'So I'm owed a favor and I'm calling it in right now.'

'Okay, okay.' He grimaced as he stood up. The snake venom had swollen his leg. It felt tight.

Hurt like a sliver of red-hot iron had been forced into his flesh.

Pamela's anger changed to concern. 'Can you walk okay?'

'I'll be fine. Let's just get to that truck.'

Norman limped from the dining room into the kitchen. If he kept walking he reckoned that maybe the tightness in his leg would ease.

Can't do much about the burning sting, though.

Pamela opened the trailer door to let in the desert sunlight. Even though the day was headed toward evening its radiance was still fiercely bright. Norman followed her down the three steps to the dusty ground. She waited for him.

Took his arm.

That feels nice. The gentle pressure of her fingers around my arm. A guy could get used to this.

'Keep walking, Norman. I'll help.'

'I'll try.'

'Try hard as you can. We don't want to stop until we're in that truck.'

Pamela was right. Norman wanted to be in that truck. He wanted to drive out of here as fast as those big old tires could carry them. It was the bit about the sheriff's office that he wasn't too happy about.

They moved away from the trailers, heading toward the parking lot with its line of abandoned cars. Beyond the lot lay the cafe. Just a few yards beyond that was the gas station. He could see a truck parked beside it. That had to be Wes's truck. Just another three minutes, and—

'Norman. What happened to you, bud?'

He stopped dead. Duke's voice.

Oh, shit . . .

'Yeah, Normy.' Boots's little-girl tones. 'We wuz worried that you might have got hurt.'

Norman stopped, turned. Pamela stood beside him, supporting him.

'Guys,' he said with a forced smile. 'Am I glad to see you.'

Duke scowled. Norman saw himself reflected in the tough guy's shades. 'You *sure* you're glad to see us?'

'Sure I'm sure.' Norman made it sound like he'd been having fun.

Boots nodded. 'You found Pamela, then?'

'Yup. I found her.'

'Why didn't you come back to the house, Norman?' Duke eased the big revolver out of his belt.

Norman saw that Boots's gun was in her hand as her arms hung loosely by her side.

Gun? Oh, fuck!

Realization hit Norman like a deluge of ice water.

I've left my gun on the table in the trailer.

'Norm, buddy.' Duke's voice was chilling. 'I asked why you didn't return to the house when you'd found runaway Pammy here?'

'We couldn't,' Pamela told him.

'He wasn't asking you, Miss Smarty Pants,' Boots said.

Norman faked an easygoing shrug, but in reality he was getting anxious. 'It's embarrassing to admit this,' he said.

'What's embarrassing?'

'In truth, Duke, I got bitten by a snake.'

'So?'

'I needed treatment. Pamela helped me.'

'She sucked out the poison?'

Norman nodded. 'Look, Duke, you can see where the rattler's fangs went through my pants.'

Boots was impressed. 'See that, Duke? He really did get bit.' She looked at Norman. Her eyes were big and dewy. 'Does it hurt, Norman?'

'Nothing I can't handle,' he replied.

'Okay, Norm.' Duke chewed an idea over. 'I buy the snakebite. But where were you headed now?'

'The cafe,' Pamela said. 'They've got a first-aid kit there.'

'But ain't that square pad in your pants a dressing, Norman? Or is it your time of the month?'

'Uh? Oh, a *temporary* dressing.'

'He needs painkillers, too,' Pamela added quickly.

Duke looked from them to the cafe. 'It ain't no direct route. You were heading toward the gas station. And there's a truck parked just there.'

'No, Duke. Like I said, we—'

'A truck,' he interrupted. 'All gassed up and good to go. And ain't those the truck keys in Pammy's hand?'

'Oh, Normy.' Boots looked as if she was going to cry. 'You weren't figurin' on runnin' out on us?'

'No.'

'We're your bestest friends in the whole wide world, Normy.'

Norman tried to change the subject. 'Shouldn't we be getting back to the house? The others will be making a run for it, too.'

'We locked them in the attic,' Boots said.

'Like maybe we should've locked *you* in, Norman,' Duke hissed. 'Then you wouldn't have been tempted to double-cross us.'

'I didn't.' Norman heard his voice rise into a squeal of protest.

Gotta persuade Duke I wasn't deserting him and Boots. If I don't, he's gonna use that Magnum on me.

Duke considered.

Norman stood beside Pamela. Boots stood beside Duke. The two pairs faced each other. The sun had taken on a rusty tint as it sank toward the hills. The highway was deserted. The silence was so intense that it almost hurt Norman's ears.

What would Duke decide?

Norman looked at Boots. She stared at Pamela with those dead brown eyes of hers. She lifted one of her dirty white boots an inch, then set it down, then raised the other. As if marching on the spot.

Weird.

Duke slid a cigarette from a pack. He lit it. Then:

'I want to believe you, Norman. But you can see my dilemma.'

Richard Laymon

'God's honest truth, Duke. I wasn't planning on leaving you and Boots here.'

'I'm thinkin' I need proof of your loyalty.'

'Anything – I'll do anything.'

Duke nodded at Pamela. 'You got your test, Norman,' he said. Then he handed Norman the Magnum. 'Shoot her in the head.'

'Pardon?'

'"Pardon?"' Duke mimicked. 'Why doesn't it surprise the everlasting shit outta me that you still speak all polite like a duchess?'

'But—'

'You heard me, Norman. Prove your loyalty to me and Boots. Blow Pamela's bitchin' brains out.'

Norman hefted the gun. It was heavier than the Glock automatic. He looked up at Pamela. She was moving backward, stumbling through the dust. She was shaking her head.

'No, Norman,' she whispered. 'Please don't do it.'

'You *can* do it, Normy,' Boots encouraged. 'Just pop one of them caps into her face.'

'Won't feel a thing, Normy.' Duke grinned. 'Ya'll be doin' her a favor. Now she'll never grow old and wrinkled and suffer from arthritis, and piles and shit.'

Norman raised the revolver. The blue metal barrel glinted.

Pamela was gasping while she backed away. 'Please, Norman. Don't kill me. Not after what I've done for you. You won't—'

'Shut up!' Norman snapped.

'Addaboy,' Duke praised him.

Then Norman turned. Fired.

Fired at Duke. The guy jerked sideways.

Lost his balance. Went down.

Did I hit him?

Norman raised the gun as Duke sat up. He was ready to fire again.

Wanted to fire again! Right plug-fuck center of Duke's chest. But his hand shook so much that the gun jumped out of his sweat-slippery fingers. It fell in the dust.

Duke looked dazed for a second. Blood streamed from a nick at the edge of his ear where the big-caliber round had brushed it.

So I did hit him. Only just.

Duke's eyes cleared behind his sunglasses.

Dragging the shades from his face he snarled at Boots: 'Kill them both.'

As Boots raised her revolver Pamela flew at her.

If Norman expected a catfight he was mistaken. Pamela swung her fist to deliver a hell of a punch at Boots's piggy face.

Boots squealed.

Dropped down.

But not out. She climbed up onto all fours in two seconds flat. She raised the hand that held the revolver.

Pamela followed through with a full-blooded kick.

The sneaker thudded into Boots's chunky side right where one of her kidneys was.

Boots gave a cry that sounded strangely orgasmic. The kick didn't stop her, either; slowed her, though.

Panting, she shuddered so hard that Norman saw her small breasts jiggling like jello. Then she started to climb to her feet again. The pistol was still in her hand.

Norman glanced at Duke. He moved on all fours to where the hefty Magnum revolver lay in the dirt.

Do I make a run for the pistol? Kill them both? he asked himself. But at that moment Pamela turned to him, hair flaring out, eyes flashing with urgency.

'Norman! *Run!*'

Norman didn't ask *where* they were running. Simply followed Pamela. Her long legs covered the distance in an easy sprint. Norman limped. His teeth were gritted. He grunted with pain.

The snakebite burnt like fury. His leg felt so tight. And heavy, as if it were clad in iron.

Can't run, can hardly walk . . .

A gunshot rang out. The bullet whined past him to smack into the ground, kicking up a splash of dust twenty yards in front of him.

Now Norman ran.

Pain or no pain.

He caught up with Pamela. They ran side by side.

'This way,' she panted.

He followed as she hurtled round one of the trailer homes. Now the fifty-foot aluminum box was between them and the two maniacs with guns.

Crack . . . crack-crack!

'They're still firing,' he gasped. 'Morons!'

'Don't bank on them not hitting us. Those trailer walls are like foil.'

Norman glanced back. Pamela was right. Boots and Duke must have fired again from the other side. Bullets came busting through the trailer's flimsy aluminum walls. Right through them to ricochet off stony ground close by.

'Where now?' Norman asked, running hard. 'To the house?'

'Nope.' Pamela's stare was fixed on the horizon. 'To the hills.'

Norman's leg hurt. The snake venom must have been fizzing in his leg muscle. He looked up toward the rocky hills that were turning red in the setting sun.

Panting, he gasped out the words. 'Pamela. I don't think I'm gonna make it.'

Chapter Fifty-one

Norman realized a rock-solid truth: *I'm gonna be dead by tonight.*

Prospects weren't good. Here he was, running up through Pits's cemetery with Pamela. The pair of them were being chased by Boots and Duke. Two crazy people with guns.

Crazy people with a proven track record of killing in cold blood. *Nope. The bottom line is: it doesn't look hopeful at all.*

'You've got to run faster, Norman.' Pamela panted the words as they exited the cemetery. Ahead was the old house on the hill. Beyond that, a craggy landscape littered with rusting mining gear.

'I am running as fast . . . as I can.' Norman struggled to breathe. 'Snakebite. Hurts . . . hurts like hell.'

Pamela might have intended to offer words of encouragement. But the crazed pair behind, letting loose with their handguns, was all the encouragement Norman needed.

Bullets buzzed through the evening air to ricochet off the rocks around them or chew flesh out of a cactus.

'That's better,' Pamela gasped as Norman piled on the speed.

Sweat blinded him, a stitch began to dig into his side. He risked a glance back.

Boots had fallen back. Now she was hobbling through the cemetery, clutching her side. A stitch like Norman's? Or had that kick of Pamela's finally made itself felt through her sluggish – her *hoggish* – nervous system?

Duke continued to run strongly. He was lean. Fit.

Muscular.

That guy wasn't going to tire easily.

So much for the government telling you that cigarettes were bad for you, that they silted up your lungs and clogged your arteries. Duke chain-smoked. But he ran like an athlete.

'We can't keep running forever,' Norman panted.

'We've got to make it into the hills again. Need somewhere to hide.'

'For God's sake . . . keep out of the canyon this time . . . dead end.'

'Don't I know it.'

Norman glanced at Pamela. Her clear-eyed gaze was locked on the path ahead. Blond hair flew out around her head. Her breasts moved in time with the rest of her body. A pleasing motion. Not a loose wobble.

God, is she something?

Something special.

If we make it outta here alive, maybe we could—

CRACK!

The sound of Duke's Magnum stopped that particular line of thought. The round passed so close to Norman's head that he felt its slipstream snatch at his hair.

The leg that had been pierced by the rattler's fangs ached like nothing on Earth. He was sure that it had swollen to twice its normal girth.

'Keep running,' Pamela urged him. 'Once we're in the hills we can give him the slip.'

'Might be time to say a prayer to your guardian angel,' Norman panted back.

He glanced over his shoulder.

No fair!

Duke was maybe forty yards behind them. And closing.

The guy didn't look tired.

Hadn't lost his cool.

A killing machine in human form.

Norman's legs quivered as though the strength was pouring out of them. Any second now he knew that he'd drop to his knees with exhaustion. Then . . . *Blam-blam! It's the BIG sleep for Norman Wiscoff . . .*

'Bear left,' Pamela told him. 'There's a track leading . . . leading into the hills by all that machinery.'

'But we're running uphill.' Norman's breath whistled through his throat. He could hardly inhale.

Still managing to run, he glanced down at his fingers. They were swollen. He couldn't even see his knuckles, his flesh was so puffed.

Snake venom. This exertion was pushing it through his veins.

His heart seemed to beat uncannily loud. Maybe the toxins were invading the cardiac muscle.

He staggered.

'What's wrong?' Pamela asked.

'I can't run anymore.'

'You've got to, Norman.'

'I know ... but I can't ... My leg's seizing up. I can't breathe.'

She's going to run on and leave me. That realization struck Norman hard. He'd been running for days. He couldn't carry on.

The moment of reckoning.

Oh, God ...

But Pamela wasn't quitting on him yet. 'In here,' she shouted.

He could scarcely walk now. Never mind run.

Pamela gripped his arm, then dragged him across a stretch of ground that was covered with fine stones. They lay so deep and thick that Norman sank up to his ankles in them. They shifted when he tried to lurch forward on his stiffening leg.

He glanced back. Duke was thirty yards away.

The man paused, aimed.

Squeezed the trigger, and—

Click!

Even from where he stood Norman heard the hammer fall on a spent cartridge.

Duke began to reload. After ejecting the empty shell cases from their chambers in a glittering stream onto the ground, he took fresh rounds from his shirt pocket. Began to reload one by one.

He grinned at them. 'No point in running, folks. Pammy? You might live if you're real nice to me. Normy? Stop running away like a kid. Come here and take your punishment like a man.'

'Don't listen to him,' Pamela hissed.

She yanked Norman by the arm again and guided him across the carpet of loose stones that were so hard to walk on. Ahead, he saw the crumbling structure of a mine building. There was no roof to speak of. Not much in the way of walls, either. Just a course of bricks about waist high, with a few weathered boards hanging from a timber frame.

Through the holes in the walls, Norman could make out hunky lumps of machinery that had been by turns sandblasted, then ravaged by rust, and finally crusted white with bird droppings.

Probably was a desirable residence for scorpions too.

Yeah, why not get a scorpion sting on the other leg, Norm? It might even up the snakebite.

'You can't run,' Duke called after them as he coolly reloaded the powerful handgun. 'Not much of a place to hide.' He laughed. 'Unless you figure on shrinking yourselves down to the size of bugs.'

Toiling up the hill behind Duke came Boots.

Oh, great.

Now Boots is gonna watch me weep and beg for my life. Not that Duke's the kinda guy who favors groveling. I'm still gonna get a bullet in the head.

'Keep moving!'

Pamela kept urging Norman on as she dragged him through the doorway into the building. The floor was covered with windblown sand. There were a couple of tumbleweeds. The sloughed skin of a snake – a yellow, papery thing. There was even the skeleton of a dog or coyote in the corner.

'Not much of a place to a hide,' he panted.

'If we can't hide, we'll fight.'

My God, is she feisty! Norman was impressed.

'We don't have any weapons,' he reminded her.

Pamela looked round. Her eyes were razor sharp. She was assessing everything for its assault potential. A length of chain that was orange with rust. A shovel with a broken handle. A couple of perished truck tires.

There were more gaps than wall. Norman could see the desert hills rearing up into the dark blue of the evening sky.

'No helicopter. No machine gun,' he observed.

'Sarcasm won't help us, Norman.'

A revolver round smacked into the timbers.

'It's your time, Norman.' Duke's voice sounded frighteningly close.

'Yeah, come on out.' This was Boots. She still sounded winded from her climb up from the trailers.

Norman limped round an engine that must have been the size of an ice-cream truck. It had cogs the size of bicycle wheels. Levers longer than his arm. A conglomeration of valves, tubing, drive belts (long perished), dusty gauges. But nothing to use as a weapon.

Pamela followed him.

Another bullet smacked into the machinery. It rang like a church bell.

'Damn, that was close,' Pamela hissed. 'What we going to do, Norman?'

Norman looked up at the remains of the wall that faced the sunset. Through foot-wide gaps in the boards he saw that tonight's dusk was a dazzling red. Two figures – one tall and lean, one short and squat – stood in dark silhouette.

We're caught like rats in a trap.

'Okay,' Duke told them. 'You've had your fun. The chase is over, guys.'

'We win, you lose,' Boots said.

Norman stepped back, his feet drawing furrows in the dust.

'Pammy,' Duke said. 'Keep your hands up. Now walk forward to the door.'

'She's cute.' From the tone of her voice Boots must have been smirking. 'Can I have her tonight, Duke? Pleezer-weezer, just for li'l ol' me.'

'Sure. You've earned some fun time.'

Pamela knew what was in store for her. She groaned, 'Oh, dear Lord in Heaven.'

Norman took another step back. This time his foot didn't step into dust.

Nothingness.

Fresh air.

Surprised, he glanced back.

A hole. Four foot by six.

A dark hole. An abyss kind of hole.

The bottomless-pit variety.

Warm air flowed up from it. Air that stank so bad he nearly upchucked there and then.

'Stand perfectly still, Norman, old bud.' Duke's voice grew colder. 'If I get a good clean shot, it shouldn't hurt you none . . . at least, not *too* much.'

'Okay,' Norman said. 'You've no objection to me turning my back to you so I don't see you fire the gun?'

'No objection at all, Normy. I should be able to plant a round smack between your shoulder blades.'

'Poor Normy,' Boots sympathized.

Norman figured that from this angle Duke and Boots couldn't see the opening of the mine shaft in the ground.

He turned round, his hands held high.

'Want me to count you down, Duke?' Boots asked.

'Sure.'

'Three . . . two . . .'

Before 'one' Norman grabbed hold of Pamela by the sweater. He heard the rip of fabric.

Heard her aggrieved 'Hey!'

But when he jumped she toppled with him.

Into the pit.

Madness, he thought as both of them fell.

But when you're faced with death by shooting or death by falling, which one do you pick?

Norman didn't want to give Duke the satisfaction of blowing him to hell and gone.

The fall was a long one. Longer than he'd thought possible.

Pamela screamed.

Kept screaming.

Until . . .

Chapter Fifty-two

Pamela screamed until they hit the bottom of the shaft.

Norman expected hardness. Hardness like you wouldn't believe. Bone-breaking, head-cracking.

Sharp debris. Discarded mining tools. Boulders. Shards of rock.

Instead.

Squelchy. Wet. Soft. Uncannily soft.

Wet?

And when he recovered from the slight concussion he detected something else, too.

Pamela voiced it first. 'Oh! That smell. What is it?'

Norman realized that everything he'd eaten in the last twenty-four hours was doing its darnedest to hurtle back up his gullet. He gulped.

'What a stink . . . it's suffocating.'

Asking Pamela if she'd been uninjured by the fall was moot now. Both of them were focused on the appalling smell at the bottom of the pit.

'Welcome to the pit that put the *pit* into Pits,' Norman managed to say. 'But – sheesh – what an odor.'

'It's so thick you could cut it with a knife.'

Norman looked round. Too dark to see anything this far down. Above them he saw the bright hole through which they'd fallen, though. Parts of the upper walls of the shaft were illuminated by the bright setting sun.

But down here—

Darkness.

Darkness and stink . . .

A sweet smell, only nauseating. Decay. Fermentation. On the shitty side as well. Like an almighty crap done by someone after gorging on chocolate.

Norman said, 'Feel round . . . use your sense of touch. Feel what we've fallen onto.'

'Oh . . . my . . . God.' Pamela knew what they'd fallen into.

Norman knew, too. 'Damn . . . this can't be happening.'

Pamela's voice whispered from the dark. 'We've found where Pits dumped its leftovers.'

'I think I've just picked up a hand,' Norman said. He felt stiff fingers. The wrist appeared to be sawn through. His own finger felt a stub of cut bone.

'I've just put my hand on a head,' Pamela told him. 'Ugh . . . I can feel the eyes – ick – no, I can feel where the eyes *were*.'

'Anything else?'

'Feels like body parts. Can you see yet?'

'Not a thing. Probably for the best.'

'Ugh, what a stink . . . I don't know how much more of this I can take.'

Norman agreed. 'And we know who created this.' He gulped. 'This is where the good people of Pits dumped the bodies. Or what's left of them.'

'Jesus. They must have been dropping human remains down here for decades. There might be hundreds.'

'Lucky they did,' he told her. 'Least the cadavers broke our fall.'

'Oooh-eee. I'm covered in corpse juice. Can you feel how sticky your skin is?'

'Don't . . . it's on my lips, too.'

Norman heard scrabbling. Pamela must still have been searching the debris in the dark.

'Find anything?' he asked.

'As well as you-know-whats – heads and arms and shit – there's plastic bags full of stuff.'

He felt around too, until his hand closed over a crackling membrane. 'Seems like a sack of clothes.'

'Probably the possessions of these people.'

He heard a squelch followed by a rattling sound.

Pamela said, 'I think I've just sat on someone's belly . . . Oh God, post-mortem farts . . . they're the worst, aren't they?'

Norman would have agreed, only he was fighting the urge to vomit.

Just as he began to forget a very real threat that should have been uppermost in his mind he heard a voice wavering down from above. 'Oooh, Norman. Coo-eee! Are you all right down there, Normy?'

'Oh shit, *those* two,' he whispered.

Neither of them replied to Boots's call.

Then Duke shouted, 'Hey Norman, reply to the lady. Don't make me come down there!'

The gruesome twosome on the surface thought this was funny. They both laughed.

Then a second later Norman heard a noise someplace between a thud and a *squish*.

Pamela warned him: 'Norman, they're throwing stuff down at us.'

Norman looked up at the circle of light that was the entrance to the shaft. He made out two heads looking down from about thirty feet away. He also saw a truck tire sailing down through the air toward them.

He flung himself to one side.

Thud.

'Pamela, you okay?'

'Fine. I suggest we get out of the line of fire.'

Just for emphasis one of the pair above fired a revolver down the shaft.

Crack . . . splat.

A body part got that one.

'Norman,' Pamela hissed. 'Over here.'

'Where the hell is over here?'

'Here. Follow the sound of my voice.'

'What's wrong?'

'I'm in the entrance of a tunnel . . . I think I am, anyway . . . if you follow me in they won't be able to hit you.'

'It's so dark they're firing blind anyway.'

Crack . . . a ricochet whine, then another *splat*.

'But then again,' he added, 'if you shoot into the dark you still might hit something – and I don't want to be that *something*.'

'Then quit gabbing and follow the sound of my voice.'

Norman didn't have a clue where Pamela's voice was coming from. Instead, he reached out with groping hands until he found the side of the shaft. Then he followed it. The snakebite still stung his thigh. The air stank. His body was sticky with sweat – and with ichor leaking from body parts. But he kept going.

Until he reached the tunnel mouth. Then he fell forward onto a piece of living anatomy.

'Ouch. Norman, you've just landed on me.'

'Sorry, Pamela. I can't see squat.'

'Shuffle back here – away from the shaft.'

'What now?'

'Wait. They'll get bored.'

They sat there, side by side. Norman could feel Pamela's shivering body against his. Every so often she flinched when she heard the report of a gun as Boots or Duke fired blindly down the shaft.

'Keep quiet,' Norman whispered. 'If they don't hear us they'll think that they managed to hit us. Or that we're already dead from the fall.'

All they could do was sit in the stinking tunnel.

And wait.

Norman could tell by the luminous face of his watch that they'd waited nearly half an hour when he heard Boots calling down to them.

'Normy . . . Normy? I shouldn't be telling you this, Normy. Duke'd get mad, but me and you had a thing, didn't we? We could've been a couple and done nice stuff together.'

Norman kept his mouth shut.

'But, like, for old times' sake I gotta tell you this. Listen. Normy. Duke's gone to get more ammo and a flashlight. He's gonna come down there after you. He said he'd . . . uh-oh.' Her call turned into a whisper that Norman could only just make out. 'He's coming back. Run, Normy, while you've got the chance.'

Norman found Pamela by touch. He moved forward until her hair brushed his lips. Now he could whisper into her ear without being overheard.

'Pamela. What Boots has just said. What do you think?'

Pamela whispered back. 'Could be the truth. It will be dark soon. They probably don't want to risk leaving us, just in case we find a way out.'

'Stay here, I'll take a look up the shaft.'

'Careful, Norman. Could be a trick.'

Groping his way over rotting human carcasses, Norman made it back to the shaft. When he looked up he could see Boots with her halo of short blond hair. She was looking down into the hole. From the way she didn't react when he peeped up he guessed she couldn't see him.

He couldn't see much, either.

Just the entrance to the shaft. A few roof timbers above it. No actual roof. Streaks of red cloud in the sky.

Wait . . .

He could make out the inner rim of the entrance to the pit. Beneath that were the walls of the shaft. He could discern patches of gray rock. Also he could see something that made his stomach drop. An iron ladder was bolted to one of the walls. He couldn't see how far it extended because just a few feet down from the surface the shaft walls were hidden by darkness.

But wanna bet the ladder comes all way down here?

Norman crawled back to Pamela.

'Looks as if a ladder extends to the bottom of the shaft,' he whispered.

'So Duke's gonna follow us down.'

Right on cue, Norman heard voices from above.

'Pamela,' Norman hissed, 'we've got to get away from here.'

'How?'

'Chances are this tunnel leads somewhere.'

'In the dark? Norman, we can't see anything.'

Norman's mind whirled into action. *Gotta think our way out. Find a solution.*

A crash sounded from the bottom of the pit.

Too much to hope that Duke or Boots has fallen down. Nice thought, though.

'Sounds like they're dropping rocks to spook us into shouting out.' Norman touched Pamela's bare arm. 'Listen, these sacks full of stuff – there might be something in there that we can use.'

Pamela's doubting voice came from the darkness. 'Like a gun, or a magic-carpet ride out of here? Get real, Norman.'

'Just look. There might be something.'

'Okay. It's worth a try.'

Norman heard the rustle of plastic as Pamela tore at the bags. He found one by touch and ripped it open.

Shoes. A comb? Clothes. A spectacle case? Hard to tell in the dark.

'Try and search the pockets,' he told her.

'I'm trying . . . it's not easy in the dark. Ugh, I think I've found a pair of underpants here. Big ones.'

'A lady's purse. Feels like lipsticks inside. But then, it could be rifle rounds. Shit, this is harder than I thought.'

'What are we looking for exactly, Norman?'

'I don't know. I'm hoping we'll know when we find it.'

'Great.'

More crashes from the pit. Duke must have hefted some of the heavy machinery over the edge.

'Probably hoping to squash us before he comes down,' Norman said. 'Aw, crap.'

'What is it?'

'Thought it was a flashlight. It's just a cellphone.'

'Pass it here.'

'Why? You'll never get a signal down here.'

'Just pass it, will you, Norman?'

'I don't know where it is now,' Norman confessed. 'I just threw it to one side.'

'Find it. It might help.'

'You going to hit Duke with it?'

'No, don't be ridiculous. Just find the phone, will you?'

Norman searched through thighbones, rib cages, moldering assholes, discarded shoes, jackets – all by touch, then—

'Here's your phone,' he told Pamela. 'For what good it is.'

'There might still be some charge in the battery—'

'I don't see what—'

'There!'

'My God.'

'See?'

'Pamela. You're a genius.'

With a bleep, as she pressed the power button, the cellphone's screen glowed a green-yellow. It wasn't all that bright but it was enough.

Norman could see Pamela's grinning face in the dim glow. He looked at the cellphone's keypad and screen glowing in her hand. She moved the phone over the bottom of the tunnel.

The downside was that now they could see the decomposing arms, legs, torsos, hearts, lungs and spinal cords of dozens of men and women.

'No wonder it stinks,' Pamela gulped. 'These people are putrefying.'

At the bottom of the pit shaft was a rounded mound of more bodies. Norman was beginning to think that the illuminated cellphone screen was brighter than he could have imagined when he realized that the light was coming from above.

Duke was coming down the ladder. He shone the flashlight down to make sure that no one below had an unpleasant surprise waiting for him.

'Shit,' Norman breathed. 'Here he comes.'

'Hang on – we can't walk by the light of the cellphone. See? It goes off every few seconds.' Pamela pressed one of the keys. With a bleep the light came on again. But only for five seconds.

'Shine the light on the bags. There's got to be some matches here.'

As quickly as they could they searched the plastic sacks by the feeble light of the phone.

'Wait,' Pamela said. 'You go through the bags, I'll keep the light near your hands.'

Now they worked together. Pamela helped Norman by repeatedly depressing a button to keep the cellphone screen glowing. When it was lit she held the device as close to his searching hands as possible.

'Hurry up, Norman ... I can hear him climbing down the ladder.'

Now Norman could see drivers' licenses, pens, combs, car keys, maps, travel itineraries, socks, women's lingerie, novels, music-cassette tapes, spectacles ... Then: *Bingo!*

'Look.'

'A cigarette lighter,' Pamela said. 'Does it work?'

'Here goes.'

Norman rotated the wheel on the top with his thumb. A yellow flame popped from the metal casing. Norman saw that the lighter was a retro model, complete with a cannabis leaf printed on the side.

'As far as I can tell, it's full of lighter fuel,' he told her.

'We've gotta risk taking that. Duke can't be far away.'

Norman kept the small flame burning as he stood up. To lift himself to his feet he pushed down on a torso, using the hand that held the lighter. The corpse was decomposing in style. There was no head.

An oozing hole formed a cleft between the shoulders. The chest and belly were rounded with gas. Chest hairs stood on end. Even the belly button protruded. The dead body's internal pressure must have been formidable.

The moment Norman pressed down on the bloated belly the torso farted through the neck hole.

A loud, rich raspberry of a fart.

An instant later the decomposition gas met the flame of the lighter. Norman flinched as a ball of fire rolled past his face, singeing his eyebrows.

Before the flame died it lit the tunnel in vivid detail. He saw the marks of miners' picks on the walls. Saw the rails once used by the ore hoppers. They ran into the distance along a dead straight tunnel.

He saw Pamela's startled face as the gas generated by putrefying internal organs flared off. Her face had a strained, tight look. A tightness that trembled. She was wet and shiny all over. Streaks of brown cadaver juice marked her cheeks.

Norman saw that when he'd dragged her over the edge of the abyss he'd torn her sweater. A rent reached down from her collar to her breastbone. It exposed the gleaming upper half of her breast. A smooth globe of perfection.

Norman's flesh tingled. This time the snake venom wasn't to blame.

When the release of inflammable gas had burnt itself out she said, 'Come on. He can't be far from the bottom.'

Pamela didn't bother with the cellphone now. It was way too dim compared with the cigarette-lighter flame. Even so, she slipped it into the pocket of her shorts.

'Just for reserve,' she told Norman.

Now they hurried as fast as they could along the old mine working. In the flicker of the lighter's flame they could see timber supports, along with twin rails that were smothered with dust.

'Gotta hope there's another way out,' Norman told her.

'Either there is, or we die trying.'

'Succinctly put.'

A white light reflected from the stone walls.

'Oh, God,' Pamela hissed. 'He's here.'

Norman glanced back. They'd covered close on a hundred yards since leaving the bottom of the pit with its rich deposit of rotting body parts. Although Norman couldn't see it now. All he saw was a dazzling mass of light.

Duke was aiming the flashlight straight at them.

Not only the flashlight.

A ricocheting bullet went screaming past them.

'Nowhere to run to, old buddy.' Duke's voice boomed along the tunnel. 'If you stop running I'm gonna promise to make it painless. You won't feel a thing.'

Norman's legs weakened. The snakebite was slowing him down again.

No . . . that's not it. There's another reason.

'We're running uphill,' he panted.

'Could be a way out up ahead.'

'Pray God there is.'

'And Duke might be doing us a favor?' Pamela glanced at the lighter in Norman's hand. 'Kill it.'

'Right! Duke's flashlight!'

Norman snuffed the flame. Duke lit their way as well as his. Without having to worry about the lighter's burning wick going out they could move faster.

Ahead, they could see an opening cut in the rock. The tunnel had branched into two.

'Rockfall to the right,' Pamela said, breathless. 'Go left.'

This tunnel ran even more steeply uphill. After a few paces it opened into a gallery where miners had once worked the seams. Then they must have loaded the ore into wheeled trucks that ran under the force of gravity to the bottom of the shaft that Norman and Pamela had fallen into. There machinery would have hauled the ore to the surface.

The gallery that they'd entered had deep gray walls that glittered with speckles of ore.

'Jeez. This is big enough to put a house in.' Pamela looked up, awed, at the high ceiling.

'Yeah, but I wish they'd ventilated the place. I can hardly breathe.'

'It'll be a buildup of gas.' Pamela too was struggling for breath.

Norman noticed the way her lips were growing pale. When she sucked in breath her breasts rose as her rib cage expanded. He saw the curve of them through the rip in the sweater.

'We can't wait here any longer,' Norman gasped. 'Duke's not far behind. See the light?'

He was right. There was still no need to use the cigarette lighter. Duke's flashlight sent a wash of white light into the miners' gallery.

'Gotta keep moving.' Pamela heaved in a lungful of toxic air. 'Right.'

They walked on. Running was impossible. The stone floor was humped in the middle. A seam of harder rock had forced the miners to dig upward before the obstacle dipped down again. It forced Norman and Pamela to walk up a steep incline before descending the other side. At the top of the mound Norman's throat stung, his eyes watered.

When they'd passed the highest point he spluttered the words, 'That's where the gas was densest.'

Pamela nodded. Her eyes streamed with tears.

Now they could hear footfalls.

Duke must be close.

All they could do was continue. The spacious gallery narrowed back to a tunnel. They followed the tracks into the gloom.

When they reached an old ore cart on the tracks Pamela stopped her companion.

'Norman,' she said, 'I've got an idea.'

Chapter Fifty-three

Norman stared at the miners' ore truck as it sat on the rails. A wedge-shaped block of wood had been forced under a rusty iron wheel to stop the truck running away. Probably done by the last miner to walk out of here eighty years ago.

Norman gasped for air. His leg hurt where the rattler venom still saturated the muscle tissue. Even his hand tingled where Priest, the crazed cannibal, had chewed on it.

At last he found the breath to speak. 'Pamela, I hope you're gonna tell me we can get in that thing and ride outta here.'

'Nope . . . the tunnel runs uphill. If we climb in the truck and get it rolling it'll take us right to Duke.'

Norman glanced back down toward the gallery. The flashlight was growing brighter. 'Well . . . Duke . . . Duke's getting closer all the time.' He licked his dry lips. 'What's the plan?'

'Give me your shirt.'

'Huh?'

'Your shirt. Quickly!'

From the bottom of the tunnel Duke sang out: 'Fee, fi, fo, fum, I smell the blood of a college bum.' The guy laughed. A mad-sounding laugh.

Kind of laugh you make as you slice someone into pieces.

'Norman? Shirt!'

'Okay, okay.' Norman ripped off his shirt without bothering to undo its buttons. Quickly she tied the shirt to the front of the ore-hopper truck, around the iron device that would have hooked into the next truck in line.

'Lighter.' Pamela held out her hand.

Norman handed it to her.

She rolled the metal wheel to ignite the wick. Then she held the blue flame to Norman's shirt. With a crackle it started to burn.

'Great,' he gasped. 'You've tied my shirt to a truck. You've set it alight. Now what?'

'Kick the wedge out from under the wheel.'

'Anything to please a lady.' Norman was light-headed now. These actions made no sense to him. But he did as Pamela asked anyway. With a few kicks he knocked clear the timber wedge that acted as a brake.

'Norman, stand back!'

He stood back against the tunnel wall, out of the way.

Nothing happened.

'The axles will be rusted,' he told Pamela. 'It's stuck . . . stuck like shit to a baby.'

'Norman!' Duke called. 'What you doing playing with rusty trucks, bud? Gonna cut yourself.'

Norman couldn't see Duke properly but he guessed the man had just entered the section of tunnel that contained Pamela, himself and the truck. The resolutely stationary truck.

Pamela hissed, 'Get behind it. *Push!*'

'You really think it's gonna run him down?'

'Just get this truck rolling, Norman.'

He limped behind the truck to help Pamela who had her shoulder against the hopper. He helped her to push.

Through clenched teeth Norman panted, 'Wouldn't we be better running away . . . rather than doing this?'

'We can't outrun the guy. He's armed. We're not. This is our last hope.'

'Gee, some hope.'

'Get it moving before the shirt burns out.'

'Like that makes perfect sense.'

'Listen to me. When you set fire to the gas pooping out of that body earlier – it was methane gas. A by-product of putrefaction.'

'So?'

'Methane. It's odorless, colorless. It's lighter than air . . . uh, come on, it's starting to move.'

The truck's wheels squealed as they turned for the first time in decades.

'Norman?' Duke's voice. 'You playing with matches up there? I can see somethin' burning.'

'Methane's inflammable,' Pamela gasped.

'Why didn't we blow up when you set fire to the shirt?'

''Cos of the hump in the gallery floor down there. Remember when we couldn't breathe? Methane's gathered in a pocket where the floor of the mine rises up in that hump.'

'From all those rotting bodies?'

'Yup, those dead people are a regular gas factory.'

'It's going!' Norman cried out as the wheels unstuck themselves and began to roll. Axles shrieked. He straightened to see the truck moving faster and faster downhill toward the light source that was Duke's flashlight. The thunder of iron wheels against the track was almost deafening.

'Get back against the tunnel sides!' Pamela shouted above the racket of the runaway ore truck. 'Cover your ears with your hands. Keep your mouth open; otherwise the shock wave will pop your eardrums.'

Shock wave? Sounded as if the truck with Norman's burning shirt tied to the front was about to go nuclear.

The rumble of the truck receded. Then came Duke's scornful laughter.

'You really thought you could run Duke down with that heap of junk! Man, you've gotta try harder than that!'

The rattle of wheels faded.

The sense of anticlimax nearly caused Norman to weep.

All that effort! For what? Jesus, we would have been better—

Norman didn't so much hear the explosion.

All he really remembered was a blue light of such intensity that he could still see it when his eyes were tight shut. Then he was flying through the air. Then he was lying with something soft on top of him.

There was darkness. He seemed to be breathing dust.

Jeez. At least he was breathing.

The darkness seemed to last a long time. Norman was too dazed to do much except lie there.

After a spell he heard a noise in the stillness. An electronic bleep.

A green face floated in front of his.

'Are you all right, Norman?'

'Pamela?'

'Yeah, sorry, I seem to be lying on top of you.'

'Believe me, that ain't a problem.'

Pamela moved the cellphone so that she could reveal a little of their surroundings.

They couldn't see much. Dust misted the air. With the light of the cellphone it created an eerie, greenish fog.

'Duke,' Norman said. 'If we're in one piece, then—'

'Relax,' Pamela told him. 'When your burning shirt detonated the methane you could say truthfully that Duke sorta went to pieces.'

The light on the phone went out again.

She pressed another key.

Bleep.

The light came on. Norman saw bits of Duke. Big bits. Small bits. Charred bits. Bloody bits. His head lay in the center of the tunnel, looking back at them. He still wore his disdainful sneer, the lip curling up. Only there was no body.

'Appears as if Duke's gone to the bad-boy convention in the sky.'

'Yup.' Pamela smiled. 'Duke. RIP. Rest in pieces.'

They stood up. Dusted each other down. Norman had had the good sense earlier to replace the lighter in his pocket. He lit it again.

'Okay,' he announced. 'Let's find the exit.'

Chapter Fifty-four

When Norman stepped out of the mine's ventilation shaft it was night. Even so, he saw the light.

Not that he was suddenly overcome by the sweet love and boundless mercy of Almighty God.

Nor any revelation concerning Jesus, Buddha or Shiva.

No.

Norman saw Pits in the moonlight below him, and then he saw 'the light' of his own personal revelation. He thought: *Duke's gone. I'm still here. I'm going to take over.*

That town is mine.

Pamela said, 'Take care where's you're stepping, Norman. This path runs right along the edge of the cliff.'

'Don't worry,' he told her. 'After what happened tonight I've gotta be indestructible.'

'I wouldn't push your luck. That's a sheer drop.'

Norman felt good. Duke was dead. Boots wouldn't be a problem. This moon was so bright that he could clearly see the narrow path that hugged the edge of the cliff. He glanced down to his left. The rock face plunged down maybe a hundred feet to a scree of rubble at the bottom. Probably old mine waste thrown out of the shafts that pockmarked the hillside here. In the distance a coyote howled in the hills. Some animal part of Norman howled back.

A desire that was nothing less than wolfish began to burn in his belly. He stopped. Glanced back at Pamela who was following him along the narrow path.

She looks good by moonlight. Skin glows silver. Hair like gold.

363

He saw her bare shoulder where her sweater had been torn open earlier when he'd pulled her into the mine shaft so that they could escape Boots and Duke. That bare shoulder burned in the moonlight. Norman burned inside.

He wanted her.

Hell, he'd earned her. He'd every right to take Pamela for his own. After all, Duke had promised Norman that he could have her first, hadn't he?

'Norman?' Pamela's voice wavered, as if she'd seen something in his expression that worried her. 'Norman, we need to go to the house and free my friends. Then we've got to find Boots. She's still armed, remember?'

'Me and you,' he breathed.

'Me and you what?' She tried to smile as if he was joking. In the bright moonlight he saw clearly enough that the smile died on her face.

'Me and you,' Norman whispered again. 'King and Queen of Pits.'

'King and Queen of Pits? What on Earth are you talking about, Norman?'

'Pamela, don't you see? We've got brains. We're brighter than the other bozos who live here. We could take over here.'

He stared at her as she stood with the rocky hills bathed in moonlight behind her. A shooting star streaked through the heavens like an omen.

Pamela was stunned for moment. Couldn't speak. Then, 'Norman, you're not being rational. Why should we want to take over Pits? They're nice people here, they saved my—'

'Pamela, listen. We can do it. There are guns in my trailer. We can force Lauren, Nicki and the rest to do what we want. We can live here like royalty.'

'Norman, the shock of that explosion must have confused you. You're sounding crazy. You're talking like . . .' She paused.

'Like Duke?' He felt a smile spread across his face. 'Yeah, you could say I inherited the Dukedom.'

'Norman, you don't know what you're saying.'

'Pamela, come with me. We can rule together.'

'Norman – no!'

She turned to walk away from him.

At that moment Norman couldn't say if he went crazy, or revealed his real character that had been hidden for years, or whether the spirit of bad boy Duke really did ghost through his flesh to take control of his brain. But he snarled.

Lunged at Pamela.

Grabbed hold of her.

'Once you've been with me,' he grunted in her face, 'you won't want anyone else. Other men will seem like a heap of wet rags compared to me!'

'Norman. You *are* crazy! You're a nobody who got hooked up with two weirdos. They've sent you insane.'

'Nobody? I'm *not* a nobody. Listen, Pamela.' He held his hands up in front of her face, the fingers splayed. 'I've killed men with these bare hands. Today I killed Terry.'

'Terry ... you killed him?' Pamela shook her head in horror. 'I don't believe you.'

'I cracked his skull like a nut. I can show you where I left the body.'

'Please, Norman, come down to the trailer. You've got to lie down and rest.'

'I'm gonna lie down, all right. With you!' He grabbed hold of her sweater again. Started tugging.

Pamela tried to pull away. She put one foot over the edge of the cliff. Her leg swung a hundred feet above jagged stones.

Norman gripped her arms and dragged her back onto the path.

'See?' he told her. 'I've just gone and saved your life all over again. You owe me a blood debt now.'

She struggled. 'Norman, please.'

He twisted her round so that he could hug her from behind. In a parody of a dance move he embraced her, his chest pressing against her back, his head jutting forward so that he could press his cheek against hers.

'Pamela. You see Pits down there, all shining and beautiful in the moonlight? That's ours now. Our Dukedom.'

'You're holding me too tight ... I can hardly breathe.'

'In a minute I'm going to undress you. Then I'm going to make love to you – right here on the path overlooking the town that we're going to own.'

'No!'

Pamela struggled. Kicked back with her heel.

Norman laughed. He grabbed her sweater where it was torn. He pulled. The gash in the fabric opened wider, ripping, exposing the upper part of her breast.

This's gonna be good ... real good. His heart thudded. His groin tingled. He could even hear Duke's voice inside his head urging him on. *'Way to go, Normy, old buddy. Nail her for me. Screw her so hard she can't walk for a week.'*

'Norman, please don't do this ... please!'

Then a calm voice. 'Pamela's right, Norman.'

'Uh . . .'

Norman looked up at the boulders on the hillside. A figure was standing there. Norman blinked. Moonlight played tricks with his vision. For the human figure appeared to have wings that jutted from its side.

'Sharpe.' This was Pamela crying out in relief. 'Sharpe, thank God.'

'Sharpe. That really you?' Norman asked. Suddenly his sense of macho power vanished. His legs felt rubbery.

Easily now, Pamela wriggled free of him.

She moved to one side until she stood maybe ten feet from Norman.

Meanwhile, Norman stared at the man with the wings. It was Sharpe standing there in the moonlight. Norman blinked. Looked harder.

No. Those *weren't* wings. Sharpe stood with his hands on his hips. Moonlight and shadows did the rest to create the illusion of angel wings jutting out from either side of his torso.

'Norman, you were hurting Pamela. No real man would force himself on a woman.'

'I wasn't,' Norman protested. He stared up at Sharpe's face veiled by shadow. His flat-top haircut made his head look almost square in silhouette. His white short-sleeved shirt seemed to glow with its own light in the radiance of the moon.

Sharpe was motionless.

Sharpe was calm.

And Norman sensed that Sharpe had passed judgment on him.

Norman's heart pounded in his chest. 'You're going to kill me, aren't you?'

'Worse,' Sharpe said.

'Worse? What can be worse than killing me!'

The Glory Bus

'I'm gonna put you on my bus, then I'm going to take you home to your family. And then I'm going to stand there while you confess to your mother and father all the bad things you've done.'

'No, you can't . . . *you can't!*' Norman's voice rose in a scream as he imagined the scenario.

Him.

Quaking there in the living room. Admitting to his mother and father how he had killed the cops. How he had killed Terry.

Then had tried to rip off Pamela's clothes.

Oh, Jesus. No way.

Guilt came in dark, sickening waves. Remorse was as bitter as bile rising in his throat.

He had to escape. He couldn't let Sharpe take him back home to face that kind of shame.

Norman turned, ran.

Ran blindly. Straight over the edge of the cliff.

Fell.

Fell a long, long way.

The cool night air rushed past him. In the moonlight he saw the ground come speeding upward to meet his falling body.

I'll be fine, Norman told himself. *Sharpe will save me. Sharpe's got wings . . .*

Then he remembered that the wings he'd seen were a trick of the moonlight. Just an illusion.

Not like those hard rocks just seconds away.

Norman wanted to cry.

But he didn't have time.

Chapter Fifty-five

Appetizers

Pits enjoyed its celebration party.

Its inhabitants' personal thanksgiving that the danger to them was over.

All the people of Pits had turned out. All seven of them. Sharpe, Priest (in his wheelchair), Lauren, Nicki, Wes, Hank and Pamela.

They lit a big fire under the summer stars where they flame-cooked delicate little blood sausages as an appetizer for the main course. Then Lauren broiled steaks on the barbecue. In tubs of ice were about a hundred bottles of beer and sodas of different varieties.

'You ready for your steak, Wes?' Lauren asked.

'Could eat a horse,' he replied.

'Horse is one thing that isn't on the menu.'

Wes sat beside Pamela at a long wooden table. Sitting opposite were Nicki and Sharpe, who had a space beside him for Lauren. Priest sat at one end, his bald head gleaming like a silver dome in the firelight.

At the other end at the head of the table – in his rightful place as mayor – was Hank, looking quite the gent in his best Stetson. Everyone was in good spirits. All were having fun.

Just one week ago the madness had ended.

Of course, this might be another kind of madness, Pamela thought. *But it's a peaceful, well-ordered madness. A happy madness.*

After Pamela and Sharpe had walked down from the cliff top that had claimed Norman's life they'd circled round the hill to Boots, who had still been guarding the pit shaft, gun in hand. Sharpe had distracted her while Pamela had introduced the pig-girl's head to a piece of lumber. The hard way.

The Glory Bus

When Boots woke up she was almost relieved that Pamela had survived. She was full of optimism for a future without Duke and Norman.

'I always thought they was gonna be trouble,' she'd confided.

'How's the steak?' Pamela asked with a wink. 'Tough as old boots?'

'Hey, I heard that,' Lauren protested as she sat down beside Sharpe. 'Only kidding.'

'You know,' Wes said, 'it really *does* taste like pork.' He smacked his lips in appreciation of the meat's flavor.

Priest sang out, 'Now, didn't I always tell everyone? You've not lived until you've eaten your fellow man – or, in this case, woman.'

Hank raised his bottle of beer in a toast.

'*Haw!* Here's to Boots. A woman who can satisfy the inner man.'

They all hoisted their bottles. '*Boots!*' Spontaneous applause broke out around the table.

Meanwhile, Boots, or what little remained of her, sizzled over the hot coals of the barbecue.

Entrees

A week after the meal that'd had Boots as dish of the day there was another celebration when Hank did his rightful duty as mayor and conducted a marriage ceremony for which the good people of Pits had been waiting for a long time. Across the town's two main buildings – the gas station and the cafe – hung banners that announced:

LAUREN & SHARPE
CONGRATULATIONS ON YOUR SPECIAL DAY!

Pamela smiled as she flipped the special-recipe Pitsburgers for the wedding feast. Then she slipped them onto buns for Nicki to distribute. It wasn't every day that Pits celebrated the wedding of two of its townsfolk. People came from miles around to watch Sharpe slip that band of gold onto Lauren's finger. Many of the well-wishers were men, women and children whom Sharpe had saved in the past.

Pamela's smile broadened. She'd never seen a couple more in love.

'Ouch.' The final burger on the skillet spat a drop of hot fat onto the back of her hand. Shaking her head, she used a pair of long-handled

369

kitchen tongs to grab the offending burger. As she did so, she couldn't resist scolding the meat that had stung her. 'That's the last time you ever hurt anyone, Norman Wiscoff.' She laid the Pitsburger on a bed of lettuce, then dropped a slice of cheese on top of the steaming patty of meat.

Norman meat, to be precise. After all, Priest had insisted that it would be a waste of perfectly good eating to leave Norman at the bottom of the cliff for the vultures and the coyotes.

Norman had always wanted to be cool. In the end he got what he wanted. He wound up in the cafe's deep freeze.

That was after he'd been expertly rendered into cutlets, fillets, chops, spare ribs and burgers.

'Pitsburger to go!'

'Is that the last one?' Nicki asked as she collected the plateful of food.

'The *very* last one,' Pamela announced, beaming.

'Well, come out and join the party.'

They walked out into the sunshine, where the party was in full swing.

Just Deserts

That evening, after everyone else had gone home, Pamela joined the other residents of Pits as they waved Lauren and Sharpe off on their honeymoon. The setting sun hung low, flooding the Mojave Desert with a light of pure gold. Cacti stood in the sand; they looked as if they were waving, too.

When the bus pulled away, with Sharpe at the wheel and Lauren sitting right behind him on a bench seat, the good folk of Pits cheered and whistled and waved.

Lauren glanced back into the body of the bus. Okay, it might be unusual to take a bus full of passengers on your honeymoon.

But Sharpe was different, she reflected.

Come to that, the bus's passengers were different, too.

The mannequins sat silently upright in their summer clothes.

Right in the front two seats were three newcomers.

Sharpe has unique ideas. Some might call him a visionary. Though not everyone understands his motives. But Lauren did.

The Glory Bus

Because the three new passengers on the bus were Boots, Duke and Norman. Or, at least, they were three plastic clothes-store mannequins that Sharpe had artfully made to *look* like Boots, Duke and Norman.

Boots with her short bleached hair, wearing her skimpy tank top and white cowgirl boots.

Norman sat beside her in a white T-shirt and beach shorts, his eyes staring glassily ahead.

Duke lounged by himself in the middle of a seat designed for two. He wore a white T-shirt like Norman's, blue jeans and motorcycle boots. Sharpe had painted his features well. The bad-boy upper lip still curled. One plastic arm reached back to rest on the seatback. On that arm a tattoo read BORN TO RAISE HELL. Even though the body was synthetic, he still looked cool.

Why had Sharpe brought replicas of these three onto his bus? Lauren had wondered about that. The other mannequins were Sharpe's reminders of the people he'd saved from the killing heat of the desert.

At last she realized that these three dummies were a warning.

They were saying:

If you ever come to Pits, California, pop. 7, you'll be greeted with the warmest of welcomes. But, take care. If you arrive with the intention of causing hurt, then you might end your days just like Boots, Norman and Duke here.

Out on the desert highway.

Riding the Glory Bus until the 'sweet by and by . . .'

And that, my friends, means until Judgment Day.

Friday Night
in Beast House

Chapter One

Mark sat on the edge of his bed and stared at the telephone.

Do it! Don't be such a wuss! Just pick it up and dial.

He'd been telling himself that very thing for more than half an hour. Still, there he sat, sweating and gazing at the phone.

Come on, man! The worst that can happen is she says no.

No, he thought. That isn't the worst. The worst is if she laughs and says, 'You must be out of your mind. What on earth would ever possess you to think I might consider going out with a complete loser like you?'

She won't say that, he told himself. Why would she? Only a real bitch would say a thing like that, and she's . . .

. . . wonderful . . .

To Mark, everything about Alison was wonderful. Her hair that smelled like an autumn wind. Her face, so fresh and sweet and cute that the very thought of it made Mark ache. The mischief and fire in her eyes. Her wide and friendly smile. The crooked upper tooth in front. Her rich voice and laugh. Her slender body. The jaunty bounce in her step.

He sighed.

She'll never go out with me.

But jeez, he thought, why not *ask*? It won't kill me to ask.

Before today, he never would've seriously considered it. She belonged to another realm. Though they'd been in a few classes together since starting high school, they'd rarely spoken. She'd given him a smile from time to time. A nod. A brief hello. She never had an inkling, he was sure, of how he felt about her. And he'd intended it to remain that way.

But today at the start of lunch period, Bigelow had called out, 'Beep beep!' in his usual fashion. Alison hadn't dodged him fast enough, so he'd crashed into her with his wheelchair. Down she'd gone on the hallway floor at Mark's feet, her books flying.

'Jerk!' she yelled at the fleeing Bigelow.

Mark knelt beside her. 'Creep thinks he owns the hallways,' he said. 'Are you all right?'

'Guess I'll live.'

And the way she smiled.

'Can you give me a hand?'

Taking hold of her arm, he helped her up. It was the first time he'd ever touched her. He let go quickly so she wouldn't get the idea he liked how her arm felt.

'Thanks, Mark.'

She knows my name!

'You're welcome, Alison.'

When she stood up, she winced. She bent over, lifted the left leg of her big, loose shorts and looked at her knee. It had a reddish hue, but Mark found his eyes drawn upward to the soft tan of her thigh.

She fingered her kneecap, prodded it gently.

'Guess it's okay,' she muttered.

'You'll probably have a nice bruise.'

She made a move to pick up one of her books, but Mark said, 'Wait. I'll get 'em.' Then he gathered her scattered books and binders.

When he was done, he handed them to her and she said, 'Thanks, Mark. You're a real gentleman.'

'Glad I could help.'

He stared at the telephone.

I've got to call her today while it's fresh in her mind.

He wiped his sweaty hands on his jeans, reached out and picked up the phone. He heard a dial tone. His other hand trembled as he tapped in her number. Each touch made a musical note in his ear.

Before pushing the last key, he hung up fast.

I can't! I can't! God, I'm such a chickenshit yellow bastard!

This is nuts, he told himself. Calm down and do it. Hell, I'll probably just get a busy signal. Or her mom'll pick up the phone and say she isn't home. Or I'll get the answering machine. Ten to one I won't even get to talk to Alison.

He wiped his hands again, then picked up the phone and dialed . . . dialed *all* the numbers.

His arm ached to slam down the phone.

He kept it to his ear.

It's ringing!

Yeah, but nobody'll pick it up. I'll get the answering machine.

If I get the answering machine, he thought, I'll hang up.

Hang up now!

'Hello?'

Oh my God oh my God!

'Hi,' he said. 'Alison?'

'Hi.'

'It's Mark Matthews.'

'Ah. Hi, Mark.'

'I, uh, just thought I'd call and see if you're okay. How's your knee?'

'Well, I've got a bruise. But I guess I'm fine. That was really nice of you to stop and help me.'

'Oh, well . . .'

'I don't know where Bigelow gets off, going around crashing into everybody. I mean, jeez, I'm *sorry* he's messed up and everything, but I hardly think that's any excuse for running people *over*, for godsake.'

'Yeah. It's not right.'

'Oh, well.'

There was a silence. A long silence. The sort of silence that soon leads to, 'Well, thanks for calling.'

Before that could happen, Mark said, 'So what're you doing?'

'You mean now?'

'I guess so.'

'Talking on the phone, Einstein.'

He laughed. And he pictured Alison's smile and her crooked tooth and the glint in her eyes.

'What're *you* doing?' she asked.

'The same, I guess.'

'Are you nervous?'

'Yeah.'

'You sound nervous. Your voice is shaking.'

'Oh, sorry.'

'The answer is yes.'

'Uh . . .'

'Yes, I'll go out with you.'

I can't believe this is happening!

'That's why you called, isn't it?'

'Uh, yeah. Mostly. And just to see how you're doing.'

'Doing okay. So . . . I'll go out with you.'

OH MY GOD!!!

'How about tomorrow night?' she suggested.

Tomorrow?

'Sure. Yeah. That'd be . . . really good.'

'On one condition,' she added.

'Sure.'

'Don't you want to hear the condition first?'

'I guess so.'

'I want you to get me into Beast House. Tomorrow night after it closes. That's where we'll have our date.'

Chapter Two

'Have you ever been in there at night?' she asked.

'Huh-uh. Have you?'

'No, but I've always wanted to. I mean, I've lived here in Malcasa my whole darn life and read the books and seen all the movies. I took the tour *before* they started using those tape players, and I know the whole audio tour by heart. I bet I know more about Beast House than most of the guides. But I've never been in there at night. It's the one thing I really want to do. I'd go on the midnight tour, but you have to be eighteen. Anyway, it's a hundred bucks apiece. And besides, I think it'd be a lot more cool going in by ourselves, don't you? Who wants to do it with a dozen other people and a guide?'

'But . . . how can we get in?'

'That's up to you. So what do you think?'

'Sure. Let's do it.'

'Where have I heard *that* before?'

He shrugged. 'I don't know, where?'

'From all the *other* guys who promised to get me in . . . and didn't.'

He felt a strange sinking sensation.

'Oh.'

'But maybe you'll be different.'

'I'll sure try.'

'I'll be at the back door at midnight.'

'Your back door?'

'The back door of Beast House. What you probably need to do is buy a ticket tomorrow afternoon and go in before it closes and find a hiding place. The thing is, they count those cassette players they give out for the tours. They can't be short a player when they go to close up for the day. If they're missing one, they know somebody's trying to stay in the house and so they search the place from top to bottom.'

'You sure know a lot about it.'

'I've studied the situation. I *really* want to spend a night in there. I think it'd be the most exciting thing I've ever done. So how about it? Are you still game?'

'Yeah!'

'All right.'

'But . . . we'll be staying in Beast House all night?'

'Most of the night, anyway. We'd have to get out before dawn.'

'Are you *allowed* to stay out all night?'

'Oh, sure. Every night.'

'Really?'

'I'm *kidding*. I'm sixteen, for cry-sake. Of course I'm not *allowed* to stay out all night. Are you?'

'No.'

'So we'll both just have to use our heads and improvise.'

'Guess so.'

'Just like *you'll* have to improvise on getting in.'

'How am I supposed to do that thing with the cassette players?'

'Where there's a will, there's a way.'

'But . . .'

'Mark, this is a test. A test of your brains, imagination and commitment to a task. I think you're a cool guy, but the world's full of cool guys. The question is, are you *worthy* of me.'

Though she sounded serious, Mark imagined her on the other phone, grinning, a spark of mischief in her eyes.

'See you tomorrow at midnight,' he said.

'I sure hope so.'

'I'll be there. Don't worry.'

'Okay. That'll be really neat if you can do it. Thanks for calling, Mark.'

'Well . . .'

'Bye-bye.'

''Bye.'

After hanging up, Mark sprawled on his bed and stared at the ceiling. Stunned that Alison had agreed to go out with him. Trembling at the prospect of being with her tomorrow night . . . *all* night. Slightly depressed that she seemed less interested in going out with him than in getting into Beast House. And dumbfounded by the task of how to deal with the cassette-player problem.

Where there's a will, there's a way.

Usually true, but certainly not always. He could *will* himself to flap his arms and fly to Singapore, for instance, but that wouldn't make it happen.

He'd taken the Beast House tour often enough to understand the system. They gave you a player as you entered the grounds. You wore it by a strap around your neck and listened to the 'self-guided tour' through head-phones as you walked through the house. Afterward, you handed back the player and headphones at the front gate. Handed it *to* a staff member.

The crux of the problem, he thought, is the staff member.

Usually, they were good-looking gals in those cute uniforms that made them all look like park rangers.

If nobody was watching, you could just walk up to the gate, return the audio equipment (slip it into the numbered cubbyhole in the storage cabinet), then turn around and go back to the house and find a hiding place. Or have an accomplice drop off *both* players on his way out while you remain in the house.

But there *is* a gal at the gate and you've gotta *hand* her the player. They want to make very sure nobody's in the house when they shut it down for the night.

So how can I do it? Mark wondered. There must be a way.

It's just a matter of *thinking* of it.

Bribe the girl at the gate?

Create a diversion?

He lay there staring at the ceiling of his bedroom, trying to come up with a plan that might work. Might work when you're just a regular sixteen-year-old real kid, not Indiana Jones or James Bond or Batman.

He came up with ideas. His only good ideas, however, involved the use of an accomplice.

I've gotta do this on my own, he thought. If I drag Vick or someone into it, they might screw up the whole deal.

So he kept on thinking. The thoughts filled his head, cluttered it, whirled, bumped into each other. They didn't make his head *hurt*, but they certainly made it feel heavy and useless.

Without realizing it, he fell asleep.

He woke up at the sound of his father's voice calling from downstairs. 'Mark! You better get down here fast! Supper's on the table. Come on, man. Move it. *Arriba! Arriba! Andalé!*'

On his way down the staircase, breathing deeply of the aroma of fried chicken, he heard a gruff Mexican voice in his head. It said, 'Tape players? We don't need no steeenkin' tape players!'

He grinned.

Chapter Three

Plans and hopes and fears swirling through his mind, Mark lay awake most of the night. But he must've fallen asleep somewhere along the line because his alarm clock woke him at seven in the morning.

Friday morning.

He lay there, staring at the ceiling, trembling.

I don't *have* to go through with it, he thought.

Oh yes I do. I've gotta. If I screw up, that'll be it with me and Alison.

But what if I get caught?

What if I get killed?

What if *she* gets killed?

By now, these were old, familiar thoughts. He'd gone through them all, again and again, while trying to fall asleep. He was tired of them. Besides, they always led to the same conclusion: getting a chance to be with Alison tonight would be worth any risk.

He struggled out of bed and staggered into the bathroom. There, he took his regular morning shower. Afterward, instead of getting dressed for school, he put on his pajamas and robe and slippers. Then he headed downstairs.

By the time he entered the kitchen, his father had already left for work and his mother was sitting at the breakfast table with a cup of coffee and the morning newspaper. She lowered the newspaper. And frowned. 'Are you feeling all right?'

He grimaced. 'I don't think so.'

She looked worried. 'What's the matter, honey?'

'Just . . . a pretty bad headache. No big deal.'

'Looks like you're not planning on school.'

'I *could* go, but . . . we never do much on Fridays anyway. Most of the teachers just show movies or give us study time. So I guess, yeah, it'd be nice to stay home. If it's okay with you.'

He knew what the answer would be. He made straight A's, he'd never gotten into any trouble and he rarely missed a day of school. The few times he'd complained of illness, his mother had been perfectly happy to let him stay home.

'Sure,' she told him. 'I'll call the attendance office soon as I'm done with my coffee.'

'Thanks. I guess I'll head on back to bed.'

As he turned away, his mother said, 'Will you be okay by yourself? This is my day to work at the hospital.'

'Oh yeah, that's right.' He'd known full well that she worked as a volunteer at the hospital every Friday. It was perfect. Many of her regular activities kept her in town, but not this one. For the privilege of doing volunteer work in the hospital gift shop, she had to drive all the way to Bodega Bay. More than an hour away. She would have to leave very soon. And she wouldn't be getting home until about six.

By then, Mark thought, I'll be long gone.

'I'll be fine by myself,' he said.

Frowning, she said, 'I'll be gone all day, you know.'

'It's no problem.'

'Maybe I should call one of the other girls and see if I can't find someone to fill in for me.'

'No, no. Don't do that. There's no point. I'll be fine. Really.'

'Are you sure?'

'I'm sure. Really.'

'Well . . . I'll be home in time to make dinner. Or maybe I'll pick up something on the way back. Anyway, why don't you make yourself a sandwich for lunch? There's plenty of lunchmeat and cheese in the fridge . . .'

'I know. I'll take care of it. Don't worry.'

Upstairs, he took off his robe and slippers and climbed into bed. He lay there, gazing at the ceiling, trembling, trying to focus on his plans but mostly daydreaming about Alison.

After a while, his mother came to his room. 'How are you doing, honey?'

'Not bad. I'll be fine. I took some aspirin. I probably just need some sleep.'

'You sure you don't want me to stay home?'

'I'm sure. Really. I'll be fine.'

'Okay then.' She bent over, gave him a soft kiss on the cheek, then stood up. 'If you start feeling worse or anything, give me a call.'

'I will.'

She nodded, smiled and said, 'Be good.'

'I will. You, too.'

She walked out of his room. A few minutes later, he heard her leave the house. He climbed out of bed. Standing at his window, he watched her drive away.

Then he went to his desk, took a sheet of lined paper from one of his notebooks and wrote:

Dear Mom and Dad,
    I'm very sorry to upset you, but I had to go someplace tonight. I'll be back in the morning. Nothing is wrong. Please don't worry too much or be too angry at me. I'm not upset or nuts or anything. This is just something I really want to do, but I know you wouldn't approve or give permission.
    Love,
    Mark

He folded the note in half and put it on his nightstand. After making his bed, he got dressed. He'd thought a lot about what to wear and what to take with him.

Down in the kitchen, he made two ham-and-cheese sandwiches. He put them into baggies and slipped them into his belly-pack. He added a can of Pepsi from the refrigerator. Realizing its condensation would make everything else wet, he took it out, put it inside a plastic bag, then returned it to his pack.

In the kitchen 'junk drawer,' he found a couple of fair-sized pink candles. He put them, along with a handful of match books, into his pack. After fitting his Walkman headphones into the pack, there was no room left for the Walkman itself.

I don't need it anyway.

He put on his windbreaker, then glanced at the digital clock on the oven.

8:06.

Perfect.

Patting the pockets of his jeans, he felt his wallet, comb, handkerchief and keys.

That should do it.

He looked around, wondering if he was forgetting anything.

Yeah, my brains.

He grinned.

Chapter Four

Outside the house, he took a deep breath and filled himself with the cool, moist scents of the foggy morning.

A wonderful morning, made for adventure.

He trotted down the porch stairs and headed for Front Street.

In the early stages of making plans, he'd considered trying to sneak out of the neighborhood to avoid being spotted by friends of his parents. Friends who would blab. After a while, however, he'd realized there was no point. He might be able to sneak into Beast House and keep his rendezvous with Alison, but his parents were certain to discover his absence from home tonight. Thus, the note.

And thus, no need for sneakiness. Not here and now, anyway.

They're gonna kill me, he thought.

But not till after my night with Alison.

And if something goes wrong and I can't make it into Beast House, I'll just come home and destroy the note and nobody'll ever know what I almost did.

That might not be so bad, he thought.

It'd be *awful*! I've *got* to get into the house and be there at midnight.

Walking along, he thought about how surprised Alison would be when he opened the back door for her.

'My God!' she would say, 'you really *did* it!'

And then she would throw her arms around him, hug him with amazement and delight.

Would that be a good time to kiss her? he wondered.

Probably not. You don't go around kissing a girl at the *start* of a date. Especially if you've never gone out with her before. You've got to lead up to it, wait until the mood is just right.

We'll have *hours* together. Plenty of time for one thing to lead to another.

At Front Street, Mark stopped and looked both ways. Only a few cars were in sight, none near enough to worry about. He hurried to the other side and continued walking east for another block. The barber shop was already open, but he didn't glance in. The candle shop hadn't opened yet. Neither had Christiansen Real Estate or the Book Nook or most of the other businesses along both sides of the road. Generally, not much was open in Malcasa Point before 10:00 a.m., probably because that was when the first tour buses arrived for Beast House.

Coming to the corner, he turned right. Though bordered by businesses, the road was empty and quiet. He followed its sidewalk southward. Because of curves and low slopes, he couldn't see where it stopped. The DEAD END sign and the fence and rear grounds of Beast House wouldn't come into view for another couple of minutes.

Almost there.

Then the fun starts, he thought.

But the fun started early.

Two blocks ahead of Mark, a police car came around a bend in the road.

Oh, shit!

Just act normal!

Trying not to change his pace or the look on his face, he turned his head slightly to the right as if mildly interested in a window display.

Mannequins in skimpy lingerie.

Terrific, he thought. The cop'll think I'm a pervert.

Looking forward, he started to bob his head slightly as if he had a tune going through it.

Just a normal guy out for a walk.

He glanced toward the other side of the road.

In his peripheral vision, he saw the patrol car coming closer.

He turned his gaze to the sidewalk directly in front of him.

The cop'll get suspicious if I avoid his eyes!

Trying to seem *very* casual, still bobbing his head just a bit, he glanced at the cop. He planned to cast the officer a friendly, uninterested smile then look away, but couldn't.

Holy shit!

In the driver's seat of the police car sat the most beautiful woman in town – and by far the most dangerous – Officer Eve Chaney.

I thought she worked nights!

Heart thudding, Mark gaped at her. Though he'd seen Officer Chaney a few times at night and admired her photo in the newspaper every so often, this was his first good view of her in daylight.

My God, he thought.

She turned her head and stared straight back at him as she slowly drove by.

'Hi,' he mouthed, but no sound came from his mouth.

She narrowed her eyes, nodded, and kept on driving.

Face forward, Mark kept on walking. His face felt hot. He was breathing quickly, his heart thumping.

How'd you like to spend the night in Beast House with HER?

The prospect of that was frightening but incredibly exciting.

He suddenly felt guilty.

Hearing a car behind him, he looked over his shoulder.

Oh jeez, here she comes!

She drove slowly, swung to the curb and stopped adjacent to him. Her passenger window glided down. Mark bent his knees slightly and peered in.

Beckoning him with one hand, Officer Chaney said, 'Would you like to step over here for a moment?'

'Me?'

She nodded.

Heart clumping hard and fast, Mark walked up to her passenger door, bent over and looked in.

He'd never been this close to such a beautiful woman.

But she's a cop and I'm in trouble.

He could hardly breathe.

'What's your name?' she asked.

'Mark. Mark Matthews.'

'I'm Officer Chaney, Mark.'

He nodded.

Though this was October, Officer Chaney made him think of summer days at the beach. Her short hair was blowing slightly in the breeze that came in through the open windows of her patrol car. Her eyes were deep blue like a cloudless July sky. Her face was lightly tanned. The scent of her, mixed with the moist coolness of the fog, was like suntan oil.

'How old are you, Mark?'

He considered lying, but knew it was useless. 'Sixteen.'

She nodded as if she'd already known. 'Shouldn't you be in school?'

'I guess so. I mean, I guess it all depends.'

'How's that?'

'My mom called in sick.'

'Your mother's ill?'

'No. I mean, she called in sick for me. So I'm officially absent today.'

Officer Chaney turned slightly toward him, rested her right elbow on top of the seatback, and smiled with just one side of her mouth. Mark supposed it would be called a smirk. But it sure looked good on her. 'So you're staying home sick today?'

'That's right, officer.'

'In that case, shouldn't you be home in bed?'

'Well . . .'

He felt his gaze being pulled down to her throat, to the open neck of her uniform blouse, on a course that would soon lead to her chest. He forced his eyes upward, tried to lock them on her face.

'Well?' she asked.

I can't lie to her. She'll see right through it!

'The thing is, I'm not all that sick. And I'm a really good student anyway and Fridays at school are always pretty much of a waste of time and it's such a nice morning with the fog and all.' He shrugged.

Eyes narrowing slightly, she nodded. Then she smiled with both sides of her mouth. She nodded again and said, 'Have a good day, Mark.'

'Thank you, Officer Chaney. You, too.'

She looked away from him, so he quickly glanced at the taut front of her blouse before she took her arm off the seatback. Facing forward, she put both hands on the steering wheel.

Mark took a step backward but remained bent over.

Just when he expected her to pull away, she turned her head again. 'Don't do anything I wouldn't,' she told him.

'I won't. Thanks.'

She gave him another nod, then drove slowly away.

Standing up straight, Mark watched her car move down the road, watched it turn right and disappear.

'Wow,' he whispered.

Chapter Five

When Mark resumed walking, his legs felt soft and shaky. He seemed to be trembling all over.

He could hardly believe that he'd actually been stopped by Officer Eve Chaney, that he'd gotten such a good look at her. It was almost like something too good to be true. But even better – and more un-believable – she hadn't balled him out, hadn't lectured him, hadn't busted him or driven him back to school or back to his house. She'd not only been friendly, but she had *let him go*.

Let him go with the caution, 'Don't do anything I wouldn't.'

What was *that* supposed to mean?

He knew it was just a saying. But it didn't really make a lot of sense when you considered that he didn't know enough about Officer Chaney to judge what she might or might not do. All he knew for sure was that she was a local legend. Since coming to Malcasa Point about three years ago, she'd made a lot of arrests and she'd even been in gunfights. She'd shot half a dozen bad guys, killing a couple of them.

Don't do anything I wouldn't?

'Good one,' he said quietly, and grinned.

Still shocked and amazed but feeling somewhat more calm, Mark came to the corner. He turned his head and looked toward Front Street, hoping to see Officer Chaney's car again. But it was gone.

He shook his head.

Continuing across the street, he found himself wishing that she *hadn't* let him go. If she'd busted him, he would've gotten to sit in the car with her. He would've had a lot more time to be with her.

Maybe she would've frisked me.

'Oh, man,' he murmured.

But he supposed it was just as well that she'd let him go. Nice as it might've been, it would've wrecked his plans for sneaking into Beast House. He still wanted to go through with that, or at least give it a good try – even though Alison suddenly seemed a little less special than usual.

It's just temporary, he thought. Like sun blindness. After I've been away from Officer Chaney for a while, it'll all go back to normal.

'Eve,' he said quietly. 'Eve Chaney.'

He sighed.

Hell, he thought. If Alison's out of my league (and she is), then what's Eve? Like a grown-up, improved version of Alison, and probably at least ten years older than me. Not a chance, not a chance. The best I can ever hope for is a little look and a little talk. With Eve, it'll probably never be better than what just happened.

Forget about her.

Yeah, sure.

He suddenly found himself only a few strides away from the dead-end barricade. A little surprised, he turned around. Nobody seemed to be nearby, so he waded into the weeds, descended one side of a shallow ditch, climbed the other side, and trudged through more weeds until he stood at the black iron fence.

Beyond it were the rear grounds: the snack stand; the outdoor eating area with chairs upside-down on table tops; the restroom/gift-shop building; and the back of Beast House itself.

He saw nobody.

The parking lot, off in the distance, looked empty.

Now or never, he thought.

After another quick look around, he leapt, caught the fence's upper crossbar with both hands and pulled himself up. The effort suddenly reminded him of gym class.

He struggled high enough to chin the crossbar, then hung there, wondering what to do next. He tried to go higher, couldn't. He tried to swing a leg up high enough to catch the crossbar with his foot, couldn't.

Muttering a curse, he lowered himself to the ground.

There's gotta be a way!

The rear side of the fence, extending along the eastern border of the lawn at the base of a hillside, was overhung in a few places by the limbs of trees outside the fence. Maybe he could climb one of the trees, crawl out on a limb to get past the fence, and drop inside the perimeter.

The limbs looked awfully high.

Climbing high enough to reach any of them might be tough. And if he succeeded, the drop to the ground . . .

He murmured, 'Shit.'

If only I'd brought a rope, he thought. I could rappel down. If only I knew how to rappel.

Screw a rope, I should've brought a ladder.

He'd heard that there were places where you could crawl *under* the fence, but he had no idea where to look for them.

There were also supposed to be 'beast holes' in the hillside . . . openings that led to a network of tunnels. But he didn't know anyone who'd ever actually *found* one.

If only I'd brought a shovel, he thought. I could dig my way under the fence.

If I'd had a little more time to prepare . . .

I've gotta get in somehow! And fast!

He glanced at his wristwatch. Ten till nine. By nine-thirty, the staff would start arriving.

He sighed, then hurried back to the street and broke into a run.

The last resort.

He'd intended to hop over the fence. While planning the details of his adventure, it hadn't seemed like such an impossible task. He'd seen people do that sort of thing all the time on TV, in movies, even in documentaries.

James Bond, he thought as he ran, would've hurled himself right over the top of a simple little fence like that.

Shit, Bond would've *parachuted* in.

As Mark ran, he realized that the *real* people he'd observed performing such feats in documentaries were Marines, Navy Seals, Army Rangers . . . not a sixteen-year-old high-school kid whose idea of a good time was reading John D. MacDonald paperbacks.

What would Travis McGee do?

Friday Night in Beast House

The fence would've been a cinch for Travis. But he might do what I'm gonna do.

The new plan was risky. He'd kept it in the back of his mind only as a last resort.

If all else fails . . .

All else *had*.

Nearing the front corner of the fence, Mark slowed his pace from a sprint to a jog.

If anybody's watching, he thought, they'll think I'm just running for exercise.

A car went by on Front Street. He glanced at it, saw the driver, didn't recognize him. A moment later, the car was gone and he found himself staring at the Kutch house in the field across the street.

The sight of the old brick house sent a chill racing up his back. He knew what had happened there. And he couldn't help but wonder what might *still* be happening within its windowless walls.

Old lady Kutch lived in there like some sort of mad hermit.

There were rumors of beasts.

Of course, there were *always* rumors of beasts.

The real things were probably long gone or all killed off.

But old Agnes Kutch was beast enough for Mark. Walking too close to her house late at night, he'd once heard an outcry . . . almost like a scream, but it might've been something else.

He looked away from the Kutch house and watched Beast House as he ran toward its ticket booth.

Blood baths had taken place inside Beast House. Men, women and children had been torn apart within its walls. But the place didn't seem nearly as creepy to him as the Kutch house. Maybe because he'd been inside it so many times before. Maybe because it was flooded with tourists day after day.

Looking at the old Victorian house as he ran alongside its fence, the place seemed almost friendly.

He slowed down as he neared the ticket booth.

Looked around.

Saw a car in the distance, but it was still a few blocks away.

He walked casually to the waist-high turnstile and climbed over it.

Easy as pie.

On his right was the cupboard where the cassette players were stored. It had a padlock on it.

He walked past the cupboard, stepped around the back of the ticket shack, took a deep breath, then raced for the northwest corner of Beast House.

Chapter Six

In the area behind the house, Mark found several metal trash cans, one just to the left of the gift shop's entrance. He dragged it a few inches closer to the wall, then climbed onto it. Touching the wall for support, he rose from his knees to his feet and stood up straight.

His head was only slightly lower than the roof.

This I can do, he thought.

He sure hoped so, anyway.

Not with the belly pack on.

Releasing the wall, he used both hands to unfasten its belt. Then he put one hand on the wall to steady himself. With the other, he tossed his small pack onto the roof. It landed out of sight with a quiet thump.

Now I *have* to get up there, he thought.

Hands on the roof, he leaped, thrust himself upward and forward and imagined his balance shifting, saw himself falling backward. But a moment later, he was scurrying and writhing, digging at the tarpaper with his elbows and then with his knees until he found himself sprawled breathless.

Made it!

He raised his head. His belly pack was within easy reach. The roof stretching out ahead of him had only a slight slope. A few vent pipes jutted up here and there. Near the middle was the large gray block of the air-conditioning unit, nearly the size of a refrigerator.

He picked up his pack, crawled over to the air-conditioner and lay down beside it. Braced on his elbows, he looked around.

Nobody should be able to spot him from the ground. Anyone on

397

the hillside would be able to see him, but people mostly stayed away from there. His main problem would be the back windows of Beast House itself, especially the upstairs windows. The air-conditioner would do a fair job of concealing him, but not a *complete* job.

He was lucky to have the air-conditioner. He hadn't known it would be here. Making his plans, however, he'd figured that the roof of the gift shop might be the only hiding place available to him.

He'd never intended to stay here all day, anyway.

He lowered his face against his crossed arms. Eyes shut, he tried to concentrate on his plans, but his mind kept drifting back to his encounter with Officer Chaney. He told himself to stop that. If he wanted to daydream he should daydream about Alison.

He imagined himself opening the back door of Beast House at midnight, Alison standing there in the moonlight. 'You *did* it!' she blurts.

'Of course.'

'I'm so proud of you.' She puts her arms around him.

Some time later, Mark heard voices that weren't in his head.

He lay motionless.

Just a couple of voices, then more. Some male, some female. He couldn't make out much of what was being said, but supposed the voices must belong to the guides and other workers.

Soon, they seemed to hold a meeting. After a few minutes, it broke up and the voices diminished.

By the sounds of jingling keys and opening doors, he guessed that people were opening the snack stand, the restrooms and gift shop.

Mark raised his face off his arms and looked at his wristwatch.

9:55.

In five more minutes, the first tourists would start heading down the walkway to the front of Beast House. They would be stopping at Station One to hear about Gus Goucher, then entering the house and going into the parlor for Ethel Hughes's story. Then upstairs. There, the earlier portions of the tour took place in areas toward the front of the house. Not until the boys' room would there be a window with a good view of the rear grounds.

The first tourists probably wouldn't reach the boys' room until about 10:30.

Making his plans, Mark had figured that he ought to be safe on the gift shop's roof until then.

Might be pushing it, he thought.

After all, the tour's self-guided. He'd done it often enough to know that some visitors were more interested in seeing the crime scenes and gory displays than in listening to the whole story, so they pretty much ignored the audio tape and hurried from room to room.

Only one way to be *sure* nobody saw him from an upstairs windows: get off the roof as soon after ten o'clock as possible. But he didn't want to leave his hiding place *too* early; he needed others to be around so he could mingle with them.

So he waited until ten past ten. Then he belly-crawled around the air-conditioner and saw the dog.

His mouth fell open.

The dog, big as a German shepherd, lay on its side a few feet from the far corner of the roof. It looked as if it had been mauled by wild animals. *Hungry* wild animals that had disembowelled it, torn huge chunks from its body . . .

Where's it's head? Mark wondered. Did they *eat* its head?

How the hell did it get on the roof?

Feeling a little sick, he belly-crawled toward the remains of the dog. He didn't want to get any closer, but it lay between him and the corner of roof where he needed to descend.

Flies were buzzing around the carcass. It looked very fresh, though, its blood still red and wet.

Must've *just* happened, Mark thought. Not too long before I got here. If I'd shown up a little earlier . . .

His skin went prickly with goosebumps.

There didn't seem to be a great deal of blood on the roof under and around the dog.

This isn't where the thing got nailed, Mark thought. It must've been hurled up here afterward. Or dropped?

He found his head turning toward Beast House, tilting back, his gaze moving from the second-floor windows to the roof.

Nah.

A bear could've done something like this, maybe. Or a wildcat. Or a man. A very strong, demented man.

Suddenly wanting badly to be off the roof, Mark scurried the rest of the way to its edge. He peered down. Nothing behind the building except for a patch of lawn and the back of Beast House.

For now, nobody was in sight.

Mark swung his legs over the edge. As they dangled, he lowered himself until he was hanging by his hands. Then he let go and dropped. Dropped farther than he really expected.

His feet hit the ground hard. Knees folding, he stumbled backward and landed hard on his rump.

It hurt, but he didn't cry out.

Seated on the grass, he looked around.

Nobody in sight.

So he got to his feet and rubbed his butt. Walking casually toward the far back corner of Beast House, he removed the Walkman headphones from his belly pack.

By the time he arrived at the front of the house, he was wearing the headphones. The cord vanished under the zippered front of his windbreaker, where it was connected to nothing at all.

At least a dozen tourists were milling about the front lawn or gathered in front of the porch stairs. They all wore headphones, too. Not exactly like his, but close enough.

Mark wandered over and joined those at the foot of the stairs.

He stared up at the hanged body of Gus Goucher.

He'd seen Gus plenty of times before: the bulging eyes, the black and swollen tongue sticking out of his mouth, the way his head was tilted to the right at such a nasty angle – worst of all, the way his neck was two or three times longer than it should've been.

They stretched his neck, all right.

The sight of Gus usually bothered Mark, but not so much this morning. As gruesome as it looked, it seemed bland compared to the actual remains of the dog he'd just seen.

Gus looked *good* compared to the dog.

Gazing up at the body, Mark stood motionless as if concentrating on the voice from his self-guided tour tape.

A breeze made the body swing slightly. Near Mark, a woman groaned. A white-haired man in a plaid shirt was shaking his head slowly as if appalled by Gus or the story on the tape. A teenaged girl was gaping up at Gus, her mouth drooping open.

She didn't look familiar.

None of the people looked familiar.

Not surprising. Though plenty of townies did the tour, the vast majority of visitors came from out of town, many of them brought here on the bus from San Francisco.

Several of the nearby people, including the teenaged girl, clicked off their tape players and moved toward the stairs.

Mark followed them.

Up the porch stairs, past the dangling body of Gus Goucher, across the porch and through the front door of Beast House.

I'm in!

Chapter Seven

From now on, *staying* in would be the trick. To manage that, Mark needed a hiding place.

He glanced at the guide in the foyer. A heavy-set brunette. Busy answering someone's question, she didn't notice him. He followed a few people into the parlor.

Though not here for the tour, he figured he should *look* as if he were, and try to blend in with the others. Besides, he really liked the parlor exhibit.

Ethel Hughes, or at least her wonderfully life-like mannequin, was a babe. On other side of a thick red cordon, she lay sprawled on the floor, one leg raised with her foot resting on the cushion. She was supposedly the first victim on the night of August 2, 1903, when the beast came up from the cellar and tried to slaughter everyone in the house. It had ripped her up pretty good. Better yet, it had ripped up her nightgown.

The replica of her nightgown, shredded in precise accordance with damage to the tattered original (now on display in Janet Crogan's Beast House Museum on Front Street), draped Ethel's body here and there but left much of it bare. For the sake of decency, narrow strips of the fabric concealed her nipples and a wider swath passed between her parted thighs. Otherwise, she was nearly naked.

A year ago, taking the tour by himself, Mark had noticed that one of the strips was out of place just enough to let him see a pink, curved edge of Ethel's left areola. He'd gazed at it for a long time.

Today, nothing showed that shouldn't. He found himself staring at Ethel, anyway. So beautiful. And almost naked. What if a wind should come along . . . ?

How? The windows are shut.

Cut it out, he thought. She's nothing compared to Alison or Officer Chaney. She's not even real.

But she sure looked exciting down on the floor like that.

The image returned to his mind of the day he'd seen Ethel with the shred of cloth off-kilter.

Quit it, he told himself.

Only one thing mattered: hiding.

Late last night in his bedroom, Mark had pulled out his copy of Janice Crogan's second book, *Savage Times*. In addition to containing the full story of Beast House, along with copies of photos and news articles, it provided floor plans of the house. He'd studied the plans, used them to refresh his memory of what he'd observed during the tours, and searched them for good a place to hide.

So many possibilities.

Behind the couch in the parlor? Under one of the upstairs beds? In a closet? Maybe. But those were so obvious. For all Mark knew, they might be routinely checked before closing time.

He needed someplace more unusual.

The attic seemed like a good possibility. Though visitors weren't allowed up there, its doors were kept open during the day. He'd heard that it was cluttered with old furniture, even some mannequins that had once been on display. He could probably hide among them until closing time . . . if he could get into the attic unseen.

That would be the hard part. A guide was usually posted in the hallway just outside the second-floor entrance. And even if he should find the door briefly unguarded (maybe if he created a diversion to draw the guide elsewhere), he would hardly stand a chance of making it all the way to the top before being spotted.

I'll at least go upstairs and check it out, he thought. The attic would sure be better than the alternative.

After giving Ethel a final, lingering gaze, Mark turned around and stepped out of the parlor. The heavy-set guide was keeping an eye on people, but paid him no special attention. He turned away from her and started to climb the stairs.

Halfway up, someone behind him said, 'Is this fuckin' cool, or what?'

He looked back.

The wiry guy who'd spoken, a couple of stairs below Mark, was maybe twenty years old, had wild eyes and a big, lopsided grin. He wore his headphones over the top of a battered green Jets cap.

'Pretty cool,' Mark agreed.

'It's fuckin' bullshit, y'know. I know bullshit when I see it. But it's fuckin' *cool* bullshit, know what I mean?'

'Yeah. It's cool, all right.'

'Beast my fuckin' ass.'

'You don't think a beast did this stuff?'

'Do *you*?'

'I don't know.'

'Only one sorta beast does this sorta shit – *homo-fuckin'-sapien*.'

'Maybe so,' Mark said.

At the top of the stairs, he joined several people who'd stopped at Station Three. Reaching down inside the zippered front of his wind-breaker, he pretended to turn on his tape player.

The guy from the stairs knuckled him in the arm.

'Love this Maggie Kutch shit,' he said. 'Man, she must've been fruitier than fuckin' Florida.'

Mark nodded.

'Name's Joe,' the guy said. 'After Broadway Joe, not that fuckin' twat in *Little Women*.' He cackled.

'I'm Mark.'

'Biblical Mark or question mark?'

Mark shrugged.

'First time?'

'In Beast House? No, I've been here a few times.'

'Where you from'

'Here in town.'

'I came up from Boleta Bay. I gotta come up and do the house two, three times a year. It's like I'm fuckin' addicted, man. I stay away too long, it's like my head's gonna blow up like fuckin' Mount St Helen.'

Mark nodded again, then turned his face away and pretended to listen to his audio tour.

Beside him, Joe's player clicked on.

Around him, people were starting to move toward Lilly Thorn's bedroom. He heard a faint, tinny voice from Joe's headset. Though he couldn't make out the words, he knew they came from Janice Crogan and he knew what she was saying.

. . . After finishing its brutal attack on Ethel, the beast ran out of the parlor and scurried up the stairs, leaving a trail of blood . . .

She then gave instructions to leave the player on and follow the replica blood tracks into Lilly Thorn's bedroom.

Joe turned toward Lilly's room, looked down at the tracks on the hardwood floor and smirked at Mark. 'Bloody footprints,' he said. 'I fuckin' love it.'

Mark walked beside him into Lilly's room. About a dozen other people were already inside, listening to their headphones and staring at the exhibit.

Behind the red cordon, a wax dummy of Lilly Thorn was sitting up in bed. Unlike Ethel, Lilly looked alive and terrified. This was how she might've appeared immediately after being awakened by the noise of the beast's attack on Ethel. Soon afterward, she had blocked her bedroom door shut and escaped through a window . . . surviving . . . but leaving her two small boys behind to be raped and murdered by the beast.

Joe chuckled and muttered, 'Fuckin' pussy,' in response to something he heard on the tape.

What if he STAYS with me?

He won't, Mark thought. He's just doing the tour.

Let's just see . . .

Mark turned around and took a step toward the bedroom door. Joe grabbed his arm. 'You gotta listen to the spiel, man.'

'I've heard it before. Lots of times.'

'Yeah, me too. But you know what, you get new stuff every time.'

Mark shook his head. 'It's always the same.'

'Yeah, the *words*. But not *you*. Every time you hear 'em, you're a different dude so they *mean* different stuff. You pick up new shit, know what I mean?'

'I guess so.'

'So you gotta listen to the whole thing, *really* listen. Got it?'

'Got it.'

Joe let go of his arm.

Mark, nodding, reached down inside his windbreaker and pretended to turn on his tape player again.

Chapter Eight

He's just hanging out with me during the tour, Mark told himself. All I have to do is walk through it with him, then he'll go his way and I'll go mine.

Maybe.

Or maybe he'll say we should have some lunch together or why not take a walk down Front Street and have a look at the museum?

That's not what'll happen, Mark thought. Long before anything like that goes on, Joe is going to notice that my headphones aren't connected to anything.

The pretense of being on the tour was only meant to fool casual observers. Mark had never considered the possibility that someone might latch onto him.

If Joe finds out I've got no tape player . . .

No telling what he might do. For starters, he'll probably ask a lot of questions. Then he might report me.

Mark put his hand on Joe's shoulder. Joe shut off his player and turned his head.

Grimacing, Mark said, 'Gotta go.'

'What's up?'

'Don't know. Something I ate. Feels like the runs. Gotta go.'

'Okay, man. Later.'

Bent over slightly, Mark walked quickly out of the room. In the hall, he didn't look back.

If he comes with me, I'm screwed.

In case Joe was following him, Mark stayed hunched over on his way down the stairs. Plenty of people were on their way up, so he kept to the right. None paid him much attention. He could hear people behind him, too.

Please, not Joe.

At the bottom, he glanced back.

Five or six people were on their way down, but Joe wasn't among them.

Mark continued toward the front door. He was almost there before he caught himself, remembered that he *didn't* need to use the restroom, and changed course.

'Excuse me, are you all right?'

He turned toward the voice.

It belonged to a girl wearing the tan blouse and shorts of a Beast House guide. This wasn't the husky one he'd seen earlier. This guide was slender with light brown hair and a deep tan. Mark quickly looked away from her and mumbled, 'Bathroom.'

'The restrooms are around back. Just next to the gift shop.'

Nodding, he muttered, 'Thanks.'

Just great, he thought.

He started toward the front door.

Now I'll have to leave and come back in.

'A lot quicker if you go straight through,' the guide said.

He stopped and turned toward her. 'Huh?'

She pointed at the hallway beside the stairs. 'Take the hall, go through the kitchen and out the back door. When you leave the porch, the restrooms'll be straight ahead.'

'Am I allowed to go out that way?'

'Anybody tries to stop you, tell 'em Thompson says it's okay.'

'Okay. Thanks a lot.'

He hurried past her, past the foot of the stairs, and into the hallway. With a glance back, he saw that she wasn't following him. He was alone in the hallway. He quickened his pace and entered the kitchen.

Nobody in the kitchen, either.

My God, I don't believe it!

Believe it, he thought.

He hurried through the kitchen, but not toward the back door – toward the open pantry.

He entered it. Before he could reach the stairs, however, he heard voices from below.

Of course, he thought. Obviously, I can't be *that* lucky.

The cellar was at the *end* of the audio tour . . . the *pièce de résistance*. Nobody actually following the audio tour should be here yet, but some had obviously ignored the tape and rushed on ahead.

Damn!

Starting down the stairs, Mark reminded himself that his plans had never included the idea that he would find the cellar deserted. He'd just figured, if one thing led to another and he ended up *needing* the cellar as a last resort, that he would find other people here and he would need to play it by ear.

It's not exactly a last resort yet, he told himself.

But things happened and I'm here.

In the light from the dangling, bare bulb, Mark saw only four people in the cellar. A young man and woman were standing at the cordon, peering down at the hole in the dirt floor. Next to the woman stood a small girl, maybe four years old. The woman was holding her hand. Off to the side, a husky, bearded guy stood staring into the Kutch tunnel through the bars of the door.

The little girl didn't have headphones on. She looked over her shoulder at Mark and said, 'Hi.'

Mark smiled. 'Hi.'

The mother frowned down at the girl. 'Don't bother the man, honey.'

'It's all right,' he said.

The bearded guy turned around and said to Mark, 'A shame they don't open up the tunnel.'

'Yeah,' Mark said.

'I'd love to see the tunnel.'

'Me, too.'

'*And* the Kutch house.'

'Yeah. Same here.'

'I mean, that's where half the good stuff happened and we don't even get to see it.'

'Well, it's still occupied.'

'I know that,' the man said, seeming a bit miffed that Mark doubted the breadth of his knowledge. 'Maggie's daughter. What I hear, she's as deranged as her mother was. Five'll get you ten she's got a critter or two over there right now.'

'Maybe,' Mark said. He turned away from the man, approached the cordoned-off area around the hole in the floor, and stepped up beside the little girl. The mother and father looked at him, then returned their attention to the hole.

Mark looked at it, too, though he'd seen it many times before.

Just a hole in the dirt, probably only a couple of feet in diameter. Can I fit in there? he wondered. Sure. I must. It's big enough for the beasts and they're bigger than me.

'That's where the beast comes out,' he explained in a voice plenty loud enough for everyone to hear.

The little girl looked up at him. Her parents turned their heads.

'We know,' said her father. 'We've seen the movies, too.'

'Have you read the books?' Mark asked.

The father shook his head and resumed looking at the hole.

'What're you looking at?' Mark asked.

'What do you think?' the father asked.

The mother gave Mark a tiny frown.

'Waiting for the beast to come out?' Mark asked.

'Please,' the man said.

'It might, you know.'

The girl, gazing up at him, raised her eyebrows.

'Yesterday,' Mark said, 'a beast came popping up out of this very hole and snatched a little girl.' He put a hand on her shoulder. 'She was just your size.'

'Don't touch my daughter,' the mother said.

'Excuse me.' He removed his hand.

The father glared at him.

'And stop trying to scare her,' the mother said.

'I'm not trying to scare her. I just wanted to warn her. This big white naked beast actually popped up yesterday and grabbed a little girl no bigger than your daughter and dragged her down into the hole with it.'

The daughter looked good and scared.

Her father whirled toward Mark. 'Look, kid . . .'

'The girl was *screaming*.'

The mother said to her daughter, 'He's making this up, Nancy. He's a *mean* person and . . .'

Crouching low enough to look the girl straight in the eyes, Mark said, 'It *ate* her up!'

409

She screamed.

The mother threw her arms around the girl.

The father stomped toward Mark. Red in the face, he stormed, 'That's enough out of you, young man! That's *more* than enough!'

Putting up his open hands, Mark backed away. 'Hey, hey. Take it easy, okay? I'm just concerned about your little girl, man. You don't *want* her to get eaten up by a beast, do you?'

The girl screamed again.

'We're getting out of here,' the mother blurted. She picked up the girl. 'You, too, Fred. Come with us right now.' She hurried toward the stairway.

Fred glared at Mark, then looked at his wife and said, 'I'll be right with you, honey.'

'*Now!* He's just a trouble-maker. He probably wants you to hit him so he can sue us. Don't give him the satisfaction.'

He nodded. 'I'll be right with you.'

'No you won't. You'll come *now!*'

Fred sighed. Then he leaned in close to Mark and snarled, 'What I oughta do, you little fuck, is rip off your head and shit down your neck.'

'What you oughta do,' Mark said, 'is lay your hands on some original material.'

Fred cried out in rage and reached for Mark's neck.

As Mark lurched backward, the wife yelled, '*FRED! NO!*' and the bearded man leaped out in front of Fred to hold him back.

'It's all right, fella,' the bearded guy said. 'Take it easy, take it easy. The kid's just a little wise-ass. Don't let him get to you. Huh? Come on, now. Come on.'

Holding Fred like a friend, the bearded guy walked him toward the stairway.

With the sobbing child in her arms, the mother climbed the stairs backward to keep her eyes on the situation.

Fred, still held by the bearded guy, started up the stairs. He muttered, 'It's okay. I'm fine. You can let go.'

But the bearded guy held on.

Near the top of the stairs, the mother halted. In a shrill voice, she announced, 'You, young man, should be ashamed of yourself. You're a nasty, horrible creature. What's the *matter* with you, saying such awful things to an innocent little child! I hope your skin falls off and you rot in hell forever! And rest assured, we *will* report you! You'll be out of here on your insolent little ass!'

They resumed their climb up the stairs.

The moment all four were out of sight, Mark swung a leg over the cordon. He hurried over to the hole, sank to his knees, then leaned forward and lowered himself headfirst into the darkness.

Chapter Nine

I did it! I did it!

Feeling gleeful and scared, Mark skidded and scurried downward. The slope beneath him was very steep at first. After it leveled out, he belly-crawled forward a little farther. Then he stopped and lowered his head against his arms.

He was breathing hard. His heart was thudding. Though he felt sweaty all over, the air in the tunnel was cool. It smelled of moist earth, but the dirt beneath him didn't seem wet.

I can't believe I made it, he thought.

I can't believe I *did* that!

Damn! he thought. Hope I didn't warp the little girl for life.

He laughed, but kept it quiet so the quick bursts of air only came out his nostrils and he sounded like a sniffing dog.

Stop it, he told himself.

For a while, he heard nothing except his own heartbeat and quiet breathing. Then came faint voices. A man's voice. A woman's. He couldn't hear them well, or what was being said, but he imagined the little girl's father was in the cellar with one of the female guides – maybe the pretty one, Thompson, who had given Mark directions to the restroom.

The bastard was right here.

Well, he doesn't seem to be here now.

He imagined the two of them roaming through the cellar, looking behind the various crates and steamer trunks scattered about the floor.

Maybe he went down in the hole.

That's not very likely, sir. What he probably did was hurry upstairs as soon as you left.

I happen to think he's hiding in the hole. Would you please check?

Then Mark heard a voice clearly. It did sound like Thompson. 'All I can say is we'll keep an eye out for him and toss him out on his ear if we run into him. Let me know, though, if *you* see him again.'

'You can count on that, young lady.' Fred, all right.

'But I imagine he probably took off after his little stunt.'

'He *terrified* my little Nancy.'

'I understand. I'm sorry.'

'I don't know what kind of outfit you people are running here, letting a thing like that happen.'

'Well, we have a lot of visitors. Once in a while, someone gets out of hand. We do apologize. And we'll be more than happy to refund . . .' Her voice began to fade.

Mark pictured them walking away, heading for the cellar stairs. He still heard Thompson and the man, but couldn't make out their words. Then their voices were gone.

I've really made it now, Mark thought. I'm home free.

He felt sorry about causing trouble for Thompson. She seemed nice, and it was his fault she had to deal with the girl's father.

Hell, he thought, she probably has to contend with crappy people all the time. It's part of her job.

What if she comes back?

She won't, he told himself.

Maybe she suspects, just didn't want to mention it in front of Fred.

He imagined her coming back without the angry father. But with a flashlight. And maybe with a pair of coveralls to put on to keep her uniform from getting dirty.

She has temporarily closed off the cellar to tourists.

Standing just outside the cordon, she takes off her tan blouse and shorts. This surprises Mark somewhat, even thought it's only happening in his own mind. He thinks maybe she is removing her uniform so it won't get sweaty when she crawls through the hole.

Apparently, she doesn't want her bra or panties to get sweaty, either. Mark can hardly blame her; who would want to spend the rest of the day wearing damp underclothes?

Now she is naked except for her shoes and socks. Balancing on one foot, she steps into her bright orange coveralls.

No longer comfortable lying flat on his belly, Mark pushed with his knee and rolled a little so most of his weight was on his right side.

Why bother wearing the jumpsuit? he thought. Why not just crawl in naked? She can hose herself off afterward.

For a few moments, Mark was able to picture her coming through the tunnel naked on her elbows and knees, her wobbling breasts almost touching the dirt.

She wouldn't do it naked, he thought. She's coming in after *me*, so she'll be wearing the jumpsuit.

But *just* the jumpsuit.

Its top doesn't have to be zipped all the way up. It can be like halfway down, or maybe all the way to her belly button, and . . .

'This is it?' asked a woman's voice.

'This is it.' A man.

'It's just a hole.'

'It's hardly *just* a hole. It's the *beast* hole. It's how the beast came into the house.'

'I'm sure.'

'Well, I think you'd feel differently if you'd read the books.'

'I saw the movies.'

'It's not the same. I mean . . . this is the *beast* hole.'

'And quite a hole it is.'

'Jeez, Helen.'

'Sorry.'

They went silent.

A little while later, a male voice said, 'I suppose it's all quite Freudian, actually.'

Someone giggled.

'Am I being naughty?' the same man asked.

'Shhhh.'

More voices.

Voices came and went.

As time passed, it seemed ever less likely that Thompson or anyone else would be coming into the hole to search for Mark.

This is so great, he thought. I've really made it. Now all I have to do is wait here until the place closes.

He imagined himself opening the back door at midnight, Alison's surprise – *My God, you really did it!* – and she steps into the house and puts her arms around him, kisses him.

'HELLLLLLL-OOOOOHHHHH!!!'

He flinched.

'HELLL-OOOHHHH DOWN DARE, LITTLE BEASTIE BEASTIE!'

Apparently, just a zany tourist.

As time passed, he found that yelling into the hole was a favorite pastime of people visiting the cellar.

Every so often, a loud voice came down to startle him.

'Yoo-hooo! Any beasts down there?'

'Hey! Come on up! Ellen wants to check out the equipment!'

'Guten Morgen, Herr Beast! Was gibt?'

'Hey! Come on up and say hi!'

At one point, a woman yelled, 'Yo, down there! I'm ready if yer willin'!'

A while later, a man called, *'Bon jour, Monsieur bete!'*

He heard languages that made no sense to him. Some sounded Oriental, some Slavic. Some people who called into the hole spoke the English language with accents suggesting they came from the deep south, the northeast, Ireland, France, England, Italy, Australia. One sounded like the Frances McDormand character in *Fargo*.

Men shouted into the hole. So did women. So did quite a few children.

When women shouted, their husbands or boyfriends seemed to enjoy it.

When guys shouted, their female companions sometimes laughed but more often told them, 'Stop that' or 'Don't be so childish.'

When children shouted, some mothers seemed to find it cute but others scolded. 'Hush!' And, 'What do you think you're doing?' And, 'Quit that!' Sometimes, immediately after shouting a cheerful, *'Hiya, beast!'* or, *'Betcha can't catch me!'* into the hole, kids cried out, *'OW!'* Some squealed. Others began to cry.

A couple of times, Mark heard mothers warn their kids, 'The monster'll come out and get you, if you don't behave.'

Mark listened to it all, sometimes smiling, sometimes angry, often grinning as he imagined himself springing up out of the hole at them.

Oh, how they would scream and run!

Except for the shouts, most of the voices weren't very loud. Some, so soft that Mark couldn't make out the words, formed a soothing murmur. He found himself drowsing off. It hardly surprised him, considering that he'd spent most of last night lying awake.

He fell asleep without realizing it, listening to the voices, his mind often wandering through memories and fantasies but eventually taking a subtle turn into dreams that seemed very real and sometimes wonderful and sometimes horrid. Then a shout would startle him awake. Sometimes, he woke up frightened, grateful to the shouter. Other times, the shout came just in time to prevent Alison or Officer Chaney or Thompson from coming naked into his arms and he woke up aroused and wanted to kill the shouter.

He never knew quite how long he'd been asleep.

Though he wore a wristwatch, he tried to avoid checking it. The more often you check the time, he thought, the more slowly it goes by.

So he waited and waited.

At last, figuring that it must be at least three o'clock in the afternoon, he raised his head and pushed the button on the side of his watch. The numbers lit up.

12:35.

He groaned.

'I heard it!' a kid yelled. *'I heard the beast!'*

Chapter Ten

'You didn't hear shit,' said someone else. The kid's sister?

'Watch your tongue, young lady.' Her father?

'I heard it, Dad! I heard it groan! It's the beast! It's in the hole!'

'There's no such thing as beasts, dipshit.'

'Julie!'

'So sorry.'

The boy said, 'It made a noise like, *uhnnnn*.'

'Oh, sure.'

'You just didn't hear it 'cause of your earphones.'

A moment later, the father said, 'It doesn't appear that anyone else heard this groan of yours, either.'

'It's not *my* groan, it's the *beast's*! And they've *all* got earphones on! Everybody's got earphones on! There's a *beast* in the hole! We gotta *tell* somebody!'

'Is there a problem?' asked a new voice. It sounded like a middle-aged woman.

'I heard a beast in the hole!'

'Really? What did it say?'

'Didn't say nothing.'

'Anything,' the father said.

'It went, *grrrrrrr*.'

Now the kid's going weird, Mark thought.

'Edith?' Another new voice. A man.

'This young fellow says he heard a growl coming from the hole.'

'Haven't heard anything like that, myself.'

'You had your earphones on,' the boy argued.

'I'm afraid my son has a very active imagination,' his father said. 'At home, he has a monster under his bed and another one in his closet and . . .'

'Don't forget the green monster in the basement,' the sister chimed in.

Thank you thank you thank you, Mark thought.

'But I *heard* it. It came from the hole.'

'*You're* the hole.'

'Julie!'

'Just kidding.'

'Come on, kids. We're disturbing everyone. Let's go.'

'But *Daaaaad*.'

'You heard me.'

'Don't be too hard on the boy,' said the voice of Edith's husband. 'An imagination's a good thing to have.'

'But I didn't . . .'

'*Ralph!*'

'Okay, okay. I didn't hear nothing.'

'Anything.'

'Dip.'

'Julie.'

'Have a nice day, folks,' said Edith.

'Thank you.' The father's voice faded as he said, 'Sorry about the disturbance.'

That was a close one, Mark thought.

Then he thought worse.

What if Ralph tells Thompson what he heard? Instead of passing it off as a figment of the kid's imagination, she might put two and two together.

They've probably browbeaten the kid into silence, Mark thought.

The chances of Thompson hearing about the groan were slim to none.

But he waited, listening, so tense he could hardly breathe, ready to scurry deeper into the tunnel at the first sound of trouble.

If it's going to happen, he thought, it'll happen soon. In the next five or ten minutes.

He looked at his wristwatch.

12:41.

Only six minutes since my groan!

He lowered his face onto his crossed arms, took a deep breath and almost sighed. But he stopped the sigh and eased his breath out quietly.

It'll be all right, he told himself. Nobody's going to come down here looking for me . . . unless I make more noise!

Sounds sure do carry through here.

He wished he'd gone farther into the tunnel before stopping. Too late, now. He didn't dare to move.

Only twelve forty-one. Maybe forty-two by now.

Five hours to go before the house closes.

Five hours and fifteen minutes.

Time enough to watch five episodes of *The X Files*. Ten episodes of *The Simpsons*. You could read a whole book if it wasn't too long.

Five hours. *More* than five hours.

Almost one o'clock, now . . .

I haven't eaten all day!

He suddenly thought about the two ham-and-cheese sandwiches in his pack. A can of Pepsi in there, too. He felt the weight of them against his back, just above his buttocks. He could get to them easily, but there would be noise when he unzipped the pack . . . more noise when he unwrapped a sandwich . . . and how about the *PUFFT!* that would come if he should pop open the tab of his Pepsi?

Can't risk it, he thought.

I'll have to wait. After six, I can have a feast.

Soon, his stomach growled.

Oh my God, no!

No comments came.

His stomach rumbled.

Maybe no one's there right now, he thought. Or they're all listening to the audio tour.

People with headphones on, whether listening to music or talk radio or the Beast House tape, always seemed to be off in their own little worlds.

'*Monstruo!*'

Jeez!

'*Buenas dias, Monstruo!*'

That's enough, he thought. He lifted his head, stared for a few moments into the total blackness, then began squirming forward,

419

deeper into the tunnel. He moved very slowly and carefully. Except for his heartbeats and breathing, he heard only the soft whisper of his windbreaker and jeans rubbing the dirt.

As the guy topside yelled what sounded like, '*No hay cabras en la piscina!*,' Mark realized the voice was giving him cover noise. He suddenly picked up speed.

'Don't you saaaay that,' protested a female voice. 'He think you loco, come up 'n bite you face off.'

'He fuckin' try, I kill his ass.'

'You so tough.'

As the male grumbled something, Mark halted and lowered his head. He had no idea how much farther into the tunnel he'd squirmed. Another six feet? Maybe more like ten or fifteen.

No way to tell, but the voices from up top were muffled and less distinct than before.

Time to eat!

He rolled onto his side, unfastened the plastic buckle of his pack belt, and swung the pack into the darkness in front of him. Propped up on his elbows, he found the zipper. He pulled it slowly, quietly.

The voices far behind him were barely audible.

How about some light on the subject?

He took out a candle and a book of matches.

Lunch by candlelight.

He would need both hands for striking a match, so he set the candle down. Then he flipped open the matchbook and tore out one of the matches. He shut the cover. By touch, he found the friction surface. Then he turned his face aside, shut his eyes and struck the match.

Its flare looked bright orange through his eyelids.

An instant later, the flame settled down and he opened his eyes.

The tunnel, a tube of gray clay, was slightly wider than his shoulders but higher than he'd imagined. High enough to allow crawling on hands and knees.

In front of him, the yellowish glow from his candle lit a few more feet of tunnel before fading into the darkness.

He picked up his candle. Holding it in one hand, he tried to light its wick as the match's flame crept toward his thumb and finger. Just when the heat began to hurt, the wick caught fire. He shook out the match.

The candle seemed brighter than the match had been.

Bracing himself up on his right elbow, he reached forward and tried to stand it upright on the tunnel floor. He tried here and there. Each time, the ground was hard and uneven and the candle wouldn't stay up by itself.

He reached out farther and tried another place. Just under the dirt, something wobbled.

A rock, maybe.

If he could get it out, the depression might make a good holder for the candle.

He worked at it.

The object came up fairly easily.

Someone's eyeglasses.

Chapter Eleven

Mark planted the candle upright at one end of the slight depression the glasses had left behind. When he let go, the candle remained standing. It was wobbly, though. He packed some dirt around its base and that helped.

Then he picked up the unearthed glasses. Braced up on both elbows, he held them with one hand and brushed them off with the other.

The upsweep of the tortoise-shell frame made him suppose the glasses had belonged to a woman. The lens on the left was gone, but the other lens seemed to be intact. It was clear glass, untinted.

Except for the missing lens, the spectacles seemed to be intact. Mark unfolded the earpieces. Their hinges worked fine. He looked more closely. Dirty, but not rusty.

How long had the glasses been down here? A few days? A month or two? A year?

How the hell did they *get* here?

All sorts of possibilities, he thought. Maybe a gal was hiding down here the same as me.

But why did she leave her glasses behind?

Easy. Because they got broken.

No. If you lose a lens, you don't throw away the whole pair of glasses. You keep them and get the lens replaced.

She might've *lost* them.

What, they fell off her face?

Fell off her face, all right. *While she was being dragged through the tunnel . . .*

Mark's stomach let out a long, grumbling growl.

He set the glasses down, reached into his pack and removed a ham-and-cheese sandwich. He opened one side of the cellophane wrapper. As he ate the sandwich, he peeled away more of the cellophane, keeping it between his filthy hands and the bread.

He decided not to bother with his Pepsi. It would've been too much trouble. Besides, his sandwich was good and moist.

As he ate, he wondered what to do with the glasses. Leave them where he'd found them? He couldn't see any purpose in that. He might as well keep them.

And do what? Take them to the police?

You found them where, young man?

In the beast tunnel.

In the WHAT?

Yeah sure, he thought. Thanks, but no thanks.

But they might be evidence of a crime.

Might not be.

What if I show them to Officer Chaney?

Show them to her in private, like 'off the record', and we can work on the case together?

He imagined himself coming down into the cellar late at night with Officer Chaney to show her where he'd found the glasses.

They both have flashlights. At the edge of the hole, she hands him a jumpsuit. She has another for herself. *Don't want to get our clothes dirty*, she explains. Then she starts to remove her police uniform.

Like *that'll* happen, Mark thought.

What'll really happen, I'll end up getting reamed for being down here in the first place.

I can at least show the glasses to Alison, he decided. She'll probably think they're pretty interesting and mysterious.

Done eating, Mark used the cellophane to wrap the glasses.

He put them into his pack.

Then he reached out, pulled the candle from its loose bed in the dirt, and puffed out its flame. A tiny orange dot remained in the darkness. Slowly, the dot faded out. He waited a while longer, then found the wick with his thumb and forefinger. It was a little warm. Squeezing it, he felt the charred part crumble.

He returned the candle and match book to his pack, then zippered the pack shut, slid it out of the way, and settled down to continue his wait.

Though he tried to relax, his mind lingered on the glasses.

There hadn't been a beast attack in years. The last two situations had taken place all the way back in 1978 and 1979. In Janice Crogan's books, *The Horror at Malcasa Point* and *Savage Times*, Mark had seen photos of all the women involved: Donna Hayes and her daughter, Sandy; Tyler Moran; Nora Branson; Janice herself, and Agnes and Maggie Kutch, of course. From what he could recall of the photos, he was almost certain that none of the women wore glasses. Maybe *sun*glasses. One snapshot had shown Sandy Hayes, Donna's twelve-year-old daughter, in sunglasses and a swimsuit.

She disappeared!

She was never seen again after the slaughter of '79.

Had she been wearing *prescription* sunglasses in the photo? Could these be her *regular* glasses? Had she been dragged away by a surviving beast and lost them here in the tunnel? Or maybe lost them while escaping through here?

Difficult to picture a cute little blonde like Sandy – who'd looked a lot like Jodie Foster at that age – wearing such a hideous pair of tortoise-shell eyeglasses.

Besides, she'd vanished almost twenty years ago. These glasses *couldn't* have been in the dirt of the tunnel for that long.

If they're not Sandy's . . .

They could've ended up in the tunnel in all sorts of ways, Mark told himself. But they obviously suggested that a woman had been down here not terribly long ago. And that she hadn't been able to retrieve them after they fell – or were knocked – off her face. Meaning she was probably a victim of foul play.

Someone must've dragged her through this very tunnel.

Someone, something.

A beast?

They're all dead, he reminded himself. They were killed off in '79.

Says who?

Chapter Twelve

Mark lifted his head off his arms and gazed into the blackness.

What if they're wrong? he thought. What if one of the beasts survived and it's *in here* with me? Just up ahead. Maybe it knows I'm here and it's just waiting for the right moment to come and get me?

Quit it, he told himself. There isn't a beast in here.

Besides, even if there is, the things are nocturnal. They sleep all day.

Says who?

The books. The movies.

That doesn't make it true.

Into the darkness, he murmured, 'Shit.'

And he almost expected an answer.

None came, but the fear of it raised gooseflesh all over his body.

I've gotta get out of here.

Can't. I can't leave now. Not after all this. Just a few more hours . . .

In his fear, however, he decided to turn himself around. No harm in that. He would need to do it anyway, sooner or later, unless he intended to crawl all the way back to the cellar feet-first.

He took hold of his pack.

Is everything in it?

He thought so, but he didn't want to leave anything behind.

Just a quick look.

He unzipped his pack and found the matchbook. Opened it. Plucked out a match. Pressed its head against the friction surface.

Then thought about how it would light him up.

And saw himself as if through a pair of eyes deeper in the

tunnel ... eyes that hadn't seen him before ... belonging to a man or beast who hadn't known he was here. But knows *now*.

Don't be a wuss, he told himself. Nobody's down here but me.

Who says?

Anyway, I've got everything. I don't have to light any match to know that.

We don't need no steenkin' matches!

He lowered the zipper of his windbreaker, then slipped the matchbook and the unlit match into his shirt pocket.

Now?

He shut the pack, pulled it in against his chest and began struggling to reverse his direction. The walls of the tunnel were so close to his sides that he couldn't simply turn around. He didn't even try. Instead, he got to his knees in hopes of rolling backward.

The tunnel ceiling seemed too low. The back of his head pushed at it. His neck hurt. His chin dug into his chest.

As he fought to bring his legs forward, he almost panicked with the thought that he might become stuck. Then he forced one leg out from under him. Then the other. Both legs forward, he dropped a few inches. His rump met the tunnel floor and the pressure went away from his head and neck and he flopped onto his back. He lay there gasping.

Did it!

Would've been a lot easier, he supposed, just to crawl backward. But he'd succeeded. It was over now.

What if I'd gotten stuck?

Didn't happen. Don't think about it.

He still needed to roll over, but he didn't feel like doing it just yet. Lying on his back felt good.

If I'd brought my Walkman, he thought, I could listen to some music and ...

My headphones!

He touched his head, his neck.

The headphones were gone, all right. The loss gave him a squirmy feeling.

Where are they?

He knew for sure that he'd been wearing them when he ran into Thompson near the front door. And he'd kept them on when he went down into the cellar. And when he'd said that stuff to the little girl. But what about after her father went after him?

He didn't know.

He tried to remember if he'd still been wearing the headphones when he dived into the hole.

No idea.

He sure hoped so. If he'd lost them in the tunnel, no big deal; he would probably find them on the way out. But finding them wasn't his main concern.

If they'd fallen off his head *before* the tunnel, then someone might find them in the cellar and put two and two together.

Someone like Thompson.

But she'd already been down in the cellar looking for him. If the headphones had been there, she – or that girl's asshole of a father, Fred – probably would've found them.

I lost them down here, Mark told himself. It's all right. They're here in the tunnel somewhere.

With the small pack resting on his chest, he raised his arms and put his folded hands underneath his head. His elbows touched the walls of the tunnel.

I'll probably find them on my way out, he thought. And if I don't, no big deal.

Someone coming into the tunnel next month . . . or next year . . . or twenty years from now might find them and wonder how they got here and wonder if they'd fallen off the head of a victim of the beast.

Little will they know.

The truth can be a very tricky thing, he thought.

A voice, muffled by distance, called, '*Heeeerre beastie-beastie-beastie!*'

Dumb ass, Mark thought.

'*Heeerre, beastie! Got something for you!*'

He imagined himself letting out a very loud, ferocious growl. It almost made him laugh, but he held it in.

A while later, he thought about looking at his wristwatch.

But he felt too comfortable to move.

Why bother anyway? It's still *way* too early to leave. It'll be hours and hours.

Hours to go . . .

A couple of years ago, Mark had memorized Frost's poem, 'Stopping by the Woods on a Snowy Evening.' Now, to pass the time, he recited it in his mind.

He also knew Kipling's 'Danny Deever,' by heart, so he went through that one.

Then he tried 'The Cremation of Sam McGee,' but he'd only memorized about half of it.

After that, he started on Poe's 'The Raven.' Somewhere along the way, he got confused and repeated a stanza and then it all seemed to scatter apart . . . *dreaming dreams no mortal ever dared to scheme before . . . scheming dreams . . . dreaming screams upon the bust of Alice . . . still is screaming, still is screaming . . .*

It *had* been a raven. He thought for sure it had been a raven at first, but not anymore. It was still a very large bird, but now it had skin instead of feathers. Dead white, slimy skin and white eyes that made him think it might be blind.

Blind from spending too much time in black places underground.

But if it's blind, how come I can't lose it?

It kept after Mark, no matter what he did. He felt as if it had been after him for hours.

It'll keep after me till it gets me!

Gonna get me like the birds got Suzanne Pleshette.

Peck out my eyes.

Oh, God!

Mark was now running across a field of snow. A flat, empty field without so much as a tree to hide behind. Under the full moon, the snow seemed almost to be lighted from within.

No place to hide.

The awful bird flapped close behind him. He didn't dare look back.

Suddenly, a stairway appeared in front of him. A wooden stairway, leading upward. He couldn't see what might be at the top.

Maybe a door?

If there's a door and I can get through it in time, I can shut the bird out!

He raced up the stairs.

No door at the top.

A gallows.

A hanging body.

Gus Goucher?

Maybe not. Gus belonged on the Beast House porch, not out here . . . wherever out here might be. And Gus always wore his jeans and plaid shirt, but this man was naked.

Naked and dangling in front of Mark, his bare feet just above the floor and only empty night behind him . . . empty night and a long fall . . . a fall that looked endless.

Mark had no choice.

He slammed into the man's body, hugged him around the waist and held on for dear life as they both swung out over the abyss. The rope creaked.

What if it breaks?

'Gotcha now,' the man said.

The voice sounded familiar. Mark looked up. The face of the hanged man was tilted downward, masked by shadow.

'Who are you?' Mark blurted. 'What do you want?'

'First, I'm gonna rip off your head.'

Fred!

Though they were now far out over the abyss, Mark let go. He began to drop – then stopped, his head clamped tight between Fred's hands.

'You aren't going anyplace, young man. Not till I'm done with you.'

With a sudden wrench, the hanged man jerked Mark's head around.

Mark stared out behind himself, knowing his head was backward, his neck was broken.

Oh God, no. I'm killed.

Or maybe I'll live, but I'll be totally wrecked for life, a miserable cripple like Bigelow.

And out in the moonlit night not very far in front of his eyes flapped the dead white, skin-covered bird.

'Get out of here!' Mark yelled at it. 'Leave me alone!'

'Nevermore, asshole.'

A moment later, Mark's neck gave way.

Fred's bare legs caught his torso and kept it.

Apparently, he had no more use for Mark's head.

Falling, Mark gazed up at the swinging naked man and at his own headless body.

Oh my God, he's really going to do it! And I'll get to watch! I don't want to see him do THAT to me!

Then Mark saw the fleshy white bird swoop down at him and realized it meant to grant his wish.

'*Yah!*' he cried out, and lurched awake in total darkness.

He was gasping, drenched with sweat, still sick with terror and revulsion.

Jeez!

For a moment, he thought he must be home in bed in the middle of the night. But this was no mattress under him.

Oh, yeah.

Better stay awake a little while, he told himself.

He'd heard you can get the same nightmare back if you return to sleep too quickly.

Not much danger of that, he thought.

For one thing, he felt wide awake. For another, he needed to urinate.

Man, I don't wanta do that in here.

Might have to, he thought. I can't leave here till after six, and it's probably . . . what? . . . three or three-thirty?

He brought his hands over his face, pushed the cuff of his windbreaker up his left arm and pressed a button on the side of his wristwatch.

The digital numbers lit up bright red.

6:49.

Chapter Thirteen

He'd actually slept *past* the Beast House closing time!

Fan*tas*tic!

He turned himself over. Holding the belly pack by its belt, he started squirming forward through the darkness. Soon, the fingers of his right hand snagged a thin cord.

All right!

He pulled at the cord and retrieved his headphones.

Holding the headphones in one hand, his pack in the other, he continued to squirm forward. He stopped when he came to a steep upward slope ... the slope he'd skidded down head-first when he plunged into the hole.

Almost out.

No light came down into the tunnel. No sound, either.

The whole house should be locked up by now, everybody gone for the night.

Everybody but me!

He grinned, but he felt trembly inside.

This is *so* cool, he thought.

Then he realized that his mother and father should both be home by now. Had they found his note yet? Probably.

They're probably both mad as hell, he thought.

And worried sick.

He felt a little sick, himself.

I had to do it, he thought. How else was I going to get a date with Alison?

In his mother's voice, he heard, *Maybe you should think twice about WANTING to date a girl who would ask you to do something like this.*

'Yeah, sure,' he muttered, and scurried up the steep slope. Not stopping at the top, he crawled over the edge of the hole and across the dirt floor of the cellar until his shoulder bumped into a stanchion. The post wobbled, making clinky sounds.

Mark went around it, then stood up. It felt good to be on his feet. He fastened his belly pack around his waist, put his headphones inside it, then closed the pack. Hands free, he stretched and sighed.

I've really made it! I've got the whole place to myself!

And about five hours to kill.

First thing I'd better do, he thought, is take a leak.

But the public restrooms were outside. Now that he was in, he had no intention of leaving, not even for a few minutes.

If the house had an inside toilet, it wasn't on the audio tour and he had no idea where it might be.

Might not even be hooked up.

Well, the cellar had a dirt floor.

What if I bring Alison down here?

He imagined her pointing at a patch of wetness in the dirt. *What's that?*

Oh, I had to take a leak.

And you did it right here on the floor? That's disgusting. What, were you raised in a barn?

No, she wouldn't say anything like that. Would she?

How about doing it in the hole?

No, no. What if Alison wants to see where I found the glasses?

Hey Mark, it's sorta muddy down here.

He chuckled.

She wouldn't *really* want to go in the hole, would she?

Who knows? She might. I'd better not piss in it.

Maybe over in a corner, behind some crates and things.

He took a candle out of his pack, removed the matches from his shirt pocket and lit it. The candle's glow spread out from the flame like a golden mist, illuminating himself, the nearby air, the dirt of the cellar floor, the brass stanchion and red plush cordon, and the hole a few feet beyond the cordon. Just beyond the hole, the glow faded out and all he could see was the dark.

Do I really want to go over there?

Not very much.

Even while in the cellar for tours during the day, he had never gone roaming through the clutter beyond the hole. Partly, he'd been afraid it might be off limits and a guide might yell at him. Partly, though, he'd always felt a little uneasy about what might be over there . . . maybe crouching among the stacked crates and trunks.

He certainly didn't want to venture into that area now, alone in the dark.

Especially since there was no real *need* for it.

Pick somewhere else, he told himself. Somewhere *close*.

He turned around slowly. Just where the glow from his candle began to fade, he saw the bottom of the stairway. He continued to turn. Straight ahead, but beyond the reach of his candle light, was the barred door to the Kutch tunnel. Though he couldn't see it, he knew it had to be there.

An idea struck him.

He chuckled softly.

Awesome.

He walked forward and the door came into sight. So did the opening behind its vertical iron bars. From the tours, books and movies, he knew that the underground passageway led westward, went under Front Street and ended in the cellar of the Kutch house.

Agnes Kutch still lived there. The locked door was meant to protect her from tourists.

And maybe to protect tourists from Agnes . . . and whatever else might be in her house. Even though all the beasts were supposed to be dead . . .

You never know.

And so with a certain relish and a little fear, Mark walked up to the door. Level with his chin was a flat, steel crossbar. He dripped some wax on it, then stood the candle upright.

Both hands free, he lowered the zipper of his jeans. He freed his penis, made sure he was between bars, then aimed high and let fly.

When Alison sees *this*, he thought, she'll never suspect it was me.

I ought to make *sure* she sees it.

Oh my God! she might say. *Look at that! Somebody . . . went to the bathroom there!*

Somebody, Mark would say. *Or someTHING. Maybe the rumors are true.*

And she says, *Thank God this gate is locked.*

When she says that, maybe I'll put my arm around her and say, *Don't worry, Alison. I won't let anything happen to you.*

After he says that, she turns to him and puts her arms around him and he feels the pressure of her body.

Imagining it, he began to stiffen. By the time he was done urinating, he had a full erection. He shook it off, then had to bend over a little and push to get it back inside his jeans and underwear.

After zipping up, he pulled at the candle. Glued in place with dried wax, it held firm for a moment before coming off . . . and Mark felt the door swing toward him.

His heart gave a rough lurch.

He took hold of an upright bar, gently pulled, and felt the door swing closer to him.

Chapter Fourteen

Mark groaned.

He eased the gate shut, leaned his forehead against a couple of the bars and looked down between them. The lock hasp on the other side was open. The padlock, always there in the past, was gone.

Oh, boy.

In his mind, he whirled around and raced up the cellar stairs and ran through the house. He made it out safely and shut the front door behind him.

In the next version of his escape, he got halfway up the cellar stairs before a beast leaped on his back and dragged him down.

Take it easy, he told himself. If one of those things *is* down here, it hasn't done anything yet. Maybe it isn't interested in nailing me. Maybe it *wants* me to leave.

Hell, there isn't any beast down here. Who ever heard of an animal taking a *padlock* off a door?

Maybe Agnes Kutch took it off.

Someone sure did, that was for certain.

I could go through and take a peek at the Kutch house.

No way, he thought. No way, no way.

Leaving the gate shut, he slowly backed away. Then he turned toward the stairs.

Just take it easy, he told himself. Pretend nothing's wrong. Whistle a happy tune.

Man, I'm *not* gonna whistle.

On his way to the stairs, he listened. His own shoes made soft brushing sounds against the hard dirt floor. No sounds came from behind him. No growls. No huffing breath. No rushing footfalls. Nothing.

He put his foot on the first stair and started up. The wooden plank creaked.

Please please please.

Second stair.

Just let me get out of here. Please.

Third.

No sound except a squeak of wood under his weight.

He wanted to rush up the rest of the stairs, but feared that such sudden quick movements might bring on an attack.

He climbed another stair, another.

So far, so good.

Now he was high enough for the glow of his candle to reach the uppermost stair.

Almost there.

I'll never make it.

Please let me make it! I'm sorry I scared the girl. I'm sorry I pissed through the bars.

He climbed another stair and imagined a beast down in the cellar suddenly springing out from behind some crates and coming for him.

Silently.

I'm sorry! Please! Don't let it get me! Let me get out of here and I'll go home and never pull another dumbass stunt in my life.

Almost to the top. And maybe the beast was almost upon him even though he couldn't hear it and didn't dare look back, so he took the next step slowly. And the next. And then he was in the pantry.

Go!

He broke into a run. The gust of quick air snuffed his candle.

Shit!

But the way ahead had a gray hint of light and he ran toward it. Suddenly in the kitchen, he skidded to a halt and whirled around and found the pantry door and swung it shut.

It slammed.

Mark cringed.

He leaned back against the door. Heart thudding hard and fast, he huffed for air.

Made it! I made it! Thank you thank you thank you!

But he suddenly imagined being hurled across the kitchen as the beast crashed through the door.

Gotta get outa here!

He lurched forward, turned and hurried through the kitchen. By the vague light coming in through its windows, he made his way to the back door. He twisted its knob and pulled, but the door wouldn't budge.

Come on!

He found its latch.

The door swung open. He rushed out onto the back porch.

About to pull the door shut, he stopped.

What if I get locked out?

Doesn't matter! I'm going home!

He let go of the door. Leaving it ajar, he backed away from it. He watched it closely.

The porch, enclosed by screens, was gray with moonlight, black with shadows. It smelled slightly of stale cigarette smoke. It had some furniture along the sides: a couch, a couple of chairs and small tables. In the corner near the kitchen was something that looked like a refrigerator.

Mark backed up until he came to a screen door. He nudged it, but it stayed shut. Turning sideways, he felt along its frame. It was secured by a hook and eye. He flicked the hook up. Then he pushed at the screen door and it swung open, squawking on its hinges.

Holding the door open, he stared out at the moonlit back lawn, the gift shop, the restrooms, the patio with the chairs upside-down on the table tops, and the snack stand. All brightly lit by the full moon. Some places dirty white, others darker. A dozen different shades of gray, it seemed. And some places that were black.

I made it, he thought.

He stepped outside and stood at the top of the porch stairs.

Safe!

Done with the candle, he opened his pack. As he put it inside, he felt the hardness of his Pepsi can. And the softness of his second sandwich. So he trotted down the stairs and walked over to the patio. He hoisted a chair off the top of a table, turned it right-side up, and set it down.

Standing next to the table, he put his hand inside his pack, intending to take out the sandwich. He felt cellophane, realized his fingers were on the eye-glasses, and pulled them out. He set them on the table, then reached into his pack again and removed the sandwich. Then the Pepsi. He put them on the table and sat down.

With his back toward Beast House.

He didn't like that, so he stood up and moved his chair. When he sat down this time, he was facing the house's back porch.

That's better, he thought.

Not that it really matters. I never would've made it out if there'd been a beast in there.

What about the padlock?

Who knows?

Somebody had obviously removed it. Earlier, the bearded guy had been standing at the gate, complaining about not being allowed to go through the tunnel to explore the Kutch house. The padlock must've been on it then.

Maybe not.

Anyway, I'm outa there.

He picked up his Pepsi, opened the plastic bag and pulled out the can. It felt moist, slightly cool. He snapped open the tab and took a drink.

Wonderful!

He set it down, peeled the cellophane away from one side of his sandwich, and took a bite.

The sandwich tasted delicious. He ate it slowly, taking a sip of Pepsi after every bite or two.

No hurry, he told himself. No hurry at all.

I'm already screwed.

If he hadn't left the note for his parents, he could walk in the door half an hour from now and be fine. Make up a story about getting delayed somewhere. Apologize like crazy. No major problem.

But he *had* left the note and they'd almost certainly found it by now.

I'll be back in the morning.

I'm *so* screwed, he thought.

We've always trusted you, Mark.

Where exactly did you go that was so important you felt it necessary to put your mother and I through this sort of hell?

We're so disappointed in you.

Sometimes I think you don't have the sense God gave little green apples.

Did it never occur to you that your father and I would be worried sick?

Maybe you should try thinking about someone other than yourself for a change.

He sighed.

It would be at least that bad, maybe worse. What if Mom *cries*? What if *Dad* cries?

All this grief, he thought, and for nothing . . . didn't even make it till midnight for my date with Alison.

Says who?

Chapter Fifteen

He kept his eyes on Beast House, especially on the screen door of the porch.

When he was done with his meal, he put his Pepsi can into the plastic bag. They went into his belly pack. So did his sandwich wrapper and the eye-glasses.

He turned the chair upside-down and placed it on top of the table.

Then he walked over to the men's restroom. The door was locked. No surprise there. But the area in front of the door was cloaked in deep shadows. He would be well hidden there. He sat down and leaned back against the wall.

And waited, keeping his eyes on Beast House.

Also watching the rear grounds.

Ready to leap up and run in case of trouble.

The concrete wasn't very comfortable. He often changed positions. Sometimes, his butt fell asleep. Sometimes, one leg or the other. Every once in a while, he stood up and wandered around to get his circulation going again.

When 11:30 finally arrived, he went to the other side of the gift shop. There, standing in almost the same place where he'd jumped down from the roof that morning, he began to pee in the grass. And he remembered the dead dog on the roof.

It's probably still up there.

How did it *get* up there?

He tilted back his head and looked at the upper windows of Beast House.

He could almost see the dog flying out into the night, tumbling end over end . . .

Thinking about it, he felt his penis shrink. He shook it off, tucked it in and raised the zipper of his jeans. He hurried around the corner of the building, out of the shadows and back into moonlight.

Much better.

Waiting in the wash of the moonlight, he checked his wristwatch often. At 11:50, he walked very slowly toward the back porch . . . his gaze fixed on its screen door.

Nothing's gonna leap out at me, he told himself. It hasn't done it for the past four hours and it won't do it now. There's probably nothing in the house *to* leap out at me.

His back to the porch, he sat down on the second stair from the bottom.

Okay, he thought. I'm ready when you are.

As eager as Alison had seemed on the phone, he expected her to show up early.

He turned his head, scanning the grounds, looking for her. Of course, the various buildings blocked much of his view.

He wondered if Alison planned to climb the spiked fence.

What if she tries and doesn't make it?

He could almost hear her scream as one of the spear-like tips jammed up through the crotch of her jeans.

Five, six inches of iron, right up her . . .

Stop it.

Anyway, she'll probably hop over the turnstile, same as me. If she does, she'll be coming around from the front of the house.

He looked toward the southeast corner.

Any second now.

Seconds passed, and she didn't come walking around the corner.

Minutes passed.

12:06.

Where *is* she?

What if she doesn't show up at all? Maybe she got caught. Maybe she forgot about it. Maybe the never *meant* to show up, and it was all just a trick.

No, no. She wouldn't do that. She *wants* to come. If she doesn't make it, it's because something went wrong.

Says who?

Me, that's who. This wasn't any trick. She wouldn't do that sort of thing.

And then she came jogging around the corner of Beast House.

Someone did. A figure in dark clothes.

What if it's not Alison?

Has to be, he told himself.

The approaching jogger seemed to be about Alison's size, but not much showed. A hat covered her hair and she seemed to be wearing a loose, oversized shirt or jacket that hung halfway down her thighs. Or *his* thighs. For all Mark could really see, the jogger might not even be a girl.

He sat motionless on the porch stair, watching, ready to stand up and bolt.

The jogger raised an arm.

He waved and stood up.

Slowing to a brisk walk, she plucked off her hat. Her hair spilled out from under it, pale in the moonlight. 'Hiya, Mark.'

Alison's voice.

His throat tightened. 'Hi. You made it.'

'Oh, yeah. I wouldn't miss this.' A stride away from him, she stopped and stuffed her hat into a side pocket of her jacket. She took a few quick breaths, then shook her head. 'But I guess I wasted my time, huh?'

'I hope not.'

'You knew the rules, Mark.'

'Yeah.'

'Damn. I don't know why, but I really figured you'd be able to pull it off somehow.'

'I sorta *did*.'

Her mouth opened slightly.

'I've *been* inside.'

'Really?'

'I just . . . figured I'd meet you out here.'

'Okay. Great. Let's go in.' She started to step around him.

He put up his hand. 'No, wait.'

She halted and turned to him. 'What?'

'I'm not so sure it's safe.'

442

She chuckled. 'Of *course* it's not safe. Where'd be the fun in that?'

'No, I mean it. I really don't think it'd be such a great idea to go in. I think somebody might be *in* there.'

'What do you mean? Like a night-watchman? A guard?'

'I mean more like somebody who *shouldn't* be in there. Maybe even . . . you know . . . one of the *things*.'

'A *beast*? How cool would *that* be?'

'Real cool, except it might kill us.'

'Then *we* could be exhibits.' She sounded amused.

'I don't think we should go in.'

'Oh.'

'I really like you a lot and everything. It'd be fantastic to go in the house and explore around with you. I mean, God, I sure don't want to *disappoint* you. But I don't want to get you killed, either.'

In silence, she nodded a few times. Then she said, 'You didn't make it in, did you?'

'Huh?'

'You just figured you'd meet me out here anyway and hope for the best.'

'No, I got in. I did. It's open.'

'Let's go see.'

She turned away. Mark almost grabbed her, but stopped his hand in time.

She trotted up the porch stairs, opened the screen door and looked around at him. 'Well, *this* isn't locked.'

'I know.'

She went in.

Mark hurried after her. 'No, wait.'

She didn't wait. She walked straight across the porch.

'Alison. Wait up.'

She stopped and gave the kitchen door a push. It swung open. 'Hey,' she said. She sounded surprised and pleased.

'I told you.'

She turned around. 'You really *did* it. Good *going*, Mark. I had a feeling about you.'

'Well . . .'

She came toward him, stopped only inches away and put her hands on his sides. She looked into his eyes for a few seconds. When she

443

pulled him forward, his belly pack pushed at her. 'Let's get this out of the way,' she said. She slid it around to his hip, then wrapped her arms around him and tilted back her head.

They kissed.

He had often imagined kissing Alison, and now it was happening for real. She seemed to be all smoothness and softness and warmth. She had a taste of peppermint and an outdoors aroma as if she'd taken on some of the scents of the night: the ocean breeze and the fog and the pine trees. She held him so snugly that he could feel each time she took a breath or let it out.

Though her breasts were muffled under layers of jackets and shirts, he could feel them.

He started to get hard.

Uh-oh.

Afraid it would push against her, he bent forward slightly.

Alison loosened her hold on him. 'I'm ready if you are,' she whispered.

Chapter Sixteen

'Huh?' Mark asked.

'Ready?'

Still holding each other, but loosely with their bodies barely touching, they spoke in hushed voices.

'Ready for what?'

'To go in.'

'Oh. I really don't think we should.'

'Sure we should. I've been waiting for this for *years*. It's gonna be *so* cool. Come on.' She lowered her arms, turned toward the kitchen door, then reached back and took hold of Mark's right hand. 'Come on.' She pulled at it.

He followed her into the kitchen. And stopped. 'Wait. I have to tell you something.'

She turned toward him. 'Okay.'

'I was down in the cellar. That's where I hid till closing time.'

'Really?' She sounded interested.

'Down in the beast hole.'

'My God. *Inside* it?'

'Yeah, there's like a tunnel.'

'Wow.'

'I stayed in there all day.'

'My God. How cool! Weren't you scared?'

'Sometimes.'

'So how did you return the tape player?'

'I didn't. I never got one in the first place. I came over really early and jumped the turnstile and hid until they opened the house. Then I just blended into the crowd and pretended to be a tourist till I got down into the cellar.'

'Good going.'

'I was pretty lucky. I had a couple of minutes by myself, so I crawled down the hole and stayed.'

'So *that's* how it's done.'

'How *I* did it, anyway. But the thing is, when I came out of the hole, I took a look around. You know how there's always a padlock on the Kutch side of the door down there?'

'Sure.'

'It's gone. The padlock.'

'Gone?'

'Yeah. And I'm pretty sure it was there this morning. So somebody must've taken it off while I was down in the hole.'

'The door isn't locked at all?'

'It opens. *I* opened it, just to see.'

'Did you go through?'

'The tunnel? No. I got out of there.'

'But it goes to the Kutch house.'

'I know.'

'Nobody *ever* gets to see the Kutch house. This is the chance of a lifetime.'

'Yeah, a chance to die.'

'Oh, don't be that way. Nobody's going to die.'

'That's because we're getting out of here.' Turning away, he pulled at Alison's hand.

She jerked her hand from his grip. 'Not me,' she said. 'I'm not leaving till I've checked the place out.'

'The *padlock's* off.'

'Right. Meaning we can go through the tunnel.'

'Maybe someone *already* came through. From the other side. Doesn't that *scare* you? We oughta get out of here right now. We're lucky we haven't already gotten . . .'

'Nobody's stopping you.'

'What do you mean?'

'You can go.'

'I can't leave *you* here.'

'Well, I'm not going.' She sounded so calm.

'But . . .'

'Okay, so the padlock's off. Did you get chased or anything?'

'No.'

'See anything? Hear anything?'

'No.'

'So as far as you know – except for the padlock being off – the house is as safe as ever.'

'But the padlock . . .'

'Did you actually *see* it today?'

'No, but I'm pretty sure it was there.'

'But you didn't see it with your own eyes. So maybe it *wasn't* there. When was the last time you actually *saw* it?'

'I guess maybe . . . early July.'

'I did the tour last month,' she admitted. 'I saw it then. So that's the last time we can be sure it was on the door. A month ago. So maybe it's been gone for *weeks*.'

'I don't think so. That door's *always* locked.'

'Okay. Maybe it is and maybe it isn't. But even if someone took the lock off *today*, it doesn't mean they're in the house right *now*.'

'I guess not,' he admitted.

'Come on. Let's take a look around.'

'I don't think we should. Really.'

'I do. Really.'

'Alison . . .'

'Mark. Come on. It took a lot of guts to do what you did today. You don't want to bail out now, do you?'

'Not really. But . . .'

'Then don't. Come on.' She took his hand and led him through the kitchen.

'Not the cellar,' he whispered.

'Of course, the cellar.'

'Why don't we go through the rest of the house first? Don't you want to wander around and see all the exhibits? I thought that was supposed to be the main idea.'

'It was. But this is our chance to see inside the Kutch house. Maybe our *only* chance ever.'

'I think it's a really bad idea.'

447

In an oddly chipper voice, Alison said, 'I don't,' and led him into the pantry.

She suddenly stopped.

'What?' Mark whispered.

'My God, it's dark in here.'

'Even darker in the cellar.'

'Do you have something?' Alison asked.

'A couple of candles.'

'Good. I meant to bring a flashlight. Glad *you* came prepared.'

'Thanks.' He let go of Alison's hand, reached over to his right hip and slid open the zipper of his pack. When he tried to put his hand in, the headphones got in his way. He took them out. 'Can you hold these?'

Alison found them in the darkness and took them.

'Thanks.'

He put his hand into the pack.

'Headphones?' Alison asked.

'To make me look like a tourist.'

'Hmm. Smarter than the av-uh-ridge bear.'

Cellophane crinkled softly.

'What's that?' she asked.

'Wrappers. I had my lunch in here. I've also got an empty Pepsi can.'

His fingertips found the match book. He took it out, opened its flap and plucked out a match. He snicked it across the score and tiny sparks leaped around the match head, but it didn't catch.

He tried again.

The match flared.

'Now we're cookin',' Alison said.

She looked golden in the glow of the small flame. Mark smiled when he saw that she was wearing the headphones.

'Why don't I hold this?' Mark suggested, 'and you reach in and get out the candles.'

'Sounds like a plan.' She slipped her fingers into the opening, then smiled at him. 'You don't have anything nasty in here, do you?'

'I don't think so.'

Her hand came out holding a pink candle. 'Here's one,' she said. She raised it and held it steady, its wick touching the flame of Mark's match.

When the candle wick caught fire, Mark shook out the match. Alison gave the candle to him.

'Thanks,' he whispered.

'I get the other one?'

'Sure. We might as well use them both.'

She put her hand into the pack again. 'What's this?'

'What's what?'

She removed her hand from the pack. And showed him.

'Somebody's glasses. I found them down in the beast hole.'

'Really? Can I have a look?'

'Sure.'

The cellophane made quiet crackly sounds as she unwrapped the glasses.

She raised them into the light of Mark's candle.

Her eyes opened very wide.

She said, 'Oh my God.'

Chapter Seventeen

Mark suddenly felt sick. Again. 'What's wrong?' he asked.

'They're *hers*.'

'Whose?'

'Claudia's.'

'Claudia who?'

'You know, *Claudia*. I don't know her last name. That grody kid. Sorta fat and dumpy. She showed up for a while last year.'

'Oh.'

'Remember?'

'Sort of.' He vaguely recalled a pudgy girl with hair that had always looked greasy. 'She was only in school a couple of weeks, wasn't she?'

'Try three months.'

'Really?'

'I should know. She spent them all *hanging* on me.'

'Oh. She *was* always, like, following you around the halls.'

'Yeah. Like a dog. She wanted to be my friend. I hated to be *mean* to her, you know? She seemed nice enough. But *too* nice, if you know what I mean.'

'Fawning.'

'Yeah. That's it, fawning. God, she was aggravating. She would never take a hint. She never knew when to quit. She would like *invite* herself places, stuff like that. There was one time, I told her she should try to find herself some *new* friends and she said, "You're all the friend I could ever want." She was *so* awful.'

'And she disappeared?' Mark asked.

Alison stared at the glasses. Nodding, she said, 'Yeah. I mean, it wasn't like she *disappeared*. I never heard of search parties or anything. One day, she just didn't show up for school. I figured she'd stayed home because she was upset at me. I'd really laid into her the day before. Told her I was tired of having her in my face all the time and how she was driving me nuts. I was pretty rough on her. But, jeez, what're you gonna do? I mean, it was like having a stalker.'

'That was the day before she disappeared?' Mark asked.

'Yeah. And when she didn't show up for school, I was really glad about it at first. But after a couple of days, I started to feel guilty. I mean, I don't want to go around *hurting* people . . . not even her. So I finally went over to where she lived, figuring maybe to apologize. I'd been to her place once before. It was this grody trailer over in the woods . . . know where Captain Frank's old bus is?'

Mark nodded.

'Over there. So I paid a visit to her trailer and her mom said she didn't know where Claudia was. She hadn't seen her in three or four days. Figured she must've run away from home. And, "Good riddance," she said. What she really said? I couldn't believe my ears. "Good riddance to bad rubbish." Can you imagine someone saying that about her own daughter?'

'That's pretty cold,' Mark said.

'I couldn't believe it. Anyway, she seemed to think Claudia had run off to San Francisco "to live with the dykes and bums." Those are her words, not mine. "Dykes and bums." Jeez.' She turned the glasses in the candlelight. Then she muttered, 'Guess that isn't where she went.'

'They probably aren't Claudia's.'

'Oh, they're hers, all right. I mean, nobody wears glasses like these. Nobody except maybe a stand-up comic *trying* to look like a doofus. And Claudia. You'd better show me where you found them.'

'Well . . . Okay. Wanta light the other candle?'

Alison returned the glasses to Mark's pack and took out the second candle. 'Need anything else out of here?'

'I don't think so.'

She shut the zipper, then tilted her candle toward Mark and touched her wick to his. Her wick caught fire, doubling the light.

'I'll go first,' Mark whispered, hurrying past her.

451

He didn't want to go first, but he didn't want Alison going first, either. Besides, he was the guy. When there might be danger, the guy is always supposed to lead the way.

He started down the cellar stairs, moving slowly. With the candle held out in front of his chest, he could see his feet and a couple of stairs below him. The bottom of the stairway and most of the cellar remained in darkness.

Alison was a single stair above him, but over to his right.

'This doesn't seem like such a good idea,' Mark whispered.

'It's fine,' Alison said. She put a hand on his shoulder. 'Don't worry.'

His legs felt weak and shaky, but he liked her hand.

We'll be okay, he told himself. I was down here all day and nothing happened.

Anything could be down here. Crouching at the foot of the stairs. Hiding *behind* them, ready to reach between the planks and grab his ankle.

We'll be fine, he told himself. Nobody's been killed in here in almost twenty years.

Says who?

At last, the shimmery yellow glow found the cellar's floor.

Nothing was crouched there, ready to spring.

Mark stepped onto the hard-packed dirt. Alison's hand remained on his shoulder as he walked straight toward the beast hole. When he came to the cordon, he stopped. Alison took her hand off his shoulder and stood beside him.

'How far in did you go?' she whispered.

'Pretty far. I don't know.'

'Want to show me where you found the glasses?'

'You mean go in?'

'Yeah.'

'Not really.'

'Come on.' She unhooked the cordon from its stanchion, let it fall to the dirt, then walked almost to the edge of the hole.

Mark followed her. 'We don't really want to go down there, do we?'

'I have to.'

'No, you don't.'

'You can wait up here if you want.'

'Oh, and let you go in alone?'

'No big deal.'

'It *is* a big deal. For one thing, it's awfully tight. I almost got stuck.'

'So stay here.'

'This is crazy.'

'If you say so.'

'It's just a stupid pair of glasses.'

'*Claudia's* glasses.'

'Even if they are . . .'

'Maybe *she's* down there, Mark. Maybe it's not just her glasses. I have to find out.'

'No, you don't. Anyway, she disappeared *months* ago. If she *is* down there, it'll just be her . . . you know, her body.'

'Whatever. Hold this.' She handed her candle to Mark, then began to unfasten the buttons of her denim jacket.

'You *don't* want to go down there.'

'Mark. Listen. Here's the thing. She knew.'

'Huh?'

'Claudia. She knew. She was always hanging on me. She was with me when a guy asked me out. Jim Lancaster. She heard me tell him the condition.'

The one condition.

I want you to get me into Beast House. That's where we'll have our date.

'Jim said I must be out of my mind,' she explained. 'No way would he try a stunt like that. So I told him he could forget about going out with me. After he went away, I said to Claudia, "Cute guy, but yella."'

'What did she say?'

Alison shrugged. 'I don't know.'

She turned away from the hole, took off her denim jacket, hung it over the top of the nearest stanchion and came back. The long-sleeved blouse she wore was white.

'Probably just laughed and said, "You're awful." Something like that. But this was only a week or so before she disappeared.' Looking into Mark's eyes, Alison slowly shook her head. 'Never even crossed my mind. She didn't run away to San Francisco. She came *here*. Just like you. To hide and stay till after closing time so she could let me in.'

'She didn't tell you anything?'

'She probably meant to sneak out later and surprise me. But I guess she never made it out.'

Chapter Eighteen

'Even if you're right,' Mark said, 'that's no reason to go *down* there.'

'It's my fault.'

'It is not. You didn't force her to do anything.'

'She did it for me. Now I've got to do this for her.' Alison bent over and peered down the hole.

'They might not even *be* Claudia's glasses.'

'They're hers.' She turned her head toward Mark. 'Are you coming with me?'

'If you go, I go.'

'Thanks.'

'You're gonna get filthy, you know. That white blouse.'

She glanced down at it, then looked at Mark.

Will she take it off?

'I didn't figure on crawling through dirt,' she said and looked toward her jacket.

'You can wear mine,' Mark said. 'It's already a mess.' He gave both candles to her, then unbuckled his belly pack, let it fall, and took off his windbreaker. She handed one of the candles back. He gave her the windbreaker.

'Thanks.' She poked the dark end of the candle into her mouth and kept it there, her head tilted back while she put on Mark's windbreaker and fastened it. When the zipper was up, she took the candle out of her mouth.

'Ready?' she asked.

'Not really.'

'Look, you stay here. I'll just go on down by myself.'

'No. Huh-uh. I'll go with you.'

'Just tell me how far in . . .'

'I don't know. Maybe twenty feet. Twenty-five?'

'Good. Wait here. It'll be a lot quicker that way, too. I'll just scurry in, have a look around. If I don't find anything, I'll come right out and we'll have plenty of time to do some exploring and stuff.'

'Well . . .'

'Anyway, you've already spent enough time down there. It's my turn.'

'I don't know . . .'

She sank to her knees. Looking over her shoulder, she said, 'You wait here, Mark. I'll be right back.'

'No, I'll . . .'

It came up fast, shiny white, almost human but hairless and snouted.

Alison was still looking at Mark and didn't see it.

But her face changed when she saw the look on his face.

Before he could shout a warning, before he had a chance to move, the thing grabbed the front of the windbreaker midway up Alison's chest and jerked her forward off her knees. She cried out. The candle fell from her hand. Head first, she plunged into the hole as if sucked down it. In an instant, she was gone to her waist.

Mark dropped his candle and threw himself at her kicking legs.

The flame lasted long enough for him to see that she was gone nearly to the knees. Then his body slammed the dirt floor. His head was between her knees and he clutched both her legs and hugged them to his shoulders as blackness clamped down on the cellar.

Gotcha!

Down in the hole, she was squealing, '*No! Let me go! Leave me alone! Oh my God! Mark! Don't let it get . . .*' Then she yelled, '*Yawww!*'

Though Mark still clutched the jeans to his shoulders, he felt sliding movements inside them. He tightened his grip. The jeans stayed, but Alison kept going. Under the denim, her legs tapered. He felt her ankles. Then her sneakers were in his face and then they came off and fell away and he lay there hanging over the edge of the hole with Alison's empty jeans in his hands.

'*Alison!*' he yelled into the blackness.

'*Mark! Helllllp!*'

He pulled her jeans up, flung them aside, then squirmed forward over the edge and skidded down through the opening on his belly.

He bumped into her sneakers, shoved them out of the way, and scurried toward the sounds of Alison sobbing and yelping with pain and blurting, '*Let me go! Please! It hurts! Don't.*'

Mark wanted to call out and tell her it would be all right. Even if it was a lie, it might give her hope.

But he kept silent. Why let the beast know he was coming?

Maybe I can take it by surprise.

And do what?

He didn't know. But staying quiet made sense. It might give him *some* advantage.

Though he scrambled through the tunnel as fast as he could, the sounds from Alison seemed to be diminishing. She continued to cry and yell, but the sounds came from farther away.

How can they be faster than me? he thought. It's *dragging* her.

Though his eyes saw only utter blackness, his mind saw Alison skidding along through the narrow tube of dirt, on her back now, kicking her bare legs. The beast no longer dragged her by the front of the windbreaker; now, she was being pulled by her arms. Stretched as she was, the windbreaker didn't even reach down to her waist. From her belly down, she was bare except for her panties.

It must really hurt, he thought. It must *burn*. Like rug burn, but worse, her skin getting scuffed off.

That'll be the least of her problems. When the beast gets done dragging her . . .

That's when I can catch up.

Yeah, right. And get myself killed. It'll take care of me in about two seconds.

But maybe those couple of seconds would give Alison a chance to get away.

It'll be worth it if I can save her.

Worth dying for?

Yeah. Fucking-A right, if I can save her.

Anyway, he told himself, you never know. It might not come to that. Anything can happen.

One of his hands slid over something slippery in the dirt. Her panties? The way she was being dragged, she'd been sure to lose them. Mark snatched up the skimpy garment, stuffed it inside his shirt and kept on scrambling forward.

The sounds from Alison seemed farther away than ever.

He tried to pick up speed.

What if they lose me?

According to the books and movies, there might be a network of tunnels behind Beast House, going all the way out past its fence and into the hills.

What if it really is some sort of maze?

The thing drags her off into side tunnels and loses me, I might have a chance of living through the night.

So far, the tunnel seemed mostly straight but with minor bends and slopes sometimes. If other tunnels had intersected with it, Mark hadn't noticed.

Though the sounds were far away, they still seemed to come from in front of him.

That's a good sign, he thought.

Sure it is. Good for who?

And a voice whispered in his mind, *I don't have to keep going. I can stop right now. Turn around and go back to the cellar and get the hell out. Let the cops take care of it.*

Better yet, don't tell anyone. Nobody has to know about any of this.

'Yeah, right,' he muttered.

And kept on through the darkness, out of breath, heart thundering, every muscle aching, his clothes clinging with sweat, his hair plastered to his scalp, sweat running down his face.

I can't keep this up forever, he thought.

So quit. That's what you want to do.

I don't want to quit, just slow down.

He stopped.

Just for a second.

Lying on his belly, head up, elbows planted in the dirt, he wheezed for air and blinked sweat out of his eyes and gazed into the blackness.

He couldn't hear Alison anymore.

It doesn't mean I lost her, he told himself. Maybe she stopped crying and yelling. Maybe she passed out.

In his mind, he saw her stretched out limp on her back, being dragged by her wrists, the windbreaker even higher than before so that she is bare from the midriff down. Her panties are gone. Mark can see between her thighs. Her legs bounce as she is dragged over the rough dirt of the tunnel floor.

'*ALISON!*' he shouted.

No answer came.

Chapter Nineteen

Mark wished he hadn't yelled. His shout had probably carried through the whole length of the tunnel.

I can't hear them, he thought, so maybe they didn't hear me.

What if they're just being quiet?

And it *heard me.*

In his mind, he saw the beast slither over Alison's limp body and come scurrying back through the tunnel.

Get the hell out!

He shoved himself up to his hands and knees, but the back of his head struck the dirt ceiling. He dropped flat.

Even if he *could* turn himself around, he knew he had no chance of out-racing the beast.

It'll be on me any second!

He listened. Silence except for his own heartbeat and gasping.

He would never see it coming. Not down here. Even something dead white would be invisible in such darkness. But he would hear its doglike snuffs and growls.

So far, he heard only himself.

What if it's still dragging Alison and they're getting farther and farther away?

Mark started squirming forward again.

Might as well, he thought. If it's coming, it'll get me anyway.

He picked up speed.

Get it over with.

In his mind, he saw himself and the beast scurrying straight toward each other through the tight tunnel like a couple of locomotives.

It's a locomotive, he thought. *I'm* a dog on the tracks.

He remembered the dog on the roof of the gift shop. Disembowelled and headless.

Is that how I'll end up? Or Alison?

As the tunnel began sloping upward, he wondered what was taking the beast so long.

Should've gotten here by now.

Maybe it *isn't* coming.

He struggled up the incline. All his muscles ached and trembled. His clothes felt soaked. Sweat poured down his face, stung his eyes.

And he saw gray.

Not actual light, but a hint of darkness that wasn't totally black.

He made his way toward it, shoving with his elbows and knees and the toes of his shoes at the hard dirt floor of the tunnel and forcing himself forward, higher, closer to the gray.

Then he noticed a breath of air that smelled like fog and sea, that cooled the sweat on his face.

A way out?

That's why he'd stopped hearing Alison. That's why the beast hadn't come to get him . . . it hadn't heard his shout.

They aren't in the tunnel anymore!

And now the gray tunnel in front of Mark seemed to slant straight up. He tried to climb it, skidded backward, then got to his feet. Standing, he reached up and found rough, cool surfaces of rock.

He found handholds and started to climb. Soon, he was surrounded by large blocks of stone. Surrounded *and* covered. Looking up, he couldn't see the sky. But he did see a patch of pale, misty light from an area eight or ten feet above his head.

He climbed toward it, moving as fast as he dared up the craggy wall.

Hard to believe that the beast had made such an ascent dragging – or carrying – Alison. But it had somehow dragged her with great speed through the entire length of the tunnel. If it was capable of that, he supposed it could do this.

Boosting himself over a rough edge, he found the opening in front of him. Not much. The size of a small window. But big enough.

He clambered toward it.

Beyond it, the night looked pale and fuzzy. Moonlit fog?

He crouched just inside the opening and peered out. Through the fog, he could see an upward slope of ground and he knew where he was; at the back of a rock outcropping just beyond the Beast House fence, a short distance up the hillside. He'd seen it many times. Never from the inside, though. Until now.

Outside, trees and rocks looked soft and blurry.

Nothing moved.

Where *are* they?

He stood up and saw the beast behind a thicket off to the left. Just its head and back, nearly invisible in the fog. It was hunched over as if busy with someone out of sight on the ground.

Mark crouched. Head down, he searched the area near his feet and found a good chunk of rock. It filled his hand. It felt heavy and had rough edges. Keeping it, he stayed low and hurried in the direction of the beast.

He didn't try to look at it again. If he could see it, it could see him. But he knew where it was. And he listened.

His shoes made hardly any noise at all as he hurried over the rocks and the long damp grass. The night seemed oddly still. All the usual sounds were muffled by the fog. Somewhere, an owl hooted. From far away came the low, lonely tones of a fog horn. He thought he could hear the distant surf, but wasn't sure.

Turning his head to the left, he looked downward and saw the back fence of Beast House with its row of iron spikes. Beyond the fence, there was only fog. Beast House was there, buried somewhere in the grayness. As he tried to glimpse it, he heard a snuffling sound.

Then a whimper.

He hurried on.

The sounds became more distinct. Moans and growls, panting sounds, whimpers and sharp outcries.

Some came from Alison.

She's alive!

But, oh God, what's the damn thing doing to her?

Though Mark knew he must be very close to them, they remained out of sight. The beast had chosen a very well-concealed place for his session with Alison. It seemed completely surrounded by thickets and boulders.

Mark climbed a waist-high rock and looked down at them.

The monster, white as a snowman in the moonlit fog, was down on its knees, hunkered over Alison's back, thrusting into her. Her clothes were gone, scattered nearby. She still wore her white socks, but nothing else.

She was on her knees, drooping forward. She looked as if she would fall on her face except for the creature's hands that seemed to be clutching her breasts. Each time it rammed into Alison, her entire body shook and she made a noise like a dog getting kicked.

Mark leaped off the boulder.

The beast turned its head. Its eyes found him, but they didn't go wide with surprise. They stayed half shut. The beast seemed blasé about this human running toward it with an upraised rock.

But it very quickly stood up, still embedded in Alison, hoisting her off her knees and swiveling, letting go of her breasts and clutching her hips as she swung so that her head and torso swept downward and crashed against Mark, knocking him off his feet.

He slammed against the ground, rocks pounding his buttocks and back, one bashing his head. He heard the *thonk!* Felt a blast inside his skull. Saw bright red. Smelled something tinny like blood. Barely conscious, he gazed up at Alison.

She loomed above him. The beast's long, clawed fingers were clutching the sides of her ribcage, holding her like a life-sized, beautiful doll, working her forward and back.

Her chest and belly were striped with scratches, with gouges. Wetness fell off her and pattered onto Mark.

Her arms hung down as if reaching for him. But they weren't reaching, they were limp and swinging. Her head wobbled. Her hair, hanging down her brow and cheeks, swayed with the motions of her body. Her small breasts, nipples pointing down at Mark, jiggled and shook as the beast jerked her forward and back.

She sniffled and sobbed. She let out a hurt yelp each time the beast jerked her toward it, plunging in deeper.

Mark raised his head.

The beast kept on working Alison.

Mark couldn't see much of it. Just its hands with their long white fingers and dark claws clamping both sides of Alison's ribcage. And its muscular white legs between Alison's legs.

Alison's legs were dangling, her feet off the ground. They gave a little lurch each time the beast rammed in. Through her sobbing and yelps and the beast's grunting, Mark could hear her buttocks smacking against the creature.

Smacking faster and faster.

The beast, grunting with each thrust, worked her forward and backward with increasing speed and power. Alison's arms and legs flopped about. Her hair swung. Her breasts lurched. Her yelps came faster.

It's killing her!

Mark's hands were empty. He turned his head and saw rocks nearby. He stretched his arm out and grabbed one and brought it closer to his side.

Above him, Alison's head flew backward. Mark thought the beast had tugged her hair, but its hands remained on her ribcage as it furiously slammed into her. Her head stayed back. Her mouth gaped. She gasped, '*AH-AH-AH!*' And then her arms stopped flapping. They bent at the elbows and she clutched her own leaping breasts and massaged them, squeezed them, tugged her nipples.

Chapter Twenty

What's she doing?

Mark *knew* what she was doing. Appalled, excited, he watched her growing frenzy.

All wrong, he thought. So wrong.

When the beast came, Alison's whole body twitched and bounced and she cried out and Mark was pretty sure she was having a climax of her own.

For a while afterward, the beast kept her in position. Her head and arms and legs hung limp. She hardly moved at all except to pant for breath. Then the creature eased her forward and upward. Its thick shaft appeared between her legs, and Mark saw it slide out of her.

Bending over, the beast lowered Alison toward him.

Does it think I'm dead?

Mark lay perfectly still as it put Alison on top of him. Her chest, hot and wet and heaving, covered his face. Hardly able to breathe, he turned his head to the side.

And waited.

Nothing happened.

Alison stayed on top of him, done in as if she'd just finished running a mile-long gauntlet.

But the beast did nothing.

What's it doing, watching us?

Just play dead, Mark told himself. If I make any sort of move at all, it'll probably drag Alison off me and rip me apart.

Though her moisture had soaked through Mark's shirt almost

immediately, he soon felt a heavy warmth spreading out near his waist. It seemed to come from Alison, from between her legs.

My God, she's bleeding to death!

But the fluid felt thicker than blood.

Mark suddenly knew what it was.

It spread over his belly, rolled down his sides, soaked through his jeans so he could feel its warmth on his leg.

Must be a gallon of it.

As he lay there motionless, the night air turned the semen chilly. But it still felt warm where Alison's body was on top of him.

How long had she been there? Five minutes? Ten? Maybe longer. During that time, Mark had seen and heard nothing from the beast.

He felt Alison raise herself slightly.

'Don't move,' he whispered.

'Huh?'

'Play dead.'

'But it's gone.'

'Huh?'

'It went away . . . a long time ago.' Trembling, she scooted herself down Mark's body. She flinched and made hurt sounds. She said, 'Ugh.' Then her face was above his, her hair hanging toward him much as it had done when she was higher above him in the clutches of the beast. Now, however, she was nearly motionless and her hair hardly moved at all. He wished he could see her face, but it was masked by shadow.

'You came after me,' she said.

'Didn't do much good.'

'You tried.'

Her head slowly lowered. It tilted slightly to the side. She whispered, 'Thank you.' Then her mouth pushed softly against his mouth. Her lips were warm and wet and open.

We need to get away, Mark thought. It might come back.

But Alison was on top of him and kissing him and naked. He didn't want *that* to stop. He could feel her breasts through the damp front of his shirt. He could feel her ribcage and belly and groin and he was growing hard inside his wet jeans.

She lifted her face.

'We'd better get out of here,' Mark whispered. 'It might come back.'

'Don't worry.' Sitting on him, her buttocks on the soaked front of his jeans and heavy on his erection, she leaned forward and began to unbutton his shirt.

'What're you doing?'

She spread his shirt open, then eased herself down. Almost on top of him, she paused and swayed, brushing her nipples against his chest. Then she sank onto him, smooth and bare all the way down to Mark's waist. Her skin felt chilly at first, then warm. She kissed him again.

Has she lost her mind?

But the feel of her . . .

This was what Mark had always wanted, to have her like this, naked and eager. And how great to have it happening in the tall damp grass of a hillside late at night in the silence and the fog!

She pushed herself up.

'We've gotta go,' Mark said.

She started scooting backward. 'What's the hurry?'

'It'll come back and kill us.'

'I don't think so.'

'It *will*!'

'Why would it do that?'

'It's the *beast*!'

A corner of Alison's mouth curled up. 'If it wanted to kill us, why didn't it?'

'I don't know.'

'Neither do I,' she said. Squatting over Mark's thighs, she bent down and unbuckled his belt. 'But here we are, and it's gone.'

He pushed himself up to his elbows and looked around. The hillside and boulders and trees looked soft in the pale fog.

'It's gone,' Alison said again. She unbuttoned the waistband of his jeans, pulled down the zipper.

Some of Mark's tightness eased.

I can't believe this is happening.

'Maybe it got what it wanted,' Alison said. Scuttling backward on her knees, she tugged at Mark's jeans. He raised his rump off the ground. His jeans and underwear slid out from under him.

He was free and rigid in the moist night air.

'Now it's our turn,' Alison told him.

'But it *raped* you! It . . . it dragged you away and . . . look at you, you're all scratched and torn up . . . It . . . it *fucked* you!'

'It sure did,' she said. Crawling over him, she whispered, 'And we never breathe a word about this to anyone.'

'We've got to! You're all ruined!'

'I'll heal.'

'We've *gotta* tell.'

'Never. It'll be our secret. Just between you and me. *Everything* about tonight. Promise.'

Mark shook his head.

'Do you want me?' she whispered.

He nodded.

'Then promise.'

'But . . .'

She eased down and he felt a soft wet opening push against the head of his erection. It nudged him. He felt himself go in half an inch. Then she withdrew.

'Promise me, Mark.'

'What'll you tell your parents?'

'Nothing.'

'But you're all messed up.'

'Most of it won't show when my clothes are on. If they notice anything, I'll say I crashed my bike.'

'But . . .'

'Promise?'

'Okay.'

'Cross your heart and hope to die?'

'Yes.'

'Cross mine.' She moved forward and down so her chest was above his mouth. 'Use your tongue.'

He licked an X on the skin of her chest, tasting sweat and blood, feeling the furrows of scratches.

'Hope to die?' she asked.

'Yes.'

'Okay then.' She eased herself down and backward and Mark felt himself slide in. She was warm in there. Warm and slippery and snug.

He knew the beast had been in before him, plundering her, flooding her. He'd heard crude guys talk about 'sloppy seconds' and he guessed that was what he was getting but he didn't mind very much.

Didn't mind at all, come to think of it.

Chapter Twenty-one

Near dawn, wearing what remained of their clothes, they made their way down the hillside. They stayed just outside the back fence and followed it. Alison could hardly walk. Mark held her. Sometimes, he picked her up and carried her for a while.

They came out of the field near some homes. Except for a few porch lights, nearly all the houses were dark.

They saw a cat. Once, a car went by a block away and they hid behind a tree. They saw no people anywhere. Only each other.

Soon, they arrived at Alison's house. All the windows were dark. So was the porch.

'I left the back door unlocked,' she whispered.

They went around the house. On the stoop outside the back door, Alison took off Mark's windbreaker and gave it back to him. Her white shirt was tattered, one sleeve missing and her right breast poking out through a split. Her legs were bare all the way down to her white socks.

'Are you sure you'll be all right?' Mark whispered.

'Pretty sure.'

He put on his windbreaker and zipped it up.

'Nice and warm?' Alison asked.

'Yeah.'

'I'm freezing.'

'You'd better go inside.'

'Not yet.' She took his hand and placed it on her naked breast. 'That's better.'

'Yeah.'

She held his hand there and whispered, 'I had a great time tonight, Mark.'

'You *did*?'

'Well . . . it had its ups and downs.'

'Jeez.'

She laughed softly, winced, then stared through the darkness at him. 'It *was* great.'

He felt goosebumps crawl up his body, but wasn't sure why.

'We'll have to do it again sometime,' she said.

'You mean . . . ?'

'Go out together. You know.' She pressed his hand more tightly against her breast. 'You want to, don't you?'

'My God. Sure I do. Of course.'

'Me, too.'

Then Mark laughed softly and whispered, 'No conditions next time, right?'

'Only one.'